LOOK! UP IN

Lucas stopped speak
he said in an entirely different voice.

Paul and I swung around. And then I felt it, a surge of enormously powerful magic which could only come from the wizard Theodora and I had been unable to find. Townspeople started looking up too, following Lucas's arm.

"Look! Don't you see it? It's coming!" cried Lucas.

Now I could see it. It could have been a bird, but it was far too big. It flew faster than any bird, across the fields and straight into town toward the cathedral. It was five times the size of a man, and it had the wings of a bat.

Several of those around us began to scream. "Our swords!" Lucas yelled at Paul. "We must get our swords!" The two princes raced off while townspeople darted for cover. I saw the mayor upended in the rush, then he scrambled to his feet and ran, his gown hitched up to his knees. The priests flung themselves against the tide of people still coming out of the cathedral, fighting their way back inside.

Only I stood still, while the creature settled on top of the half-completed tower, the tower that was not yet consecrated, and stared down at me with burning eyes. Though vaguely human in shape, it was covered with scaly hide, and its mouth and fangs were much bigger in proportion to its face than any human's could be. This was no illusion. This was real.

And this was why I was in the cathedral city. I took a deep breath and, without the slightest idea what I would do, launched myself into the air.

BAEN BOOKS BY C. DALE BRITTAIN

Tales of the Wizard of Yurt
A Bad Spell in Yurt
The Wood Nymph and the Cranky Saint
Mage Quest
The Witch and the Cathedral

Voima

The Witch & The Cathedral

C. Dale Brittain

BAEN

THE WITCH AND THE CATHEDRAL

A Baen Books Original

Baen Publishing Enterprises
P.O. Box 1403
Riverdale, NY 10471

ISBN: 0-671-87661-9

Cover art by Newel Convers and Courtney Skinner

First printing, April 1995

Distributed by Simon & Schuster
1230 Avenue of the Americas
New York, NY 10020

Printed in the United States of America

DEDICATION

For Bruce and Doug,
who thought it would be mushy

CONTENTS

PART ONE

The Cathedral

I

That morning I thought my main problem was the three drunk newts. But that was before I got the telephone call from the chaplain. He was not in fact the chaplain anymore, but then a minute ago the newts had been three drunk students.

I had been sitting in on Zahlfast's class at the wizards' school. He paused in his description of the basic transformations spell to explain the dangers inherent in its use. Any magic spell, even illusions, can have repercussions far beyond the expected, and advanced spells if not done properly can lead to loss of identity or even life.

The three drunk wizardry students, sitting together and laughing quietly in the back, had apparently decided to test for themselves what these dangers might be.

We dived for the newts before they had a chance to disappear into cracks in the floor. "Hold on to those two, Daimbert," said Zahlfast. "I'll start on this one."

The newts wiggled in my hands as I tried to hold their smooth bodies gently. The loss of a tail or a leg as a newt would mean permanent damage to the student as a human, and if they escaped as newts we might never be able to return them to themselves. They were quite attractive, light green with bright red spots, but their tiny newt eyes looked up at me with human fear.

The rest of the class had retreated to the back of the room. Zahlfast glared at them. "What are you waiting for? This is all the demonstration you'll get *today.*" The students left in some confusion, and he returned to his spell.

It is harder to undo someone else's spell than one of your own. As I started on one of the newts I was holding, Zahlfast finished with his, and suddenly a student stood before him, or rather slumped. He was slightly green, but I think that was from feeling ill rather than the aftereffects of being a newt.

I finished with mine and handed the third to Zahlfast. "How can they be drunk so early in the day? I didn't think the taverns down in the City were even open yet."

Zahlfast spoke the final words in the Hidden Language to break the spell. "Bottles in their rooms," he said as the last dazed and frightened newt became a dazed and frightened wizardry student.

"We never had bottles in our rooms when *I* was a student here," I said self-righteously.

Zahlfast looked at me sideways, a smile twitching the corner of his mouth. "As I recall, you had plenty of trouble at the transformations practical exam, even perfectly sober."

I preferred not to recall all my embarrassment with those frogs, even twenty years afterwards, so I loftily ignored this comment. I had, after all, become a perfectly competent wizard in the meantime—or at least had managed to persuade the wizards' school of my abilities enough that they had invited me back for a few months as an outside lecturer.

"Now," said Zahlfast to the students. "Are you sober enough to listen to reason?"

"Spill a spell, spoil a spell," blurted one and collapsed on his face. I was interested to see that they still excused themselves for magical mixups with the same catch-phrase we had used years ago.

At that moment one of the other young wizards came in. "Telephone call for you, sir," he said to me. I excused myself and followed him out and down the hall.

I felt as I always did a stir of pride in using a telephone with a magical far-seeing attachment, allowing one to see as well as hear the person at the other end. Although I had invented the attachment essentially by accident, as my first and only success in technical wizardry, it had over the years become widely adopted.

The view-screen lit up, showing the face of the man waiting to talk to me: gaunt, with deep-set eyes over high cheekbones and a mouth that looked as though it rarely smiled. It was Joachim, dean of the cathedral of Caelrhon.

His dark eyes looked at me unseeing. Without a far-seeing attachment on his own telephone, he could not tell I was there until I spoke. The bishop, always dubious about magic, had doubtless considered it enough of a concession to institutionalized wizardry to allow the installation of even an ordinary magic telephone.

"Hello!" I said. "I haven't heard from you in ages!" Although traditionally priests and wizards never get along, Joachim and I had been friends, at least most of the time, since I had first taken up the position of Royal Wizard of Yurt and found him Royal Chaplain there.

"I'm glad I was able to reach you, Daimbert. I need your help." Joachim had never been strong on social chit-chat. "As you may have heard, we're just starting construction here in Caelrhon on a new cathedral. But now something very odd is happening—something which may involve magic."

I was flattered but surprised. Since Joachim had become dean of the cathedral, he had studiously acted as though wizardry had nothing to offer a priest. "What kind of problem is it?"

He hesitated. "I would just as soon not explain over

the telephone, especially as I haven't talked to the bishop yet. Is there any way you could come here?"

It must be serious, then. "I would, Joachim, but there's one difficulty. Caelrhon's not my kingdom. You need to talk to your own Royal Wizard. He would be furious to find another wizard interfering in his kingdom."

I didn't mention that long-ago incident, when I had been in Yurt only a year, when the king of Yurt had told the king of Caelrhon that if his wizard couldn't install a magic telephone easily he could offer *my* services. I had innocently assumed that Sengrim, Caelrhon's wizard, knew all about it, but he had come home to find me seated like an invader at his desk, his books scattered all over his study. When he burst through the door, I was so startled I dropped and smashed the glass telephone I was working on—the spells hadn't been working right anyway—and gasped, "Spill a spell, spoil a spell," which hadn't helped. Neither had sending him as a peace-offering an inscribed copy of Zahlfast's new edition of *Transformations for Beginners* when it came out the next year. He had returned it with a frosty note saying that he had no books for beginners in *his* library. Ever since then, Sengrim had done his best to suggest that I was incapable of even the simplest illusions.

The dean lifted an eyebrow a fraction. "I would have asked for that wizard's help," he said dryly, "except for one thing. I officiated at his memorial service last week."

"He's *dead*?" I demanded with a rather slow grasp of the obvious, and feeling instant remorse for all the times I had thought of Sengrim as a bitter old man who wasn't nearly as good a wizard as he wanted to be considered. "Nobody here at the school has heard about it! Do you know what happened?"

"He seems to have blown himself up in his study," said the dean slowly, "taking half the tower with him. Apparently he had just had some sort of a quarrel with his crown prince, and most likely his anger made him careless with his chemicals and herbs. There was not enough left of him to bury. . . ."

I had to tell the masters of the school about this at once. They avoided checking up too often on all of us Royal Wizards of the western kingdoms, but they would certainly want to know that Sengrim was dead. And the royal court of Caelrhon would doubtless be asking soon for a new Royal Wizard.

"So," said Joachim, "can you come?"

"The series of lectures I'm giving will finish this afternoon," I said, dragging my attention back from the image of Sengrim blowing himself up in the royal court of Caelrhon to the question of magical problems in the cathedral city, ten miles down the road. "I'd been planning to return home shortly, but I can visit you first. Would tomorrow be all right?"

He did smile then. "Tomorrow would be excellent." He rang off, and I hurried away to find Zahlfast again.

The rest of the day was very busy, as I gave my last lecture, talked afterwards to several of the more promising (or least discouraging) students, then packed up my clothes and books to have them shipped back to Yurt. Those who had known Sengrim were saddened, although the students' reaction didn't go much beyond commenting that they were just as glad that modern wizardry had essentially eliminated herbs and chemicals. At the end of the afternoon I went to talk to the Master of the school.

There had been talk of my organizing some workshops after the lecture series was over, but I was just as happy to abandon this project. They had assigned me to the technical wizardry division although as a student I had managed to avoid any courses there. More than once I had felt like a fraud, lecturing away to a group of intensely serious and pale-faced young wizards who, in at least some areas, must know more magic than I did.

I had only found enough to say to fill the lectures by trying to make them think about magic beyond their textbooks. What would they do, I challenged them, if they discovered themselves in a situation where the dry series of spells which modern wizardry does so well failed them and they had to improvise? They had given me puzzled looks and asked me to write out the improvised spells so they could memorize them. Some of the other teachers had started coming to my class, sitting quietly at the back of the room, and I was fairly sure they were collecting stories about my experiences.

The Master was in his study. Years ago I had gotten over my old terror, but I still stood in awe of him. The story was that he had started the wizards' school a hundred and fifty years ago as a retirement project, but his ice-blue eyes were as sharp as ever.

He was (gratifyingly) sorry I was going, but not (disappointingly) because he wished he could enjoy my company longer. Rather, he was concerned that I was going to help a cathedral dean. "You know wizards try to stay aloof from the Church and their worries about sin—after all, we don't want priests interfering in magic."

I had heard all this many times. It is best not to get involved in the Church because the priests think they have the right answers, whereas instead we wizards have the right answers all the time. "He's not interfering in magic—as soon as he ran into a magical problem, he had the sense to send for a wizard."

He nodded slowly. "All right, but remember: our responsibility is to help mankind, and mankind would be helped more by technically trained wizards who also knew how to improvise than by priests talking about the supernatural."

I thought he was through, but after a moment's hesitation he spoke again. "While I don't want to sound as though I'm accusing your friend, there have been rumors, stories, the last month or two, apparently centered in the twin kingdoms of Yurt and Caelrhon. . . . Some members of the aristocracy are starting to talk as though they don't need wizards, even as though they resent us. Something like this must have been behind the quarrel Sengrim had just before his death. Though I must say he had been acting erratic lately; he even became furious with me because none of us here were interested in some ideas he had about teaching different kinds of magic. But his behavior must have intensified local opposition to wizardry. When I telephoned the royal constable of Caelrhon a short time ago, he was *very* brusque and unhelpful and said his king had no intention of hiring a new wizard. Our first idea, of course, is that these rumors are being fueled by the priests. So while you're at the cathedral, keep your eyes open."

In spite of going to bed late, I awoke before dawn. I rolled over with the feeling that I was being pulled away from something indescribably sweet and realized that I had been dreaming about Yurt. It was little more than a sensation, but I recognized in the dream the kingdom as it had been when I first arrived there, while everyone was still alive, before anyone started to grow old.

I looked out my window toward the eastern sky, where a faint yellow glow presaged the sunrise. In many ways my life as Royal Wizard had grown better and better over the years, as I became more sure of my abilities, as I was able to work out plans and programs and see them take effect. But six years ago, during the terrible winter of bitter cold and raging fever throughout the western kingdoms, the old king of Yurt had died. Starting then, I had begun to feel nostalgic, sometimes even melancholic, as though the best part of my life had already passed by.

It was also that winter that several members of the cathedral chapter of Caelrhon had died, including the dean. Joachim, who a few years earlier had finally yielded to pressure to leave the royal court and join the cathedral, had immediately been elected to replace him. With his new responsibilities as the chapter's senior officer, I doubted that he had any time to look back nostalgically to what once had been.

I swung my feet out of bed, too awake to go back to sleep. I was much too young to start living in the past—I probably had a good two hundred years to go, barring run-ins with demons or dragons. During these last months at the school there had been hints that I would be welcome if I decided to stay on. I would not of course join the small group of permanent faculty members, all far older than me and much better at magic, but there was plenty of other occupation available here, assisting in advanced courses or aiding in administration, as well as giving the occasional series of lectures.

I had always brushed aside such hints. Being back in the great City with money to spend had somehow not turned out to be as exciting as I had imagined when an impoverished student. But now I found myself considering whether I ought to take the opportunity once I had solved the cathedral's problems for them. Leaving Yurt for the school would be better than allowing myself to be permanently homesick for a life that no longer existed.

II

Zahlfast came to see me off. We stood on the little plaza in front of the wizards' school, on the highest point of the City. Clouds whipped miles above us across a pale blue sky.

"I'm glad you were able to give your lecture series," Zahlfast said. "I'm sure the students benefited."

"How are the newts today?"

He laughed. "Once they'd sobered up, I think they were thoroughly frightened—now I just hope that none of the other students try something similar."

"Is it my imagination," I asked, "or are some of the students even more irresponsible now than they were when I was here?"

Zahlfast shook his head ruefully. "If you're imagining it, then so am I. You know we used to warn students against summoning, and normally wouldn't even teach them the spell? Well, now we don't even mention it exists for fear that the warning would only incite them."

I had a secret about the summoning spell, but as the secret was now twenty years old it would keep a while longer.

"Elerius has been saying we need to tighten down on the students," Zahlfast commented, "give them real discipline from the beginning rather than allow them as much room to find their own way."

"Elerius?" I asked in surprise. Elerius, three years ahead of me, was rumored to have been the best student the school ever produced. He was now Royal Wizard of one of the largest and wealthiest of the western kingdoms. I had always viewed him with a certain suspicion, but I had never been sure how much of that was merely jealousy of his abilities. "I hadn't realized you were putting him on the faculty."

"No," said Zahlfast with a smile. "I doubt we'll add anyone to the permanent faculty for years, though it's always worthwhile to hear the thoughts of our former students. The Master and I haven't felt that wizardry needed a more rigid structure—but if there's a recurrence of newts I may change my mind. Elerius always has ideas; not long ago he even tried to persuade us to teach the magic of fire here on top of everything else."

Zahlfast and I chatted for a few more minutes, the slightly awkward conversation of two people when it is time for one of them to go, and yet their friendship makes them want to delay the parting.

And then Zahlfast startled me much more than I wanted to admit, by speaking to me directly, mind to mind. "Beware of the Church. The priests hate and fear wizardry, and they seek to destroy you."

His eyes held mine steadily. I shook my head without responding. Although all young wizards learn in their final years of training to communicate with each other without speaking, telepathic communication is extremely rare at the school. In speaking mind to mind one's own mental fences are down, and in an atmosphere of unruly students it is usually safest to keep one's thoughts sealed up securely. All I could think was that Zahlfast wanted to impress his warning on me with special emphasis.

The alternative was that someone was watching us from hiding, and Zahlfast wanted to warn me without him overhearing, but this seemed highly unlikely. Whatever odd stories there might be about priests and the aristocracy resenting wizardry, I doubted it had progressed to spies infiltrating the school.

"Good-bye," I said, shaking Zahlfast's hand. "Thank you again for having me here." I took off flying, soaring high over the City's spires and then inland, where the dense urban area quickly gave way to the fields, woods, and isolated villages of the western kingdoms.

It was a beautiful day of late spring, and the earth below me was spread with a hundred shades of green, but I thought less of the scenery than of Zahlfast's warning. It was tantalizingly unspecific. Several times I had wondered if the older wizards deliberately withheld information from us, perhaps as self-sufficiency training or even as a test, and they might be doing it again. I didn't like it, especially since I hadn't been their student for close to twenty years.

The magic required for flying is hard mental and physical work, so it was with relief several hours later that I saw the sharp cathedral spires of the little city that served as commercial and religious center of the twin kingdoms of Yurt and Caelrhon. To preserve the sensibilities of cathedral priests who might not know their dean had sent for a wizard—and who apparently hated and feared me—I dropped to the ground half a mile from the city and walked in.

A band of Romneys was camped in the meadow in front of the city gates. Horses and goats were tethered behind their brightly painted caravans. The smoke of a dozen fires rose lazily upwards. Several children came running to meet me, black eyes shining.

"A magic trick, a magic trick!" the oldest cried, while the younger ones whispered to each other in the Romney language. Even the smallest girl wore big gold hoop earrings.

"All right," I said with a smile. A lot of people were suspicious of the Romneys, but I liked them. There were stories that they practiced a little magic themselves, secretly and without proper training, which meant that the unwary were in constant danger of slipping over into black magic. I myself had never seen anything either evil or magical about them.

I put a few words of the Hidden Language together and in a few moments had created an illusory scarlet dragon. It reared back on its fourth and final pair of legs, roaring silently and growing until it stood ten feet high.

The children seemed oddly unimpressed. "Well, it's a *nice* dragon," said the oldest boy. He reached his hand toward the metallic gleam of the scarlet scales, and a vicious but insubstantial set of claws passed harmlessly through his arm.

Even though illusions are among the first things taught at the wizards' school, it takes years of practice to be able to do them quickly and consistently. The first time I had ever made an illusory dragon, it had not been nearly this good and yet it had thrown the royal court into a blind panic. Whose illusions had these children been seeing that they could refer to my dragon as "nice"?

"Rather than just an illusion," continued the boy, clearly

disappointed in me but trying to be polite, "could you show us some real magic? Maybe some invisibility, or a cloak of fire?"

Before I had a chance to answer, a woman in a red shawl came hurrying up. Both her front teeth were gold. She spoke quickly in Romney to the children, who dispersed reluctantly, looking back over their shoulders at me and my now dissolving dragon.

"I'm sorry, sir, if the children bothered you," she said. "They're just so curious, and they love to see magic. How about if I tell your fortune to repay you for your trouble? I'll even do it for free!"

I was standing in what I thought of as my wizardly pose, absolutely still except for slow breathing, hands folded and eyes fixed intently on whomever I was facing. I had picked it up from the older wizards at the school and had become quite good at it.

But the Romney woman gave me a good-natured smile. I abandoned attempts at dignity and smiled back. "How will you tell my fortune? You know natural magic is useless for predicting the future, and I hope you aren't stirring in a little of the supernatural!" I was able to speak lightly because I had already probed delicately for magic and not found any.

"We have our ways," she said. If she was trying to be awe-inspiring, she was having no more success than I. "Now let me see!" She walked around me slowly, examined the front and back of my head, squeezed my arm above the elbow, plucked out a hair and held it up to the light, and finally stared at my shoes.

"Yes," she said at last, and this time without a smile. "I can see your future. Shortly you will meet someone beautiful and mysterious, and you will fall deeply in love."

This was so stereotypically what Romney women told young men at the fairs—and not even for free!—that I had to laugh. "Don't you have any other fortunes? You know wizards never marry."

"Love and marriage are two different things," she said as though the platitude had great significance. "Now, if you will excuse me, sir."

She returned to the caravans where the children had been watching us impatiently, and I continued toward the city gates. Although I was not particularly concerned about meeting someone beautiful and mysterious, I did wonder who had given the children a demonstration of magic. It is far harder to make something invisible than to make an illusion appear, and to be able to surround oneself in real fire without being burned takes powerful magic indeed.

Inside the gates, I threaded my way through the narrow streets to the little plaza in front of the cathedral. The last time I had been here it had been full of the carts and stalls of farmers, merchants, and foodsellers. Now it was a construction site, jammed with lumber, heaps of cut stone, workmen's huts, the vats where mortar was mixed, and the wooden forms used to lay out the stonework patterns on the ground before they were hoisted up. A huge windlass was being erected, its treadmill big enough for three men.

I paused for a moment at the edge of the site. The old cathedral was still intact, and they seemed to be planning to build the new, larger church around it. So far they had concentrated their efforts on the west front, building a new façade and towers thirty feet in front of the old main steps. One of the new towers, hung with scaffolding, was already as tall as the towers of the old cathedral.

After working out the route that would be least likely to end in something being dropped on my head, I hurried across the plaza toward the church's entrance. Above the old doors, the figures of Christ and the apostles still stared stonily down, and the figures of the damned and the saved still pleaded or prayed at their feet.

All around the air was loud with the shouts of workmen

and the sounds of hammers and stone chisels, and my nose was assailed by the mixed smells of mortar, sweat, and the sausages someone was grilling for lunch. But when I went through the heavy doors of the old cathedral I passed from noise and bright sunshine into the dimness and stillness of the church's interior.

While I was still blinking a young man came up, a junior priest or a seminary student. "The dean's expecting me," I told him.

III

There was a quick step outside the little office off the nave where the young priest had put me to wait, and Joachim came in. "Good," he said. "I'm glad you've come."

I seized his hand, delighted to see him, even though lately he had always seemed older than I remembered. His handshake was still much stronger than mine, but the once black hair was gray at the temples, and his face had lines I had forgotten. My own hair and beard had turned snow white before I was thirty, but other than that I looked almost exactly the same as when I graduated from the wizards' school. When I had learned the complex spells that slow down aging, I had not counted on all my friends leaving me behind.

"Sit down," said the dean without preamble. "I have only a few minutes now, and I need to tell you about our problems."

"Do you think you could have a demon here?" I asked cautiously. I had been wondering what would be serious enough to make Joachim call me.

"Of course not," he said with a faint smile, about all he ever allowed himself. "Would a priest ask for help from a wizard against the supernatural? I think the problem's natural, but it's magic."

I was fine as long as I stayed away from the supernatural

battle between angels and demons. "So you think someone's practicing renegade magic?"

"That seems the most likely explanation. Construction on the new cathedral goes well during the day, but something happens at night. The watchmen have seen lights, even what looks like a flame flickering on the new tower. In the morning, the workmen sometimes find material moved around, stones, scaffolding, things no one should be able to move unaided."

"The Romneys," I said. "It must have something to do with what the Romney children saw."

He nodded slowly. "Several members of the cathedral chapter have thought it was the Romneys' doing. You must have seen them as you came in—*are* they capable of casting powerful spells?"

"Not the Romneys themselves. But I talked briefly to some of the children—I even made them an illusory dragon—and they seemed disappointed in my illusions. They hinted they had recently seen someone else doing much more powerful magic."

"This band has been camped outside the walls for about six weeks. The bishop, the city mayor, and the constable of the castle have all been unhappy about having them there, but they do not hurt anyone so there has been no reason to drive them away."

"What is it," I said, "maybe ten years since the Romneys first started to appear in the western kingdoms? I wonder where they were before then."

"Probably in the eastern kingdoms," said Joachim without interest. "Look. I shall be busy all afternoon, but I want to have dinner with you and we can talk more then. Do you think you could go up on the new tower to search for magical influences? Now is a good time, while the workmen take their noon break."

Far above us, a bell began ringing. Joachim stood up and pulled a silk stole across his shoulders. "I must go; I'm performing the noon service at the high altar." But he paused at the door to smile before he was gone. "It *is* good to see you."

Being the head of the cathedral chapter, I thought, had given him an attitude of command he had never had in Yurt. I didn't mind him ordering me around, but I wondered if he even realized he was doing so. I watched his black-clad figure hurry down the nave toward the high altar, where an acolyte was lighting the candles.

As I went back out through the heavy cathedral doors I was immediately struck again by the sounds, the smells, and the brightness of noon. Workmen were starting down from the scaffolding. I would have liked some lunch myself, but I had been told to look for magical influences.

First I found the crew foreman. "The dean's asked me to look over your construction site. I'm a wizard, and he told me you had been having some sort of problem."

"All right," said the foreman. His manner was not insolent, but it was certainly not respectful either. "If you're a wizard I guess you can fly, so I'll let you have a look. But I wouldn't let anyone else!"

He was short, thin and wiry, with very long fingers. I glanced down at his bare feet; his toes too were unusually long. The workmen now assembling were all built similarly. I remembered hearing that there was a valley somewhere far to the north that produced men both strong enough to move great stones and agile enough to carry them up a precipice.

The lower part of what would become the main stairs of the southern tower was finished, so I started climbing. The recently quarried stone was smooth and light-colored, still covered with a fine coating of dust. I didn't want to fly, at least at first, because I hoped to tell better what was happening from close up.

By the time I reached the fifth landing my legs had begun to ache, but I kept on. The last workmen shot by, jumping down whole series of steps with little apparent regard for their safety. What would one day become highly complex stone sculptures on the wall were now just roughed in, and the many windows were still no more than openings in the walls, without their tracery or glass.

And then the stone stairs ended and I was out in the open. I could just detect a faint hint of magic, as though a spell had been cast nearby sometime earlier.

The tower continued above me, though in much less complete form. Rough wooden steps continued upwards, and after a brief pause to catch my breath I followed them. Wind whirled around me, tugging at my clothes and hair.

The wooden steps were succeeded in turn by a series of toeholds. I glanced down and wished I hadn't. The tower zoomed downward, narrowing dizzily at what seemed an impossible distance. The workmen, their sheds and fires, and all the piles of materials were reduced to indistinct lumps. I could hear voices but very faintly, like the voices of insects.

But the magical influence seemed stronger here. I breathed deeply for a moment and began climbing again.

With sheer force of will I made my hands, one after the other, leave the crevices they were gripping and feel upward for the next. My knees trembled so hard that it was difficult to make my toes follow my hands. I had climbed as high as the towers of the old cathedral, and was abruptly startled by the sound of the bells. I plastered myself against the vertical stone face of the half-finished tower. If I could I would have held on with my ears.

When the bells stopped ringing, I made myself continue to the final scaffolding where I sat quietly, careful to make no movement that would start the board swaying on its ropes, waiting for my heartbeat to return to normal.

This is ridiculous, I told myself. I was supposed to be a competent wizard. The workmen went up and down here all the time, and they couldn't even fly! But knowing that I could save myself even if I suddenly hurtled toward the ground was not reassurance enough.

I tried to distract myself by probing again for magic. Although there was no other wizard on the tower at the moment, the faint trace of magic certainly suggested someone had been here earlier—probably someone who had had the sense to fly up, rather than letting his body discover, by climbing every step, just how high he had ascended.

But what would a wizard be doing here? Someone trained in the school would have received all the same warnings I had about getting involved with the Church. I tried to analyze the faint traces of magic; it was hard to be certain, but I did not think it was a school spell. It might have been cast by a very old wizard whose training predated the school.

There could also have been a magician here, I told myself, or even a witch. A magician would know a little magic, probably from a few abortive years of training at the school. But most of the young men who left without finishing the wizardry program also left without learning to fly.

Witches I knew less about. Women were not admitted to the school, although the possibility had sometimes been raised in recent years. But there were always rumors of women who had learned a little magic, doubtless dark and arcane. I had never actually seen a western witch, but the one witch I *had* met, in the East, had mixed the supernatural power of evil into her spells.

I recalled again the Romney children and their disappointment over my spells. They had clearly seen someone working magic more powerful than the illusions a magician might use to make a living at the fairs, more complex than something a witch might be expected to know. But speculation was neither stopping whoever had been on the tower nor getting me down. I took a deep breath, deciding there was nothing more to be learned here, and forced myself to let go.

As I dropped into open air, I had half a second's doubt

whether vertigo might have made me forget how to fly. But I swooped downward easily as I had on a thousand other occasions and landed in the middle of the construction site, where the workmen had just finished the sausages.

"I'm through checking the tower for now," I told the crew foreman. "I won't be in your way any longer."

He smiled at me almost impudently, wiping the grease from his mouth. I wondered if he guessed my terror up among the scaffolding. "And what did you find out?"

"Someone has certainly been practicing magic up there, probably another wizard, although not today."

"The priests worry a lot," he said, having apparently no more respect for them than he did for me. "We were concerned at first; after all, we don't want anything stolen or our work set back. But then we realized it's nothing serious. My men and I have been working construction in this part of the world for many years, but in the valley we came from, far up in the north, you learn not to worry too much about the Little People or fairy lights at night."

Fairy lights, I thought. This was a different interpretation than the flickering fire Joachim had mentioned. I wasn't sure I believed in fairies. They were a popular feature in children's stories, and hearing my grandmother's stories about them when I was little was probably one of the reasons I had been attracted to magic in the first place, but they had always had an unreal quality to them. On the other hand, the dragons that also appeared in children's stories were certainly real.

"Well," said the foreman, "it's time we were back at work."

I excused myself and found a path out of the construction site, then turned to look back at the half-finished tower. The small figures of workmen were already clustered along the scaffolding, and several were on the treadmill, winching up a load of stones.

An inn opened onto the street in front of me. Feeling a strong need for lunch after my experiences, I ducked my head and went inside. I wondered if the mothers in the northern valley worried about their children climbing too high or going too close to precipices, or whether they encouraged them in such explorations.

After a plate of sausages and a mug of beer, the terrors of clinging to the vertical side of a tower a hundred and fifty feet up had receded nicely. Since Joachim had said he would be busy, I went to see what diversion the little city of Caelrhon offered.

I had come here relatively frequently over the years. It was the closest city to the royal castle of Yurt, even though located in the adjacent kingdom, and the royal family of Yurt owned a small castle here. They came for fairs and carnivals and occasionally for services in the cathedral—the late king had married his queen here, over twenty years ago.

After spending the last three months in the great City by the sea, however, I found the streets and shop windows here held little to interest me. After wandering around for a quarter hour, I decided to try again to talk to the Romney children. I went out through the open gates toward where they had been camped that morning.

But the brightly painted caravans were gone. Less than four hours earlier, dozens of men, women, and children had been here. Now there was only a broad patch of trampled grass and the ashes from their dead fires. I walked around the abandoned campsite for several minutes without finding anything of interest other than a single gold earring, small enough to be a child's, which I slipped into my pocket.

I hesitated, wondering if I should follow the Romneys. They couldn't have been on the road for long, and their shaggy horses would not be able to pull loaded caravans very rapidly. Flying, I could quickly search all the roads leading out of the city.

But was there any reason to find them? They had, according to Joachim, been camped outside the city for six weeks, which I thought was fairly long for them. It must be simple coincidence that their decision to move on came the same day as my arrival.

Playing with the earring in my pocket, I wondered if returning it to its owner was excuse enough to catch up to the Romneys and decided that it was not. If their departure was indeed coincidence, then they would have nothing to tell me that I needed to know. But if they *had* moved off as a result of my appearance that morning, fearing that I would further question the children about the person they had seen working powerful magic, then even if I caught up to them they would deny any knowledge of anything.

I turned to go back through the city gates. If whoever had been casting magic spells on the new tower, fairy or wizard, was with the Romneys, then maybe I had scared him off and Joachim's problems were over. But I didn't believe in fairies and had been, at least a few hours ago, fairly sure that no one in the Romney encampment knew magic.

IV

Late afternoon found me in the cathedral listening to the organ.

From the main doors I had followed the Tree of Life worked in mosaic tiles the length of the nave. I started with the tree's roots and walked across branches and leaves among which appeared first fish, then insects, serpents, toads, rabbits, and deer. Now I leaned against a pillar at the transept, my feet among men and women, old and young, lords and peasants, sinners and saints.

Even before coming through the doors I had heard the organ. From outside, its notes competed awkwardly with the lighthearted songs the workmen were singing as they closed down for the night, but inside the organ swept all other sounds away. The sun's horizontal rays poured through the stained glass, lighting up a church interior that had seemed dim at midday. The row of organ pipes, ranging in size from scarcely bigger than my finger to the diameter of a young tree, glowed like red gold. A high melody rose in a hymn of praise while great chords rolled below. The pillar against which I leaned, the stones under my feet, and the very air around me vibrated with the bass.

The organist finished with a flourish. As the thunder of music died away, I became aware of Joachim beside me. I had no idea how long he had been there. "It would make someone believe in God even if he didn't already," I commented.

He gave me a quick, sideways look. "That *is* the idea. Come to dinner, and we'll talk."

We went out a small side door and around to the back of the cathedral. Here on a quiet cobbled street, at the opposite end of the church from the new construction, the cathedral priests had their houses. As we walked down the street a priest emerged from a covered porch to stare at us. "Father Joachim," he said in greeting, dipping his head to the dean, but me he glared at as though I had the word WIZARD (or even DEMON) emblazoned on my forehead.

"Father Norbert," Joachim replied with a nod. When we were past he said in my ear, "Don't mind him. He's never had much use for wizards."

The dean's house was at the far end. The carved wooden porch and the cathedral looming over the street made the entrance very dark, but as we stepped inside we were greeted by light. Many-paned mullion windows on the far side of the house looked out over a hillside that sloped sharply down toward the river and the tiled roofs of the artisans' quarter of the city.

A servant in black livery met us. "We'll just wash up, and then we'll eat right away," Joachim told him. "Once we are served, you can leave us." The servant nodded silently and disappeared.

A senior officer of a cathedral, I thought as I dried my hands, lived fairly well. But good living had not filled out Joachim, and his face was as gaunt as ever. I wondered briefly if I should suspect *him* of being behind some veiled attack on organized magic—which Brother Norbert appeared ready to join—but I dismissed this. I had known Joachim too long, and, besides, he had asked for my help.

The servant lit the white candles on the table, served us from a large platter, and withdrew, still without a word. As we ate, the sky outside the window became gradually dim, and the candle flames seemed to grow brighter and brighter, their light reflected from the polished surface of the woodwork.

"I climbed up the new tower after I talked to you," I said once I had finished a plateful of chicken. "How did you find those construction workers? It's terrifying being up on the scaffolding, yet they seem totally fearless. Maybe their long fingers and toes allow them to cling to a surface like tree frogs."

"I did not hire them myself. Even though I am the elected head of the cathedral chapter, the provost and the chancellor are in charge of the cathedral edifice itself and of raising money to pay for its upkeep. There had already been discussion for years before I arrived about building a new cathedral. The provost had heard good things about this construction crew from the priests of another church on which they had worked."

"They also aren't very concerned about the strange lights at night," I continued. "They come from somewhere far up north, and they seem to consider magical occurrences fairly ordinary. After all, I gather that if one went only a little further than their valley one would reach the land of dragons. And up there it's all wild magic, not organized and channeled as in the western kingdoms."

"My colleagues do not like any kind of magic, wild *or* organized," said Joachim, a glint in his eye. He paused to refill my wineglass. "I'm sorry if I seemed abrupt earlier. I have a lot on my mind." Tact had never been his strong point; although he had become no more tactful over the years, at least he worried about it more. "When I told the bishop today I had sent for you, he was very unhappy about bringing a wizard into the affairs of the Church."

"You can tell him that the wizards at the school weren't any happier about it," I said cheerfully.

This seemed to surprise him, but he made no comment. Instead he asked, "And could you tell if the lights at night and the material being moved around on the tower were due to a magic spell?"

"Someone's certainly been working magic up there. But I'm hoping he may have left with the Romneys." I told him about the Romney woman's eagerness to chase the children away and the abrupt departure of the entire camp that afternoon.

"That would indeed solve the problem," said Joachim thoughtfully, twirling the stem of his glass and looking somewhere over my head. "But you say the children expected to see something spectacular, as though the last magic-worker they had seen had *not* been a member of their band but an outsider like yourself. They hoped for as good tricks from the new wizard they had just spotted as they had from the last."

I ignored his implication that my scarlet illusory dragon had been less than spectacular. "If the magician or wizard is still here," I said, "the most direct approach would be to put a spell on the tower, a magical shield that would keep any further spells from working."

"And could you do it?"

I knew he'd ask that. "Actually, no. I know such spells are possible, but it's very advanced magic, and I don't have my books with me."

"What else can you do?"

"The other possibility would be to sit on the construction

site every night, watching for signs of magical activity, and then go up and confront the magician if he reappears." Joachim did not answer at once, and I hoped he was not summoning his small supply of tact to ask me to spend the summer with the watchman. "Why are the members of the cathedral chapter so concerned anyway? The crew foreman said it hasn't been much of a problem. He told me he thought it was Little People."

Joachim fixed me with his enormous dark eyes. "I thought fairies were just a story."

"Down here, in the western kingdom, they probably are, but I'd believe anything of the land of dragons."

"Fairies or wizards," said Joachim, "it's sacrilegious. The bishop feels that someone is violating the sanctity of a new edifice that will be consecrated to God."

"And that's why he didn't like it when you sent for me? He felt that being saved by wizardry is scarcely an improvement over being violated by wizardry? I hope you explained to him that bringing in a wizard to deal with a magical problem is much more effective than trying to pray it away. The saints have better things to do than to worry about whether the new cathedral has fairies living in it. Besides, it may even be good for the bishop's soul to have to deal with magic, and I'm sure the saints know that."

Joachim gave me a look without answering, having had long practice in ignoring my humor.

"Do you want to go out and see if we can spot the magician tonight?" I asked.

It was now full dark, and we had been slowly finishing the cheese. Joachim pushed back his chair and rose at once. He lit a lantern, and we stepped out his door under the low porch into the street.

"How long is it going to take to finish the cathedral?" I asked. We walked slowly because of the unevenness of the cobblestones; neither the lantern nor the shuttered windows of the other priests' houses did much to light up the street. Shadows danced crazily around our feet.

"Originally they had spoken of being done within fifteen or at the most twenty years. But I think the provost may have changed his calculations. The workmen are certainly working hard, but there is a limit to how fast anyone can erect that much stonework. Some of the supplies are proving much more expensive than the chancellor had hoped; it's possible construction may have to stop for a time while we raise more money. It is good that it was decided to leave the old cathedral intact, within the circle of what will be the new one, as long as possible—it may even be generations before the new edifice can be dedicated." His voice was troubled. Since Joachim was dean, I reminded myself, the cathedral was his as much as Yurt was my kingdom.

We came around the side of the cathedral to the edge of the construction site. So far, they had completed half a tower. I didn't want to think what this part of the city would be like once they had to start tearing down houses and moving streets to accommodate the new, wider size of the rebuilt church.

"I like your cathedral," I said. "Why not just leave it as it is?"

"It's six hundred years old," replied Joachim. "It's dark, it's old-fashioned, and its roof is too low, even compared to some of the regional parish churches that have gone up in the last decade or two. A cathedral is the heart of the Church's administration and care of souls, and it must reflect the glory of God."

The watchman on the construction site came toward us when he saw our light, holding up his own lantern to illuminate our faces. "Good evening, Father," he said, recognizing the dean. "There have been no disturbances so far tonight."

"I have brought a wizard to check for the presence of magic," said Joachim.

We made our way through the maze of materials, even

more difficult to negotiate at night than during the day. Quick, cool breezes, twisted and turned by the piles of building materials, whirled around us. There were lights in the workmen's huts at the far side of the site, but the bulk of the tower was completely dark. We leaned our heads back, looking up to where it blocked out the stars.

"Maybe I'll go up again to where they've got the scaffolding," I said. "Do you want to come?"

"I'm not going to climb up in the dark, if that's what you mean."

"I'm going to fly. I can take you with me." I knew this was audacious. Not only had I never suggested such a thing to Joachim before, but it was potentially dangerous to lift anything heavy while concentrating on one's own flying. But the night breezes and the wild shadows cast by our lantern had made me reckless.

Although I expected him to refuse at once, instead he hesitated so long that I started to wonder if he was outraged or indeed had even heard me. "The bishop would not like it," he said at last.

"But the bishop isn't here. No one will see us." The watchman had not followed us, and the workmen were out of sight.

Maybe the night had made him reckless too. "Just don't drop me," he said, setting down his lantern with what might have been a chuckle. "It would be hard to explain in the morning."

I paused for a few seconds to find the right words in the Hidden Language, then rose slowly and majestically up the face of the tower, Joachim at my shoulder. His vestments fluttered slightly in the breeze. I had been right that afternoon. Without the process of climbing, my body had no sense of how high we had risen and no irrational fear of hurtling downwards. I set us on the ledge at the top of the last flight of wooden stairs with a sense of triumph.

"Are you all right?" I asked Joachim. He had not made

a sound while we were moving upward, perhaps not even breathing.

He let out his breath all at once. "Yes. I'm fine. It's a strange sensation. It— It must be what ascension would feel like."

As there had been earlier, there was a hint of someone's magical spell, but faint and distant, as though cast several days earlier. "Certainly no one but me is practicing magic here at the moment," I said. "Maybe the magician *did* leave with the Romneys."

I turned back toward Joachim to ask if he wanted to catch his breath for a few more minutes or if we should go even higher, then suddenly staggered. Delicately, fleetingly, another mind had touched mine.

I stumbled against a wooden brace, leaned on it, and probed in return, but found nothing. Holding on hard to the brace, I let my mind slip lightly from my body, searching more widely while never allowing myself to forget for a second where I was standing. Below us in the city were a great mass of minds, many of them already asleep. A few I could recognize, such as the crew foreman, but most were unfamiliar and hence indistinct. None of them seemed to be practicing magic.

Had I imagined it? Far beyond the old cathedral, a half moon rose slowly above the eastern horizon. The wind was rising. With the workmen talking of fairies and Joachim of ascension, it was possible to imagine anything tonight.

V

The dean was whistling almost soundlessly, but I could recognize the hymn the organist had played that afternoon. "Are you ready to go back down?" I asked. If the magician or wizard was somewhere in the city, probing for my magic as I was probing for his, he was at any rate not up on the tower.

Our descent was again silent. I was glad that I had

not felt that fleeting touch while trying to lift Joachim, or I really would have had a lot to explain to the bishop.

We recovered the lantern and picked our way back out of the construction site. "Good-night," Joachim said gravely as we passed the watchman, the first thing he had said since leaving the tower. But he whistled again as we walked back to his house.

Inside, however, in the light of the relit candles, his eyes looked distressed. "Would you like some tea?" he asked distractedly.

"Let's just finish the wine." I wondered if I should mention a delicate mental touch I was still not completely sure I had felt.

He emptied the bottle into our glasses. "I'm in much too responsible a position to enjoy magical flying," he said bitterly.

I thought about this, sipping my wine slowly. He *had* enjoyed flying, and he had telephoned me to come help him in spite of the bishop. "Tell me what's really troubling you," I said. I considered adding, "Confession is good for the soul," but rejected the thought.

He hesitated. I waited, knowing that at a certain level anything he said to me was a betrayal of his position in the Church. For that matter, Zahlfast's warning to me may have included conversations such as this one.

"The bishop has been bishop for nearly forty years," Joachim said at last. "He had already been here for many years when I first came to Yurt."

I nodded, studying his face. It had always been hard to read, and I could only see now how truly worried he was about something.

"This last year, he has become extremely weak. His mind is as clear as ever, and he still directs the affairs of the diocese. But he never leaves his house, even to go to service in the cathedral, and for the last month he has not even left his bed. The doctors say he does not have long to live."

I contemplated the blow it would be if I heard the old Master of the wizards' school was dying and nodded again.

"When they made me dean, I knew that most commonly a new bishop is elected by the cathedral priests from among the senior officers of the chapter. Any member of the Church could of course be elected, but cathedral priests usually have a preference for their own officers. But since I've only been dean for a few years, I had not thought this would be a concern in my case. I had in fact always assumed that Norbert, the cathedral cantor, would succeed. He is quite a venerable scholar if not a senior officer, and very dedicated to the Church's welfare—you saw him in the street this afternoon."

"And aren't you the youngest of the senior officers?"

He did not seem to hear me. "This last week both the provost and the chancellor spoke to me, separately and privately. Neither mentioned Father Norbert. Both said they were too old and comfortable in their present offices to seek the position of bishop. When the old bishop dies, I fear they may elect *me* bishop in his place."

"But that's wonderful," I said. "It's an enormous honor."

"It is an enormous responsibility," he answered with a flash from his dark eyes. "And I know I am not worthy."

"I'm sure the old bishop thought exactly the same thing when they elected him," I said encouragingly.

"But why *me*? What have I done to deserve this?"

"You were Royal Chaplain of Yurt for years," I suggested.

"A position as chaplain to an aristocratic court has never been considered a great sign of spiritual purity."

"And you've been to the Holy Land."

"So have several other members of the cathedral chapter, including the chancellor. What special merit can they imagine I have?"

I took a sip of wine I did not want while wondering

whether to remind him. "You brought someone back from the dead."

"That had nothing to do with my merits," he said, staring straight ahead. "Besides, it was so long ago I doubt they remember, even if they heard about it in the first place."

When there was that note in his voice, I knew better than to argue with him. Instead I said, "I think you'd be a very good bishop."

The edge of his mouth twitched in what might have been a wry smile. "The good opinion of a wizard is not what I need."

I knew him too well to worry that this might be an insult. "At least if you were bishop you wouldn't have to worry about someone else's disapproval if you needed help with another magical problem."

He leaned forward, resting his forehead on his fists for a moment, then shot me one of his piercing looks. "I realize wizardry does not demand the same level of spiritual commitment as religion, but maybe I can explain it to you. I know my own weaknesses. My fears of being unworthy are not a meaningless or automatic response. Do you remember the very first day I met you, when you had just become Royal Wizard of Yurt? You were talking about the land of wild magic and said that you had never been there because you were 'not yet worthy of the voyage.' Do you remember?"

"Yes, I might well have said that."

"Have you been there yet?"

"Well, no. They used to have field trips from the wizards' school, but I was never invited to go. I guess I could have gone myself any time in the last nineteen years, but somehow I haven't." Wild magic had been to meet *me* once too often; I had no desire to go meet it.

"Then even you, with the audacity wizardry gives a man, know what it is like to feel unworthy."

Actually I had always had an excellent idea of what it

feels like to be unworthy, or at least incompetent, but I had never let it bother me.

He sat back as though he had just explained something important. I still thought he would be an excellent bishop. "If they do elect you," I said, "I'll go to the land of wild magic. Maybe I can find the Queen of the Fairies and make her stop sending her fairies to your cathedral."

Joachim said nothing but just looked at me.

"Or," I added, warming to the topic, "you and I could try to arrange better relations between wizardry and the Church, so that bishops aren't always warning young priests and old wizards warning young wizards against each other."

I was pleased to see that this idea distracted him. He played with his empty wineglass, thinking about it.

"There are three who rule the world," I quoted, "the Church, the wizards, and the aristocracy."

"And the greatest of these is the Church," he said absently.

"Hey! They never added that when *I* learned the proverb!"

This actually made him smile. "Did they tell you that the greatest were the wizards? It *is* a good saying. The Church is concerned with the souls of men and women in this world and their salvation in the next, and wizards with keeping the peace and keeping dragons away."

"And the aristocracy with law-giving and administering justice, with wars—when we let them—and with the extremely vital mission of providing the income for priests and wizards. We don't actually say that wizards are the greatest, you know, even if we are; after all, we've always served the kings."

"That leaves the peasants and the artisans and the merchants."

"Of course they don't have time for anything as foolish as ruling the world," I said. "They're too busy producing what everybody else needs."

Joachim smiled again and worked the cork out of another bottle. I was delighted to see him feeling less bitter. Maybe sometime he'd even want to go flying again. "But we are not discussing social theory," he said. "You're trying to cheer me up, and it may be the sin of despondency to resist such cheering, even from a wizard." He filled our glasses; he had switched from white wine to red, and it glowed the color of rubies in the candlelight. "I still often feel like a callow priest fresh out of the seminary, but maybe even the most powerful men feel that way sometimes."

I remembered him having an air of mature gravity from the day I met him and very much doubted he had ever been callow and shallow—unlike the young priest who was now chaplain of Yurt. But I did not mention this, and also did not mention that he seemed to have done a very good job of overcoming the same fears of unworthiness when he was first invited to join the cathedral chapter.

"Lately I've found myself wishing," I told him instead, "that we could go back to Yurt the way it was when we first arrived there."

"Of course you have to remember," he said thoughtfully, "that 'Yurt as it first was' is different for me than for you. I had already been royal chaplain for several years when you arrived. I remember the queen's old nurse living in the chambers they later gave you."

I had never quite gotten over the feeling that I would have been much more awe-inspiring in a dungeon or a tower, but I very much liked my chambers in the royal castle, looking out into the courtyard through a tangle of climbing roses. It was by now far too late anyway to become frightening and mysterious.

"Speaking of the queen," added Joachim, "I meant to tell you. I received a letter from her yesterday."

I was jealous at once. I hadn't had a letter from her since the first week I had been in the City.

"I had not heard from her in months, maybe a year, but she wants to find out what she needs to do to reserve the cathedral."

"The cathedral?"

"Yes. She is thinking of marrying again."

I stared at him, unable to answer. I was devastated. The old Romney woman, in prophesying that I would fall deeply in love, had been almost twenty years too late. I remembered my wineglass just in time not to drop it. "But she can't get married!" I finally managed to gasp.

"Why shouldn't she? She has been a widow for some six years, so remarriage would show no disrespect to the king's memory. Doesn't Paul come of age this summer? Once he is eighteen her regency will be over, and she will be free to leave Yurt if she wishes."

This was even worse. "She can't leave Yurt!"

Joachim looked at me quizzically. "You seem very disturbed by this."

"I *am* disturbed," I said desperately. "I've never told you this before, but I love the queen."

"Of course. Everyone who knows her must love her. That is why we should welcome anything that makes her happy."

I thought, not for the first time, that it was a good thing he was a priest.

"You can see her letter if you like. She did not tell me the name of the man she is thinking of marrying."

He got it from his desk. It was a real letter, not one of the tiny rectangles that were all the carrier pigeons could handle. She must have found someone heading to the cathedral city to carry her letter by hand. I read it avidly, looking for hidden clues as to why she should suddenly have made such a bizarre decision, but there was nothing in it besides what the dean had already told me. I found myself remembering various men over the years who had looked admiringly at the queen, all of whom I now detested. Joachim was right that everyone loved the queen, and not everyone was a priest.

"I'll have to go back to Yurt at once." When Joachim gave me another puzzled look, I added lamely, "They'll need the Royal Wizard to help prepare for the wedding festivities."

"I had hoped you could stay at least a few days. If she is only just now inquiring about the availability of the cathedral, she cannot be planning to marry in less than six months."

He was right, of course. And if I had left the wizards' school earlier than planned to help out an old friend, I couldn't very well abandon him after only twelve hours in town.

Joachim tipped up the bottle. "This is almost empty; we might as well finish it. There is a guest house down the street we use for visitors to the cathedral. Or you can stay here with me; I have an extra room."

"Thank you. I'd be very happy to stay here." I sipped the last of my wine, listening to the wind. The moon outside the window kept appearing and disappearing behind shreds of clouds. I hadn't mentioned that mental touch up on the tower, and I was still not sure how real it had been, but if someone was practicing magic with evil intent—or if there really was priestly intrigue against organized wizardry here in Caelrhon—I felt much safer with Joachim than I would somewhere down the street.

But how could I go on as Royal Wizard of Yurt if the queen moved away, married to somebody else?

PART TWO

The Queen

I

I stayed with Joachim for four days. The cantor Norbert avoided me pointedly, the rest of the cathedral priests ignored me, and none of them showed any sign of trying to destroy me.

Every night I went out to check for magical influences on the new construction, and every night I found nothing. Although in the evenings the dean and I caught up on some of the conversations we had not had since he left Yurt, there was little for me to do during the day except fret about the queen. I did not even feel again the fleeting mental touch which I now concluded I had imagined.

"Telephone me if anything else happens," I told Joachim as I prepared to leave. "But I really do think the magician or whoever was responsible must have been warned by the Romneys. Once he realized a wizard had arrived in town, he decided it was safest to stop his mischief."

"I would certainly like to think so. Give my best wishes to everyone in Yurt."

Though I left the quiet cobbled street behind the cathedral on foot, once I had made my way through the city streets and out the wide gates to where the Romneys had been camped I soared upward for the flight home. The whole way, I was trying to imagine what could have possessed the queen to want to marry again.

I came over a stretch of thick forest and saw before me the fields and castle of the kingdom of Yurt. It always looked from the air like a perfect child's toy of a castle, with its whitewashed turreted walls and the pennants snapping from the towers. As I swooped down I noticed someone working in the old king's rose garden, just outside the moat, so I landed there.

She saw me descending and came to greet me. I was flabbergasted. It was the queen, and for the first time in six years she was not wearing black.

"You're home!" she said with delight. She had a smile that lit up her whole face and made whoever saw it want to smile too. "When your books arrived from the City, I knew you couldn't be far behind!"

"I've been down in the cathedral city of Caelrhon, visiting the dean for a few days," I said, wondering how I could possibly have stayed away as long as three months.

She gestured toward the garden. "As you can see, I was pruning the king's roses. But I've just finished. Shall we go inside?"

The queen swung the gate shut and slipped one arm through mine, holding her gardening gloves and pruning shears in the other hand. She was wearing a very simple, but also undeniably very bright red dress. Red had always gone well with her complexion and her midnight hair. Although her hair now had an attractive white streak in it, red still suited her. She was, as she had always been, the most beautiful woman I had ever met.

I squeezed her arm with mine and said, "It's good to be home."

"If you've seen the dean, maybe he's told you my news," she said gaily as we crossed the drawbridge into the castle. "I'm thinking of marrying again!"

I realized from the thud of my heart that I had been hoping for four days that it was not true. But hearing her talk about it so blithely made it real in a way that seeing the words on paper had not. "Who are you marrying?" I asked and was surprised to hear my voice sound almost normal.

"His name is Vincent," she said, again with that smile but this time not directed at me. "I'm sure you've met him, as he's visited here several times over the years. He's the younger son of a king—in fact the king of Caelrhon, where you've just been."

I did indeed remember Vincent, well enough to detest him now. "But a king's younger son!" I protested. "He is not worthy of you, my lady!" I stopped myself just in time from adding that he was much too young for her.

"You forget that I myself was only a castellan's daughter before I became queen of Yurt," she said with a laugh. Then she answered my unspoken comment as well by saying, "With him I feel almost like a girl again! Vincent is very different from King Haimeric, but I'm sure he would be delighted to see me happy again."

She was at least right, I thought gloomily, about the old king of Yurt. He would have approved of the marriage even though I did not. "What do your parents think?"

"They're pleased, of course. But you ask," she added with another laugh, "as if I were still a girl too young to know my own mind!"

It was not hard to think of her as a girl in spite of the white streak in her hair. She gave a quick little whirl, almost a dance step, and said, "Vincent's coming tomorrow so you can renew acquaintances. Your chambers should be ready. The constable put your books inside, but he didn't unpack them—he was afraid his eye might fall on a spell accidentally and he would turn himself into a frog!" And she went off laughing at her own joke.

I was gloomily reshelving books when I heard a knock at the door. "Come in!" I called, hoping it was the queen come to say her plan to marry Vincent was just another joke, and in rather poor taste.

But it was Prince Paul, royal heir to Yurt. He seemed to have shot up several inches in three months and had to duck through the doorway. "Welcome home! I just heard you'd arrived. Did you have a pleasant stay in the City?" His good manners did not mask the intensity of whatever had brought him here. I had barely begun a congenial response when he added, "I need to talk to you privately. Can you come for a ride?"

Paul loved riding and was very good at it. I thought ruefully that I was going to be made stiff after months of not being on a horse, especially at the pace I was sure he would set. He led the way across the courtyard with rapid strides; his legs still had the slenderness of a boy's, but they were appreciably longer than mine.

In a few minutes we were mounted and riding out across the bridge, me on an old white mare and Paul on a gelding. "I think Mother's going to get me a horse for my eighteenth birthday," he said in a low voice, smiling in anticipation. Temporarily, his other concerns seemed forgotten. "I heard her talking to the constable about horse breeders and about the horse fairs this summer. They didn't know I was listening so I had to slip away, but I'm fairly sure she knows I want a roan stallion."

"Your mother is a good judge of horses," I said. "She used to ride a magnificent black stallion before you were born."

"I know," he said regretfully. "I still don't understand why she sold him. But then," with a grin, "I've never liked black horses that well anyway." Paul kicked his horse to a faster pace. He was bareheaded, and the wind swirled his hair. When he was young his hair had been so blond it was almost white, and even now it formed a golden halo around his head.

We rode for a mile, more rapidly than I would have liked but not as rapidly as I had feared, down the hill from the castle and then along a deep tree-shaded lane by the meadows. Larks soared over the long grass, and in the distance I could see people starting to harvest the hay.

Paul tied his reins to a branch and threw himself down on the grassy verge. "No one will overhear us," he said, intense once again.

I reminded myself as I eased out of the saddle that I couldn't treat him like a boy. Legally he would be of age in another three months, and with his mother's fire and his father's sweetness of temperament he would be a formidable king. If I let his boyish enthusiasm for horses remind me too strongly that I had given him horsie-rides on my knee not long ago, I was never going to have his confidence. "What's bothering you?" I asked, seating myself beside him. "Is it your mother's remarriage?"

"Yes," he said gloomily, lying down with his hands under his head. "It wasn't hard to guess, was it?" He jerked back up to a sitting position. "How can she do it? Why would she want to marry *anyone*, after Father? If she *has* to marry somebody, why does it have to be Prince Vincent?"

Since I had been asking myself exactly these questions, I found it difficult to answer.

Paul was now examining one of his riding boots, rubbing his thumb on a scrape. "I even tried talking to Aunt Maria," he said. "If Mother remarries it will affect the entire kingdom." He shifted his attention to the other boot. "But she just said something foolish about how a woman like her deserves her happiness."

As I had been about to say something similar, I was glad I had not spoken. Instead I asked, "What are you afraid will happen to the kingdom?"

"Vincent will move here," said Paul from the depths of despair, "and nothing will ever be the same again."

"You mean your mother isn't planning to leave Yurt?" I asked, trying with only moderate success to keep the excitement out of my voice.

"Why should she?" said Paul, ignoring my tone if he even heard it. "She's a queen, and back home in his kingdom he's just the young prince. He'll come here and change everything."

"But there's a limit to what he'll be able to do. After all, you're going to be king, not he."

"I don't mean he's going to introduce bad laws or anything," Paul said in irritation. "But we've been so happy and comfortable here, and now everything will be different."

I observed with interest that nostalgia was perfectly possible even for someone thirty years younger than I. The afternoon breeze was a caress. The thought that the queen would not be leaving was so cheering that it was hard to be properly sympathetic.

"So what can we do?" He looked straight at me for the first time, waiting for an answer. He had the same brilliant green eyes as his mother.

Short of assassinating Prince Vincent I had no good suggestions. I was still unable to speak reassuringly of how the marriage was really best for the queen, especially since this was apparently what everybody else had been telling him. "I honestly don't know, Paul. I was just as upset as you are when I found out."

"So that's all we can do, be upset together?"

"And learn to live with it. People can learn to live with a surprising number of problems. Yurt has gone on without your father, though when he died I never thought it would."

Six winters ago, I reminded myself, was far more recent to me than it was to Paul. He did not find my comment reassuring. "Mother's certainly recovered nicely from her loss," he grumbled. "You would have thought at her age she'd be much too old for love."

Since I knew no good way to contradict this foolish idea without also pointing out that I thought eighteen was much too young to know anything about love, I said nothing.

"And this Vincent is younger than she is by at least

five years; she won't tell me exactly. I think he's deceiving her terribly. She goes around telling people she feels like a girl again, while it's clear that his only interest in an old woman is to get hold of her kingdom."

I had to smile at this, but since Paul had rolled over onto his stomach he fortunately didn't see me. I would have been in love with the queen even if I had been eighteen and she was forty-three. "Do you know when they're planning the wedding?" I asked with remarkable calmness.

"Not yet—I guess there's still hope she'll discover her mistake before it's too late. She told me she didn't even want to start plans for the wedding until after I come of age, and the dean of the cathedral sent her a note that if she wanted to get married there she would have to reserve the church six months ahead of time. And she said she didn't want to get married during the winter."

So they might not be getting married for close to a year. I agreed silently with Paul; the longer the wedding was put off, the more likely that she would have the sense not to go through with it.

He changed the subject abruptly, turning toward me with arms wrapped around one knee. "So what have you been doing the last few months in the wizards' school?"

"I ended up teaching improvisational magic to technical wizardry students. In spite of all the formulas and books we have, you still have to be able to create your own spells—and to know when to try something unusual. Of course," I added with a chuckle, "sometimes the unusual is not a good idea." I went on to tell him about the three drunk newts.

Paul laughed, pulling up and twisting together blades of grass. "I think I'll go study at the wizards' school," he said thoughtfully.

This made me sit up sharply. "Do you mean that?"

He looked at me with surprise. "Is there a reason why I shouldn't?"

"No, but— Usually members of the aristocracy don't become wizards. The training is too long and too hard and the rewards too negligible in comparison to aristocratic rule."

"But aristocrats become priests sometimes."

"Well, yes, but I've never heard of a king doing so. And there are a lot more priests than there are wizards. I assume a lot of men have a religious calling or something."

"So would I be the only king at the wizards' school?"

"That's right," I said, hoping desperately he was just casting around in his mind for an alternative to living with Vincent.

"What is it, an eight-year program?" he asked, positioning a blade of grass between his thumbs. He blew on it and seemed pleased to produce a high, blatting tone. "Maybe you could just teach me a little magic here."

"I could certainly teach you a few simple spells," I said, trying to hide my relief. I liked Paul tremendously, but I could not imagine him in the wizards' school—nor imagine Yurt abandoned by its new king. "Real wizardry training," I went on, "has almost all taken place at the school for the last century and a half. There are thousands of aristocratic courts in the western kingdoms and probably hundreds of seminaries, but only one wizards' school. Since the old apprentice system died out, everyone's been trained the same, and most of us know each other. But there are still a number of people, not wizards, who know the odd spell or two. Your father tried to learn to fly once though he never got very far. And your Great-aunt Maria wanted me to teach her wizardry; her problem was that she got bored with the first-grammar of the Hidden Language."

"I never knew she was interested in magic," said Paul in surprise. "The last couple of months, while you've been gone, she claims to have gotten very interested in theology."

It was my turn to be surprised. The Lady Maria had a lively mind and had made early chapel service every morning for years, but she had always become quickly bored by anything intellectual. "Your father was interested enough in religion to go on pilgrimage," I said.

"But Father was different. Besides, that was when the old chaplain was still here," meaning Joachim. "He wasn't too bad, and I also liked that priest whom the old chaplain had take over for him. But last winter, when he got a chance to go be a chaplain in the City, we ended up stuck with the chaplain we've got now.

"If you ask me," he added in tones of disgust, "it isn't religion she's interested in at all, but that young chaplain. She acts moonstruck when he's around. I decided I had to speak to her firmly. 'Aunt Maria,' I said, 'I hope you remember that priests have to swear a vow of chastity.' And you know what she said? She told me I had an 'impure mind.' All I can say, there are too many people in this castle who ought to know enough to act their age."

Since I didn't like the young chaplain either, I didn't say anything. The problem with being mature was that I was always feeling that I ought to tell young people things for their own good when they were things I wouldn't have wanted to hear myself.

"I'll tell you who has an 'impure mind': it's that chaplain."

"Have there been any particular incidents of impurity?" I asked in some alarm.

"Of course not. Everybody but me thinks he's fine." I relaxed again. "But I can tell from his laugh and his handshake that he's really a goat."

Since these had never conveyed anything of the sort to me, I attributed this statement to Paul's dislike of any change of personnel in Yurt. But an uneasy thought sent cold fingers walking down my spine. I had assumed that Zahlfast, in warning me against priests who would destroy me, was warning me against the cathedral. He might instead have been warning me against the young chaplain of Yurt.

Paul jumped to his feet, looking as satisfied and resolute as though we had decided something, which as far as I could tell we had not. "Race you back to the castle," he said, reaching for his horse's reins.

II

At dinner that night the queen formally welcomed me home to Yurt. We ate as we always did in the great hall of the castle. A brass choir, seated on a little balcony, played as the serving platters were brought in. Suspended beneath the high ceiling were the magic globes made many years ago by my predecessor as Royal Wizard, casting a sparkling light on the crystal and silver. The tall windows stood wide open, but a blazing fire on the hearth took the chill out of the spring air.

As regent, the queen sat at the head of the main table where the king had once sat, and Paul sat at the opposite end. I wondered where Vincent would expect to be seated once he married the queen.

I dined as I always had with the Lady Maria on my right hand and the chaplain facing me across the table. Paul's Great-aunt Maria now had hair as white as mine, but her manner had scarcely changed since she had worn her golden curls in girlish locks bedecked with bows.

"It was not the same here while you were gone," she said, fixing me with wide blue eyes. "All that arcane wisdom you wizards acquire makes you uniquely capable of counseling a court on all *sorts* of worldly matters, not just those involving magic." She paused for a bite. "But there are other matters," she added, "where even a wizard's wisdom does not reach: these are the affairs of the soul. And it is the inner soul, the inner heart, that drives women and men. I may seem to be an old woman leading a quiet life in a small kingdom, but within this heart are *scores* of adventures, of triumphs, of tragedies, of fears and hopes each day."

I had forgotten in my months away how irritating the Lady Maria could sometimes be. This sounded like the result of what Paul had characterized as theological discussions with the young chaplain.

He smiled and bobbed his head at her. To me he seemed much too young to have the responsibility for the souls of the royal court—he was even younger than I had been when I first came to Yurt. He had a very wide, congenial smile, but somehow I had never felt it was sincere. If Joachim did become bishop, I thought, I would ask him for a different chaplain.

"We know what you wizards do down at that school," continued the Lady Maria, jabbing me playfully with her elbow. "You plan to coordinate all your efforts, both against the western kings and against the Church!"

"We certainly try to coordinate our wizardly efforts for best effect," I said, startled to find that I was considered one of the wizards down at the school. "It's always hard, though. I'm sure you know that wizards are generally in competition with each other—and not always friendly competition. And if wizardry and the Church are rivals," I added graciously but insincerely, "I think the Church may be winning."

"But is it really true," the Lady Maria asked, "that your school now intends to put a wizard not just in every royal or ducal court, but in every castle and manor house?"

The young chaplain widened his eyes at me as though trying to signal that he was not responsible for her. I found this highly unlikely.

"I wouldn't call it an intention," I said uneasily. What had the young chaplain been telling them while I was gone? It was a good thing that Joachim's call had taken me away from the school sooner than I had planned, or there might have been a full-fledged plot against institutionalized magic here by the time I finished making improvisation into an organized discipline. "It's certainly true that more noble households have hired wizards during the last generation or so, but that's only because the school has made more fully qualified wizards available."

I added to myself that it was a good thing I had graduated when I did. Without an honors certificate or even areas of distinction, I might not be able today to become Royal Wizard at even as small a kingdom as Yurt, and I could instead be casting spells in a ramshackle manor house in the foothills of the mountains.

We were interrupted at this point by the arrival of dessert, raspberry pudding, my favorite. I looked over to the side table where the servants were sitting and signaled my approval to the cook. She smiled back, highly pleased. The cook was now a full-bosomed matron and had a daughter almost as old as she had been when I first met her, but we had been friends ever since she was a saucy kitchen maid.

If it had not been for the Lady Maria and her questions, I would have assumed that the whole court was as happy to see me again as I was to be here. Now I was beginning to wonder.

"Wizard!" called the queen down the table. "We missed your illusions while you were gone. Could you entertain us over dessert as you used to?"

My entertainments went over very well. I made the same scarlet dragon I had tried on the Romney children, and this time it got the appreciation it deserved. I finished by creating a pair of golden crowns, glittering with enough jewels to be worth a small kingdom by themselves if they were real, and had them whirl through the air and settle on the queen's and Paul's heads.

"Thank you!" said Paul with a laugh. "Everybody else keeps trying to remind me that I still have three months to go!"

As the illusions faded away, people began to disperse. The young chaplain startled me by touching my elbow. "Would you care for a final glass of wine in my chambers?"

For a moment I was unable to answer. Even aside from my suspicions of him, coming back to Yurt had revived long-forgotten memories of the day I first arrived here. We had eaten in the same hall, its doors and windows open to the air; I had had the Lady Maria beside me; and after dinner I had asked Joachim to have a glass of wine in my chambers.

The young chaplain seemed to take my silence as a symptom of abstemiousness. "The Apostle tells us to take 'a little wine for thy stomach's sake,' " he said with a genial chuckle, patting the organ in question, "and we shouldn't disobey the Apostle, now, should we?"

"I'm sorry," I said. "I was thinking of something else. I'd be very happy to join you."

I turned toward the stairs that led up to the small room both Joachim and his immediate successor had had, but the young chaplain turned the other way. I hurried after him, recalling some problem which had made him ask for different chambers.

"So how are you settling into your new duties?" I asked as I caught up. "You'd been here a month with the previous chaplain, but you'd only been on your own for a few weeks when I left." I wondered jealously if he now thought of Yurt as *his* kingdom.

"Very well, I hope. But maybe you shouldn't be asking *me*," he added with another chuckle, "but those I try to serve!"

He opened his door and motioned me to precede him. I observed at once that he had more space than I did. But I was also relieved to see that his chambers did not suggest an impure mind. The rooms were furnished sparsely, with nothing on the walls but his seminary diploma and the crucifix at the head of the narrow bed.

"You probably wondered why I asked you to join me,"

the chaplain said, opening a bottle, "especially after the Lady Maria seemed to imply that you and I ought to be fierce competitors!" He gave a broad smile and handed me a glass. Even though it had always bothered me that Joachim had a rather limited sense of humor, I would at the moment have preferred his sober intensity.

"So she's been taking her instruction in directions you hadn't intended?" I asked, taking a sip. The first night I had met Joachim, we had put away several bottles of City vintage between us. I had been determined to show him that no priest could outdrink a wizard, and although I had never asked him about it, I had the impression he didn't want to let a wizard think he could outdrink a priest.

"Well, her comments have put me in a delicate position," said the chaplain with well-modulated cheerfulness. "You may not believe me" —I didn't— "but it was not I who originally pointed out to her the growing role that wizards are taking in all noble courts. While naturally I have stressed the position of the Church in my little chats with her, it was someone else who planted the first seed of the idea that wizards are manipulating the secular rulers of society."

"Then who was it?"

"Christian charity forbids me from speaking his name."

Prince Vincent, I thought with sudden conviction. He must be behind the rumors the Master of the school had heard.

"But I will try to make amends," continued the chaplain, "by asking you to join us in a conspiracy!"

I barely avoided choking on my wine. "What sort of conspiracy?"

"We want to make sure the queen does not make the error of marrying Prince Vincent."

Immediately I liked the young chaplain much better. I could sort out all these strange rumors later. "And who is *we*?" I asked with an accommodating smile.

He looked down for a moment as though embarrassed,

then smiled again. "Well, I sounded pretty self-important there for a moment, didn't I! So far, the conspiracy is mostly myself. The Lady Maria is of course in agreement with my purposes."

"I would have thought she'd adore the romance of a love match."

"In a way she does, but there is a core of wisdom in what you might think is just a silly head."

I did not point out that I had probably known the Lady Maria since he was a child begging his mother for extra snacks. "How about other members of the court?"

"No," he said, shaking his head regretfully. "When I tried to broach the topic to one of the knights, he said something—I know you'll find this hard to credit—about the Church needing to stay out of the affairs of the aristocracy!" So if members of the court were being taught to distrust wizards, I noted with interest, they also distrusted the chaplain. "I would like to bring Prince Paul into our plans," he added, "though at his age it is hard to trust his judgment."

I thought uncharitably that the chaplain was not very much older. "I can understand why Paul doesn't like the thought of his mother's remarriage," I said. "He's had her all to himself, and he doesn't want any disservice to his late father's memory. But I don't understand your own objections."

He leaned forward and spoke gravely. The candlelight made flickering points of light in his eyes. "A woman, once widowed, does better to devote herself to God than to another temporal spouse."

"So you think widows should never remarry?"

"The Apostle tells us it is best that they do not. I can see that she felt she had a moral obligation to raise her son to manhood before retiring, but a woman of true religious sensibilities would now be planning her retreat to a nunnery. The Nunnery of Yurt has an excellent reputation for holiness and was in the past, I understand, supported by generous and pious gifts from the royal family of Yurt."

I was unable to answer at once. The queen had in fact, when very young, contemplated entering a nunnery rather than marry someone she detested, but she had instead married the king, whom she loved. I could not see her in a nunnery, then or now.

"Have you mentioned this to the queen?"

"I tried to suggest to her delicately that perhaps remarriage would distract her from the higher affairs of the soul, but she just laughed."

I gave him my wizardly look. "Surely I do not need to tell you that to force a soul into suitable religious behavior will not help that soul's salvation." I rose to my feet without waiting for an answer. "Thank you for the wine. It is good if representatives of wizardry and the Church can agree on issues of mutual importance."

As I strode with self-conscious gravity from his chambers and crossed the courtyard toward my own, I found myself wondering if a belief that the queen's soul would be improved by a nunnery was his only consideration. Might he have some ulterior motive for wanting her out of the castle?

III

I awoke to the chapel bells the next morning with the happy realization that I was back home in Yurt, far from technical-division wizardry students. This cheerful thought was followed however almost immediately by the distressing knowledge that Prince Vincent was coming today.

He had telephoned that he planned to reach Yurt in the afternoon. The queen was busy bringing heaps of roses into the great hall, arranging them in vases and attaching bouquets to the dark stone walls. I myself wandered out across the drawbridge, gloomily convinced that he was the mysterious person inciting aristocrats to distrust their wizards. At least the queen and Paul seemed unaffected so far. I looked down the hillside sloping away from the castle, past the walled graveyard where the king was buried.

A distant group of tiny horsemen emerged from the woods, far earlier than anyone had expected. Faint on the wind came a trumpet call. Knights and ladies poured out across the bridge behind me. Even the queen, flushed, laughing, and pinning a white rose into her hair, came running out.

The trumpet sounded again, and the horsemen kicked their steeds for the last ascent. The man in the lead, whose golden surplice left no doubt he was a prince, was mounted on a red roan stallion. I looked surreptitiously for Paul, who I knew would be furiously jealous. He stood motionless among the members of the court.

With a jangling of bells and clatter of hoofs, the knights pulled up their horses. Vincent vaulted from the stallion and swept the wide velvet hat from his head. "My lady!" he cried and knelt before the queen. The jeweled scabbard of his sword and the long feather of his hat dragged unheeded on the brick road. With one hand he took both her hands and kissed them gravely.

She blushed charmingly and tugged to bring him to his feet. He leaped up, smiling all over his face. He was graceful and muscular, with hair that glowed like burnished copper, and very obviously in love. He was, I thought ruefully, a truly glorious knight. Thirty years ago, before I had decided to become a wizard, I would have wanted to be just like him.

"We had not expected you so early," said the queen. "You must forgive me if you find me in some disarray."

"You should have known, my lady, I would not stay from your side one moment longer than I could help. And I came to see *you*, not your array."

The other knights were dismounting. "Where is Prince

Paul?" Vincent called in a high, ringing voice that cut across the other voices. "I have something to give you!"

Paul came slowly forward. His mouth was grim, but he determinedly looked Vincent in the eye. I knew him well enough to realize that he did not want anyone to think that he was sulking.

"My prince!" cried Vincent. "When I left here three weeks ago, everyone was talking of preparations for your coming of age ceremony later this summer. I remember what it was like to be eighteen, and how long a few months could be. I thought then that you might not want to wait for all of your gifts, so I brought you one now. It's this stallion: he's yours, I bought him for you, take him!"

For a second all the color drained out of Paul's face, then he stepped closer, stiffly, unbelieving, unable to speak. Vincent handed him the reins.

I had to fight against my initial hope, that Paul would refuse the gift and would cast the reins into Vincent's face with a rebuke for the patronizing note I thought I had heard.

But I need not have worried. I saw all of Paul's objections to Vincent cracking and dissolving away like ice in the sun. A smile started small and stretched until it threatened to crack his face. He found his voice at last. "Thank you! How did you know? He's exactly what I wanted, more than anything!"

He swung up into the saddle. The stallion arched its neck and took a few quick steps. In spite of the long trip to Yurt which had left the other horses lathered, the stallion seemed nearly fresh. Paul brought him around, the horse answering instantly to the reins. Then, reluctantly, the prince slid back to the ground. "You've just been riding him rapidly, and I don't want to push him, even though I can tell he's ready to go again. Thank you!" It was going to be hard after all for the young chaplain to incorporate Paul into his "conspiracy."

"I thank you too," said the queen to Vincent, her

emerald eyes dancing with delight although she managed to keep her manner sober. "You have done my son a signal honor. Now, would you enter my castle?"

I watched jealously to make sure they weren't holding hands, but they walked side-by-side in perfect dignity across the drawbridge and through the castle gates. Stable boys came to take the horses, although Paul took charge of the stallion himself, and the constable directed our new guests to their quarters. I lingered outside the castle for a moment, looking across the green hills of Yurt, wondering if the queen had secretly loved Vincent for years as I was sure he must always have loved her, or if her feelings were only a product of a few short weeks of courtship while I was not there to stop it.

When I looked into the great hall a few minutes later, to see Vincent and the queen finishing arranging vases of roses, she motioned me over, smiling with a tenderness I knew was not meant for me. "Vincent, I'm sure you remember our Royal Wizard."

"Of course, though it's been several years," he said. "You performed some really spectacular illusions after dinner." Flattery was not about to win me, but I nodded my head. For the queen's sake I had to be polite. At least if he thought all wizards were plotting to take over the western kingdoms, he was too well bred to say so.

"You've been in the City, I understand?" he went on. "You missed what I gather has been the talk of Yurt, our whirlwind courtship!"

"Don't make it sound *too* rapid," said the queen with a laugh. "We had after all known each other for years, and it was scarcely my fault when I invited you to stay for a week that you stayed for eight!"

"And even so, when I left three weeks ago you still wouldn't say you'd marry me."

The queen laughed again. "I waited a week before I telephoned him to say Yes, and I still told him he couldn't come back right away. Do you think me very heartless, Wizard?"

"Entirely heartless," I agreed. I was sure the fact of their eight-week courtship was accurate; they wouldn't tell me something anyone might contradict. But I wondered why they should go out of their way to tell me, when it was none of my business, that the queen had initially hesitated to accept Vincent's proposal, and why they should do so in a manner so ostentatiously cheerful, affectionate, and in perfect dignity.

Were they trying to distract me from why Vincent had left and why he had come back now? Was it accidental that the queen had invited Vincent to visit shortly after I had left for the City? Had something happened during those eight weeks he was here, something they hoped was hidden from everyone else and they didn't want me to look for? Then I had to smile at myself. Now *I* was developing an "impure mind."

"We want you to know," the queen continued, "that you'll continue to be a valuable part of Yurt even after Paul becomes king and Vincent and I are married. We wouldn't dream of getting rid of our Royal Wizard."

This came as a serious shock. *I* had certainly never dreamed of this. That she would even bring it up meant that they had indeed considered it.

Though my first reaction was horror at realizing how close I had come to having to leave Yurt and join the Romneys, my second thought was to wonder why Vincent—he must be responsible—wanted to get rid of me. Was their cheerful unanimity a mask for severe disagreements, of which the question of whether to fire the wizard was only one? If so, the queen had apparently won this round, but might she lose the next?

"I thank you, my lady, my lord," I managed to say and retreated before they could spring any more devastating surprises.

The decorations were for the dance the queen had

planned in Vincent's honor, and in the late afternoon I could hear from my study the brass choir being tuned. Reluctantly I was drawn back to the hall; I had always liked the royal musicians' playing.

In spite of several suggestions from the ladies of the court, most playful, some even serious, that I join in, I sat obstinately in the balcony and watched. Even Paul was dancing, leading around women his mother's age with charming grace.

The queen and Vincent led every dance. The last of the sunlight, the flickering fire, and the glow from the magic lamps made the room bright as though the dancers themselves were filled with light. Vincent really was younger than the queen, maybe ten years younger rather than the five that Paul had guessed.

But there was nothing about him to support Paul's suspicion that he wanted the queen's kingdom rather than her person. He had his eyes on her constantly as she turned in the intricate steps of the dance, with an open affection that was almost too personal to watch. Even though for the most part her own expression was amused or even mocking, he several times said something in her ear that turned her laugh into a smile of undisguised pleasure.

They were only a couple in love, I told myself, and their unanimity, their cheerful picking up of each other's lines, did not show any plotting or planning but only how closely their minds and spirits were intertwined. I only wished I believed it.

IV

In the morning I heard from my chambers the clatter of horses being brought from the stables. A surreptitious glance out the window confirmed that the queen and Vincent were going hawking. I would stay in my study, I decided, until they were gone.

I was leafing through the third volume of the *Arcana*, looking for spells that might help the cathedral keep fairy lights off their new tower, when there was a knock on the door. "Come in!" I called, assuming it was the kitchen maid come to get my breakfast tray.

But the door burst open with a bang that the kitchen maid would never dare. I swung around to see my doorway blocked by a dark form, silhouetted beyond recognition by sunlight outside. But unmistakable was the naked sword it held.

I didn't even think. Two words in the Hidden Language and the figure staggered; three more and the sword clattered to the flagstones while the figure dropped as though hit with a plank. I strode across the room to retrieve the sword, then turned to see who had unwisely tried to attack a wizard.

It was Vincent. He sat up and tenderly felt his ribs. "I guess there's nothing broken," he said and gave me a rueful smile. "Help me up?"

I took the proffered hand and pulled him to his feet, but I held on to his sword.

"I'm sorry!" he said with apparently real penitence. "I was going to ask if you wanted to come hunting, and I thought it would be fun to pretend to attack you—just a joke, you realize, just to show you a trained warrior's power! I had no idea you'd react like that."

"Wizards always react rapidly," I told him sternly. "Suppose a trained warrior burst into *your* room. Wouldn't you draw your sword first and inquire who it might be afterwards?"

"I guess I'm lucky you didn't kill me, in that case," he said cheerfully, brushing himself off. "After my brother's experiences, I should have known better! Let me have my sword back, and I'll certainly never try a joke like that on a wizard again. Now that I'm here, *do* you want to go hunting?"

I handed him his sword since I could think of no excuse

to keep it. "Thank you for the offer," I said, more sternly than ever, "but I need to spend the day in the perusal of my magic spells." What could Vincent mean by his brother's experiences?

"We'll see you later, then," he said, uncowed. I closed the door firmly behind him and sat at my desk, doing nothing but listening until I was sure the hunting party was gone.

Then I did turn again to my books, looking for a spell that might protect against the action of any other spell. In an hour I determined that there actually was no such thing, but with enough effort I might be able to create one.

I put the volumes back onto the shelf, hoping I would not have to try. Even the simplest spell can have unforeseen results, and a spell against magic would create enough tensions within the natural fabric of the cathedral city that I might end up with the whole church sinking into a giant hole in the earth.

Instead I reached for another book. If I saw the Romney children again, I wanted to be ready with something to impress them.

It had been years since I had tried to make myself invisible. When I first came to Yurt, I had become quite good at making my feet disappear, but I had never been able to become invisible above the waist. Now, after reviewing my books, flipping back and forth between several volumes with fingers and three pencils marking different places, I thought I finally understood the problem.

I stood up, took a moment to review the spells in my mind, and began. As the heavy syllables of the Hidden Language rolled into the silent room, I slowly became invisible, starting at the feet and working up to my head. I looked into the mirror with delight. Nothing was there.

There was a sharp rap on the door. "Come in!" I called without thinking.

This time it *was* the kitchen maid. "I'm sorry, sir," she said, coming in. "But with the extra people staying, I'm afraid I lost track of your breakfast tray, and so—" She stopped, not seeing anyone. I smiled to myself and tried not to breathe. "Sir?" She looked directly through me to my bedroom beyond.

She shrugged then and picked up the tray. For a moment I was tempted to break the spell and appear abruptly before her, preferably with a flash and a lot of smoke. I went as far as to tiptoe over to the doorway where she would pass directly by me.

But I resisted. She was a very young kitchen maid, and it would not be fair to make her suffer for Vincent having surprised me. Besides, I didn't want to have to sweep a lot of broken crockery off my clean flagstone floor. I stepped silently aside and let her pass.

As she swung my door back open, sunlight poured in from the courtyard. She didn't see it, but I did: my shadow stretching out from invisible feet. The door swung shut and the shadow was gone, but I was left considering. My spell of invisibility made me and my clothing invisible to the human eye, but apparently not to the sun.

I snapped my fingers, said the two words to break the spell, and reappeared in the mirror. I doubted even the wizard or magician the Romney children had seen could have made his shadow disappear. Now all I had to do was to find a way to make a cloak of fire.

Since the spring morning was so warm, I had not lit a fire. Now I knelt at my hearth and put a pile of kindling together. Some wizards, I had once heard, could create fire straight from the air, but that was something never taught at the school.

The challenge with a cloak of fire would be to surround oneself with living flames yet emerge unscorched. Once I had a small fire burning, I pulled another book off the shelf and started putting a promising spell together. Sitting with one hand holding the volume, I tentatively reached the other hand toward the flame and then rapidly drew it back. This particular protective spell didn't seem to do anything against heat.

I tried a different spell, one that I knew was effective against arrows. But it worked no better against fire than the first. The third spell I tried seemed to have potential until I realized that I was able to put my hand closer to the flame only because the flame was dying.

I stood up, sucking the burnt back of one knuckle. "If the Romney children aren't satisfied with illusions and invisibility, then it's no use even trying to satisfy them," I told myself and went out.

Gwennie, daughter of the cook and the constable, was crossing the courtyard, staggering under a pile of leather-bound ledgers. I hurried to help her, putting a lifting spell on the volumes. "Where are these going?"

She gave me a quick and grateful grin and pushed the hair back from her face with a dusty hand. "To the storeroom. I decided Father doesn't need all these old ledgers cluttering up his office. Some of them even date from before I was *born*!"

I had to smile because I well remembered when she was born, which didn't seem long ago to me. "I would have thought you'd be helping your mother in the kitchens instead of your father."

Gwennie shook her head hard. "Not me! I'll never be a cook. I've decided I'm best at organizing and keeping track of things. I'm going to be constable of Yurt some day, like my father."

"Do you think people will approve of a woman constable?" I asked, amused.

"Well, Paul approves," she said proudly, adding, "Prince Paul, that is," after a very brief pause. She flushed a little and looked away as I considered her thoughtfully. She and Paul were nearly the same age and had been childhood playmates, but I had assumed the prince and the cook's daughter had drifted apart in the last ten years.

"I want to tell you, Wizard," she said hastily as though wanting to change the subject, "that the staff all support you." She unlocked the storeroom and showed me where she wanted the ledgers. "*We* don't think that wizards have to be stopped before they wrest control from the aristocrats. After all, we've known you for years, and you'd never be able to take power from anybody!"

She realized at the last minute that this was not coming out the way she intended and started to blush again. I excused myself before she could become any more embarrassed. But as I crossed the courtyard toward the main gates I decided I had better find out more of what Vincent seemed to have been telling the court.

On the grass beyond the moat a table was set up. The young chaplain and the Lady Maria sat in the sun, playing chess.

"Checkmate!" cried the Lady Maria in delight as I came toward them. If she was indeed moonstruck by the chaplain, as Paul had suggested, it wasn't stopping her from beating him. "You moved right into my trap!" The chaplain gave me a complacent smile over her head as though to suggest that he and I both knew he had deliberately let her win. He didn't fool me for a minute.

"Did Prince Paul go hunting with the others?" I asked.

"He rode out by himself," said the Lady Maria. "He took his new horse and told his mother she wouldn't be able to keep up with him!"

The chaplain was busily putting the chess pieces back in the box, clearly in no mood for another game.

I leaned on the back of the Lady Maria's chair and smiled down at her. "The chaplain tells me you're opposed to the queen's marriage yourself, even though you did tell Paul a woman like her deserves her happiness. I would have thought you'd love it: after all, who else could plan the wedding but you?"

"Surely, as I told you the other night, in the case of a widow—" the chaplain began, but I ignored him.

"Well," Maria began, confused now and not wanting to meet my eyes, "I did hope to reassure the boy. And normally I *would* love planning the queen's wedding. You never saw anything as beautiful as her first one, so many years ago! And although of course she wouldn't wear a white dress for her second nuptials, I had thought that pink, both for her dress and for her bouquet, or maybe light blue—"

The chaplain cleared his throat meaningfully.

"But in the last few weeks I have come to think about it differently," Maria continued resolutely. "The chaplain has made it clear to me that, at a certain age, only a *heavenly* spouse will do."

"Are you going to join the Nunnery of Yurt, then, my lady?" I asked in mock surprise.

"Of course not!" she replied in real surprise. "I've never married—at least not *yet!*—so it wouldn't apply in my case."

I moved in rapidly with my real question. "Aren't you worried that if Vincent *doesn't* marry the queen, there will be no one here to protect Yurt against the conspiracy of the wizards' school?"

Her brow crinkled in distress and her blue eyes widened. "When I mentioned that— When I repeated what Vincent had told us— I hope you realize, Wizard, I never meant you!"

"Yes, yes, I realize that now," I said in reassurance. No question then that the prince of Caelrhon was behind this oblique attack on wizardry, and not the priests as the school had thought. Regretfully, I gave up my suspicions of the chaplain. I would have to telephone the school and also have a long chat with Vincent; my dislike for him now felt entirely justified.

But would Zahlfast have been so insistent that priests were seeking to destroy wizardry only on the basis of some foolish statements made by the younger son of the king of Caelrhon?

I looked up to see someone riding toward us. It was Paul. "Back so soon?" I asked.

His expression was radiant, almost as though he had had a religious vision. The stallion snorted and tossed his head as Paul reined in and dismounted.

"I'm almost frightened of him," he said. "I've never seen a horse this good. Walk with me; I want to cool him down."

I nodded to the Lady Maria and the chaplain; I wasn't sure Paul even realized they were there. Maria, recovering quickly from her distress, said to the chaplain, "Don't tell me you put the chess pieces away already. We still have time for another game before lunch."

"He's as fast as the wind," said Paul, "probably faster. He jumps like a dream—and I really mean a dream, one of those where you feel yourself floating effortlessly through the air."

I nodded, knowing what he meant. I still intermittently hoped, usually when half asleep, that flying could be like that instead of a lot of hard work.

"I know he'd be willing to run all day—look at him now, still ready to go. But he never fights the bit, takes commands almost before I give them. I can't do any more now."

We continued our circuit in silence for a moment. Paul was breathing much harder than the horse.

"Do you remember me asking about fairyland?" he said suddenly. "It was years ago. My nurse told me about a place where you could go and see the fairies, and I asked you how to get there."

"And what did I say?"

"You gave me a very good answer. You said that there was indeed a land of wild magic thousands of miles away, but that if I wanted fairyland, the real fairyland where lights glitter, the trees are covered with gold and flowers, and dreams come true, I would have to find it here in Yurt."

I couldn't answer, being much too embarrassed that I had ever been that sententious.

"When I was young, of course," Paul continued, "I took your advice literally. I kept on peeking out my window at night, hoping to see the fairy lights, and when I walked in the woods I went quietly so that I might surprise them. Then as I got older, I thought I understood what you really meant. But now Vincent gave me this stallion, and it's as though I finally found fairyland after all. This horse is like something I looked for when I was six, that I'd long since realized was only a metaphor, but suddenly it's here."

I glanced sideways at his shining eyes, decided it would be completely inadequate to agree that this was indeed a fine stallion, and remained silent.

We walked on slowly for another minute, then Paul turned toward me, really looking at me for the first time this morning. "You know what I like about you, Wizard?" he said with a grin. "You're the best person to talk to I've ever known."

"I'm sorry you never had more boys your own age here," I said. "Then you might have had more people to talk to." If this stallion stepped in a rabbit hole and broke its leg, Paul might never recover.

"Oh, I've missed them sometimes," said Paul. "But I know why it's been like this. 'Only a count's or duke's son is fit to be raised with a future king,' as I've heard often enough. Neither of Yurt's counts had sons old enough to start knighthood training with me, and the duchess only has daughters. I guess I could have gone to live at the royal court of a larger kingdom, but I never wanted to and Mother didn't want me to go, especially after Father died. Besides, first I had my nurse to talk to, then my tutor, and all the time you!"

I felt depressed at this enormous responsibility I had apparently had without even realizing it. We finished circling the castle and returned to the chess players by the gate. The Lady Maria had already captured several of the chaplain's pawns and both his bishops.

The stallion shook his head, ringing the bells on the bridle. Paul laughed suddenly. "He knows he's a real horse, not just a vision, and he knows he can run a lot farther today!" I gave the prince a boost, and he scrambled up into the saddle and sat for a moment, silhouetted above me against the sky. "I'll be back later!"

He touched his heels to the stallion's flanks and was off, down the field and across the meadows, sailing effortlessly over the hedges until horse and rider disappeared into the distance.

V

I was waiting by the gates at the end of the afternoon when Vincent and the queen returned from hawking. Paul had finally come in an hour earlier, looking transformed, as though beyond happiness. It was a relief in a way to see that the engaged couple were merely extremely happy.

"You missed some good hunting," said Vincent, swinging down from the castle gelding he had been riding, the game bag in his hand. "We'll have geese for dinner tomorrow. You know," he added to the queen with a smile, "I can't even begin to tell you how much better it is to be here than at home."

"How nice," I said, not interested either in Vincent or in geese. "My lady," to the queen, "I need to talk to you. Now. It's about Paul."

"Of course," she said, naturally surprised. "Give me ten minutes."

While I waited for her I wondered what I was actually going to tell her, since I wasn't sure I trusted myself to speak coherently. I intended to have a long talk with Vincent tomorrow, so I need not bother her yet with his perverse views of wizardry. But I did feel a need to warn her that

Paul had been bewitched by a horse, but there was also much more. What I really wanted to say was that she couldn't marry Vincent under any circumstances but that I couldn't explain why.

The queen came back out, still wearing her riding habit. "Can we go somewhere to speak privately?" I asked.

A vision of being invited to her personal chambers flashed through my mind, but instead she said, "I've been riding all day and feel a little stiff. Let's go for a walk until dinner."

She went first, holding the narrow train of her habit looped over one arm, the polished leather of her boots brushing through the sun-warmed grass. She sang softly as she walked, and our shadows stretched out long behind us. I had a new vision, of sinking into the grass with her in my arms, but while it was fairly easy to imagine myself kissing her, it was much harder to imagine her kissing me back.

She paused half a mile from the castle. Swallows swooped across the meadow, passing close to us as they dove for insects. Although the sun was near the horizon the sky was still fully blue, and the day seemed caught in a never-ending pause between afternoon and evening.

"What did you need to talk to me about?"

"Paul doesn't want you to marry Vincent," I said, much more abruptly than I had intended.

She looked thoughtfully out across the countryside and started slowly walking again. I strolled beside her. "I know he doesn't," she said after a minute. "It's not surprising—at seventeen, he only thinks of me as his mother, not as a woman. He's had a happy youth in Yurt, and he distrusts anything that might interfere with that. But there will be many changes, most of them good, once he comes of age, so my marriage will seem less threatening. And after our whirlwind wooing, we may want to wait a few months to marry!"

A suspicious thought flashed through my mind, that

Vincent had no intention of marrying the queen, that he had wooed her only because, as a welcome visitor to Yurt, he now had the opportunity to carry out some nefarious plan of his own. I found this thought so appealing that I wished I could believe it.

"So I hope that Paul will become reconciled to the idea," the queen continued. "I wouldn't want to marry in the face of his opposition. But," looking up with a smile, "don't you think he may already be changing his mind?"

"The roan stallion seems certainly to have been well thought out as a means to reconcile him to Vincent."

She laughed. "You make it sound like some sort of conspiracy. I'd had no idea Vincent was going to give him that horse, although it was no secret that that's what Paul wanted—I had been hoping to find him a suitable stallion myself for his birthday. I think it shows a real sweetness on Vincent's part!"

I actually agreed, but I wasn't about to say so. "In fact I'm rather worried about Paul's reaction to that horse. He not only likes it, he loves, he adores it. I think at the moment it means more to him than any of us do, or even the kingdom of Yurt."

She laughed again. "It's the novelty. You sound as though you thought this attitude would continue. I'm not worried."

I looked at her profile as we continued walking. She had very faint lines at the corners of her mouth, the result of years of smiling. The air around us was fragrant with mown grass and moist earth.

For nineteen years I had known the queen, and I had been in love with her since the first moment I saw her, but in some way I felt I hardly understood her. If I did know her, I thought, or if she really knew me, I would be able to explain better my concern about Paul.

But then I wasn't entirely sure myself what was worrying me. She was right, of course; a boy could become quickly and entirely enthralled with the horse of his dreams without losing track of all else in his life.

Paul was not my principal concern and never had been. "My lady, I don't want you to marry Vincent either."

She stopped and turned toward me. Her emerald eyes danced with amusement—I wondered suddenly what Vincent had told her of his mock attack on me. "If you were still worrying that a king's youngest son is not worthy of a queen, or whatever you were trying to tell me, I hope that seeing him here has cleared up your concerns."

"It's not that," I said, amazed at my own audacity. "I couldn't bear to see you married to someone else."

"Someone other than King Haimeric?" she asked, looking at me with a faint, puzzled frown.

Now that I had started I couldn't stop. "Someone other than me."

All the laughter went out of her face. For a horrible moment I feared she would recoil in disgust, but her only expression was one of distress. She slowly started walking again, looking not at where she was going but at me. Her eyes went over my face as though she had never seen it before.

"I thought wizards never married," she said as though from a considerable distance.

"They don't. I don't care. I'd give up wizardry for you."

"But you're a very good wizard."

I was about to protest, to tell her that I hadn't even known how to make myself completely invisible until this morning, then realized that she was trying to shift the conversation. "It doesn't matter. Nothing matters. I've loved you since the first day I met you. I loved the old king as well, and as long as I could serve you both, and as long as you were caught up in his memory, I could say nothing. But now I find you are ready to love again and I have to speak."

Her foot caught on a tussock of grass, and she stumbled and almost fell. I caught her by the elbow and steadied her just in time. Once I touched her I couldn't pull my hand back again. Her eyes were turned away, but the curve of her cheekbone was only inches from my face. I moved my hands to her shoulders, drawing her toward me. I could feel her shoulder blades, her rib cage through her clothes. Someone's heart was pounding terribly loudly; it might have been mine.

She kept her face down so I couldn't find her lips. But I could hear her voice, faint against my shoulder. "Don't. Please don't."

I let go of her as though she were made of fire. I turned abruptly away, feeling my face go scarlet. It was growing dark at last; the sun hesitated on the horizon but would be gone in a moment. "Forgive me, my lady," I managed to gasp. "I'm sorry, I'm terribly sorry. Please don't think too ill of me. I would never have forced you."

She did not reply. Her breathing was broken, and in a moment I made myself turn toward her again. She had her hands over her face, and I thought I could see tears running between her fingers. I stifled the impulse to take her in my arms and comfort her and instead sat down in the damp grass.

In a minute she sat down too, a few feet away. I looked away. "I shall leave Yurt, of course," I said to the darkening sky. "I think they'd like to have me stay permanently at the wizards' school as an assistant. It would be a good position, and I could make sure that you and Paul got a competent new Royal Wizard." I noticed with detachment that the swallows had all gone for the night.

"I never knew!" the queen burst out suddenly, as though she had not heard me. "I've lived beside you, what is it, close to twenty years, since before Paul was born, and I never knew! And all the time I thought I understood you. Maybe I don't understand anyone in Yurt."

"Maybe no one fully understands anyone else—we may not even understand ourselves."

Fortunately she also did not seem to hear this highly

inadequate platitude. "I think I thought of you as I did the chaplain," she went on, her voice somewhat steadier, "someone serving a function, someone I liked and appreciated, but never someone I thought of as a man. I must have been so cruel to you, and I never even knew it! Do you think you could ever forgive me?"

"There is nothing to forgive," I said stiffly, looking out across the twilight landscape. "The fault is entirely on my side, for presuming where I had no right to presume. Unless—" I had thought I had frightened her with the impetuosity of my embrace, but she was now sitting next to me with no suggestion of fear. For two seconds I allowed myself to hope that she had been frightened not of me but of herself, that she had been about to give way to passion. "Unless you could love me instead of Vincent."

When she did not answer, I turned slowly to look toward her. She shook her head hard, her hands over her face again.

"Do you truly love him, my lady?" I asked gently.

This time she nodded.

"And he loves you?"

"I know he does."

"Then why are you crying?"

She wiped the tears from her cheek with an almost angry gesture. "Because I am terribly sorry to have hurt you!"

I had imagined so many times over the years telling the queen I loved her that our conversation seemed almost unreal. But I knew I was not imagining this. If I had been, it wouldn't have been going this badly.

Neither of us spoke for several minutes. Then she struggled to her feet. I stood up as well. Her face now seemed composed but the smile that almost always lurked near her lips was gone. It did not seem worth asking her again if she might change her mind.

She turned toward me and slowly reached out both

hands, first to touch my beard and then to cup my face. It was rapidly becoming dark, but her emerald eyes seemed to glow at me. With one finger I delicately traced the line of her jaw.

I waited for her to speak, but when she did not, I finally said, "I hope you realize, my lady, that in a minute I'm going to kiss you."

"I owe you a kiss, at least," she said and tilted back her head.

Though I told myself that I would not take a kiss given only because it was owed, I found myself kissing her before this thought had had time to take effect. With one arm around her shoulders and the other hand still lightly touching her cheek, I kissed her for what seemed about half an hour. She kept her hands to her sides and her body drawn back an inch from mine.

She turned her head away suddenly. I let her go and shivered, immediately feeling extremely cold. In a moment I would start crying myself.

"We should get back to the castle," she said in a calm, almost flat voice. "We're terribly late for dinner."

We turned together and started stumbling back across the fields. The yellow lights of the castle shone at us from narrow windows a mile away.

At the moment it was still my castle, but I did not know for how long. I had resigned as Royal Wizard, although the queen may not have heard me. Even if she had not, I did not see how I could go on living in Yurt. In a minute she took my arm. I would have told her she wasn't helping any, but then she would have let go again.

As we came up the hill toward the gates, we heard someone whistling, and a dark shape came across the bridge to meet us. "There you are," said Paul's voice. "I knew you'd be along soon."

The queen let go of my arm. "I hope you haven't been waiting all this time."

"Vincent told me you'd gone off to talk about me, so when you weren't here for dinner we knew it must be something important." His voice managed to be casual, but I could hear the intense curiosity lurking under the surface.

"It wasn't particularly important; it just took more time to discuss than we'd expected," the queen lied cheerfully. "The wizard wanted to go over all his duties with me, to review what might change and what might stay the same once you become king." She, at any rate, did not seem to realize I had resigned.

"And I have a message for you, Wizard," said Paul, seeming to accept this account. It was too dark for him to see the tear smudges on his mother's face. "The dean of the cathedral telephoned for you, maybe an hour ago. I told him I'd have you call as soon as you returned."

I excused myself and hurried off to the telephone with relief. To return to the cathedral city would give me an excuse not to face the queen again.

Joachim's black eyes burned at me a moment later, even though I knew he could not see me. "How soon can you come?"

"What's happened?" I asked, startled out of my own concerns by the intensity of that stare.

"The lights are back. And this time it's not just lights."

"What is it?"

He hesitated. "I don't know."

"Have you seen it?"

He paused for a moment as though wondering if he dared tell me, then plunged on. "It lit on the tower at twilight. Dozens of people saw it. It's enormous, five times the size of a man, and it has the wings of a bat."

PART THREE

The Witch

I

Prince Paul came into my chambers. Books were scattered across the room, their pages marked with pencils, scraps of paper, and the covers of other books. Leaning on my desk with a magic globe glowing at my shoulder, I madly scribbled spells.

"So you have to return to the cathedral city?" he asked. "I'd been hoping you were back home for good."

"So had I," I said without looking up.

"Do you need to take a lot of books?"

I slammed one book shut and tried to find my place in another. "I have to go now, tonight, and my books are too heavy for me to carry them all and fly at the same time."

Paul was clearly not interested in my books. I checked another spell, folded up the paper on which I was writing, and stuffed it into my pocket. I assumed he was hoping to hear more about the conversation I had had with his mother, but he was certainly not going to hear it from me.

"Even if you have to stay away a long time," he said, "you *will* be here for my coming of age ceremony, won't you?"

"Of course," I said, trying to sound jovial. "You didn't

think I'd forget something that important?" I had completely forgotten about it. I tossed a few of my most basic books into a box with a change of clothes, began to reshelve the rest, then decided just to leave them.

"Did you know it's starting to rain?" asked Paul.

I didn't, but at least it couldn't make my mood any worse. I turned off the magic lights and stepped into the dark courtyard. A fine rain made the cobblestones slippery. I turned to Paul. "Good-bye. Tell your mother I was very sorry not to see her again before I left."

This too was a lie. As I flew up into the black sky, I wondered what she had told Vincent. I said a prayer to whatever saint might listen to wizards that she would not tell him the real story.

It was a long way to the cathedral city. On horseback it took a day or more, and it was more than an hour's flight even in daylight, not carrying anything. But I was constantly concentrating on keeping my small box flying with me and on finding my way. The moon was hidden, and if I flew high enough to avoid the trees I had trouble picking out the road. The wet countryside was dark, spotted only occasionally with the lights of a house or village. I flew in and out of fog, of sudden rain showers. At first I tried to maintain a protective spell against the rain but I didn't have the concentration for it. I gave up and got wet.

Constantly running through my mind, interfering with my spells, were all the things the queen and I had said to each other. They burned in my brain as though written in fire, and turning them over did not improve them. I wondered if she, lying alone in bed—that is, I *hoped* she was lying alone—was awake and thinking the same thoughts.

At least she had no reason to feel my bitter shame. I was ashamed that I had tried to tell her I loved her, even though I had had nineteen years in which to realize it was foolish to do so, and ashamed that I had made her cry. The time for impetuous avowals, I told myself, was many years past. Paul was more accurate than he realized when he said there were people in the castle who should know enough to act their age.

The rain was letting up and the eastern sky was gray as I finally approached the cathedral city. Its streets were dark and quiet. I rose to the height of a quarter mile and swooped over the new construction, though I saw nothing unusual in the murky light of early dawn. Just as well—I was in no shape to meet a monster. But even at this height I could feel the presence of wild magic.

I descended to the street behind the cathedral, staggered under Joachim's porch, and knocked on his door. In a moment he answered it himself, dressed in a long nightshirt and carrying a candle. He looked understandably startled but pulled me through the door and closed it against the damp.

"When I asked if you could come at once," he said, "I meant tomorrow. I never intended you to come tonight." The candle made light and shadow flicker across his face.

"I had to. If you can give me a dry jacket, we'll go find out what was on the tower."

"Did you see something?"

"I saw nothing, but it's still nearly dark."

"It wasn't there at midnight." Joachim pushed me into a chair. "You should go to bed at once. You're exhausted. We can talk about it when you've had some sleep."

"How do you know it wasn't there at midnight?"

"I went up, of course," he said, giving me a sharp look. "The head of the municipal guard, the crew foreman, and I all climbed up with torches."

"It's a long climb."

"I know. Especially in the dark." He gave a wry smile. "Flying was a lot easier. But we were able to ascertain that, whatever it was, it had left under cover of night." He pulled me back to my feet. "I'm putting you to bed.

I'm cold and you must be frozen. We'll discuss it in the morning."

"But I can't stay here with you," I said, weakly holding back. "I've probably gotten you into enough trouble with the bishop as it is. I should stay across town in the royal castle."

Joachim didn't even bother to answer but propelled me into his spare room and threw in extra blankets after me. I peeled off my wet clothes and fell into bed. In spite of the contradictory voices clamoring through my mind I fell asleep at once.

I awoke several hours later to the smell of bacon frying. Outside the window the sun was sparkling. The clothing I had left in sodden heaps on the floor was gone, but my box had resisted the rain and my spare clothes were dry. The contents of my pockets, including my spells, were arranged neatly on the desk. I got dressed and went to find breakfast.

In the kitchen, wet clothes hung in front of the fire, and Joachim's servant was setting plates on the table. He smiled and motioned me to sit down. When I asked where the dean was, he simply nodded and started serving.

I remembered on my second serving of bacon and fourth piece of toast that I never had gotten any dinner last night. I wondered why, since food and a few hours sleep could not change what I had said to the queen, they seemed to have made it an experience I might still survive.

The front door opened and Joachim came in, dressed in his formal black vestments. He sat down across from me and poured himself some tea. He looked, as always, composed and well brushed, not like someone who had been scrambling around on a rain-soaked tower at midnight looking for a monster, or who had had his sleep interrupted after only a few hours by a wizard arriving on his doorstep.

"I certainly hadn't expected to need to call you again so soon," he said, "but it's always good to see you."

"I *had* to come right away," I said lamely. "You have a magical problem and no wizard here to take care of it."

The servant put breakfast in front of the dean and disappeared. "I've just come from morning service in the cathedral," Joachim said. "There's no sign of any damage to the tower according to the workmen, and with the sun shining like this one could almost imagine all of us were seeing things—but not quite."

"Even if it was only an illusion, someone with enormously powerful magic is operating in the city. Tell me, did it roar or bellow?"

"It just looked at us—it had eyes like coals, very visible even at a distance."

I shivered in the warm sunlight and took a hasty gulp of hot tea. "With bat wings, it could be some kind of dragon—or a demon."

Joachim met my eyes levelly. "If a demon appears in a church, it means that one of the church's priests has sold his soul to the devil."

I too hoped it was not a demon. It had been entirely on purpose that I had left my copy of the *Diplomatica Diabolica* behind in Yurt.

"Could you tell if there was a supernatural presence here?" Joachim asked.

"The whole church is full of the supernatural," I said, "but one would expect that anyway, from the presence of the saints. Magic can only indicate if there's something present from outside the natural world, not if it's good or evil."

"And a dragon?"

"Dragons are natural—wild, deadly, and unlike anything else, but natural nonetheless. They're not even, strictly speaking, magical, because they aren't formed by spells. If you *do* have a dragon, we might do better overcoming it by force than by magic."

Unaccountably, I suddenly felt almost cheerful. A dragon I thought I could deal with. It might very well kill me, but it was the sort of problem any competent wizard should be able to face with some hope of success, unlike a ruined love affair. And if I failed, I told myself, at least I would not spend the next two hundred years being melancholic.

"I told the workmen to proceed with the construction," said Joachim. "I hope I have done right."

"Of course you have. To let something like this stop the work would be to give it control over you. Oh, I was trying to tell you, rather than staying here I should go across town to the castle. It does after all belong to the royal family of Yurt."

"Stay here with me. I think even the bishop now realizes we need a wizard. Anyway, the royal heir is in the castle."

"The royal heir? You mean Paul? But he's home in Yurt!"

"I don't mean the heir to Yurt. I mean Prince Lucas, the heir to Caelrhon, this kingdom. He arrived in town early this morning, just in time for service. The chancellor is worried that he may be hoping to play a role in the first election of a new bishop here in forty years, although I discount that."

"That reminds me." I was uninterested in the political relationship between a hypothetical new bishop and a kingdom's heir but wondered if it was only coincidence that a bat-winged monster had appeared just before Vincent's brother Lucas arrived in the city. I reminded myself firmly not to let my dislike for Vincent cloud my judgment. "The queen is planning to marry the younger son of the king of Caelrhon." I tried to keep my voice casual and natural.

But I should have known better. Joachim looked at me sharply. "Is Prince Vincent in Yurt now?"

"He arrived the day after I did."

"And you do not approve of him?"

At least, I thought, whatever Joachim suspected it was highly unlikely to be me kissing the queen at twilight. "It's hard to think of her married to someone else, after the old king," I said. This was something I wasn't even going to try to explain. "Paul feels the same way, I think, although he seems to like Vincent personally."

Joachim appeared to accept my words at face value. "It's just as hard for me to imagine Paul as king of Yurt," he said. "You know, I've scarcely seen him since I left the court."

"You may not recognize him," I said. "He's really grown."

"I may go to Yurt for his coming of age ceremony," said Joachim. "The queen invited me, and I would enjoy seeing everyone again."

Paul I could talk about with no problem. For a moment, the apparition on the cathedral tower seemed comfortably far away. I mentioned Vincent's gift to Paul of a roan stallion.

"I wonder if it's the same horse," Joachim surprised me by saying. "I may have seen it earlier this spring. For a while the Romneys had a magnificent red roan for sale."

"Does anyone know where they've gone?"

"Not that I've heard." He paused, then looked at me soberly. The monster was not going to be far from his thoughts for long. "I know we'd hoped that whatever wizard was here had left town with the Romneys, but if so he must have returned on his own."

"I'll find him," I said with my best effort at confidence. "A wizard—much less a magician—shouldn't be able to hide for long from another wizard. By the way: is your servant mute?"

Joachim shook his head, a faint amused glint in his eye. "He served the old dean before me, and one night many years ago, having I believe drunk unwisely, he stood in the middle of the market square shouting the most scandalous things. Since that one lapse he has spoken as little as possible. He imagines that I never heard about the incident." He rose. "I have to get back to the cathedral."

"And I need to begin my search for renegade magic."

We were interrupted by a banging on the door. "Father Joachim! Come quickly! It's back!"

II

Joachim took the young man at the door firmly by the shoulders. "Tell us exactly what you saw."

He wore the uniform of the municipal guard. "Maybe it wasn't the same one," he said, breathing hard, "but it was horrible! It was a whole lot smaller—maybe the size of a hound." I could see him trying to concentrate under the dean's intense eyes. "It was red, like an enormous red lizard, with maybe eight legs. It had wings—and when it saw me and reared up, I could see that on its front legs it had hands."

A red winged lizard with hands. No wonder the young guard's eyes were so round. "Go on to the cathedral," I told Joachim. "Keep everyone calm. I'll deal with this." I might not be Royal Wizard of Yurt anymore, but when it came to magical apparitions I was still in command.

The construction site swarmed with activity as the guard and I pushed our way through. No one else seemed aware of the winged lizard. Cartloads of cut stone were arriving, drawn by oxen, and workmen unloaded and stacked them, easily levering the stones up and down ramps. The new tower's light-colored stonework was almost white against an azure sky. There was nothing ominous here in daylight. But it did not need very complex spells to realize that the whole city was permeated with magic.

"It was on the docks by the river," the young guard panted as we hurried through the narrow streets. "The dean led the climb up the tower last night, so I ran for him at once. I didn't tell anyone else except my captain."

"Good thinking," I said. "We don't want panic."

But the docks were no more ominous than the construction site. We wove between stacks of cargo crates, coming into the city or ready to leave. I probed for magic and found very little. The aura that lingered seemed wild and unfocused, nothing like the tightly constructed spells used for illusions—but then I had never expected any of this to be illusion.

An older guardsman joined us, lifting his eyebrows at me. "So the mayor's sent for a wizard," he commented.

I didn't have time to correct him. "What happened to the winged lizard?" I probably would have called it a small dragon myself, but "lizard" did not sound as horrible.

He shook his head. "It's gone. It disappeared with a pop, right into the air. I tried thrusting with my sword into the space where it might be, but I didn't hit anything." He paused. "Just before it disappeared, I had the impression it was picking up some of the cargo crates. . . ."

"A sword won't find it," I said grimly. "It's going to take magic. Stay on guard here in case it returns, and tell the dean at once if it does. I'll search the rest of the city for it."

As I hurried away from the river, I asked myself if a winged red lizard, the size of a hound, could have been what they all saw on the cathedral last night. But I rejected this idea—Joachim would certainly know the difference. But why should terrifying magical creatures suddenly be appearing in Caelrhon?

I turned a corner and thought I saw Prince Vincent.

After a startled second I realized the lord coming toward me could not be Vincent himself. He was slightly taller and quite a bit heavier, as well as several years older. He had the same burnished copper hair, the same wide-spaced eyes and firm jaw, but not the same easy and confident way of walking.

I gave all my suspicions free rein and stepped into his path. "Excuse me, let me introduce myself. I am Daimbert, the Royal Wizard of Yurt. You're the heir to Caelrhon, Prince Lucas if I recall correctly. We met several years ago; I don't know if you remember."

His reaction did nothing to lessen my suspicions. He gripped his sword and his eyes narrowed. "And *what* are you doing in my kingdom?" he demanded.

I took a step backwards as he thrust his face toward mine. "The monster," I babbled. "The dean of the cathedral asked me to come. I heard that your own Royal Wizard had an unfortunate accident, so—"

"We dismissed him even before his accident," said Lucas, glowering. "We have no more use for magic-workers in Caelrhon."

"But— But why not?"

"You keep it so discreet you think we won't notice," said Lucas coldly. "But after my experiences, my eyes were opened. We know you wizards are plotting to throw off the 'service' you claim to practice. 'Establishing peace throughout the western kingdoms,' you like to call it, but I know better. And now I wouldn't be surprised to learn that you're hoping to influence the election of the next bishop. *If* you really are here at the invitation of the cathedral—something I intend to find out!—then all I can say is that the bishop should know better."

Shocked at his open vehemence, I didn't reply but made him the formal half-bow and hurried away. None of this made any sense. Even though Sengrim, Caelrhon's wizard, had always treated me rudely, I could not imagine what he could have done to get himself dismissed with harsh feeling that would persist even after his death.

As I walked I kept probing with magic but found no sign of either an enormous bat-winged monster or a giant lizard with hands. Regretfully, I had to conclude that neither of the princes of Caelrhon could be responsible if they no longer even employed a wizard. I reached the gates of the city and went out into the field where the Romneys had been camped a week ago. The new grass, growing rapidly, had nearly covered the marks left by their caravans.

For a moment I hesitated, then rose into the air for the flight back to the kingdom of Yurt. If someone had brought monsters here and then taken them away again, he must have somewhere to imprison them. There was one place I knew where it might—maybe—be possible to do so, and the quickest way to find out was to look.

I scrupulously went nowhere near the royal castle of Yurt, instead heading for the magical valley at the other end of the kingdom. Prince Vincent could now persuade the court all he wanted, I told myself, that aristocrats would be better off without their wizards; it no longer mattered to me.

In the valley was concentrated a pocket of forces left over from the creation of the earth, as well as the home of a wood nymph and the shrine to Yurt's own Cranky Saint, a place where spells always worked especially well. Here it might be possible for a master wizard to find the power to bind even a monster from hell.

The saint's shrine had been served by an old hermit when I first came to Yurt, but a much younger man, ascetic, earnest, and with a shaved skull, now lived at the hermitage. I thought gloomily that this was one more example of everyone around me growing older.

I approached cautiously, but the little green valley dreamed peacefully in the sun. I slowly flew its length above the sparkling river, seeing no monsters and noting with some detachment that I was capable of being back in the kingdom, within thirty miles of the queen, without disturbing the emotional scab that had formed over my bitterness and pain.

The valley was so permeated with magic that it was hard to find specific spells, but after half an hour I was fairly sure no one had used its powers to conceal the cathedral's monster. It was afternoon when I arrived, hot and tired, back in Caelrhon, feeling intense frustration at not being able to find a monster that dozens of people had seen.

Ox carts laden with cut stone were coming toward the city gates. The oxen plodded slowly, their wagons creaking and the loads appearing to rock dangerously. Walking beside the oxen or sitting on the loads were the drivers, lazily flicking long whips, more to remind the oxen of their duties than to hurry them on.

But on one of the loads of stone rode a ragged magician.

My discouragement fell away, and I stepped casually to the edge of the road. "Greetings, Magician," I said as he drew even.

Although from the nature of the magic that had been going on in the city I had expected a fully qualified wizard, I felt I had solved the mystery at last. The unkempt beard and filthy clothes could conceal unusual abilities. After all, some magicians specialized to the extent that, in one small area of magic, they might be better than most wizards.

He gave an abrupt start. "Greetings, Wizard," he managed to say, though his voice came out an indistinct mumble. Squinty eyes stared at me from under scraggling brows. Between his eyebrows and beard, his face was almost completely obscured.

I could have tried probing magically to get a better idea what he looked like, but another magic-worker would know at once what I was doing and be grossly insulted. He was certainly old: even the best magic cannot reverse or conceal the natural forces of aging. "Why don't you get down so we can have a talk?" I suggested.

He hesitated a moment, then grunted and slid down from the moving wagon. "Thanks for the lift, driver!" he called.

"How far have you been riding?" I asked.

"Just a couple of miles," he said in a surly tone. His

small eyes kept shifting, not quite meeting mine. For a second I had an impression of great magical power here—maybe even, strangely enough, the spells of two separate wizards. But the next instant the impression was gone. I mentally shook my head. I was, I knew from long experience, highly capable of jumping to unwarranted conclusions and then convincing myself that they were true. And I so much wanted to believe that I had found here the source of the cathedral's problems.

"Look at my shoes," the magician continued. "If yours were like this *you* wouldn't walk a hundred yards farther than you had to." The uppers of his shoes were badly cracked and the soles flapped loose. "I begged a ride not far from the quarry, paid the driver with a few illusions—pretty racy ones, too!"

I had never been sure what Zahlfast had seen in me in my student days, why he had passed me in spite of the disastrous transformations practical, but I knew how perilously close I had come to being a magician making his living by selling pathetic scraps of magic wherever he could. But this magician, I reminded myself, might have made a giant bat-winged creature appear on the new cathedral tower. "Where were you last night?" I demanded.

"Asleep in a haystack, and getting pretty wet, too," he said grumpily. "But what is it to you?" the last almost in a shout. "Since when does a wizard want to keep an honest magician from earning a living?"

I would have offered him money except that I knew any such condescension would have made him even more indignant. "You were not perhaps here in the cathedral city, calling up a monster?"

"No," he said almost hesitantly, then "No!" quite explosively. "I've had enough of self-satisfied wizards like you without you starting to accuse me of nonsense!"

"Glad to hear it," I said, taking a step backwards.

He had worked himself up into a fury. Half of what

he said was unintelligible, and for the rest he seemed to group me with an apparently diabolical conspiracy of wizards from the school, all bent on starving him. He seemed to have several vicious things to say about other important members of society while he was at it. I took the opportunity while he was distracted by his own anger to check again for signs of great magical power and this time found nothing. The brief impression I had had of some sort of double power also disappeared on closer examination—just my overactive imagination again.

"The reason I asked," I said when he paused for breath, "is because whoever *is* practicing magic around the new cathedral will be in serious trouble, and I thought I should warn you to stay away."

"It wouldn't be *you*, would it?" he snorted.

I shook my head. "But if there's a renegade wizard here in the city, especially one practicing black magic, I'm going to find him."

The shifty eyes became guarded. "I don't call up monsters," he said after a minute, as though settling on a plan of attack. "I study the magic of fire."

He waved his hand, muttered a few quick words, and the grass around my feet burst into flame. I jumped back, and his beard split in a grin. But the damp grass blazed for only a few seconds, and I quickly stamped it out. A few final wisps of smoke curled up.

"That's marvelous!" I cried. "I don't know how to do that. Can you teach me how? I'll pay you well!" Elerius had apparently tried to persuade the school they should teach fire magic, but as far as I knew none of the teachers had ever learned any.

But the old magician was backing away. "I guess they don't teach you *everything*, then," he said with a bitter laugh, "even the ones of you they coddle. Be jealous of *me* for once, and see how you like it!" Empty carts were coming back out of the city gates. The old magician waved one down.

He was much too ragged for me ever to be jealous of him, no matter what skills he possessed. But I was delighted. I could no more have created fire out of air than I could have a few minutes ago, but in the moment when he made the grass blaze I at least thought I had an inkling how to begin.

As I headed back into the city I glanced over my shoulder. The magician had successfully negotiated a trade of illusions for a ride. Over the ox cart rose the insubstantial form of a naked woman, not quite life-size, moving in awkward gestures apparently meant to be obscene. I turned my back.

I wanted to tell someone what I had just realized about fire magic, but I wasn't sure whom to tell. In the meantime, although I did not like the coincidence of the magician appearing here only a day after the monster appeared on the tower, I was inclined to believe it had nothing to do with him. It was time to start searching the city itself more thoroughly.

But first, I thought as I walked through the gates, I needed to speak with the mayor. He might not be among the "three who rule the world," but the elected head of Caelrhon had the right to be consulted about a monster in his own city.

"There must be a very powerful wizard operating nearby," I told him. I had been ushered at once into the mayor's study when I told the official at the door the reason for my visit, and the mayor seemed to have abruptly left a meeting in order to talk to me. "Creatures from the land of wild magic shouldn't just appear by themselves in the lands of men. That's why the cathedral dean sent for me at once."

He played with the heavy chain of office that hung around his neck. It must have had twice as much gold in it as anything I had ever seen the queen wear. He looked as though his normal expression was genial, but it was not genial this afternoon.

"Fighting wizardry with wizardry," he said thoughtfully and tugged at an earlobe, not quite meeting my eyes. "How can we be certain you are truly here to help us and are not the wizard who made a monster appear here last night?"

If this is what the city council had been discussing when I pulled the mayor out of the meeting, I had gotten here just in time. Had Lucas's distrust of all wizards now infected the local merchants and artisans as well? "Good question," I said with all the confidence I could. "But you see, I'm school-trained."

"And why should we trust a school we've never seen, whose methods and purposes are hidden to us?"

This would have been easier with less astute questions. "Then don't trust the school," I said, seeking to be genial myself. "Trust the dean. He's known me for twenty years."

Unexpectedly the mayor smiled. It looked as though he had missed all day being able to smile. "You've chosen the best man in the city to be your guarantor. We would of course prefer not to have to rely on arcane spells. But if religion and magic can work together, perhaps we may still hope."

When I left the arched porch of the municipal building a few minutes later, the streets were still full of people, shopping, offering goods for sale, carrying water from the fountain, hurrying somewhere. Most were too absorbed in their own concerns even to notice me.

But as I passed one young woman she looked directly at me. She had amethyst eyes and a mole high on one cheek. For a second she smiled. Then she was past me and I was left looking after her, at a swirl of loose nut-brown hair over a dark shawl.

In spite of people pushing me from behind I stopped dead in the middle of the street. For reasons I did not understand her glance brought back all my shame and sense of loss with the force of ripping the top from a wound. Only a short while earlier, I had begun to hope that time had already begun to heal; now I knew that I had only been numb.

I was in exile from the royal castle of Yurt, probably permanently. I had lost any chance to see and talk freely with the queen, as I had done for close to twenty years, and with it I had lost my home, all because I had been a complete fool.

After a moment I forced myself to keep walking, trying to decide what it was about the young woman that brought this knowledge so vividly to me. It was not her appearance. As I tried to picture her face, I decided it was probably attractive, but it was nothing like the queen's. I had passed dozens of other women in the street without any such reaction.

But those women had all looked past me without even noticing. This woman had looked at me as though she were my friend.

III

"I saw a magician today," I told Joachim that evening. We again ate at the table by his eastern window, watching the sky darken.

"Did he summon the bat-winged monster?"

"I doubt it," I said, wishing I had a more productive answer. "At first I thought I sensed some strange power in him, but then I realized that was only because he knows fire magic, of a very different sort from the magic they teach us at the school." I decided not to mention my fleeting impression of two different sets of spells lingering about him, not wanting to bother the dean with my highly unlikely speculations about Sengrim's dead spirit returning bodiless to possess a carnival magician. "He probably didn't have anything to do with the monster or the giant lizard, but I still warned him away. If I'm going to find who in this city is working renegade magic, I don't want to be distracted by some half-competent magic-worker. Do you have magicians here often?"

"There is sometimes a magician in town for market day, and always for the big festivals," said Joachim. "They do magic tricks on the corners for a few coins. But tell me: When will you find out why there was a monster on the tower and make sure there never is again?"

I looked into his intent dark eyes and felt embarrassed. Both of us looked away. "I can't tell you," I said. "The whole city feels full of magic, but it's very unfocused." For some reason I was reminded of the woman with the nut-brown hair, but there was no way I could mention her or the effect she had had on me.

We were both silent for a moment. "I called the wizards' school from your office in the cathedral late this afternoon," I added then. "I hope you don't mind." The dean shook his head without looking up. I thought about that conversation, about Zahlfast's surprise that I was back in Caelrhon again. It had been disconcerting, after years of using telephones with far-seeing attachments, not to see him as I spoke to him.

"I already warned you about the priests," he had said, uncomfortably loudly and clearly considering that I was talking to him on the priests' telephone. "And Elerius tells me that Sengrim had long had disagreements with the crown prince of Caelrhon." I didn't like the suggestion that Elerius knew more than I did about the kingdom adjoining Yurt, but I did not interrupt. "You knew, didn't you, that Sengrim only received the final year or two of his training here at the school, but it's no use yet trying to persuade the royal family that a completely school-trained wizard would be less irritating to them. Let the prince's resentment die down before we introduce a new wizard into the kingdom."

"The Master was telling me there was some concern that aristocrats might be turning against their wizards," I said. "You can reassure him that there's nothing more to it than Prince Lucas."

Zahlfast had not sounded as reassured as I expected. Instead he said slowly, "We've had indications that more is involved. . . ."

Joachim poured himself another half-glass of wine but did not drink it. Instead he stared at the bottle. "The bishop wants to see you in the morning," he said at last.

"The bishop? But I thought he understood that the cathedral needs a wizard here. Has Prince Lucas been talking to him?"

"I don't think he's going to order you away," said Joachim, slowly enough that I began to fear that was exactly what he would do. Since no one wanted me here, not Prince Lucas, not the city council, and not the school, it would be entirely appropriate if the bishop didn't either. "But anyone who serves the interests of the cathedral is to some extent under his authority, and he wants to meet you."

I was not going to leave here without doing what I had come for, no matter who wanted me to go. The school, I told myself, was wrong, and I actively wanted to irritate the princes of Caelrhon. Besides, Joachim needed me. "Do you think I should entertain the bishop with some magic tricks?" I suggested.

He smiled, although rather faintly. "I thought you were a fully-qualified and competent wizard, not a magician," he said, which was apparently meant as a joke. "You won't need to do any flashy tricks; I think he mostly wants reassurance that you are not acting with any disrespect for religion."

"That depends," I thought but had the sense not to say, "on whether you're defining religion as Christianity or the organized church." Instead I changed the subject. "I was starting to tell you about this magician. His illusions are very poor; they wouldn't fool anybody. But he knows the magic of fire!"

"The magic of fire?" Joachim asked politely.

"Even you priests know there are several different

kinds of magic, corresponding to the different natural elements," I said. "Most of the magic they teach in the school, including the whole technical magic division, is the magic of light and air. But there are other sorts of magic as well. There's the magic of earth, herbal magic for the most part, which has never been incorporated into the school texts but which I learned from my predecessor at Yurt."

"Indeed." Joachim attempted to look interested.

"And there's the magic of fire." We had finished eating and were sitting back in our chairs, our legs stretched out under the table. "It's a different branch of magic, with different rules and different spells. It doesn't have very many applications unless you want to be able to start a blaze without flint and steel or to walk through fire without being burned."

"So could this be what the Romney children had seen, a magician practicing fire-magic? Might this be related to the lights the watchmen have seen on the tower?"

If he thought I was trying to distract him from his concerns about the cathedral, he must feel I was doing a very poor job. "It's possible," I said, making one more attempt, "but the children also suggested they'd seen someone make himself invisible. That's the magic of air, and hard magic—that ragged magician couldn't possibly have done it, that is unless he'd somehow gotten hold of a ring of invisibility. You can attach a spell to a physical object, you know, and then the spell will work for anyone."

"We have to find out who is summoning monsters and make him stop," said Joachim, abandoning any pretense of interest in different kinds of magic and their uses. "What will happen if enormous lizards start appearing all over the city? Half the cathedral priests are already terrified, thinking that we saw the devil last night and he'll be back for them tonight. The other half are outraged that anyone dare mock us like this.

We are trying to act for the glory of God, and we are either being threatened or laughed at by a beast from hell."

It did sound serious when he put it like that. I had been waiting to see if he would open a second bottle of wine, but instead he rose abruptly and started gathering the plates.

"We should make it an early night," he said. "The bishop will want to see you first thing in the morning."

I had expected the bishop to be tiny and frail. Instead there seemed to be a lot of him, or at least a lot of unexplained lumps under the blankets on the bed. Only his head protruded, propped up by pillows against a dark carved headboard. His skin was pale and he had no hair left.

"Come here, my son," he said in a voice that would have been appropriate for someone tiny and frail. I advanced slowly toward the bed, Joachim one step behind me. There was a faint movement under the blankets and a white hand emerged, beckoning. On the hand was a ring, an enormous ruby with a cross cut in its surface.

I started, then probed magically, just one tiny respectful spell. But this ruby ring, unlike the last one I had been acquainted with, had nothing magical about it. I went down on one knee as Joachim had told me I had to do, murmured, "Your Holiness," and kissed the ring. I just hoped the Master of the wizards' school never heard about this.

Then I took the chair toward which the bishop waved me and looked at his face properly for the first time. His wide eyes brimmed with love and intelligence but seemed to do so from a considerable distance, as though the real bishop were not lying here slowly dying.

"My son the dean has told me he asked you to help us," said the bishop. He spoke so softly that I had to lean forward to hear him. "I am afraid he called you without consulting me, but prompt action in the service of God is always commendable."

I nodded without speaking.

"But he has put us in a delicate position," the bishop continued. "If we are being threatened by magic, some of my priests feel the last person we should ask for help is another magic-worker."

Doubtless starting with the cantor Norbert, I thought. Joachim stirred beside me but I spoke first. "You aren't being threatened by wizardry in the abstract," I said. "You're being threatened by someone working spells against the cathedral, and the dean knows that the quickest way to overcome magic spells is to find someone with powerful magic to break them."

"And do your spells have power against the devil?"

"Of course not. Only God and those who serve Him have power against the devil," I said generously. "But you aren't facing the devil here. You're facing a wizard working natural magic."

The bishop closed his eyes for a moment. The blankets rose and fell slowly, and for a moment I wondered if he had even heard me. But when he looked at me again it was unexpectedly shrewdly, as though the real bishop's mind and ideas had come close to this room again. "You wouldn't be casting magic spells yourself as an excuse for the wizards to get a toehold here, would you? I hear the wizards' school in the great City is trying to expand its placement."

"I can assure you," I said with dignity, "that I am not responsible for whatever is happening here." So Lucas's and Vincent's accusations against wizardry had now even reached the cathedral. "I neither want to mock the church nor gain any 'toeholds.' "

The bishop started to cough. A young doctor in white, who had been standing silently on the far side of the room, came forward and offered him a cup. He took a sip and closed his eyes again. But when he opened them he continued as though there had been no pause. "When will you have banished evil magic from our cathedral?"

"I hope soon. I've only been here twenty-four hours, and I didn't see the monster myself. Until I have a better sense of who is working magic and what spells he is using, it may be difficult to counter him. I'll do my best to be quick and discreet."

Joachim rose to his feet, so I did as well. He knelt to kiss the bishop's ring before leaving, but I felt once was enough. The bishop's eyes closed again as we went out.

"It is an enormous responsibility he carries, and yet he seems able to do it still, in spite of his weakness," said Joachim as we reached the street. "The doctors say he may only have a few weeks, but they have already said that many times."

I considered asking Joachim if he would expect me to kiss *his* ring once he became bishop but was able to resist doing so. I realized we were entering the side door of the cathedral, on our way to early service. No hope for breakfast then until service was over. But it was a good chance for some of the other cathedral priests to see me and realize how reverent and discreet a wizard could be.

IV

I spent the morning irreverently practicing magic within twenty yards of the bishop's palace. First I tried a number of spells from the collection I had brought, shaped to reveal a hidden magic-worker. I was disappointed that none of them worked, because it would have taken a master wizard to shield his mind against all of them, but it was a further indication that whoever was working here was indeed a powerful wizard and not just a renegade magician with one good trick. I would certainly have been able to find the magician I had met the day before if he tried to sneak back into town, with his weak illusions and not enough flying ability to save his shoes. It was distracting that the face of the woman with the amethyst eyes kept appearing inexplicably in my mind in the middle of my spells.

When this search got me nowhere, I started again trying to work out the principles of the magic of fire. My books had only the faintest hints but I had a few ideas, extrapolating from the other sorts of magic that I knew. Herbal magic, I recalled from when I had first learned it, was set up with its spells quite separate from the magic of light and air, as though on a track that started parallel but quickly veered away in a different direction.

If the magic of fire worked similarly, I reasoned, I had to find the direction in which its magic veered. In the Hidden Language, one not only said specific spells but entered into the very fabric of magic's four dimensions. The direction in which one entered that fabric exerted a very powerful flow, and one had to remember that other directions were always possible.

Knowing that I was deliberately avoiding thinking about a bat-winged monster five times the size of a man and doing so anyway, I worked on a candle in my room. I could with no trouble make the wick glow and even emit a plausible cloud of smoke, but it remained obstinately cool. Yet perhaps with a spell from another angle—

I emerged from a struggle with the forces of magic and gave a shout of delight. Joachim's servant put his head in, alarmed and then puzzled. I sat by a sunlit window, triumphantly holding up a lit candle.

"It's all right," I said. "I was just excited because I lit the candle flame. Will your master be home for lunch?"

But the servant was gone, doubtless thinking that his master was harboring a madman.

I extinguished the candle and lit it again to be sure that I could. Once more, with two words and a snap of my fingers I caused a blue flame to blossom on the end of the wick. It was a real flame, too, no illusion; I nearly burned my fingers. So far I could only create fire, not protect myself against it.

I settled back, feeling a great reluctance to do anything else after my frantic efforts of the day before and then this morning's unsuccessful attempts to find another wizard. Sitting in the dean's house felt so safe and normal that I could almost imagine that nineteen years of romantic dreams were not shattered, that I had not resigned the only post I had ever had, and that an enormous monster with eyes of fire had not landed a very short distance from here. If I didn't think about any of this, maybe none of it would be true.

Again I wondered why Prince Lucas had come to the city just now, and why he seemed so furious with organized wizardry. He might have come here at his father's direction, I thought, to protect the largest community in their kingdom from a magical attack. In that case he might well suspect *me* of having something to do with the monster. But could he have learned of its evening appearance in time to arrive at dawn the next morning?

When I heard the noon bells ringing in the cathedral, I began waiting for Joachim's return. But time passed, time enough for the noon service and enough more that I realized he was not coming.

Unless I merely waited for the monster to reappear, something neither the bishop nor Joachim would want me to do, I would have to search it out. By sheer willpower I dragged myself to my feet. The cathedral tower might offer more clues if I looked again.

As I shouldered my way through the crowded streets, thinking of my best approach, I suddenly froze in the middle of a step. A light touch once brushed across my mind. This time it was not just a touch but a voice.

It spoke one word, "Wizard." It might have been a statement, or it might have been someone addressing me. I looked around wildly but could find no clue. The mental touch was gone as quickly as it had come. But that single word inside my mind had sounded as though spoken with a woman's voice.

No wonder, I thought grimly, that the town seemed full of magic. It would appear to have almost as high a density of magic-workers as the great City. Besides me, there was whoever had the power to make a monster do his bidding; plus the magician I had seen outside the gates; plus the wizard who had impressed the Romney children; and finally whatever witch had first touched my mind up on the scaffolding and had just done so again.

Then out of the corner of my eye I saw a head of nut-brown hair over a dark shawl.

In two steps I was beside her, the monster and Prince Lucas forgotten. "Excuse me," I said and touched her on the shoulder.

She turned quickly toward me, but where I had expected a startled look I found a smile that put a dimple in her cheek.

"I am Daimbert, Royal Wizard of Yurt," I said, flustered. "But I'm afraid I don't know who you are."

"My name is Theodora." Her voice was almost musical in its lilt and deeper than I had expected.

"Theodora," I said. "It is a very lovely and unusual name."

"It was my mother's and grandmother's name, and I believe my grandmother's mother's and grandmother's as well."

"Were all of them witches as well?"

She burst into laughter. "I never thought of myself as a witch. Isn't that something wicked?"

"Well," I said uncertainly, because she certainly did not appear to be wicked, "witches are women with strange powers."

"Sometimes I call on serpents from deep beneath the sea," she said, looking at me with teasing amethyst eyes.

"But they haven't answered me yet. Does that make me a witch?"

"How about bat-winged monsters?" I said, finding it coming out much more harshly than I intended. "Do you call on them too?"

"That's why the mayor sent for a wizard, isn't it," she said, sober for a moment, and I recalled that the first time I had seen her I had been coming from the municipal building. "I didn't see the creature myself, but it must have been terrible." Then her eyes danced again. "If you think I'm a witch, why are you surprised that I would want to meet the magic-worker brought in to deal with a monster?"

"Why do you think the mayor himself would have sent for a wizard?" I asked, feeling reluctant to tell a witch that the cathedral dean had invited me here.

"There are three that rule the world," she quoted, "the wizards, the Church, and the aristocracy. We who are the merchants and the artisans and the farmers don't count as rulers."

"My family ran a warehouse in the great City," I said defensively. "Most wizards don't come from ruling families."

"You have authority *now.* But this social structure gives someone like the elected mayor of a town a flexibility to do whatever he wants. He can ask for help from wizards or priests or aristocrats, whereas those three would be embarrassed to call on each other. I suppose," the dimple coming back, "if I called on monsters and they *answered,* then I probably would be a witch, but I'm not."

"If you're not a witch," I said, trying not to sound accusing, "how were you able to speak inside my mind?"

Instead of answering she took my arm. "If we're going to chat and get acquainted, let's not do it in the middle of the street. I was just going home for lunch. Won't you join me?"

Stories I had half-heard twenty years ago flashed

through my mind, stories of witches luring men into their caves, of what they did to them there in their mad lusts. The young woman beside me did not appear to be racked with mad lusts. Maybe I was developing an impure mind.

"I'd be happy to eat with you," I said, "but you may not have enough to spare for a stranger. There's an inn right around the corner; I'll even pay for both of us!"

"Now," I said again when we were seated at the inn and I had ordered, "tell me, if you're not a witch, how you can speak with me magically, mind to mind."

She bent her head to reach up and unknot her shawl. Her profile and the angle of her neck made a delightful silhouette against the window beyond her. "Are *you* a witch?" she asked me.

"I am a wizard. But only men can be wizards, because only men are trained properly in magic. A witch is a woman who has picked up a few rudiments of magic and, being untrained, uses them at best awkwardly and at worst in the service of darkness." Everything I said sounded in my ears as though I were charging her with unspeakable crimes.

"I *am* a woman," she said with a laugh, "and I do know one or two rudiments of magic, but I would not say I was untrained, and I certainly don't serve the powers of darkness!"

Our mugs of beer were brought, and she looked at me with dancing eyes over the rim of hers. I noticed how long her lashes were. I felt no touch in my mind, but her look implied that she could see all my thoughts and intentions and overall, surprisingly, rather liked what she saw.

"Were you trained by an old ragged magician?"

This she seemed to find the most amusing yet. "Of course not. My mother trained me. In fact, I taught the magician a little fire magic a few years ago. All he'd had before then were some rather flimsy illusions." If she had known him for several years, I thought, then I could give up my rather vague suspicions that he was a very powerful wizard in disguise, who had for reasons unclear come here to attack the cathedral.

Theodora looked down at her plate for a moment, then toward me again. "You're one of the wizards he told me about, aren't you, one of the ones who finished the whole program at that school?"

"Yes, I am, but that doesn't mean I know all the different sorts of magic there are. Watch this." I snapped my fingers, said two words, and the candle on the table came alight. "I worked that out this morning, but *only* this morning, and I'm afraid it's all the fire magic I know. Could you teach me more?"

"And could you teach me illusions? Yours, I know, would not be flimsy or pathetic. It hardly seemed worth it to ask the magician to teach me his magic, and I was always afraid he would think I was trying to compete with him, keeping an 'honest magician' from earning a living."

We both laughed at this. Our conversation seemed to be going nowhere, and almost every question was answered with a different question, but I felt intrigued. Something about her resisted my efforts to understand her, yet in a very few minutes I had started to feel I had known Theodora for weeks or even longer, and she seemed always to have known me.

"Are you perhaps one of the Romneys?" I asked as we ate. I brought out the gold hoop earring I still had. "Did you lose this?"

She brushed back the hair from both ears, tilting her head forward in the angle I liked. Long pendant earrings sparkled against her cheeks. "Doesn't it look like I still have my earrings?"

"But are you a Romney?" I persisted.

"No, I've lived all my life in the kingdom of Caelrhon,

and as far as I know all my ancestors have too," she said, giving me a straighter answer than most. "But I've become friends with some of the Romneys. There's one band that often camps outside the city."

I thought rapidly. "Why didn't they want me to know about you?"

"Did they try very hard to deny my existence?" she said with an amused glance.

"Maybe not. The old Romney woman implied I would meet you." I paused, remembering exactly what the woman had said. "But were they afraid of my discovering there was someone who knew magic in the city?"

"Why would they do that?" she replied.

"They certainly left town in a rush, I assume to avoid telling me."

"But if I were with them, how can I be here now? Or is that just another of my witchlike tricks?"

I was fascinated by her hair, a dark brown that caught gold highlights as she moved her head. It looked luxuriantly soft. "What are your *other* witchlike tricks?" I asked, almost wishing after all that I had accepted the invitation to her cave.

"What I actually like to do best of all isn't even magic." She paused briefly; I could tell this was very important to her. "I like to climb."

"To climb?"

"I have to do it at night for the most part. It would cause scandal in the city to have a woman scrambling around on towers in broad daylight. But it gives me a sense of mastery, of power over my own body and over the world around me, to know there is nothing too steep or too tall for me to climb if I want."

"Then you have a power over your body I don't have over mine. I went up the new cathedral tower last week, and it gave me vertigo. If you're not a Romney, are you perhaps related to those workmen working on the new church?"

"I thought they were from far away in the north somewhere," she said with another smile. "Do they enjoy climbing too?" She had not actually answered my question, but it was too pleasant to have an attractive woman paying close attention to whatever I said to worry about it.

V

Even after we finished our food we continued sitting and talking, a conversation of unrelated questions and oblique answers, where she seemed continually amused by me. At last she looked out toward the street, where the movement of the sun over the housetops had cast the cobblestones into shadow. "I have a lot to do at home," she said, as though surprised herself at how much time had passed.

"I'll walk you back."

She took my arm again. "You school-trained wizards may luxuriate in royal courts," she said with a smile, "pondering the meaning of magic, but those of us who work for a living actually have to *work*."

We walked rapidly through twisting streets. Timbered house fronts leaned over us, seeming to stare down from multipaned windows. We emerged in a quarter of small houses near the river, overlooked by the backs of the tall homes of the cathedral priests. Theodora stopped by a low door and turned her key.

"Maybe it's just as well you didn't come here for lunch," she said apologetically as she opened the door. "I'd forgotten I left everything so scattered."

Inside was a rather dimly lit but completely conventional room. I had a brief glimpse of the black and white tail of a cat disappearing under a chair. Spread out on the table and chairs were brightly colored embroidered pieces of cloth. "I do embroidery for some of the merchants and the garment retailers," she said. "The best piece I've done recently is no longer here, but if you're in the cathedral you'll see it: the cloth on the high altar."

Joachim or whatever cathedral officer bought altar cloths, I thought, must not know that the skilled local embroideress he had hired was a witch. I was not going to tell him.

"Usually I try to work at midday because the light is best," she said. "The drawback to fire magic is that you never end up with anything better than candlelight. But I did enjoy talking to you."

"I hope I'll see you again," I said.

"Of course you will. You promised to teach me some of your magic. An embroideress could use magic globes to shine beside her."

I tore myself away and started back up the hill. I thought I knew now the source of the lights the watchman had originally seen on the new tower. But I knew even less the source of the bat-winged monster.

The dean was very quiet at dinner that night, as though he had decided it would not be tactful to keep quizzing me on my progress. I took advantage of his silence to think about Theodora. But, as usual, tact lost out.

"My servant told me you were lighting candles in broad daylight this morning," Joachim burst out at last. "Are you trying your own version of an exorcism?"

"No, nothing like that," I answered vaguely. "I was working on a different aspect."

For close to twenty years, I had been the wizard of Yurt. When I had gone to the school for a few months, it had been with the assumption that life in Yurt would be the same when I returned. Now, in the last week, I had discovered the queen was getting married, had resigned as wizard of Yurt, and had met Theodora. With all my habits and suppositions shaken up, I had to remind myself that for Joachim, to whom the monster on the cathedral tower was of overriding concern, nothing was happening at all.

"I did find out one piece of information which may reassure you," I continued. "The flickering lights on the construction at night, and maybe even the disturbance of materials up on the scaffolding, were due to the influence of a harmless magical being."

"Do you mean a wizard?"

"Actually something closer to the fairies the workmen suggested," I said, avoiding the word "witch." But I wondered even while I spoke whether Theodora, even if she lit magical fires while scaling the scaffolding at night, would be capable of shifting heavy stones and equipment.

"But what about the monster?" said Joachim, looking at me with enormous black eyes. I had always found it difficult to hide anything from those eyes.

I dropped my own gaze to my plate. "I haven't made as much progress with that as I hoped," I confessed. "If it was called here by a wizard, that wizard is hiding very thoroughly from me."

Joachim started to speak, stopped himself, and then spoke anyway. "I know you don't need me to remind you that the bishop was hoping you could be quick."

"And discreet," I added. "Look on the bright side. If I can't find out what's happening, and the bishop blames you for bringing in a worthless magic-worker, then maybe the priests of the cathedral chapter won't elect you bishop after him."

Joachim took a deep breath. "Forgive me if I have in any way suggested you are a 'worthless magic-worker.' It is just hard to wait for *it* to appear again."

"It may not appear at all," I said. "Remember, while I was here last week there weren't even any flickering lights. The guard saw a giant lizard with hands yesterday morning, but that was only a few hours after I arrived, and there's been nothing further today. Maybe the monster is afraid of what *it* at least considers a highly competent wizard. I could stay here for a while, keeping it away by my very presence."

"But you want to get back to Yurt."

And Father Norbert isn't the only priest who wants one less wizard on the street, I thought. "I can stay for some time," I said airily. "For various reasons I don't need to return to Yurt right away."

Joachim stood up, and I started to rise to help him collect the dishes, but he had only gone to the sideboard for a second bottle of wine. I watched his face as he worked out the cork and filled our glasses; he seemed even more sober than usual.

"I may not always understand you," he said after we had sat in silence for several minutes, "but I know you better than you think I do. Something has upset you, upset you terribly. What is it?"

"Why do you think I'm upset?" I said lightly. I took a drink of wine to avoid looking at him.

"Or made you angry, or frightened, or filled with sorrow. I know you were a little disturbed when you heard the queen was getting married, because you felt she was being untrue to the memory of the king we all loved and served, but this goes beyond her marriage. I first knew something was wrong when you arrived here yesterday at dawn, totally drenched. Since then you've acted distracted, and I know you well enough to realize that you've been thinking inappropriate thoughts even when you are not saying them."

It was a good thing, I thought, that he didn't hear some of the more inappropriate things I had refrained from saying about the organized church.

"And then this evening," Joachim went on inexorably, "it's as though some new and very strange ideas had come to you. I'd assumed you were as worried as all of us about the magical apparitions, but I soon realized that was not all. What then is it?"

This was the one question I felt I could not answer. I knew he would be shocked if I told him I had tried to propose to the queen, even if I could make him understand why I had and why her refusal was so devastating. And I certainly couldn't tell him that I had just met an extremely intriguing witch, even though, I reminded myself firmly, our relationship was completely innocent and was going to stay that way.

"I'm more upset about your cathedral than I think you realize," I prevaricated, still not looking at him. "It's a blow to my self-esteem as a wizard not to be able to find out yet who or what caused the bat-winged creature to appear. And the wizards at the school specifically warned me about threats to wizardry from the priesthood. I know it's not you, but it makes me uneasy to be surrounded by so many priests without knowing what's behind the warning." I dared at last to look up; I had been clasping my empty glass and staring into it. Joachim reached for the bottle and poured both of us more wine.

"And you think this goes beyond the general fear by wizards of becoming involved in religion," he said, "where all the shortcomings of wizardry will be revealed?"

"I'm not sure how seriously to take it," I answered, relieved to have distracted him from his original question and deliberately ignoring the second half of this statement. "And then your bishop tried to suggest that the wizards are trying to get a toehold in all the cathedral cities. Do you know where he got that idea?"

The dean shook his head without answering.

"And did you know that Prince Lucas, Prince Vincent, the royal chaplain of Yurt, and apparently a lot of other people are talking about a wizardly plot to dominate the aristocracy?"

Joachim cocked an eyebrow. "The chaplain accused you to your face of this plot?"

"Forgive me," I said, "but I don't like that young chaplain. He gets on my nerves somehow—maybe because he's so unlike you."

"I didn't appoint him," said Joachim, "but I had thought

you'd be pleased to have someone else at court who enjoys a hearty laugh."

"Lots of people in Yurt already enjoy a good laugh," I said, "from the queen and Paul down to the stable boys. But I wouldn't call the chaplain's laugh 'hearty.' This may sound odd coming from a wizard, but I like to see a chaplain with more moral depth." What I would really have liked, though I knew it was impossible, was to see Joachim back in Yurt again.

The dean looked at me with raised eyebrows, considering. "I am afraid that too many seminary students these days do use the knowledge that the world is God's creation as an excuse to enjoy it too fully, without considering their ultimate responsibility to save human souls. It would certainly be possible to give the royal court of Yurt a different chaplain, but I would not do so without a better reason than personal antipathy from the Royal Wizard."

But then, I thought, I wasn't Royal Wizard of Yurt anymore. "Paul thinks he has an impure mind."

Joachim looked alarmed. "What does that mean?"

"I think it means that Paul distrusts the discussions the Lady Maria has with him."

"I believe the Lady Maria can defend herself from impure thoughts very well," said Joachim. If he was making a joke he looked perfectly sober. "Perhaps you should discuss this wizardly 'plot' with Prince Lucas," he continued, "while you are both here in Caelrhon."

"He won't want to talk to me. He almost attacked me today."

"Maybe some way could be arranged for the two of you to spend time together," said the dean thoughtfully.

I took a sip of wine and leaned back in my chair. "Did you ever think," I said, changing the topic abruptly, "that it might be nice to give all this up?"

"Give what up?"

"These responsibilities. I know you feel the burden even

more than I do. We're supposed to be responsible for the young wizards and the young priests, for organizing and carrying out the important functions of our institutions, but after a while who wants the aggravation?"

"What are you suggesting we do instead?"

"I think the Romneys have the right idea," I said, pushing my glass forward for more wine. "When they get tired of being in the same place too long, they leave. I know they're rumored not to be Christians, so you might not want to travel with them, but we could have our own caravan, drawn by our own pony."

"And what would we and our pony do?" asked Joachim. A faint smile hovered near his lips.

"We could go from town to town, see all of the different cities and castles—and even the pilgrimage churches—in the western kingdoms, and when we had finished with those we could start on the eastern kingdoms."

"What would we live on?"

"I could do magic tricks, and you could work a few simple miracles, and people would pay us."

Joachim poured out the last of the wine. "You realize of course," he said, "that that's your most inappropriate suggestion yet." But the smile had reached his eyes.

PART FOUR

Theodora

I

During the following weeks I saw Theodora every day. The first morning I strolled through the city for several hours, probing for wizards or magical creatures and seeing no one I knew except Prince Lucas, who turned deliberately away. Finally I spotted her coming out of a garment retailer's. But after that I abandoned all pretense and we arranged our meetings.

I did not telephone the school again. Zahlfast thought I should be home in Yurt, and I was unsure how to tell him I had resigned. And, at least so far, my presence did seem to be keeping monsters away from Caelrhon. And it was easy to find excuses to stay in the city now that I had met Theodora.

We usually got together late in the afternoon, when the light was poorer for close hand-sewing. After a few hours every morning of searching in an increasingly desultory way for a powerful wizard I did not particularly want to find, or of going through my spells once again in a fruitless search for one that might work against monsters, I was gladder each day to see her. Strolling in the fresh air outside the city walls or sitting in the grass, thick with wildflowers, where the Romneys had camped, Theodora and I discussed magic. She explained fire magic to me, and I taught her some of the magic of light and air.

"You call it the Hidden Language?" she asked. "My mother simply called it the language of magic. She said it had no grammar, only words and phrases to be memorized, but I've long suspected it must have an internal logic of its own. Otherwise, you couldn't create new spells."

I felt vaguely uneasy teaching magic to a witch. The Master of the wizards' school, I suspected, would disapprove. I rationalized that I was no longer Royal Wizard of Yurt, and that I would not want to return to the school either if they persisted in their belief that I would be good at teaching in the technical division, and thus I was not bound by the practices of institutionalized magic. Besides, this was not some witch in the abstract: this was Theodora.

The grass grew so tall around us that someone else would have spotted us and stepped on us at the same time. She sat with her legs tucked demurely under her while I sprawled back on my elbows, looking up at her. The breeze blew tendrils of hair across her face, half obscuring it. "And have you created any new spells of your own?" I asked.

"Just one that works reliably." She snapped her fingers and said the two words to light a flame, but this one appeared not on the ground but in the air in front of her. It died out of course almost immediately, but another appeared just above it, then another, until a string of twenty tiny flames, each lasting only an instant, had climbed an arc up into the afternoon sky.

"So that's what you were doing up on the cathedral scaffolding?" I asked casually.

Theodora's dimple appeared. "I knew you were going to ask me about that sooner or later. The scaffolding presented a much better challenge than anything else in the city—and since my mother and I always embroidered for the cathedral, I felt secure there. I know the priests disapprove of magic, but as the tower wasn't consecrated yet I thought they couldn't object."

"They did object." Once again I sounded accusatory. At least so far she had not seemed offended.

She looked down at me and smiled. "That's what the Romneys guessed. Isn't that why the mayor sent for a wizard, even before the monster appeared, to find the source of the lights?"

"But the mayor didn't send for me." For reasons not entirely clear to me, I had not yet told either the dean nor Theodora about the other.

She plucked a long stalk of grass and tickled my nose with it. "The Romneys always worried about me," she said. "They said I couldn't be a wizard because I didn't know how to fly. They never told me I couldn't be a wizard because I was a woman. I still don't understand why you don't let women into your school."

This topic had come up more than once. Since the more I knew her the less I agreed with the school's policy, it was hard to be convincing in my answers. "I've already told you," I attempted, "that some of the wizards have been contemplating for years whether and how the policy ought to be modified."

"Then they ought to have been able to work it out by now."

Theodora learned so quickly, and she had so much magic of her own to teach me, that I kept finding myself thinking of her as an equal. Even without what I would consider proper training, she learned faster than most of the wizardry students. I had only rarely in the last twenty years felt I was meeting someone else's mind on an equal level in the area of magic. Joachim was my friend, but our areas of expertise were so different we were sometimes strangers to each other, and even the teachers at the wizards' school had to work to remember I was no longer their pupil.

"Change can take a long time," I said, shaking my head. "The old Master must be hundreds of years old by now, and he isn't going to make innovations rapidly. But there's something else, something I've felt uncomfortable telling you. The real objection raised to training women in wizardry is that women already have a creative power men don't have. You can create life in your wombs."

"You men are just jealous," said Theodora.

"But it causes very serious problems," I persisted. "A woman with the full knowledge of wizardry could create and give birth to a monster."

"And school-trained wizards can transform ordinary creatures into monsters," she replied. "I thought your training was supposed to make sure that wizards knew the responsibilities of magic as well as its uses. Why not train the witches too as long as you're so worried?"

"I *have* been training you in the magic of light and air," I said. "I just don't care to start on women in general. For one thing, most women wouldn't have all that you have to teach *me*."

"And you wouldn't be interested in a witch if I didn't have fire magic to teach you?" she asked, giving me a sideways glance from her amethyst eyes, a glance that might have been teasing and might have been accusation.

"I wouldn't be interested in you if you weren't Theodora."

"Fear of monstrous babies has nothing to do with your school's attitude," she said. "The real reason is that men *already* feel threatened by women. You're desperately trying to keep mastery in at least one area."

I sat up and frowned, wondering if she was serious. "Theodora, what are you talking about?"

"You're smart. You'll figure it out."

I didn't answer. She started braiding stalks of grass together, not quite looking at me. I felt my irritation drain away as I watched her hands, the way she moved her head, the slow movement of her chest from her breathing.

Theodora spoke several words of the Hidden Language hesitantly, so slowly that the spell she was creating trembled on the edge of dissolving, but then the grass braid she held was suddenly diffused with light.

She laughed with excitement and looped it around her arm. "It will fade in a moment," I said. "Do you want me to put on a spell to make the light permanent?"

"No," she said, as the glow slowly dimmed. "If I put a permanent light on something, I want it to be something better than stems of grass. However," starting to rise to her feet, "the day is also dimming; I need to get home."

Without even realizing what I was doing, I took her hand, pulled her back down beside me, and kissed her lightly. "Let's go, then," I said. "What time will I see you tomorrow?"

My dinners with Joachim became almost silent as the days passed. The dean may have feared my brief visit was going to stretch on forever. I could see burning in his eyes the constant question, the constant concern for his cathedral, but he did not want to ask me again. Since I did not feel I could discuss with him any of the topics I wanted to talk about, I found that I too had little to say.

Once Joachim became bishop, I knew, he would no longer feel comfortable with our late night talks. By not arguing theology and human nature with him now, as we had done for years, or even discussing my own difficulties in tracking the monster, I was wasting what might be my last chance for such conversations.

He handed me a letter that evening at dinner. "It came via the pigeons from the City," he said, eating as though not tasting his food.

I took it in surprise, wondering who in the City even knew I was here. Then I saw it was from Elerius and had been sent from his kingdom and relayed through the City's postal system.

"Just a friendly word of advice, Daimbert," read the letter from the school's best graduate. "I hear you've gotten yourself maneuvered into trying to help the Church. The Master, I'm sure, will not be happy to hear this, especially now that the priests are conspiring against wizardry. Keep your distance, or at least keep your eyes open."

I crumbled the letter in my hand. Anyone, much less Elerius, should have known that such a patronizing "word of advice" was enough to make a wizard do just the opposite. I turned to Joachim and tried talking to him.

"I'm starting to feel as though I've lost control of my own life," I told him. "Events keep happening faster than I expect, and I do things that surprise myself."

"If you wish to go back to Yurt," he said slowly, "I shall not keep you. I understand if you feel you cannot oppose another wizard's magic."

"That's not what I meant at all!" I said in exasperation. "I intend to stay here until I find out what's happening to your cathedral. I'm just sorry I haven't made progress as fast as you hoped."

"We're grateful for whatever assistance you can offer," he said stiffly and rose to gather up the dishes.

I would have moved out, gone to the little castle across town, except that Prince Lucas was still there. I thought that he, too, might be waiting.

"Do you know why Prince Lucas is here?" I asked Theodora the next afternoon.

Rain hissed on the street outside as we sat in her house, drinking tea on a cleared spot in the middle of a table scattered with spools of thread and scraps of colored cloth. Her cat, who had become used to me, purred by the fire, its paws tucked tidily together. Some of Theodora's completed work, stacked on a nearby chest, was worked with simple designs, but some was embroidered elaborately with flowers or with geometric patterns. On all of it, whatever design she was following, Theodora used a distinctive stitch: across three threads, skip one, then across two more.

"And why should a great prince tell an embroideress why he comes and goes?" She seemed, as always, to find me highly entertaining.

"Well, you live here in the city, and I understand he comes here often." I paused for a moment, thinking. "Why, when Caelrhon is so much larger a kingdom than Yurt, does the king of Caelrhon not even have his own castle in his own cathedral city?"

"I'm sure you don't want me to tell you," said Theodora, trying to suppress a smile, "that great princes don't explain these things to embroideresses."

"Paul will know," I said. Theodora knew about Paul. I had told her a little about Yurt, hoping that in return she would tell me more about herself. But from my account she would have gathered that after the old king had died the royal heir brought himself up with the aid of his great-aunt and the castle staff, for I never mentioned the queen.

I thought, as I already had several times, that I was caught between finding Theodora highly elusive and knowing her better than I had ever known anyone. She had quickly learned everything—or almost everything—important there was to know about me, and yet I often felt there were whole aspects of *her* life that were still hidden. But then she would casually tell me something in a way that suggested she had never meant to keep any secrets.

"I'd like to meet Paul," she said thoughtfully.

Reason reasserted itself after two jealous seconds. Paul must be ten years younger than she was and would probably consider her a contemporary of his Aunt Maria.

On the other hand, I reminded myself, she was twenty years younger than I. For the first time since I had become a wizard, I wished that I looked less old and venerable rather than more so. "Has it ever bothered you that I have white hair?"

"No," she said, with a teasing smile that brought out her dimple. "I assumed that that was just an emblem of your wisdom."

"You still haven't told me," I said. "Why, when the Romneys left town to avoid telling me about you, did you seek me out yourself?"

"I had to see whether I approved, of course, of the man who was supposed to use his magic to protect the cathedral. And did you ever think you aren't like most wizards?"

I wasn't sure what this meant and thought it safest to leave it while it might still be a compliment. "Did you ever meet Sengrim, the late Royal Wizard of Caelrhon?"

"He was here in the city a number of times over the years," she said slowly. "I wouldn't say I ever actually met him." Her tone suggested that he was one of the wizards I was not like.

"Prince Lucas dismissed him, and I wish I knew why."

"A secret quarrel, clearly not suitable for witches to hear," she said with another smile. "Shall I make more tea?"

I nodded but refused to be distracted. "I have an idea about that wizard," I said. "I notice Prince Lucas's wife isn't with him."

"I remember his wedding," Theodora said reminiscently, refilling the pot with boiling water from the hearth. "It was one of the most exciting events in the city in years. They were married in the cathedral on one of the hottest summer days I've ever seen. The princess had her own gown made in the great City by the sea, but I helped make some of the bridesmaids' gowns. The princess paid better than anyone around here; I lived on the money for three months. I hope she hasn't found life in a small inland kingdom too dull—though she does have her children now."

"But she found a way to liven up her life!" I interrupted. "I think she had a torrid romance with their Royal Wizard! That's why Prince Lucas dismissed him and became so furious when I even mentioned him. You don't think—you don't think Lucas deliberately arranged for the 'accident' that killed him?"

Theodora poured out the tea, looking at me from under long lashes. "Why would a wizard have a romance with a princess? I'd always heard they were as chaste as priests."

I knew she was teasing me again but answered seriously. "It *is* traditional that wizards never marry, but it's very different from the situation in the priesthood. A wizard is not considered to have sinned against wizardry and blackened his soul by being with a woman. Most wizards just prefer to keep their own counsel."

"I see," she said, her back to me while she set the teapot down. When she turned around she was smiling. "I like your idea, it's very dramatic and romantic, but you still need to explain one thing: why would a princess possibly be interested in a wizard?"

When I left a little later, I kissed her, tipping up her face with a finger under her chin. For a moment I felt the pressure of her forearms against the sides of my neck.

"I'll see you tomorrow," she said, stepping back. "Keep practicing your fire magic until then; you seem to be a very promising pupil!"

II

We arranged to go on Sunday to the stone quarry three miles from town. Theodora said she had always wanted to climb the steep limestone outcropping from which they were cutting the blocks for the cathedral, but she couldn't go during the week while they were quarrying and said she felt uncomfortable going alone on Sundays.

"There are some rough men who camp there," she said. "It's far enough away that the municipal guard doesn't pay attention to them."

"But isn't that a problem for the men working in the quarry?"

"I think a lot of them *are* the men working in the quarry."

She was so good at some aspects of magic that I kept forgetting how big were the gaps in her knowledge. Without knowing how to fly, she was limited to running from danger. Climbing around the cathedral tower at night must have seemed less threatening than facing strange men in daylight.

First thing Sunday morning, however, I went to service in the cathedral. I sat with the servants of the cathedral priests, doing my best to look serious and not at all like a wizard. The cantor Norbert, however, standing in front of the choir, seemed to have no doubts about me.

Joachim led the service, and, watching him, I realized something that I should have realized much earlier. The reason he was always so busy was that he was already effectively the bishop. It should have been the bishop standing at the high altar on Sunday morning, the dean taking the noon service, but Joachim was doing both. In his care for the diocese, for the cathedral edifice, for the rest of the priests, for the seminary itself and all the young would-be priests, he must also be doing double duty.

The congregation came out of the cathedral into brilliant sunshine, rolled on a wave of organ music. Joachim caught up to me at the door. "We just have time for breakfast," he said, "and then I have to ride out to a village five miles from here for a baptism. The baby was born too soon, and they're afraid that bringing her into the city might kill her, but they want her baptised as soon as possible. I'll have to hurry back, because after the noon service a castle chaplain is coming for his annual spiritual examination."

After that I certainly couldn't tell him I was going to spend the day with an attractive witch. "I hope it goes well," I said gravely.

But as Theodora and I walked out the city gates an hour later, I was not thinking of the heavy responsibilities of cathedral priests. "I really should teach you how to fly," I told her. "Then you'd be able to get to *really* high places to do your climbing."

"Could you really? Could a witch learn to fly?"

By the time we had walked the three miles to the quarry, Theodora was able to lift herself about six inches off the ground, although she kept laughing, which broke her concentration.

The quarry itself was silent, and there seemed no one around but ourselves. The sun beat warm on our heads, and larks soared and sang around us. The actual quarry was a great gash in one side of the limestone outcropping, but the other side was untouched. "I'll try climbing here," said Theodora.

She unbuttoned and stepped out of her skirt—I was intrigued, but underneath she wore men's leggings—and braided up her hair. Then she rubbed a little dirt into her palms and, her head back, considered the steep surface. It was pocked with cracks and fissures; even a few flowers grew in tiny pockets of soil. Then she began to climb.

"Remember those words of the Hidden Language," I said quickly. "If you start to fall, you might be able to slow your descent with the flying spell."

Theodora finished shifting her weight from a lower to a higher toehold and paused. "Maybe I shouldn't let you teach me to fly after all," she said. "This wouldn't be as challenging if I knew I was always perfectly safe."

She went back to climbing, moving slowly but steadily, finding crevices in the rock which I would never have found, trusting herself to them when I would have been paralyzed. Although she did not have the long toes and fingers of the workmen on the cathedral, she moved with the same apparent disregard for height.

At first I watched her from the ground, then I flew up to a ledge and watched as she went by. She broke into a light sweat as she climbed, making her tunic stick to her back. She seemed to have an exquisite sense of balance and an absolute confidence that her body would obey her mind.

At the end of a half hour, Theodora had almost reached a deep crevice in the rock face. But the last few feet of cliff jutted outwards. She worked her hand into a narrow crack, made a fist so that the hand would not slip out again, and braced her weight against it as she scrambled for purchase with her toes. For a moment she became motionless, then her knees started to tremble and she began quietly swearing.

I reached with magic to catch her, but then she flung the other hand up, grabbed the lip of the crevice above her, kicked her way upward, and folded herself into it. I let out my breath all at once. "I'm going to rest here!" she called cheerfully. "I think there's enough room for you, too."

I flew up to join her. "Are you all right?"

"Of course. I apologize for the cursing. There's always a moment, usually just before you reach the top, when you think that this time you'll never make it and you have to yell at your body to keep it moving at all."

There was just room in the crevice for a second person. Although not nearly as supple as she, I managed to fit most of myself in. Our faces were very close together and our shoulders collided. I was surrounded by the scent of her, a combination of sweat, lavender, and clean hair.

"I'm extremely impressed," I told her honestly. "Did your mother teach you climbing as well as magic?"

"It was my father, actually," she said. "He died in a fall when I was only ten, but he'd already taught me everything he knew."

"Oh, I'm sorry," I said inadequately.

"It's a long time ago now. Besides, I don't think of him as being dead. I think about what he used to say to me, how he used to encourage me when he first took me out to practice on little ten-foot boulders. Sometimes when I'm climbing I can still almost hear him."

I thought to myself that theirs must have been a very unusual family. But I was distracted by the realization that her lips were less than an inch from mine. It seemed perfectly natural to start kissing them. Even though I could not embrace her, as my arms were needed to hold me in the crevice, I kept on for some time. Theodora seemed to be enjoying this as much as I was.

I had almost decided I could spare one arm to put around her when the corner of my eye caught a glimpse of empty air. If I wasn't careful, both of us would be down at the bottom of the cliff.

Very delicately, I pulled my head back. Her eyes smiled into mine. "Is this what you're imagining the princess and the royal wizard doing?" she asked.

I wasn't at all sure she believed my theory about Sengrim—I wasn't sure I believed it myself. But being reminded of him calmed me down enough that I noticed how cramped I had become jammed into the crevice. "I'm going to slip out now," I told her. "Were you planning to climb any higher?"

"This is high enough for today," she said. "It always takes longer to go down than up. We'll have to come back here again."

I rolled out into the air and hovered, watching as she extended first one long leg and then the other. She found toeholds and started easing herself down.

As she descended I hovered to one side, trying to stay far enough away that I would not distract her and yet close enough that I could catch her with magic if she slipped. She would probably object if she knew what I was doing, but her father had fallen to his death.

Somehow and quite mistakenly I had assumed going down would be easier than ascending. Instead of looking above her for the next tiny ledge or crevice, Theodora had to feel below her with a toe. When she was twenty feet from the ground I went down and stood below her, thinking that if she did fall I could cushion the impact with my body. Suddenly I heard voices.

Coming around the corner were three men. They had the massive upper arms and chest muscles of men who spend their days swinging hammers against solid stone. "Hey, look!" said one of them. "It's a girl on the cliff!"

The other two laughed. "Let's get her down!" They ignored me, an ineffectual looking white-haired man. They brushed past and looked up the cliff as though about to start climbing.

A pebble rolled past my head as I heard Theodora shifting. I looked toward her and froze. She was gone.

The men were equally startled. "Hey, where's the girl?" The leader looked at me for the first time. "What did you do with her, old man? Are you a magician or something?"

"I am the Royal Wizard of Yurt," I said loudly, doing my best to give him a piercing look. Inside my head I was yelling, "Theodora! Where are you?"

"A wizard, huh? Did you make the girl disappear? What did you do that for?"

"To keep your unwanted attentions from her, of course," I said and extended a hand. With a small bang and a burst of pink smoke, the grass caught fire at his feet.

"*Very* good, pupil!" said Theodora's voice inside my mind. I stole a quick glimpse up the rock face. The sun was at an oblique angle, and the crevices and odd bits of plant growing out of the limestone made a jumble of shadows, but there was a larger shadow where I had last seen Theodora.

The men stepped back, temporarily startled. The leader

regained his composure first. "You want to fight, is that it?" he cried and charged.

I would never have been able to hold him off if he had reached me, but fortunately I did not have to. I lifted him six feet off the ground and held him suspended. "All right," I said to the other two. "Would either of you like to take your turn?"

The man in the air kicked and bellowed, but magic held him firmly. I shifted my attention to the second man and started lifting him slowly. I did not have to lift him far. He tried to jerk away and cried out with fear as all but the tips of his toes left the ground. I let him go, and he dropped heavily. He caught his balance, spun around and began to run. The third man was already gone.

"Keep this in mind as a useful warning," I said to my remaining audience. "Never try to attack a wizard." But I went up into the air myself, above the reach of his powerful arms, before letting him down. He gave one snarl in my direction and followed his friends.

"Theodora!" I called, trying to find her shadow. But the shadow was moving. In a few minutes it had reached the bottom of the cliff and Theodora reappeared, taking one hand out of her pocket.

I put my arms around her. "Thank God. Are you all right? How did you make yourself invisible?"

"How did you lift him off the ground?" She was smiling with delight. "Is that a variation of the flying spell?"

"It's related," I said. "I can teach it to you too. But I didn't realize you knew any of the magic of light and air."

"You mean making myself invisible? Isn't a witch entitled to a few secrets?"

She was enjoying teasing me, but I had been too worried about her to be teased right now. I still had an arm around her firm, muscular shoulders. "What is it, a ring of invisibility?"

She became serious and reached back into her pocket. "I hadn't wanted to tell you at first, because I was afraid you would tell me it wasn't something suitable for a witch and try to take it away from me."

"What have I done to make you think that?" I protested.

"My mother had it before me," she said, "and her mother and grandmother before her." She had it in her palm, a heavy gold circle without any stone or ornament. I took it carefully and looked inside. It was engraved with very tiny letters, too small to see clearly without a magnifying glass, but they looked like the angular letters of the Hidden Language.

"What's the inscription?" I asked, handing the ring back.

"I don't know. It might be a spell of some sort."

"I'll read it for you if I can look at it with a glass," I said. "Do you always carry the ring?"

"Always. But I don't like to use it very often, especially since I started seeing those things."

"What 'things'?" I demanded.

But she was smiling at me. "Thank you for rescuing me. Even with my ring, I can't hide my shadow." She put her skirt back on and shook out her hair. Although I was fairly sure that, with her climbing ability and ring of invisibility, she would have been able to protect herself quite well, it was gratifying to be considered a rescuing hero.

"Rings of invisibility are rare," I told her as we started to walk back toward the city. "But the spell to make things invisible is so difficult that wizards who can master it attach that spell to rings more than any other kind of spell."

"Can you make yourself invisible with just your Hidden Language?" She gave me a challenging look from under long lashes.

"I can, but don't ask me to do it now. I know you'll make me laugh, and then it won't work."

"You're just nervous about having to see those things."

"What 'things' do you mean?" I asked again.

"I don't know what wizards call them. Those little creatures—except some of them aren't very little. I don't see them every time; I didn't see them this time."

"Oh," I said, wondering what she could possibly have seen. I would have to look at the inscription on the ring very soon.

"I've already taught you most of my fire magic," said Theodora, "even though you still need to practice the spells against being burnt. Maybe in return for your magic I should teach you how to climb the real way, without flying."

"But I don't have your suppleness or your muscles."

"That takes practice too, just as magic does," she said in the tone of a reproving school teacher.

I laughed and put my arm across her shoulders. She was exactly the right height to fit under my arm. She put her own arm around my waist and we walked hips together, matching strides, back toward town.

On the walk out to the quarry, I had thought three miles long, in spite of the sunshine and flower-scented air. Now I would have been happy to walk twice as far. At some point without noticing I seemed to have fallen in love.

III

Joachim asked me somewhat stiffly the next morning if I would mind not joining him for dinner that night. "I have invited the other officers over," he said, "so that we may discuss in perhaps a more relaxed setting than the cathedral office what we shall need to do as the bishop's illness continues."

"Of course," I said, thinking that the dean was surely hoping to get some of the other cathedral officers to take up some of the double burden he was carrying, while the rest of them were doubtless intending to accuse him of introducing into the city the wizard responsible for all their problems—and maybe even the bishop's illness itself. The cantor Norbert, whom I suspected from something Joachim had said of having long had aspirations of being elected bishop himself, would doubtless lead the accusations: from his point of view, the dean was assuring his own election by taking over the bishop's duties now. "Are you sure you wouldn't feel more comfortable if I moved out," I asked, "maybe went to stay in an inn?"

The dean looked up. "I asked you to stay with me, Daimbert," he said soberly and apologetically, "and am sorry if you are still uneasy here."

I shook my head and went out, mumbling something unconvincing about still looking for traces of magical apparitions. But Theodora was busy finishing a new dress for the mayor's wife, so I was back not much later, letting myself in quietly with the spare key Joachim had given me because I knew he would be at the cathedral and I didn't want to disturb his servant.

But as I stepped inside I heard a voice from the study. It was Norbert. "Remember," he was saying, low and fierce, "you never saw me here."

Intensely interested, I went still and amplified the sound of voices with magic.

But I heard no one answer Norbert. He spoke again. "You seem to pride yourself on rarely speaking. Trust me: your silence now will be for the good of the Church. So just don't speak this time." There was another pause. "Do you want me to tell the dean about that time you stood shouting and cursing in the middle of the market square? It happened before he moved here from Yurt, and I doubt he's ever heard the story. I'm sure he'd find it *most* interesting."

There was another silence. "Good," said Norbert with satisfaction. "Remember, I have not asked you to do anything to harm your master. Just don't tell him I was here or touch *this.*"

Rapid steps were coming my way. I made myself invisible just in time. Norbert came within an inch of brushing against me as he opened the front door. Fortunately the entry was dim and I cast no shadow. His face, close to mine, did not look evil, but there was a desperation in his eyes that contrasted with the good-natured if somewhat self-righteous lines that the years had put around his mouth.

Could *he* have summoned a bat-winged monster to the cathedral? Not without a lot of help, I concluded, just barely getting in a quick magical probe before the door slammed behind him. There was not the slightest indication that he knew any wizardry.

But what had he left in the dean's study? Still invisible, I went quietly into the room, in time to see Joachim's silent servant, his expression anguished, hurrying out the far side.

It didn't take long to find it. On the bottom shelf of a wide oak bookshelf, tucked almost entirely behind some heavy theological treatises so that no one would see it unless they were looking for it, was a book of magic.

I pulled it out carefully. To a wizard it almost shimmered with the residual spells of the magic-workers over the generations who had used it. And it *had* been used for generations. It was written on parchment sheets in a number of different hands, bound in calf made rough by long use. Half a dozen names had been written on the flyleaf, below five stars and a pentagram, but all the names were heavily crossed out. The parchment leaves were soft with much handling, but the book fell open to a place marked with a fresh red velvet ribbon. Above the words of the Hidden Language was a heading in the sharply angled handwriting of a wizard or magician who might have been dead for centuries: "How to poison a rival with a slow-acting poison."

I slammed the book shut and retreated to my room, so indignant and so furious that it was lucky for Norbert he was no longer in the house. *Nobody* was going to plant false evidence, accusing Joachim of poisoning the bishop, while I was in Caelrhon.

But once I calmed down a little I realized that transporting Norbert up to the top of the new tower and dropping him off would not help the dean. Joachim, I was afraid, would be sorrowful but forgiving when I told him about this. I somehow had to find a way to reveal Norbert's plot in a way that would discredit him so thoroughly that he would not try something similar again, but I would have to do so without warning Joachim ahead of time.

Norbert's plan was fairly clear. He had brought the book here, with the marker carefully in place, and threatened Joachim's servant with revelation of his old shame if he even mentioned the cantor's visit. He intended to "accidentally" discover it that evening, in the presence of all the cathedral officers, thus casting the dean under so much suspicion regarding the old bishop's illness that he would no longer be a viable candidate for bishop himself. Even if Joachim convincingly denied all knowledge of the book, the suspicion would fall on me, and hence reflect very poorly on the dean who should have known better than to harbor a wizard who had probably already brought a bat-winged monster to attack the new cathedral.

Should I, I wondered, weighing the worn magic volume in my hand, suspect Norbert after all of calling the monster? But it was hard to imagine someone who had resorted to a rather petty if despicable trick like this of being behind something so spectacular as having a creature five times the size of a man land on the tower.

On the other hand, where had he gotten the magic book?

I examined it again. Nothing about it gave any clue. It must long predate the school and its cleanly printed books on magic. Unless I was going to assume that Norbert himself, a cathedral priest for decades, kept a collection of arcane tomes, he must have gotten it somewhere on purpose to discredit Joachim. Perhaps he had been able to overcome his aversion to wizardry enough to find and deal with a wizard—but who? And could it be the same one who had been behind the monster, the one I still couldn't find?

Suddenly I smiled. Joachim, if I told him about it, would have called it totally inappropriate, but I had a plan.

I lurked, invisible, while the cathedral officers assembled that evening. I had started to think that Joachim was growing old, but compared to the rest of them he was positively youthful. Most had white hair and faces that had started to sag around the jawbones, but they all seemed conscientious, polite, and genuinely concerned about the welfare of the diocese. They did not go into the study as I expected but instead passed into the dining room, with a rustle of vestments and a faint scent of incense and talcum.

While they ate dinner I retreated into my own room to take a break from invisibility—always a difficult spell to maintain. Besides, I really didn't want to hear all the details of diocese management. An hour passed. Listening to the distant clinking of plates and silver, I started growing hungry enough to wonder if I could slip out to an inn for a bite and be back before anything happened.

But then I heard the scraping of chairs and the sound of feet moving toward the study. I quickly wrapped myself in a spell of invisibility and took the old magic book out of the bottom of the box where I had hidden it under my own books. Silently I slipped out into the hall, sliding the book above me along the high ceiling.

"You certainly have a good theology collection,

Joachim," I heard Norbert's voice. "I might like to borrow some of your books sometime."

I stopped outside the study door, afraid of having one of the cathedral officers bump into me, but peeked around the edge as I continued the book's progress into the room. No one looked up to see it.

Norbert bent toward the bottom shelf of the wide bookcase. "Now this work, for example—I haven't seen it since seminary!" His voice was just a little too loud and his manner nervous; he was clearly unused to plotting and deception. For a second I even allowed myself to feel sorry for someone so desperate as to resort to plots he would have denounced if presented to him in the abstract. This went far beyond jealousy of the dean—he must be genuinely worried about the church's welfare. "Let me see," he continued, pulling out a large theological volume. "But wait! Joachim! What's this I see *behind* it?"

Joachim politely bent to look. "There is nothing behind it."

"Of *course* there— Don't tell me he—" Norbert dropped to his knees to look for himself. The other priests glanced at each other in surprise.

The cantor, bent over with his face thrust into Joachim's innocuous theology collection, presented much too tempting a target for me to resist. I dropped his magic book from the ceiling and hit him square on the fundament.

He jerked, banging his head on the shelf, and spun around. "Here it is!" he cried, picking it up. "Joachim! I am deeply shocked!"

The priests all looked at each other again. "Where did that book come from?" several asked in surprise, and "The dean didn't do it," added several others.

"But look what he has on his shelves!" Norbert cried, vicious and triumphant, pushing himself to his feet and opening the volume. "Joachim, you know I don't shock easily, but I am deeply disappointed! It's— Why, look!" holding up the title page to show the others. "It's a book of magic!" He leafed through. "And here, marked with his own marker—" He stopped, unable to find the poison spell because I had taken the marker out.

There was a short silence. Norbert seemed to realize that this wasn't coming out quite the way he intended. One of the priests, the one I thought was the chancellor, asked quietly, "Why did you think the dean had such a book in his study, Norbert? And how did you know even before you opened it that it was a book of magic?"

The cantor looked around desperately. "That servant of yours—" he tried.

"I hope," said Joachim mildly, "that you did not bring this book in here earlier and threaten my servant with exposure of what he still believes is a secret, to keep him from informing me of your visit."

In the subsequent uproar everyone seemed to forget the magic book's abrupt arrival on the scene, except for Joachim, who looked thoughtfully at the ceiling. I slipped back to my room as Norbert, apparently deciding that at this point full confession would work better than denial, threw himself at the dean's feet, quite real tears running down his cheeks.

This I didn't need to see. I quietly opened my casement window, stepped out into the air, and flew off, still invisible, in search of supper.

IV

Even with a magnifying glass, it was hard to read the inscription in Theodora's ring by candlelight. I tipped the ring back and forth and wished for one of the excellent magic lamps from Yurt.

"It's a spell, certainly," I told Theodora. We sat by her hearth, where she had been trying to teach me the spell for a cloak of fire.

"It's really very easy," she had said. "Make yourself a net of anything that will burn quickly—dry grass works very well. Then ignite it while simultaneously saying the spell against being burnt." We practiced while sitting almost all the way into the fireplace. She had moved her piles of cloth well away to keep them from sparks.

"My hands do all right," I said. "You know you used to scold me about drawing them back, but I hope you notice how much better I've become. But my head still worries; my hair and beard know they're going to catch fire at any second."

This she found hilarious, and by the time she recovered her breath I decided I had had enough for today of trying to establish the same sort of authority over my body that she seemed to have without the slightest effort over hers. These recent weeks felt to me like something flaring and flashing just barely within my control, but so far—I hoped—I had avoided being scorched.

Even though Theodora's magic and mine were so different, I felt a companionship with her that I had never felt with anyone else. Now that I had admitted to myself that I was in love with her, I kept wondering what would happen next. I found it difficult to imagine being back either in Yurt or at the wizards' school with Theodora at my side. But it was equally difficult to imagine being anywhere without her.

Although I had told the queen I would give up wizardry for her, I knew I could not. It had become such a part of me that it would be like trying to give up breathing. I loved Theodora and wanted her, but it would still be impossible never to practice magic again. On the other hand, I told myself, just because I gave up all recognized posts for wizards did not mean I would have to give up practicing magic. I could be another itinerant spell-caster, just one who happened to have a degree from the school.

Maybe, I thought, Theodora and I could take off in a caravan with a pony. But I had promised Joachim he could come in my caravan, and he might not like her company. Or maybe I could settle down here in the cathedral city and do tricks in the marketplace, even if the old magician did become furious at me. I had thought when I met him that doing simple magic tricks for pennies would be a degrading way to spend one's life, but if Theodora were with me it might have unexpected benefits.

I wondered briefly if she had been falling in love with me as I fell in love with her, or if she had picked me out even before we met face-to-face. If so, was it with the intention from the beginning that we fall in love? But I didn't like this line of thinking and tried to dismiss it. "Maybe I can make your ring glow itself with a spell of my own," I suggested.

The spell worked even better than I had hoped; the gold blazed into light while the letters remained black and finally intelligible, spelling out words in the Hidden Language that I recognized.

Carefully I put the magnifying glass down, feeling stabbed with cold. "Theodora, this is a spell to reveal what is hidden. When you put on the ring, you not only make yourself invisible, you make yourself able to see other invisible creatures. You've got to tell me about these 'things' you see. Are they here in the city now?"

"I don't know," she said slowly, completely serious for once. "I try not to use my ring very often and, as I already told you, I don't see them every time."

"When was the last time you saw them?"

She closed her eyes. "I don't like thinking about them. It must have been two months or so ago."

I put a hand on her arm. "Where were they?"

She opened her eyes and put her hand over mine. "On the new cathedral tower. I had been climbing up there at night. When I was near the top, where the workmen had some cut stone piled ready for use, I noticed it was all in disarray as though the piles had been pushed over. And then as I was coming down I almost ran into the watchman. I put on my ring just in time."

I could feel her trembling and realized that she had been deeply frightened. "And then?"

"I saw two of them, almost like big lizards. I just caught a glimpse of them out of the corner of my eye. But they had wings and—and what looked like hands."

The winged red lizard the guard had spotted down on the docks. It had disappeared into the air—made itself invisible. Though I had assumed there was only one, and that whatever wizard had brought it had taken it away again, maybe there had been several of them in the city the whole time. The dean wasn't going to like this at all.

Neither one of us said anything for several minutes. This then explained the tumbled building material that had originally appeared on the new tower at the same time as Theodora's magic lights. But I still did not know what relation it might have to the bat-winged monster. The room was silent except for the occasional *tap-tap* of steps going by outside. The cat made me jump by suddenly meowing. Theodora picked it up and stroked it until it began to purr.

"Somebody's working magic here besides you and me," I said at last. "Whoever it is must be bringing creatures from the northern land of magic and making them invisible." Might the Royal Wizard of Caelrhon have been dismissed just before his death for summoning enormous lizards?

The cat was going to sleep in Theodora's lap. "Do you mean it's something to do with this city, and not with my ring?"

"Unless the world is fuller of invisible creatures than I had thought," I said grimly.

"You do know," said Theodora, "that there's another wizard in the city right now."

I took her by the shoulders so sharply that I jostled a highly indignant cat off her lap. "Another wizard? Here? Now? No, I didn't know!"

But I should have known it perfectly well. After all, Norbert had gotten that book from *somebody*. I had grabbed a quick breakfast while Joachim was still at morning service and gone out before he returned, preferring to postpone a discussion of books falling from the ceiling. Thinking about Theodora had distracted me from what I knew I should have been doing.

She pulled back as though almost frightened of me. In the uncertain candlelight her eyes looked gray instead of amethyst. I made myself loosen my fingers from her shoulders. "He's been in town all week," she said. "Haven't you felt his presence?"

I put my forehead on my fists, feeling like a fool. A wizard who had resisted my best spells to find him seemed to be transparently obvious to a witch. I stopped myself from asking Theodora why she had not told me about him. I had not asked her.

I forced myself to look up. "Where is he right now?" I judged how devastated I must look by Theodora's expression.

She put out a hand and touched my face. "I don't know where he is, but I can help you look for him."

Might it be the old magician I thought I had warned away? Someone that destitute might have been forced by hunger to sell even his tattered old book of spells if Norbert had offered him enough. Maybe, and I clenched my jaw at the thought, just as he had persuaded Theodora to teach him a little fire magic he had persuaded some wizard to teach him how to summon invisible and even demonic creatures.

"Not demonic," I said. "They're not demons."

"How do you know?" I didn't realize until she spoke that I had said it aloud.

I pulled her toward me. "I don't."

She started kissing my face, my cheeks, my eyes. In a moment I thought that she was doing a remarkably good job of making me forget my fears. "I'm afraid I haven't been entirely frank with you," I said, pulling back. "You already know that I came here to find the source of the magical apparitions here in the city. The mayor didn't send for me, however; the dean of the cathedral did."

This did not seem to strike her as a particularly startling revelation. "Maybe you haven't been able to find the other wizard because he's afraid of your powers and is deliberately hiding from you," she said, "whereas it never occurred to him he had to shield his mind from a woman."

"Well, then," I said, trying to regain my good humor, "if you can help me find him, maybe I can make sure he doesn't summon any more invisible creatures to bother you."

"Come on," she said, jumping to her feet. "We'll look for him now."

But Theodora and I were unable to locate the wizard or magician. She could find his mind quite easily but not actually touch it, so she had no information on his exact location. I could not find him at all.

"You don't sense him?" she said in frustration. "You don't find him right—*there*? Are you sure you're using the right words of your Hidden Language?"

"Maybe witches are just better at finding other people than wizards are," I said, equally frustrated. "You found me long before I found you." I was using discovery spells powerful enough that I doubted I could have shielded against them myself, school spells that should have sliced straight through the old magic of earth and herbs, without the slightest result.

"Let's not stand here being irritated any longer," Theodora said with a sudden smile, taking my arm. Market day was finishing, and we had been pushing through the jammed streets on our unsuccessful search. "Let's walk outside the walls and think about something completely different. Then if he thinks he's safe and lets his guard down, we'll have him."

In the weeks I had known Theodora, the season had passed from spring to summer. The early wildflowers were over, but the flowers that bloomed in the high grasses of summer were crowding toward the sky. While we normally had the Romneys' old campground to ourselves, today because of all the people in town for market the area was scattered with carts and tents. Even market stalls had spilled out from the crowded streets.

She settled herself among the sun-baked blades and I flopped beside her, pulling her down so that her head was pillowed on my shoulder. It was very easy like this not to think about the wizard. The late afternoon sun cast shadows across Theodora's face. She had unfastened the neck of her bodice, and with my free hand I stroked the side of her neck, then the line of her collarbone.

She smiled up at me through a veil of nut-brown hair. I wondered what she would do if my hand kept going. While wondering I started to kiss her and she kissed back, pressing herself close against me. Her fingers caressed my face, then slipped lightly across my chest and down my side and hip. Once again, it seemed, events were happening faster than I could plan or control them, and once again I seemed about to have a remarkably interesting series of experiences.

I drew back to catch my breath and look into the amethyst eyes so close to mine. There was no hesitation there, only affection. "You know," I said, "nothing like this has happened to me since— Well, not for longer than I can really say." Yurt was much too small a kingdom for private romantic interludes, and, besides, for close to twenty years I had been in love with the queen. I started kissing Theodora again.

This time she drew back, a smile flickering on her

lips. "This isn't exactly the most private place in the kingdom."

I sat up abruptly, distracted and pulling bits of grass out of my beard. She was quite right. Although lying down we were hidden from view, several groups of people were walking or standing within twenty yards of us.

"Come on," I said, standing up and holding out a hand for her. I didn't know where we were going, but I did know I had never been so excited in my life.

Theodora straightened her skirt and rose. She took my hand and led me purposefully. Having trouble focusing on anything but her, I staggered along as well as I could.

She took a shortcut between two large silken tents. Although there were voices all around us, the narrow space between the tents was sheltered from view. I clasped Theodora to me and kissed her face, her neck, her shoulders, murmuring endearments I had not realized I knew. My blood was rushing through my head so fast I felt half blind.

Then I could feel her shoulders shaking, and I pulled myself away in alarm, incoherent pleadings frozen on my lips. But she was laughing. "Do you just not like privacy?"

"This is private!"

"Until someone else decides to take the same shortcut. Come with me; I told you I knew where to go."

Once again she led me by the hand, away from the market stalls, the tents, and the people. I passed my free hand over my brow. It felt fevered, in spite of the breeze dancing around us.

We walked a mile toward a small grove of trees, at the edge of which blackberry bushes created a nearly impenetrable tangle. Theodora had started to pull long, thorned stalks back to make a path when I remembered that I was a wizard and flew both of us up and over the brambles.

Beyond the briars enormous trees stood tall and still. Very little underbrush flourished in their shade. Theodora kept on walking. The grove felt permeated with magic, the same wild mix of unfocused magic that could have concealed any number of spells as in the valley of the Cranky Saint back home in Yurt. But I had no attention to give to spells.

"No one comes here," Theodora said. The trees opened out suddenly, and a spring bubbled out of the ground in the center of an emerald stretch of grass. I saw that someone had built a little springhouse, but the stonework looked ancient. Beyond the spring, looking out of place, was a jagged boulder twenty feet high. "My father knew these woods," she continued, "and he used to bring me here to practice climbing when I was very small."

I was not interested in her youthful climbing experiences. I turned her toward me. "Is this then finally private enough for you?"

She gave me a long look from beneath her lashes. "I should certainly think so," she said with a smile, and I took her in my arms at last.

V

Afterwards we lay on the soft grass and watched the sun turn red beyond the trees. I felt happier than I ever had in my life. "Will you marry me?"

Theodora had been lying with her head on my chest. Now she sat up and scrambled around to face me. For a second she seemed almost alarmed, then she smiled, although somewhat tentatively. "This seems an odd time to ask!"

"I mean it. I'm just sorry I didn't ask you before."

She lay down beside me again, one arm across me and her lips grazing mine as we talked. "But everyone knows wizards don't marry."

I was getting tired of hearing this. "Don't you know I

love you, Theodora? This isn't just a pleasant interlude during an extended visit to town. I don't want to go on unless you're beside me."

Her amethyst eyes again looked troubled, but then she smiled. "Aren't you going to have trouble explaining this in Yurt? No king wants to have a Royal Witch alongside his Royal Wizard."

"It won't be a problem. I should have told you this long ago. When I left Yurt, I resigned as Royal Wizard."

"But what will you do?" she asked in what sounded like genuine distress.

"I thought we could have a caravan like the Romneys. If an old magician can make a living doing magic tricks at fairs, we should certainly be able to as well—after all, our magic is a lot better!"

She was silent for a moment, and I could sense a tension in her that I had not expected at what seemed to me a delightful proposal. But in a few seconds she relaxed and smiled.

"Let me give you my eagle ring, then," I said, encouraged, and started tugging at it.

She forestalled me with a hand on mine. "I can't wear a wizard's ring that's too big for me!" she said with her usual amused look. "Besides, I already have a magic ring of my own. What I have from you is much more valuable than any ring. Come on! We'd better get back to the city soon, and it won't be fun scrambling through the briars once it gets dark."

With clothes neatly arranged and hair smoothed, we walked through the silent trees like a decorous couple coming home from an innocent ramble. Once again I flew us over the briars. Outside the woods the breeze found us, cool now that the sun was setting. A mile away, the last of the sunlight glittered on the cathedral towers. I put my arms around Theodora and kissed her thoroughly. Her firm, slim body in my arms seemed like a gift: not mine by right, but given to me.

"You still haven't said you'd marry me," I said, smiling down at her.

"Isn't a woman supposed to have a little time to consider a proposal?" she said with a teasing look. "After all, it seems that if I accept you I'll be accepting a caravan and a pony."

"We can work something out," I said comfortably as we strolled back toward the city. "We could have a donkey or a horse instead of a pony."

It was nearly dark by the time we reached Theodora's house. She paused with her key in the lock. "Well, good-night."

"What do you mean, good-night? I can't leave you now!"

She stretched up to kiss me. "Your friend the dean will be horrified if you spend the night with a witch."

I hated to leave her, but she had a point. "I'll see you tomorrow, then," I said and turned away quickly before the desire to go inside with her became overwhelming.

Whistling, hands in my pockets, I walked back toward the cathedral. It was only as I reached Joachim's door that I realized that, for the first time in weeks, we had not arranged where and when to meet the next day.

A loud knocking woke me in the middle of the night. I had been happily dreaming of Theodora, and it took me a few seconds to realize where I was. The knocking was at the outside door, and in a moment I heard it open, letting in the sound of rain. There was rapid conversation, too low for me to understand, although I could recognize one of the voices as Joachim's.

There was a confused sound of further voices, the banging of box lids, rapid steps, and then the slamming of the door. The house was now totally silent. I lay tense for a moment, wondering if the monster had returned to the cathedral tower. But Joachim was highly unlikely to go face a magical apparition without the wizard he had brought in especially to deal with it. I rolled over and went back to sleep.

When I awoke several hours later the house was still silent, although I could hear, or rather, feel the heavy booming of the organ from the cathedral. Thinking it was a little late for early service and that I had never heard the bells, I dressed quickly and uneasily. When I went into the kitchen, the fire was cold. I found the tinder to boil some water and looked around for the bread. While I was rummaging through the cupboards, Joachim's silent servant came in.

"What's happening?" I asked, wondering if he would even answer me. "Where's the dean gone?"

The servant turned his eyes toward me, not with Joachim's piercing look but with something close, as though he had been trying to emulate it. On the surface he looked very sober, but there was a look of relief underneath; maybe, I thought, he had finally confessed his youthful indiscretions to the dean. He spoke for the first time since I met him. "The bishop is dead."

"Oh," I said, and then, "I'm very sorry to hear that." This then explained the sudden summons to the dean in the middle of the night. The water I had put on the hearth was close to boiling, and I realized I was standing with a loaf in my hand. "Is it all right if I make myself some breakfast?"

The servant did not speak again. He nodded gravely and left the room. I consumed tea and toast rapidly and stepped out into the normally quiet street.

It was now thick with priests, most of them sheltering under umbrellas against the continuing rain. They went in and out of the houses, in and out of the side door of the cathedral, and gathered in little knots to talk. I could usually keep myself dry against the rain with magic, but out of respect for the dead bishop I let the rain fall on my head as I hurried down the street and into the cathedral.

The inside of the church had been transformed. The altar cloths were gone from all the altars, and the crucifixes had been draped in black. The bouquets of flowers which normally clustered in front of the statues of the saints were also gone, and no candles burned. The organ, which I had heard increasingly clearly as I came down the street, played deeply and solemnly.

As I hesitated in the doorway, I heard a confusion of voices and footsteps in the street. I stepped quickly into a side aisle as a small procession came in. They paused briefly to remove the cover from the burden they were carrying, then proceeded toward the high altar. It was the bishop.

I did my best to make myself invisible without actually employing magic. Shielded by a pillar, I watched the priests arrange the bishop's body in front of the altar. He looked in death both older and smaller than I remembered. He was dressed in his full formal vestments; the brilliant scarlet made the only spot of color in the dark church. A tall white and gold hat covered his bald head. His eyes were closed peacefully, and his hands were folded across his pastoral staff. As banks of candles sprang to light around him, I could see the flash of reflected light from the bishop's ruby ring.

The organ kept playing its dirge. When the priests began to kneel, I slipped from behind my pillar and darted back out into daylight.

As soon as I was away from the cathedral I set up the spell to keep off the rain. I walked toward Theodora's house with my head down, thinking that now Joachim really might become bishop.

The news of the bishop's death had already spread through the city. I heard it discussed at open windows and where people sheltered under broad eaves. I wondered what Theodora would think of the event; the bishop had held office here since long before she was born.

But when I knocked on her door there was no answer. I peered through the window into the dark interior, seeing nothing, and rattled the door handle to find it locked. I told myself that she had probably gone around to some of the garment retailers to pick up or drop off embroidery, but I felt strangely uneasy.

When I discovered that virtually all of the shops in the city were closed, I became even more concerned. Shades were pulled, and black ribbon hung on the doors. In a cathedral city, I thought, the death of the bishop must be one of the major events of the generation. The inns were still open, but I did not spot Theodora there either. Thinking that she must have gone out and then returned home when she found the shops shut, and that I had simply missed her in the streets, I hurried back again to her house. But it was still dark and silent; my knocking did not even gain a response from the cat.

"This is silly," I told myself, trying to stem an irrational panic. "We just didn't happen to plan where to meet, and now with the bishop's death she's probably out looking for *me*." Leaning against her doorway, I closed my eyes and stepped into the flow of magic.

My mind raced across the hundreds of minds in the streets around me, not quite touching them, moving so lightly they would never know I was there. Most of the minds were unfamiliar, and I slid across them without pausing. Some were people I had come to know more or less well: Prince Lucas, one of the innkeepers, a few of the cathedral priests.

I was startled in brushing the edge of Joachim's servant's mind to find it a dense turmoil of thoughts. Somehow I had assumed his thoughts would be as silent as his voice. For a second I even wondered if *he* might be the evil wizard, but I dismissed this at once; if I could actually touch a wizard's mind, there was no way he could conceal his magic from me. I did not find Joachim or most of the other priests, but this was not surprising. Deep in prayer, their minds would have entered the supernatural realm of the saints and thus be beyond the reach of my magic.

But I also did not find Theodora. My mind slid back to my body, and I opened my eyes. There was no emotion in the deep silent tunnels of magic, but once back to myself I felt a sharp fear. Where could she be? Within the square mile or so of the city, she should not have been able to hide from me unless she were cloaking her mind thoroughly. This meant that she had either left the city and was already a good distance away or else was deliberately hiding from me.

I hurried back to the cathedral through the wet and slippery streets. All activity on the construction site had ceased. The tall front doors of the church stood open. A few townspeople were going up the stairs to them, almost shyly. None of them was Theodora. I joined them, and we entered the dim church and walked the length of the nave to where the bishop lay before the altar, surrounded by candles. After a brief pause and a brief dip of the head, the townspeople quietly walked out the front doors again, but I slipped around to the side entrance.

The street behind the cathedral was quiet once more. I hurried down to the dean's house and went inside. He was there, but I did not think he even heard me come in. He sat at the table, all in black, his face buried in his hands.

I tiptoed past him and went into the room where I had been staying. The only thing I could do was leave at once. I gathered up my clothes and books and packed everything neatly in my box.

But where could I go, and, even more importantly, where was Theodora? Maybe she had had a fit and died in the night. Maybe the old bishop, in dying, had reached out a demonic hand to take her soul with his.

This last was too unlikely, even in my worried state.

But I did not like my other ideas any better. Had she been kidnapped and dragged from the city? Had an evil wizard ambushed her and taken her to wherever he and his nefarious magic were hiding?

Or, most devastating of all, did she not want to see me?

"No," I said aloud. I could not think of this as the most devastating, no matter what it did to my self-esteem. I would rather have her alive and furious with me, for reasons I could not begin to fathom, than to have her in dire captivity or even dead.

Had Theodora felt violated by my attentions? I found it hard to accept this; it was she who had led the way to the grove. Since I was a wizard, not a priest, I had, as I had told her, not sinned against institutionalized magic by being with her. But if I had somehow, unintentionally but horribly, frightened her or hurt her, I had sinned against Theodora herself. As I thought again of our walk back to the city last night, it became more and more clear that she did not want to marry me.

Had she all along been the sort of witch I had feared when I first met her, only interested in men to satisfy her mad lusts? Maybe the woman I thought I had come to know and love this summer had all been a façade.

"Theodora!" I shouted inside my mind. "Where are you?" Any wizard or witch within five miles should have been able to hear me.

There was no response, but I had expected none. After sitting glumly on the bed for a few more minutes, I stood up abruptly to go out. Joachim had not moved. I closed the door quietly behind me as I stepped into the street.

The rain had let up. As I came around to the front of the cathedral, I saw that the numbers of townspeople coming to pay their final respects to the bishop had grown.

I headed out through the city gates and wandered through the long, wet grass, finding no clues and not even sure what I was seeking. I stared out along the road leading from the city, and, in the distance, could see a galloping horse coming toward me.

It was a red roan stallion, and in a moment I could see that the rider was Paul. No one was with him, and he rode as though pursued by demons. My heart felt as though a hand had clutched it.

With Theodora either held captive by an evil wizard or furious with me, and with Joachim lost to me forever, I had been thinking that nothing worse could possibly happen. But now I knew it could.

PART FIVE

The Funeral

I

Paul reined in the stallion and leaped off lightly. The sun broke from behind a cloud at the same time. "Wizard!" he cried with a smile. "I've come to look for you!"

I went weak in the knees as I realized that nothing could be as horribly wrong in Yurt as I had feared. "But why are you alone?" I managed to ask. "And why were you riding so fast?"

"Bonfire loves to run," he said nonchalantly. Indeed, the stallion did not seem at all winded by the gallop. "I must have left the other knights some miles back."

"It's dangerous," I said sternly, "for a prince to ride around unprotected."

Paul smiled again. I had not remembered that he was half a head taller than I. "I've got my sword and shield," he said, "and I know how to use them. And Bonfire can outrun any bandits in the western kingdoms. Besides, I don't think there even *are* many bandits anymore—haven't you wizards from the school gotten rid of most of them?"

I would have been interested in Paul's thoughts about the wizards' school, but not now. "You haven't said why you're here."

We went in through the city gates, the stallion's reins looped over Paul's arm. He saw the black ribbons along the street. "Has someone important died?"

"Yes, the bishop. But why are you here?" I persisted.

"Mother wanted to find out how you were doing, and she said she didn't like to telephone the cathedral to ask about a wizard. Did you find their monster?"

"Not yet," I said cautiously, wondering what intention of the queen's might lie behind this terse message.

"So the bishop died," said Paul. "He was very old, wasn't he? I wonder who the new bishop will be."

I realized we were walking briskly through the city streets as we talked. "Where are we going, anyway?"

"To the castle, of course," said Paul in surprise. "That's where I'll be staying."

"But Prince Lucas is there."

Paul was even more surprised. "Prince Lucas? Mother mentioned that she'd sent him permission to make a brief stay, but he should have been gone weeks ago." He grinned disarmingly. "Well, we're both royal princes, but I'll be king of Yurt in not much more than a month, whereas he may not be king of Caelrhon for years, and it *is*, after all, our castle!" He continued on, apparently looking forward to putting Prince Lucas out by force if necessary.

I hurried behind him. "I've never known," I said as I caught up again, "why only the king of Yurt has a castle here in the cathedral city when the city is located within the kingdom of Caelrhon."

"Did you never study the history of Yurt?" asked Paul.

"Of course not," I said in exasperation. I felt myself fortunate to know what little I did about the history of wizardry.

"Well, Father taught it to me. It's actually quite interesting now, with Mother planning to marry Vincent, because—"

He stopped without finishing the sentence. Before I

could do more than note that he now seemed capable of speaking of his mother's marriage without despair, he reached into his pocket. "I'm sorry, I almost forgot. Mother said to give this to you."

It was a large white envelope, sealed with the queen's crimson seal, and much too heavy to have been sent by the pigeons. The image on the seal was a tiny picture of a crowned woman, and around the edge ran the inscription, "*Regina Regensque Yurtiae,*" Queen and Regent of Yurt.

I tore the envelope open while Paul stood a short distance away, trying to appear politely uninterested in my correspondence. At first I thought the letter was shaking, and then I realized it was my hands.

In spite of Theodora, I realized as I saw the familiar black sprawling handwriting, I was still in love with the queen. A very faint scent came from the letter; it must have been a perfume she always wore of which I had never before been consciously aware.

The message was brief. "I don't know what you have thought or what you have imagined, but you are still Royal Wizard of Yurt. Come home as soon as you can. Give our love to Father Joachim." At the bottom of the page, squeezed in as though an afterthought, were the words, "Paul and Vincent and I all need you."

I was still wizard of Yurt, even if she sent her love only to Joachim and not to me. I didn't know if I was glad or not. I looked up and met Paul's inquiring eyes. "Your mother wanted to make sure I was back for your coming of age ceremony," I said.

He smiled. "But I told her you'd promised to be there! And of course," he added casually, "you'll be there for the wedding the next day."

I caught my breath between my teeth. "Her wedding?" I said slowly over the hard pounding of my heart. "I thought she didn't plan to marry for months and months!" I was the cause of this, I thought. My impetuous avowals had made the queen move up her wedding to avoid anything similar in the future.

"That's because she and Vincent had originally planned to be married in the cathedral here," said Paul. He spoke without concern, but for a second I thought I spotted behind his calm words a determination not to make a childish fuss over something he could not change. "But then they realized that as soon as I'm king, there will be nothing improper about the queen mother marrying the prince of the neighboring kingdom. So they'll have the ceremony when everyone is already assembled at Yurt for my coronation."

I found I had nothing to say. We turned a corner and reached the little castle that belonged to the royal family of Yurt. Paul stepped boldly up to the knight in Caelrhon's livery who stood at the door. "Inform your master," he said, resting his hand casually on the pommel of his sword, "that the heir to Yurt demands that he vacate this castle at once and make it available for our use."

Inwardly I smiled, distracted for the moment from the devastating news about the queen. Paul was so confident, so bold, and still so young. A stray beam of sunlight made his hair shine like a crown of pale gold. I waited, ready in case the knight tried to oppose him by force.

But after one hard glance at us the knight grunted, "Wait here," and disappeared into the castle. While we waited, I took the queen's letter back out and looked at it again. Apparently she was willing to go on living in the same castle with me on the same terms as during the previous nineteen years; the only question was whether I was equally willing.

This thought shocked me. How could I even be considering going on as wizard of Yurt when I loved Theodora?

Prince Lucas's knight returned. "He will receive you within, sir."

Paul handed him the stallion's reins. "Watch him for me until I return. But be careful. He's wild, and he'll kill anyone but me who tries to mount." He grinned as we went up the steps, leaving the knight looking dubiously at the stallion. "In fact, Bonfire is as gentle as a kitten," he said in a whisper.

Prince Lucas met us in the castle's great hall, doing his best to appear gracious; I did not judge the effort a great success. "I am delighted to see you, Prince," he said to Paul, but looking at me with thorough disapproval. "I just wish you had warned me of your coming to Caelrhon, so that we might have been prepared to greet you more suitably."

The two princes kissed each other on the cheeks, their hands stiffly placed on each other's shoulders. Paul was as tall as Lucas, although I doubted he weighed more than half as much.

"My mother and I are deeply surprised to find you still here in our castle," said Paul with comparable courtesy. "If you had warned us you wished to extend your stay, it would not now be necessary to ask you to leave."

"Let me make a suggestion," said Lucas. "We were unavoidably detained in the city by certain business, and now, with the bishop dead and the funeral scheduled for tomorrow, it seems inappropriate to leave immediately. There is plenty of room for both of us. I will vacate the royal chamber, of course, but it would be unsuitable for a prince such as yourself to stay here alone."

"I have three knights coming to town behind me," said Paul, "and of course our Royal Wizard will stay with me. But for one night we are willing that you stay here as well. The royal heirs of the twin kingdoms will be suitable representatives at the bishop's funeral."

Prince Lucas looked at me even more sourly but nodded. "May I have a few hours to make the appropriate arrangements?"

"Certainly," said Paul. "I'll be back later this afternoon." He gave me another grin as we went back out of the castle, proud at how he had handled a potentially delicate situation.

"I think I know," he said, once we were outside and he had reclaimed his stallion, "why Lucas stayed on in the city all this time. He was hoping to outwait you."

"Outwait *me*?"

"Of course," said Paul. "He must assume that you're here on some secret business of the royal house of Yurt. Since he knows he can't discover your real business, he has to wait until you actually do what you're planning to do."

"But what sort of secret business could there be?"

"That's right; you don't know anything about the history of Yurt. Remind me to tell you later. Where are we going, by the way?"

"To the cathedral," I said. "I've been staying at the dean's house and need to get my things."

Paul waited at the end of the street. Joachim's door was locked, and no one answered. I unlocked the door and went in. The house was completely silent except for the distant sound of the cathedral organ. I got my box and went out again. For a second I hesitated on the porch, Joachim's spare key in my hand, then locked the door and slipped the key under the mat. I doubted I would ever be back.

"Yurt and Caelrhon used to be all one kingdom," said Paul. We sat at a table in the inn, having dinner. The royal heir to Yurt seemed to be enjoying eating with the ordinary townspeople of Caelrhon. The last time I had been here was with Theodora.

For a terrifying moment I feared that the events of the last six weeks had all been imagined. In many ways Theodora was the woman of my youthful dreams, coming to meet me a generation later. But then rationality reasserted itself. My memories were much too vivid to be illusory. Besides, if I had been creating an imaginary woman for myself, I would not have created an amethyst-eyed witch who climbed steep cliffs unaided by magic.

I dragged my attention back to Paul, who was giving me a quizzical look. "I'm sorry," I said. "So Yurt and Caelrhon used to be all one kingdom? How long ago was that?"

"Until—" he paused to calculate "—until two hundred and fourteen years ago. That's when the twin heirs to Yurt decided not to fight any longer but divide the kingdom between them." He put down his knife and fork to explain more fully. Although I had no appetite, Paul had been eating with gusto. The three knights from Yurt, who had finally reached the city at the end of the afternoon and were seated across the room, seemed likewise absorbed in dinner.

"The one twin, the younger, took the part of the kingdom with the cathedral city in it, and indeed his share was larger in terms of total area. The older brother took the smaller share, but his had much richer land, and he kept the royal castle of Yurt. The younger brother had to settle for making what had been a small, dependent castle into the royal castle of Caelrhon. And of course it was understood that Yurt was the senior kingdom."

I paid proper attention now. "And is your mother's marriage to Prince Vincent going to reunite the two kingdoms?"

"Of course not," said Paul, with disdain for my inferior understanding. "Vincent is the younger son, not the heir, and besides, I'm going to be king of Yurt, so it won't matter whom Mother marries. But one thing I did find out from Prince Vincent—although I don't think he realizes I know this—is that certain members of the royal family of Caelrhon, especially Prince Lucas, are terrified that Yurt is planning to reconquer their kingdom."

"You aren't, are you?" I asked dubiously.

Paul laughed. "Yurt and Caelrhon will still be separate kingdoms. Prince Lucas has waited too long to be king to want to risk losing the crown."

"Would he like to unify the two countries himself?"

"He'd have to get rid of me first," said Paul, young enough to feel immortal.

"But he fears I'm the spearhead of a reconquest?" This was rapidly becoming too complicated for me in my present state of mind. "But why then is Vincent marrying the queen?"

"Vincent thinks that his older brother doesn't entirely approve," said Paul, as though this explained everything. "You know," with an expression of disgust, "they really do act as though they're in love."

And I was in love with Theodora. I dropped my forehead onto my fist and tried again to reach her mind. But I hesitated to use the most powerful spells, the ones I had already tried unsuccessfully against the wizard, which should reveal almost anyone trying to shield his mind from magic. If she was deliberately hiding from me it would be unfair to use my better knowledge of magic to force her out of hiding.

Paul was saying something, and I looked up quickly. "Are you feeling all right?"

"Oh, yes." It did not sound convincing in my own ears.

But Paul seemed ready to believe me. "Anyway, as I was saying, some of Vincent's ideas make excellent sense. On this he and his brother *do* agree. It really is true that the kings of the western kingdoms have acted in the last few generations as though we're not truly rulers of our own peoples and destinies."

Now I was alarmed. I pushed my uneaten plate of food away, half-nauseated from the vertiginous feeling of being flung from one emotion to another. "But what is Vincent planning to do?"

"Everyone knows the saying about the 'three who rule the world,'" Paul continued, staring fixedly at the candle flame. Although he spoke fairly casually, I realized he did not want to meet my eyes. "But the world is in many ways ruled only by two, the church and wizardry, and it's only because those two have a traditional rivalry that the aristocracy is allowed even the smallest role."

This did not sound at all like Paul. Won over by the gift of a red roan stallion, he seemed willing to believe whatever Vincent told him.

"The princes have relied too long on the advice of their advisers," Paul went on as though repeating something he had been told. "It is very well to be guided by the Royal Chaplain and the Royal Wizard in affairs of the soul or in magic spells. But the Church has long had its own organization and institutional goals, and the wizards have molded their school on the seminary system, only making it more centralized. Now that there are wizards being placed in every castle and manor-house in the western kingdoms, no aristocrat will be able to have an independent thought again. When the wizards first started putting an end to warfare, everyone accepted it at first as an excellent improvement. But only now, when it's almost too late, are the aristocrats realizing that the real purpose behind it all—"

I had to stop him before he went any further. Several people at adjoining tables were looking toward the prince with surprise. I put my hand on his arm, making him jump. "Paul," I said gently, "I'm a wizard, and my chief concern is the welfare of the kingdom of Yurt."

He looked at me then, his eyes wide. "I didn't mean *you.*"

"But I think Prince Vincent did."

"This isn't something Vincent told me; I worked it out for myself."

"Come on, Paul. Your Aunt Maria told me what Vincent had been saying to the court. You know that we wizards tend to fight among ourselves so much it's lucky we get anything accomplished at all." If I were conspiring to give the aristocracy more power, I thought, I would have started by trying to discredit organized religion, but the princes of Caelrhon seemed to have started with organized magic. "If you keep on believing in a wizardly conspiracy," I continued, "soon you'll start sounding like the young chaplain."

As I hoped, this brought an expression of disgust to Paul's face, and then he smiled. He glanced at my plate. "You didn't eat your lamb chop. Don't you want it? Do you mind if I take it?"

II

We arrived early at the cathedral, the two princes dressed soberly in black. I mingled with their knights, trying my best not to look like a wizard. The bishop's body still lay in front of the high altar, surrounded by candles. One of the flagstones to the side of the altar had been taken up and stood on its edge, next to a dark pit.

The church filled with town dignitaries and wealthy merchants and many ordinary citizens, everyone dressed formally and somberly. Even the workmen from the cathedral construction wore shoes over their long toes for the first time since I had met them. I recognized the mayor, who arrived wearing all his chains and medallions of office. As people slid quietly into the pews, I kept looking for Theodora.

When we had been there nearly an hour, and Paul was starting to swing his legs restlessly, the deepest bell began to toll in the tower above us. I started counting the strokes, lost track around forty, and realized they must be tolling a stroke for each year the bishop had lived. The bell went on for a long time, until the prolonged, deep strokes seemed to beat along with my heart.

The bell was still at last. All of us took a deep breath,

and then the organ began. It played deeply and slowly, all in the bass, as a young boy dressed in white proceeded down the aisle swinging a censer. Then the cathedral priests filed solemnly down the nave and took their positions around the altar. Joachim walked at their head, taller and gaunter than any of the rest. I got a close look at him as he went by, but I did not think he saw me. His face looked as though he had never smiled in his life.

He led the service, his voice ringing clearly through the packed church, but I knew him well enough to recognize the enormous strain behind the calm voice. The bishop had been a father to him for over twenty years. As Joachim spoke of the bishop's goodness, humility, and spiritual guidance, I felt my own eyes stinging.

The priests began to sing then, and the congregation rose to sing with them. We of the royal courts of Yurt and Caelrhon scrambled to our feet only a few seconds behind the rest.

When the singing ended, while the last organ notes still lingered, there was a brief scramble at the door and four seminary students came in, carrying an enormous coffin between them. There was dead silence except for the sound of their footsteps. They brought the coffin up to the altar and set it down. A priest stepped forward with a candle snuffer and one by one put out all the candles.

I understood at last what Joachim had meant when he said his cathedral was too dark. In spite of the high stained-glass windows, the church was extremely dim on this overcast day. The priests who lifted the bishop's body and placed it in the coffin were only dark shapes.

Joachim's voice rose as though disembodied. "As for man, his days are as grass. As a flower of the field, so he flourisheth. For the wind passeth over it, and it is gone; and the place thereof shall know it no more. . . .

He cometh forth like a flower, and is cut down; he fleeth also as a shadow, and continueth not."

There was more rustling by the altar. Then came the clang of a lid closing, a creak of bolts being tightened, and the faint sound of heavy breathing, even a grunt or two, as the dark shapes lowered the coffin. Finally came the hard report of stone being dropped into place.

After a long pause, the priests of the cathedral chapter began to sing. "Kyrie eleison, Christe eleison, Kyrie eleison." For a moment their song filled the dark church, but then their voices died away. Again there was total silence.

Then Joachim began to speak, and as he spoke lights sprang up on the altar. "I am the resurrection and the life: he that believeth in me, though he were dead, yet shall he live. . . . I create new heavens and a new earth: and the former shall not be remembered. I create Jerusalem rejoicing, and her people a joy. And the voice of weeping shall be no more heard in her. . . . And God shall wipe away all tears from their eyes; and there shall be no more death."

The black veils were gone from the altar, and the gold of the crucifix seemed to burn with its own light. The organ struck a new note, of utter seriousness yet great joy.

The choir began to sing again, a hymn of glory and triumph. At the same time, the sun finally emerged and struck through the stained glass to cast a brilliant glow on the replaced flagstones around the altar. The priests kept singing as the congregation slowly filed out of the church.

We emerged blinking into sunlight in the construction site in front of the cathedral. Lucas kept glancing around in a manner I considered highly suspicious. "Well, I thought they carried that off fairly well, everything considered," he said, as though wanting to make light of the whole matter and not quite daring to do so.

Paul paid no attention to his tone. "It was good that we were here," he said, extremely seriously. "A man like that, who has guided the souls of our two kingdoms for forty years, deserves every gesture of respect we can pay him as he goes to his last rest."

I found myself thinking two quite different thoughts: that if Joachim became bishop I might be attending *his* funeral in forty more years; and that by the time I finally got used to Paul alternating between being a boy and being a man he would have stopped being a boy at all.

"Yes, as representatives of royal rule, it certainly was good that we—" Lucas stopped speaking abruptly. "What's that?" he said in an entirely different voice.

Paul and I swung around. And then I felt it, a surge of enormously powerful magic which could only come from the wizard Theodora and I had been unable to find. Townspeople started looking up too, following Lucas's arm. Most of the priests had come out of the cathedral. I heard one saying, "I wonder if it would be disrespectful to go get a drink," before he caught the mood of the little group of people gathered around us.

"Look! Don't you see it? It's coming!" cried Lucas.

Now I could see it. It could have been a bird, but it was far too big. It flew faster than any bird, across the fields and straight into town toward the cathedral. It was five times the size of a man, and it had the wings of a bat.

Several of those around us began to scream. "Our swords!" Lucas yelled at Paul. "We must get our swords!" The two princes raced off while townspeople darted for cover. I saw the mayor upended in the rush, then he scrambled to his feet and ran, his gown hitched up to his knees. The priests flung themselves against the tide of people still coming out of the cathedral, fighting their way back inside.

Only I stood still, while the creature settled on top of

the half-completed tower, the tower that was not yet consecrated, and stared down at me with burning eyes. Though vaguely human in shape, it was covered with scaly hide, and its mouth and fangs were much bigger in proportion to its face than any human's could be. This was no illusion. This was real.

And this was why I was in the cathedral city. I took a deep breath and, without the slightest idea what I would do, launched myself into the air.

The creature watched my approach with interest. It had folded its wings and seemed content to sit where it was. As well as long fangs it had enormous, curved claws. As I flew closer it extended its claws as though in anticipation of sinking them into me.

My immediate need was to get it away from Joachim's cathedral. I hovered thirty feet away and tried a lifting spell. It shifted a little but that was all. Either it was too heavy or its magic too strong against mine. The evil lips pulled back in a grin, and the bat wings rose slightly.

I backed up warily. A hideous stench wafted toward me. I had defeated a dragon once, but I had had the old wizard of Yurt to help me, and I still had come remarkably close to a funeral of my own. I caught a brief glimpse of white faces far below me and wondered if they would mention in the eulogy that I had been trying to destroy the monster when it killed me.

Abruptly and with a loud bang it was gone. But not gone, I told myself grimly, only invisible. I could still smell its stench, and somewhere in the air, horribly near, I heard a hungry slobbering.

There were faint, excited shouts from below, but I ignored them. I retreated rapidly toward the main body of the cathedral and braced myself on the slates of the roof, my feet in a rain gutter, hoping it would not follow me to a consecrated church. But it might still attack the people below, especially now that it was invisible.

Desperately and without success I tried two school

spells, and then the powerful spell inscribed inside Theodora's ring, to reveal all that was hidden. I shouted the words of the Hidden Language, my fingers grating on the slates and eyes staring.

It appeared directly in front of me, its mouth wide open and one set of claws only a foot from my chest.

I spun away and fell into space, expecting to feel its touch on my skin any second. But I did not hear the slobbering behind me, and in a quarter mile I looked back. It had resettled itself on the half-finished tower.

It was not alone. Scampering around the tower were several red lizards the size of dogs. They must have been there all along and only been revealed by the spell.

But I had no time for them. I approached cautiously, watching for the monster to leap toward me. For a second I thought I glimpsed in the square below a woman's face with amethyst eyes, framed by nut-brown hair, but I could not look. I remembered Theodora's spell to create a series of tiny flames and began saying it rapidly, over and over, until the very air around me began to burn, and I hurled balls of fire toward the monster.

It sprang backwards, spreading its wings, one of which was already scorched. It gave a guttural cry as it staggered toward the pile of cut stones set ready for the masons. With clawed hands, it heaved up a piece of rock as big as I was and flung it toward me.

I whirled out of the way, but the stone hurtled downward, toward the crowd below. I flew after it, madly seizing at it with spells until its fall was slowed. People had just enough time to see what was coming and scatter, screaming, before the stone crashed into an empty spot where seconds ago a dozen had stood.

I found my feet and looked up. The monster had another enormous stone ready to hurl.

"Into the church!" I shouted, though I wasn't sure anyone could hear me through the general cries of panic. "Get inside the church!" I flew up, dodging the stone and trying to slow it with magic at the same time. Barely, just barely, I was able to reduce the speed of its descent, even guide it a little sideways. By the time it reached the ground, the construction site was nearly empty.

I could not take time to rest, but if I did not take at least a few seconds my lungs would burst. I leaned against the stone, which had shattered the paving where it landed, and took deep, sobbing breaths.

There was still wild scrambling at the cathedral doors but almost everyone was inside. One figure, however, watched with attentive interest: the foreman of the construction workers.

I flew back up. The monster's eyes glowed, but it threw no more stones. My balls of fire had lit the scaffolding timbers, which now blazed merrily, and the monster seemed afraid of fire. I eyed it warily as I approached.

The scorched wing was extended at an awkward angle as though it might not be able to fly, but I feared a trick. I wrapped myself in the spell Theodora had taught me against fire and waded into the middle of the blaze, screaming insults and challenges at the monster.

I had suspected it was trying to mislead me with its wing, but I was not suspicious enough. With a single leap it was beside me, careless of the blaze. I ducked barely in time to avoid being disemboweled by raking claws. But the monster's other arm caught me. It sprang into the air with a great flap of its bat wings and began to squeeze.

Desperately I raced through all my spells of attack, but I had never had very many of them, and none of them worked. The monster kept squeezing tighter. The only advantage I had was that I would already be unconscious when it began to eat me.

My last hope was a transformations spell. Zahlfast had taught me something important about transformations spells, I vaguely recalled, something highly important, something I ought to know right now—he had even been talking about it the day I visited his class. I did not have time to remember.

Because I could not wait to see if my spell would work, I coupled it with another spell, a spell I had never used in my life but which I, along with several of my friends at school, had looked up very late one night in the old Master's library. It was the spell to summon a human mind. To summon another human against his will, we had been taught, was the greatest sin a wizard could commit. I found and summoned the monster's mind and stuffed it into the middle of my transformations spell.

The grip around me was released so suddenly that I collapsed, losing parts of my spell against fire. My hair was ablaze and both hands were tightly grasped around something. I readjusted my spell to put out the fire and looked down. I was holding on to a frog.

I realized then I was not really flying but only floating, and not very well at that. Consciousness kept threatening to leave me, and the frog struggled in my hands. I set myself back down on the tower, away from the fire. There I found a piece of rope and, with the last of my concentration, attached the most powerful binding spell I knew to it and tied up the frog.

The red lizards all seemed to have scurried away. Still hanging on to the frog, I stepped out into space, only to recall too late that if my magic was deserting me it might have been better not to try flying.

But my spells stayed with me long enough for me to descend at only a moderate pace. I hit the ground, staggered, and fell, the mass of rope and frog a hard lump under my stomach.

"Get up!"

I could not move.

The toe of a boot kicked me. "Get up! Now!"

The toe turned me over. Prince Lucas stood over me, a naked sword in his hand and his face dark with fury.

III

I felt gentle hands then and heard Paul's voice. "Lucas! What are you doing? He conquered the monster, but he's been burned badly!"

I closed my eyes. It was quite clear that I would die before being able to get up.

"Conquered the monster!" said Lucas in utter scorn. "Can't you see it was a magical creature he summoned himself? He played with it for a while, then sent it away again. All of *us* came out of the bishop's funeral in sorrow and awe, yet all he could do was perform a few flashy tricks to show wizardry's utter lack of respect!"

This last was said in a shout, for the benefit not just of Paul but of the others who had begun gathering around. At this I did manage to open one eye.

Paul pulled back sharply. I could hardly blame him. The timing had been too good, too carefully planned to show disrespect for the old bishop. And it would be hard to explain that this tied-up frog, still very much alive and struggling in spite of being rolled on, was a monster.

For a second I thought I saw someone black-bearded, someone I did not recognize but who seemed strangely familiar, step forward from the crowd. The sight of Lucas's blade distracted me from a closer look.

"I'll kill him now to avenge the church!" bellowed Lucas. I ached so badly that death at the moment seemed rather appealing.

But if he was trying to win Paul's support, he had gone too far. I heard the metallic hiss of another sword being whipped from its scabbard. "Then you'll have to kill me first," calmly replied the royal heir to Yurt.

There was a brief pause. I could see a corner of Lucas's face, and he looked as though he realized his miscalculation. The ugly murmuring against me which had started in the rapidly gathering crowd changed its note.

A firm set of steps advanced across the pavement. "In the name of Christ!" came Joachim's voice. "The bishop has not yet been buried one hour, and the cathedral has just been successfully defended from the powers of evil incarnate, and all you princes can do is start fighting each other!"

I closed my eyes and began to believe, for the first time since Lucas had pointed toward the sky, that I might actually live. Joachim had never properly understood the fundamental difference between wild, natural magic and supernatural evil, but I didn't feel like trying to explain it now.

He knelt beside me. "Can you hear me? Do you think we can move you?"

I discovered I was still capable of speech. "Moving me couldn't possibly make me feel any worse than I already do."

"Good," said Joachim in a tone of authority. "Here, some of you, help me get him onto a board so we can carry him inside. He's saved the church in its greatest need, and we can't let him die a martyr."

I heard two swords being sheathed. People who a moment ago had been murmuring against me now came forward, volunteering to help. "He set the new cathedral tower on fire," said Lucas almost plaintively.

"Only in overcoming the monster," Joachim replied, "and the workmen already have the fire mostly out." I did my best to focus on the tower and could see several workmen scrambling around on it. To my surprise, being shifted onto a board actually did make me feel worse.

Paul saw the frog. "Ugh, what's this?" He reached for it, but I held on tight.

"This is the monster. I've transformed it, and now I've got to take it somewhere I can destroy it. I must get to a telephone."

Paul clearly did not believe me, but he decided to humor me. I rather hoped the dean didn't believe me, because he might not want even a transformed monster in his church.

"We'll take the wizard to the cathedral office," said Joachim, lifting the head of the board. Paul had the foot, and several townspeople stood around in helpful attitudes. Lucas followed slowly.

A seminary student was sent for the doctor, but even before he came I insisted on using the telephone. In a minute, I had reached the wizards' school and was talking to Zahlfast.

"I need the air cart," I said in the husky voice that was the best I could manage.

Without a far-seeing attachment I couldn't see him, but he could see me. He drew in his breath in a sharp gasp. "Where are you? Aren't you home in Yurt? What have you been doing to yourself?"

"I've been fighting a monster in Caelrhon. I don't know what it is, but it must be from the northern land of wild magic."

The foreman of the construction crew had slipped into the office with us. I wondered rather distantly if I should suspect *him*. "It was a fanged gorgos," he said quietly.

"It was a fanged gorgos," I repeated for Zahlfast, wondering with mild curiosity if there was also a non-fanged variety; if so I doubted it would be a substantial improvement. "But it isn't one anymore. That's why I need the air cart; I need to get it back north before it breaks out of the transformations spell."

"Out of the *what*?"

"I turned it into a frog."

And then Zahlfast said something I had never heard him say before. "Dear God." He paused for several seconds. I wished again I could see his face. "You realize transformations spells don't work against creatures of wild magic."

"Yes, I know. I remembered after I did it. I used a

summoning spell at the same time as the transformations spell. Please don't be angry; I know you never wanted us young wizards to know summoning, but I learned the spell years ago."

"Used the summoning spell," said Zahlfast slowly.

"And now I think I've destroyed all my own magic. I couldn't say another spell to save my own life, which may not last long anyway."

"Nonsense," said Zahlfast in something closer to his usual brisk tone. "You're just worn out. I'll send the air cart at once." But he paused then and added, "Have you remembered my warning?"

"Yes," I said wearily. At this point I neither knew nor cared whether priests hated and feared wizardry, but I did know that if Joachim wanted to destroy me I would do nothing to stop him.

Paul sat beside me, offering me drinks of water and brandy and ineffectually straightening the blanket while we waited for the doctor. He felt guilty, I guessed, for having believed, even momentarily, that I might have called the gorgos myself. "You know," he said, "I'm not sure I'd ever seen you really using your magical powers before. I've heard of course about your fight with the dragon, but that was before I was even born."

If I was going to serve Paul when he was king of Yurt, I thought, maybe it was just as well he realized that a Royal Wizard could do more than just after-dinner illusions.

"Thank you for standing up to Lucas," I told him. "Usually a wizard can defend himself, but I certainly couldn't now."

"I'm almost sorry Father Joachim stopped us," he said with a grin and a quick look across the room to make sure we were not overheard. "It would have been my first real fight." But then he became more sober. "Can that frog *really* be a transformed monster?"

I had continued to cling to the frog. It stared at me

with vicious eyes. "It is indeed. I don't know if you heard what I said on the telephone, but I'm going to take it back to the land of wild magic."

"Then I'll go with you!" said Paul in a joyous shout. "What better way to finish my minority than helping our Royal Wizard destroy a monster? I've wanted to go on a quest since I was eight years old, and this time no one will stop me!"

Lucas came and stood over me, fists on his hips. "What makes you think this wizard really *does* plan to destroy his gorgos," he demanded of Paul, "if he hasn't just hidden it somewhere and substituted a frog to deceive us? Don't you think it more likely that he is planning to call up even more monsters?"

I squinted at him suspiciously from under half-closed eyelids. Lucas had seen the monster before any of us. Even if this was merely due to excellent eyesight, he had certainly moved rapidly to take advantage of the opportunity to discredit me.

The dean looked across at him. "Then go with him, Prince," he suggested.

Startled, I pushed myself up on an elbow. Although I had certainly not planned to take Lucas with me, if I did I could keep an eye on him. And it might be good for him to see how useful and indeed necessary wizards were for the western kingdoms. "Go pack some clean socks," I told him quickly, "and blankets and enough food for all of us for two weeks."

Lucas hesitated, a hard curl to his lip. But he was rapidly losing the momentum that would allow him to refuse. "Do you not think it your duty?" the dean asked him sternly. "Do you not, as royal heir, need to witness the destruction of a monster that almost destroyed the major city of your kingdom?"

"Of course, Father," Lucas said, flustered and scowling.

The two princes started to leave together, then Paul stopped. "Wizard! Is there going to be room for Bonfire?"

"Of course there isn't going to be room for a horse," I said in exasperation. "Tell the knights from Yurt to exercise your stallion every day, and he'll be fine. And send a message to your mother to tell her where we're going. Give her everyone's love."

The doctor arrived as the princes clattered out. He clucked over me, putting ointment on the burns and pronouncing none of my ribs cracked, after an examination that I was convinced cracked several.

As he left again and the dean prepared to follow, I put a hand on the latter's arm. At least the bishop's death and the monster's attack seemed to have made Joachim lose track of whatever embarrassing questions he might once have been going to ask me about how the cathedral cantor came to be struck in the rear by a book of spells. "What do you expect me to do with Prince Lucas?" I demanded.

He cocked an eyebrow at me. "I have no idea. But if he did not go he would be here, worrying the cathedral chapter about the election of the new bishop, becoming increasingly irritable because he did not leap as Paul did at the kind of adventure he thinks is the function of the aristocracy. His younger brother would have needed no such prodding. And I have noticed this about you, Daimbert. You are at your best when everyone has been caught off balance, because you improvise better than anyone." At the moment I felt at my worst, but I did not interrupt. "You need to talk to Prince Lucas, to find out why he is accusing you of a wizardly conspiracy, and now will be your chance."

"But suppose he had refused to go?"

"It *is* his duty. And after he announced himself as protector of the Church, he could not very well refuse a suggestion from the man who is now the most powerful religious leader in the twin kingdoms."

I lay back down again. "I'm sorry," I said. "I'm sorry the bishop died, and I'm sorry I set your tower on fire."

He looked at me a moment and nodded gravely without speaking.

"Thank you for saving me from Lucas and from a riot."

Joachim gave me another long look. He did not smile, but at least his face looked as though he might once before have smiled in his life. "Thank *you* for saving us all from the monster. If Prince Lucas wants to incite a riot, he will have to do better than that." Then he was gone.

When at last, toward dusk, the air cart landed in front of the cathedral, I hobbled out to it with Paul's support. Several hours' sleep had made me feel, if not exactly better, at least as though living might be worthwhile. The air cart was the winged skin of a purple flying beast that had originally come, long ago, from the northernmost land of magic. Even after the beast had died its skin kept on flying if governed by magic commands.

Paul looked at the frog to which I continued to cling. "Why don't you just kill it here?"

"You're welcome to try. But don't cut the rope."

Paul set the frog on the paving stones and hesitated, his sword in his hand. I could tell he did not like killing a helpless creature. But he trusted me, and in a moment he lifted his blade and drove it down against the kicking green form.

His sword sprang back so abruptly it was jerked from his grip. Paul recovered it with a startled look. "What have you done to this frog? Its skin is made of iron!"

"That's what I was afraid of," I said. "You can't really transform creatures of wild magic. Spells are the orderly channeling of magical forces, but creatures like this cut right across order. The gorgos is now no bigger than a frog and looks like a frog, but I'm afraid it's still a gorgos."

"But is it going to start looking and acting like a monster again?"

"I hope not—or at least not right away. That's why I

need to get it back to the land of magic before it can recover its powers." I wondered sourly just how powerful the hidden wizard here might be, whether his magic might even be strong enough to bind *two* separate monsters at the same time. In that case, he might bring out the second while I was off taking care of the first. But I forced myself to dismiss the thought. If my opponent was that good, there was nothing I could do about it.

In the bottom of the air cart was a small box, absolutely black. I tried a gentle probing spell, the first spell of any sort I had tried for hours. It was a binding box, set about with spells to secure whatever was in it. Zahlfast must have decided to include it. I pushed the frog inside and slammed the lid.

Paul boosted me over the edge of the cart, and Lucas climbed in without a word. While I was searching for the words of the Hidden Language to guide the cart, a short, wiry figure came toward us from the huts. It was the foreman of the construction crew.

He leaned casually against the side of the cart, not quite looking at me. A pack was slung over his back. "So you're going up to the land of magic," he said at last. "Have you ever been there?"

"No." Normally I would have tried to justify or explain, but now the monosyllable sufficed.

There was another pause. "Would you like a guide?"

There was more here, I thought, than helpful concern for a confused wizard, but I was too tired to work it out. "Have *you* been there?"

"Not right up in the wild magic. But I come from the borderlands."

"Borderlands?" asked Paul.

"Of course, lad. You don't think the western kingdoms stop at a line on the map and the land of magic starts right there, do you? There's a stretch of territory several hundred miles wide in which the lands of men and the land of magic penetrate each other. Some places you can go just a few miles from an ordinary village to the castle of a will-o'-the-wisp."

Paul's face lit up. "It would be like stepping into fairyland!"

I kept a dignified silence. "Well," said the foreman, "do you want a guide or not?"

"Of course," I said. The foreman could prove useful, and I wanted to know how he had recognized a fanged gorgos. "But aren't you needed here?"

"I've been talking to the provost, and he seems to feel there's no use trying to get much work done in the next few weeks, before the new bishop is elected. My lads can repair on their own the damage the gorgos did to the tower."

"Then climb in," I said. "It's time to start."

IV

Dusk rose from the narrow streets of the city, punctuated only at intervals by the yellow gleam of lanterns, even while the sky above us was still pale blue. Laden with two princes, a wizard, a construction foreman, and a transformed monster, the air cart rose gracefully, spun around twice, and headed north. Though it flew no faster than I normally could, in my present exhausted state I could never have made the trip unaided, especially carrying a monstrous frog.

As the city dropped away behind us I leaned on the edge of the cart, looking back as intently as though I might be able to see Theodora from this height. I had not seen her for forty-eight hours.

If she had not been kidnapped, she must be hiding from me deliberately. But how could she have been so warm one day and flee me the next? Her reserve, the private inner thoughts to which I had only sometimes felt admitted, now took on an ominous interpretation.

She was, after all, a witch. Had she never loved me at all, only set out to distract me while her partner in evil, the hidden wizard, brought his gorgos to Caelrhon?

I gritted my teeth until my jaw ached. I could have sworn she loved me as much as I loved her.

"So you've got the gorgos in the box," said the foreman, leaning next to me, his long fingers folded over each other. I forced myself to stop thinking of Theodora. Cool air streamed by our faces. Everyone was avoiding the black box; Lucas especially made sure to stay on the far side of the air cart from it.

"That's right, and I hope I can keep it there until we reach somewhere I dare let it free. You know, I'm afraid I don't even know your name."

"Call me Vor," he said with a quick, sideways look that made me wonder if this really was his name.

"All right, Vor, maybe you can give me some suggestions what to do with an indestructible gorgos."

"First you have to decide," he said slowly, "whether you particularly want it dead."

I hadn't thought about it in those terms. "I would have killed it if I could," I said, "to keep it from attacking the people in the city, but I don't think I can. That's why I'm taking it north. If I let it go, do you think it will return to its gorgos shape and come back to Caelrhon again?"

"But you don't want to kill it out of revenge for nearly killing you?"

I looked at the motionless black box, a more solid piece of darkness inside the dark air cart, and wondered hopefully if the monster had suffocated. But Vor seemed to be asking something more. "No, I'm not interested in revenge."

Vor nodded as though I had clarified an important point. Below us dim hills and valleys streamed by. The air cart was high enough that it only had to rise for the steepest hills. Tiny figures of men and horses were coming in from the fields to villages where firelight welcomed them. No one looked up to see us.

"You can't actually kill a gorgos," Vor said at last. "Or, if you do, they're even worse dead than they are alive. I knew a man once who decided to kill one out of vengeance. Once it was dead it took possession of him, mind and body."

He fell silent then. I decided that I was happier not knowing the details and started putting together the spell to slow the flight of the air cart. "We must have come over fifty miles already," I told the two princes. "We'll camp in a field tonight and fly on in the morning."

It took us over a week of flying to reach the borderlands of the land of magic. The air cart did much of the flying on its own, needing only a steady low-level attention from my own spells to keep its flight smooth and on course. At first much of the land we crossed was rolling hills and farmland, similar to that of the kingdoms of Yurt and Caelrhon, but as we went north the season seemed to retreat, so that we started seeing again flowers that had already passed in the fields outside the cathedral city. Then we began to cross dense forests, where only occasionally we saw a track that might have been made by humans, and rocky, barren stretches where there were very few farms.

For most of the trip the weather was fair, and we flew during the day with the wind in our hair and slept under the sky at night. The stars were much brighter in the thin northern air, away from the smoke of the city, than I ever remembered seeing them. But one day it rained steadily for nearly twenty-four hours. I was able to rig a spell to keep us dry while the air cart flew on, but that night we had to overturn the cart in a partially successful attempt to keep the rain off, and all of us slept uneasily.

Being cramped in a small space all day was especially

hard for Paul. Every evening, as soon as the cart touched down, he was off running, sometimes for as much as an hour. Prince Lucas, gathering fuel the first night for a fire to try to stew up some of the dried beef he had brought along, grumbled that the other prince was deliberately shirking his responsibilities, until Paul came back with fresh bread and lettuce bought from a farmhouse over the hill.

Vor exercised by walking on his hands, doing bends and twists of which I would not have thought the human body capable. Prince Lucas practiced swordplay against his shadow. I, still recovering from my wounds, mostly worried about the gorgos frog.

Paul and I sat by a small fire one evening, watching the sun set behind the graceful branches of an oak. He was back from his run but the others were still gone. The heir to the throne of Yurt pulled off his boots, stretched, scratched, and flopped back cheerfully on the grass. I found myself imagining that if I had met the queen on one of her trips to the City, back when I was a wizardry student and she still only a castellan's daughter, he might have been our son.

A stream gurgled nearby, and the grass on which we sat was intertwined with wildflowers. "You know," I said to Paul, "we'll probably never see this spot again."

This didn't seem to bother him. "There are a lot of nice places," he said lazily, "many of them in Yurt. But traveling like this has made me want to travel more, to see *all* the beautiful spots in the world. Mother makes a good regent; maybe I'll just let her rule Yurt a few years more."

I did not like at all the idea of him taking off across the western kingdoms, but I let this pass in silence, hoping he would forget it as quickly as he had forgotten wanting to become a wizard.

"This is silly," Paul added after a moment, abruptly serious and looking off into the distance. "I'm going to be king very soon. I know I don't have the wisdom Father had, and I don't think I have the courage of Uncle Dominic, who loved Yurt more than his own life. He might even in other circumstances have become king instead of me. What do you think, Wizard, do I want to travel only because I'm afraid I won't be an adequate king? But then you've probably never known what it's like to feel unworthy of your position."

There was no possible way to answer this. I watched the flickering of our fire for a minute, feeling the evening air grow chill around us. "We've come so far and so fast," I said, "over land that none of us know. Sometimes I wonder if we'll ever find our way home again."

But this didn't bother Paul. "Of course we will," he said, cheerful again, lying on his back, supporting his hips on his hands and kicking long legs into the darkening sky. "If we get lost, all we have to do is go west until we reach the ocean, and then follow the coast south to the great City. It's easy enough to get home to Yurt from there."

He was right, of course, but as the days went by I kept feeling that I was astray in a strange world, with no landmarks and no way to find my way back to the world I had always taken for granted.

After a week the land below us began to rise sharply and all signs of human habitation disappeared. Soon we were crossing a jumble of sharp peaks, topped with snow.

"Wild magic starts not long after the mountains," Vor told me, looking down at the air cart's shadow far below us, darting wildly up and down the steep mountainsides.

"So you came south through the mountains?"

He nodded. "Years ago. That's why I want to go back now." He paused, then pointed down. "See that river?" A thin, dark line cut a twisting slice through the mountains. "There's a track that follows it all the way through."

At least one person, then, had known where we were going. The laconic suggestions he had made on our route in the previous days now made more sense. A cloud came toward us, looking, as always, incredibly soft, as though one could sink with delight into its feathery blue shadows. As always, when the air cart plunged into it the cloud proved to be nothing more than fog, blocking out the sun and putting drops of water on our hair and clothes.

"I know a good place to get rid of the gorgos," Vor said suddenly. But he turned away from me as he spoke, discouraging questions. I wondered uneasily if he had a plan of his own for the monster.

If only, I thought, I were more confident of my magic. So far every spell I had needed on the trip had worked. But I had the disconcerting feeling that I had, before the bishop's funeral, known more magic, and that not only the spells themselves but the knowledge that the spells existed had been wiped from my mind.

The teachers at the school had warned us against summoning as the greatest sin a wizard could commit, because it violated the integrity of the human mind. But, I thought now to myself, reckless summoning, practiced by someone remembering something he had learned twenty years earlier, might also destroy the person who practiced that spell. In summoning the monster, I might somehow have intermingled a part of its mind with my own.

"Did you ever decide where the fairy lights came from on the new cathedral tower?" asked Vor. "They weren't caused by the gorgos, were they?"

"No," I said slowly, "nor by one of your Little People. They were caused by a witch."

He nodded as though he had expected as much. "Down in your part of the world, if it's not a wizard with a heavy dose of formal magic it's probably a witch."

"Do you know anything about the witch?" I asked at

once, trying to keep the eagerness out of my voice. But he shook his head.

I looked down at the trackless snowfields below and wondered if I would ever see Theodora again.

V

A steep mountain peak rose before us, far higher than any other we had passed. Its snowy top, thrusting into the sky, glinted like gold in the early morning sun. As we flew toward it I heard, first distantly and then increasingly clearly, a call coming from it, and realized it was calling me.

I gave the magical commands to turn the air cart. Instead of circling the peak we started straight up its side.

"There's a wizard on the top of the mountain," I told the princes, who looked toward me in surprise. "I'm going to talk to him." Suddenly I did not feel as hopelessly lost as I had all week.

The air off the snowfields became rapidly colder, and we pulled blankets around our shoulders. I took mouthfuls of the thin, frigid air, my heart beating rapidly, either from the altitude or from excitement. For the first time since transforming the gorgos, I began to think I might someday be able to practice real magic again.

A sharp wind scraped ice from the peak into a swirling cloud that half obscured it. At the very top of the mountain, just under the final, jagged knife-blade of ice, was a small level area where all the snow had been swept away. Here was a bright blue house.

I set the air cart down by the door, vaulted out, and tied it to a ring in the doorpost. Leaning into the wind, I lifted a fist, but the door opened before I had a chance to knock.

A wizard put his head out. I recognized him at once. He had graduated from the wizards' school three years before I had, then stayed on as a teaching assistant. I had not seen him in nearly twenty years, but he still looked exactly the same.

"Well!" he said with pleasure. "If it isn't good old 'Frogs'!"

I stiffened. I had had no idea the other students at school had given me a nickname derived from my disastrous experiences in that transformations practical. But several comments I had half-overheard at the time now became horribly and mortifyingly clear.

"My name," I started to say in cold fury, "is Daimbert!" But I managed to stop myself. After all, I was delighted to see him.

I turned back toward the cart where the other three were hesitating. "Come on!" I called. "Prince Lucas, Prince Paul, Vor, I'd like you to meet an old friend of mine from the wizards' school."

They climbed out, and the princes gave the formal half-bow, while Vor dipped his head. "He graduated second in his class," I continued cheerfully, having an inspiration how to get my own back, "and would easily have graduated first most years. We used to call him 'Book-Leech'—behind his back, of course."

Good old Book-Leech froze for a second, then smiled. "Welcome, welcome, come in! It's much too cold to leave this door open." As we filed past him, he said modestly, "Well, I don't know if I ever could have been first in the class, as there's always someone— But Elerius *was* good, wasn't he! Do you correspond with him at all, Daimbert? I hear he's Royal Wizard now at one of the most powerful of the western kingdoms."

I graciously overlooked the inherent insult in this comment. Yurt might not be the most powerful kingdom, but I liked it best. And if the queen took me back, I would not have to live in a blue house three miles up on top of a snowy peak.

Inside the house a fire roared in the fireplace, and the

morning sun through the windowpanes made rainbows on the floor and furniture. We pulled off our ice-encrusted jackets, and the wizard hurried to make tea.

"You have no idea how pleased I was when I first sensed another wizard's mind here in the mountains," he said. "It does get lonely here, in spite of all the advantages. I'd known you would be coming across the mountains of course—they'd telephoned to warn me you were taking the air cart up to the land of magic. But I hadn't dared hope you'd come so close that I could call you and have you stop."

The water boiled and he poured it into the pot. Vor and the two princes sat rather stiffly against the wall, still startled to be suddenly in a real house again after days outdoors, much less a wizard's house on an inaccessible mountain peak. This, I thought, would be an especially useful lesson for Lucas, to see wizards serving mankind even in the northern mountains.

"What happened to you?" the wizard asked. "Your face looks burned."

"My hair caught fire," I said. "I was fighting a fanged gorgos."

"A gorgos? And you won?" He stirred the tea leaves and chuckled. "Well, you must have won or you wouldn't be here. But how did you do it? Who wants sugar?"

He poured out the tea into a row of mugs. "I transformed the gorgos into a frog," I said modestly. "I've got it out in the cart, inside a binding box. I know one shouldn't be able to transform creatures of wild magic, but I put a summoning spell on it at the same time, and at least it's now a very small and frog-shaped gorgos."

He was actually silent for a moment, looking, I thought, suitably impressed. "Well," he said to the others, "I should have known. 'Frogs' here always had a real genius for improvisation. The rest of us were always jealous."

"Nonsense," I said. "No one at the school was ever jealous of me."

"Yes, we were!" he said, quite seriously. "All of the rest of us would spend hours with our books, preparing for an exam, but you would come strolling into class late, probably not having studied, doubtless having spent the evening down at the taverns, maybe not even owning the right books."

Paul gave me an odd look. Perhaps it was good that he realize I had not always been the staid, even stodgy old wizard he doubtless imagined me to be.

"And then," the wizard continued, turning to the others, "he'd try to make up for his lack of application with sheer flair. Sometimes of course he failed spectacularly—I'll never forget the expression on Zahlfast's face that time!" He chuckled appreciatively at the memory. I did not join in. "But more likely than not, he'd manage something. You know, Daimbert, I think you were the despair of our teachers."

This at least I could agree with.

"I hear they had you teaching improvisation at the school this spring," he said, sipping his tea. "How did it work out?"

"Not quite as well as I'd hoped," I said. "Whenever I tried to explain to the students of the technical magic division that sometimes you have to put spells together in new or unexpected ways, they always wanted me to make explicit *which* ways, so that they could practice their improvisation and be ready."

"Excuse me," said Paul to the wizard, "but what are you doing here, on top of a mountain at the edge of the land of wild magic?"

"Guarding the border, of course," he said in surprise. "Your wizard must have stopped here twenty years ago to meet the border-guards when he took his field trip up here from the school."

"I was never invited to go on the field trip." I was quite sure he knew this; after all, he had been one of the assistants taken along to help guide the few chosen wizardry students. "As you said, I think I was the despair of our teachers."

"But why are you guarding the border?" Paul persisted.

"Making sure creatures of wild magic stay where they belong rather than coming down into the land of men."

"Do you mean," said Prince Lucas, speaking for the first time, "that there would be monsters down in our cities all the time if it weren't for you wizards? I must say, you can't have been doing a very good job or the gorgos wouldn't have gotten to Caelrhon."

"It's not that simple," said the wizard crossly. "Wild magic tends to stay in place north of the mountains, and it would most of the time even without us. And we can't stop a creature that's been called by very powerful or even black magic from going south. I expect that's why you had gorgos problems. There were always hermit-wizards up here, but it's all become much more orderly and reliable since the school was founded. Now we can stop most of the creatures that would otherwise wander south by accident, and we telephone the City to warn them about any unusual activity."

"So you do have a telephone." I glanced around without seeing one but assumed it was in the other room. The thought that the City was only a call away was very cheering.

"Yes indeed. With one of your far-seeing attachments, of course," he added generously.

"But doesn't it become dreary, being up here alone?" This was Paul.

"Not dreary. You lads won't understand this, but Daimbert will. There's something enormously seductive about the land of magic. All one's spells work much better. Flying isn't an effort anymore. Even here, at the border, one can feel the difference. None of us are posted here very long, and they say it's because they don't want us to become too lonely, but I think in part it's because they don't want us going over the edge.

"It *is* lonely, of course," he continued. "The air cart brings us supplies, but only irregularly, when no one else needs the cart. The school ought somehow to arrange for a second one. We can talk on the telephone, but it's not the same. I've already been here two months, and I'll be here for another two, and you're the first people I've seen."

"Then if you were at the wizards' school two months ago," I said in surprise, "you were there at the same time I was."

He waved his hand vaguely. "Well, there are always a lot of people at the school, and one doesn't see everybody." It was true that, between the teachers, the students, the young wizards, and the older ones coming and going, there were always a lot of people at the school. But he had known I was there. He had just not wanted to see foolish old 'Frogs' until now, when he had no other wizards to talk to. "So I'm delighted I'm having a chance to see you now," he added.

"I'm sorry in that case to have to leave," I said, standing up, "but we really need to get the monstrous frog up further into the borderlands, somewhere we can dispose of it. Thank you for the tea. Maybe we can stop here again on our way back."

"Then I'll hope to see you all again in a few days. Very nice meeting you young fellows."

PART SIX

The Borderlands

I

The air cart came down out of the mountains. The snow lingered on the northern slopes, but finally we dropped enough that the land beneath us was green again, and we spotted miniature flocks of goats followed by miniature goatherds. These were the first humans, other than the wizard, we had spotted in three days.

I filled my lungs with cold air and almost felt confident again of my ability to practice wizardry. But I reminded myself that this might only be due to the influence of the land of magic, not a sign of returning abilities.

Vor pointed. "There's my valley." Ahead of the air cart was a deep gash in the mountain slope, perhaps a mile wide and ten miles long. The sun had not yet reached down the sides of the rift, but I could see a waterfall pouring into it from the mountains and a dark green river winding the length of the valley.

The air cart slowly descended beside the waterfall, its roar loud in our ears. The tumbling water rushed downward like something solid, and drops of spray nearly reached us. Vor leaned what I considered dangerously far over the edge of the cart, staring ahead. The valley floor was a patchwork of fields, but there were no buildings. "So where do your people live?" I started to ask and then saw them.

Their houses were built into the nearly vertical rocky sides of the valley, half-hidden by gnarled trees. A network of steep stairs, ladders, and toeholds connected the valley floor with the doors of dwellings burrowed back into the rock. Theodora, with her love of climbing, would like this valley.

"How long is it that you've been gone?" I asked as though casually.

"Years," Vor replied briefly.

"Why haven't you been home again?" asked Paul.

"Three thousand miles is a long way on foot," said Vor. "My men and I reckoned we might not be home again in our lifetimes."

As we moved slowly downward, I could see people on the ladders, looking up. To them, I thought, we must appear as frightful, appearing without warning out of the sky, as the gorgos had appeared to the citizens of the cathedral city. "We don't want to terrify anyone into falling," I said anxiously.

Vor tore his eyes away from the valley long enough to give me a quick, amused glance. "Everyone knows these purple flying beasts aren't dangerous. The only surprise will be when they see us inside the skin."

I was interested to realize that the flying beast from which the air cart had been made was not unique, as I had always supposed. I found myself wondering if we could find an aged flying beast and induce it to come back south with us, so that after it died a natural death I could have an air cart of my own.

The air cart was now level with doors and windows, and heads protruded, staring at us. Paul waved cheerfully, and several people waved back. We landed with a bump in a meadow by the river, a mile downstream from the waterfall.

Vor leaped out at once and was off, springing from

tussock to tussock across the meadow's damp surface. Other people came running toward him, all with the short stature and unusually long fingers and toes of the cathedral's construction crew. He had seemed calm and unhurried the whole time I had known him, but now he spoke animatedly, waving his arms, pointing toward the sky and toward us. Several people threw their arms around him, and he embraced them with fervor. Everybody was talking at once; they seemed to be calling him a name I did not catch, but it was not Vor.

"That's curious," commented Lucas. "From several things he said, I had the impression he'd *had* to leave home, yet everybody seems happy to see him back again."

I had had the same impression, but all I said was, "Long absence makes quarrels seem trivial."

Paul was looking not at Vor but at the houses. "Think what it must be like to live there!" he exclaimed. "In the heat of the summer, it would be comfortably cool, and in the winter it would be as cozy as a den. Will we still be here tonight? I can't wait to see the hillsides all dotted with lamplight!"

Vor came back over to the cart. "I don't want to interrupt your reunion," I said. "Perhaps we should leave you here and continue north, until we find a good place to get rid of the gorgos."

He was smiling as broadly as I had ever seen him. "We can go dispose of the gorgos whenever you like," he said.

The air cart rose back out of the valley, and, with Vor's direction, I guided it northward. We rose over a last range of hills that protected his people's valley. The high snowy peaks were behind us, and before us a dry rocky land stretched out desolate. All of Vor's cheerfulness left him as soon as we left the valley, replaced by a tension so tight it almost vibrated.

Thirty miles beyond the valley, just as I had been about

to ask if he really knew where he was taking us, he pointed downward. "There. Put the cart down there."

I saw nothing to distinguish this particular patch of loose boulders from any other, but I obeyed. "Do you think we're far enough from your valley?" I asked. He nodded emphatically and kept peering about as we descended, apparently not seeing whatever he was seeking. I preferred to think this was good.

Just before we landed, I spotted something odd about some of the boulders. Rather than being scattered, they seemed to be piled up, as though to form a monstrous hut. I nudged Vor and pointed, but he just shook his head, and in a second the hut or whatever it might be was hidden beyond other rocks. At any rate I saw nothing alive. We hit the ground hard, and the cart tilted to one side.

"So what do you suggest?" I asked Vor, picking up the binding box from where it had slid down with the rest of our baggage.

"Just take it out and release it," he said shortly.

I put one leg over the edge of the air cart. "All of you stay here," I said. "By now you've heard me say many times the two words of the Hidden Language that will get the cart off the ground. Use them if you have to."

Carrying the heavy black box, I walked slowly away from the cart, trying to probe for magic. What I found was almost overwhelming. I was used to the orderly channeling of magic, but here magic whirled and spun in complete confusion. There was too much detail, too little focused, for me even to try to identify the source.

I closed my mind resolutely against these magical influences. This must be one of the spots in the borderlands where human habitation was only a short distance from wild magic.

Fifty yards from the air cart I set the black box down. Slowly, cautiously, I pulled open the lid and peeked inside. The frog was still there, glaring at me furiously. As soon as daylight touched it, it began to kick. The rope with the binding spell in which I had originally tied it was gone; I wondered if the frog had eaten it.

I swung the box forward, catapulting the gorgos frog out. It hit the side of a rock, rolled down, and righted itself. I realized I was trembling as I watched. It started to work itself along, although a frog's feet do not do well on rough stone.

"Go ahead," Vor called. "Turn it back into a gorgos."

I hesitated. There seemed no reason not to leave it a frog. Sooner or later it might be able to overcome the transformations spell by itself, but in the meantime we should be able to get well away.

On the other hand I feared that part of my own mind might still be attached to the gorgos. I had summoned it to me while transforming it, and there might still be enough attachment that it would be compelled to follow me.

Carefully, feeling my way into my own magic and trying to avoid the swirling alien magic around me, I put together the words to break the transformations spell. When I said the final syllables to restore the gorgos to itself, my mind leaped back out of the calm channels of magic into a body whose heart was pounding madly.

It had worked. The gorgos crouched on the ground where the frog had lain a second before. It was appreciably larger than I remembered, especially the fangs.

Both terrified and exhilarated, I started flying backwards toward the air cart. My mind was clearer than it had been for a week, and for a second I felt that nothing could overcome me and my magic. The gorgos seemed to be startled at its abrupt return to itself. It glared about with burning eyes and scratched its side with long, curved claws.

Then, behind me, I heard a shout. I spun around. It was Vor.

Beyond the tumbled boulders, in the direction in which I thought I had seen stones heaped into a hut, I heard an answering bellow.

The gorgos spread its bat wings and rose into the air, looking back toward the bellow but moving toward me. I retreated more rapidly.

And then I saw, rising over the boulders, a second fanged gorgos.

The first gorgos, my former frog, saw it too. He turned from pursuing me and, with a great flap of his wings, launched himself toward it. The two monsters rushed at each other, slavering mouths wide open, claws ready to rend each other's flesh. Just before they met, I thought I sensed something very odd about the second gorgos.

Not stopping to analyze it, I rushed after the air cart, which had taken off and by now was careening across the sky. The two gorgoi roared and screeched, apparently ripping off major parts of each other's bodies.

I caught the cart after a mile's pursuit. The magic words to lift off had put it into the air, but without further direction the purple flying beast's skin had started flying on its own with little regard for the people in it.

Vor and the two princes clung to the edge, looking ill. I dropped inside, stopped the cart's spinning, and straightened out the course. "Back to your valley?" I asked Vor, as calmly as if I dealt with gorgoi every day.

He blinked. "Yes. That would be good."

Paul looked at me wide-eyed. "I don't know how I could have gone all these years without realizing what a good wizard you are." I nodded gravely at this praise from my future king.

The cart banked and started to return. I could still hear faint bellows in the distance. I turned from Paul to address myself to Lucas. "I trust, Prince, that you will be able to report to the dean that I did indeed destroy the gorgos."

His lips tight, Lucas nodded slowly. I had plenty of questions for him now that my mind was abruptly clear again, but even more pressing were my questions for the construction foreman.

"You knew about the second gorgos, Vor," I said. "Ever since the first one appeared in the cathedral city, you've been working to bring the two gorgoi together. Now that, I hope, they're finishing destroying each other, I would like you to tell me what's really been happening."

Vor looked at me in silence for a moment. The two princes leaned back against the far side of the air cart, their elbows hooked over the side. Paul appeared interested and amused, Lucas suspicious.

"The second gorgos wasn't really a gorgos," I prompted Vor. "It's something—or someone—turned into a gorgos. Was it a person?"

He smiled suddenly and fleetingly. "The prince is right—you *are* a good wizard." I had scarcely received so many accolades in one day before. I hoped they would remember to relate all the details when we stopped at the blue house on top of the mountain on the way home.

"It used to be human," Vor continued, "a man from my valley." Once I had him talking, he seemed uncharacteristically willing to continue. "As I'm sure you already guessed, it was the man I mentioned to you, the one who determined he was going to kill a gorgos. He *did* kill it, too, but its gorgos spirit overwhelmed him, body and soul, as it died."

"And that's why you warned me not to try to kill the gorgos frog."

He nodded. "Maybe another wizard could have overcome your gorgos with wizardry." So much for the compliments! "But when it became clear that you were either going to have to take it back to the land of wild magic or else kill it by force, I decided I'd better come along. I knew where to find a second gorgos, and I knew if they killed each other they would both be dead, with no more humans taken over by their spirits."

"There's more to it," I said, watching Vor's face. His willingness to tell me all this now, I thought, was an attempt to hide something else. "You didn't merely want to dispose of the gorgos from the cathedral city. You had always known about the gorgos here, and you had been wanting to kill it for years." He blinked in what might have been agreement.

"You brought me and the transformed frog up here on purpose to kill the gorgos that was already here," I continued, holding him with my eyes. "The gorgos here, the one that used to be a person: *that* was the reason you left your home in the valley originally. What did it do to you?"

Again he gave that fleeting smile. "It killed my father," he said in his normal laconic tone.

As he seemed unwilling to add anything else, I said, "So is that why you had to leave? You couldn't live on in your valley with your father unavenged, but you couldn't avenge him without becoming a gorgos yourself?"

He did not answer. My brain, awakened fully from the miasma into which the gorgos had dragged it, had at last worked out something important. Let the others imagine that I had realized it all along. "Vor," I said with my best wizardly scowl, "this all started when you became involved in the plots of a renegade wizard. Since his gorgos nearly killed me, I think I have a right to know about it."

The two princes looked startled, but I ignored them.

"Nothing worked out as you had planned, Vor," I said sternly, "at least until the two gorgoi destroyed each other. Did you think that I would believe it was sheer coincidence that a gorgos should appear in the very cathedral city where the foreman of the construction crew wanted revenge on a gorgos? No," shaking my head, "it was not coincidence."

The air cart flapped steadily, carrying us across the brown borderlands of the land of magic. I paused to let Vor say something, but he seemed willing to listen in silence. "You had struck up a friendship with a certain wizard," I continued, "and he knew you'd come from the borderlands. He asked you, very casually, what would be a good type of creature to call to the city. And this is where things began to go wrong. Not letting yourself think about why a wizard would want to call a monster, you suggested, equally casually, that a gorgos would be just right. If the gorgos who had killed your father left the borderlands for Caelrhon, you thought, you could go home again without shame—especially if, as you let yourself imagine, the wizard planned to destroy it. But he called the wrong gorgos!"

Vor answered at last. "It wasn't like that! I would never have had anything to do with him if I'd known he was planning an attack on the cathedral. He told me the wizards' school was trying to find a good kind of monster so that the young wizards could practice their new antimonster spells."

"And even when the gorgos, the wrong gorgos, showed up at the cathedral instead of at the wizards' school," I asked, "did you still hope these 'new antimonster spells' were real?"

He did not meet my eyes, but a slow smile spread across his face. "I did admire your technique."

"But who was the wizard?" I insisted, not about to be flattered now. "Was it that old ragged magician who knows fire magic?"

Vor looked surprised. "Not *him*. *He* could never master a gorgos. It was one of you school-trained wizards, but I'd never seen him before. A relatively young one—no gray in his beard."

Lucas interrupted before I could press for details. "All right, Wizard," he said brusquely, "you've made your point that wizards may occasionally be useful against creatures of wild magic. But now you have to answer to me!" He tapped his fingers on the pommel of his sword. "You and your friend the dean—and I certainly hope the cathedral chapter has enough sense not to elect him bishop!—may have forced me to come with you, but now that you can't threaten me with your black box anymore, I think it's time to teach you your place!"

II

"I'd credited you with more intelligence than this, Prince," I replied sternly. "I don't have to answer to you, but you to me! You're three thousand miles from home, without a horse or a map. The only people here are half-fey themselves. If you try walking back south through the mountains, you will find *very* few people who have even heard of the kingdom of Caelrhon, and even fewer impressed by the crown prince of Caelrhon. It's no use trying to overpower me, because you'd be trapped here without my magic."

I took a deep breath. "Now! I'll give you a choice: between explaining why you contracted with a renegade wizard to bring a gorgos to the cathedral city, or staying in the borderlands of magic the rest of your life."

The hard curl of Lucas's lip was very pronounced. He must know I was bluffing and looked obstinate enough to dare me to leave him behind. I did not want to have to explain to the king and the royal princess of Caelrhon that he wasn't coming home. He had children, too, I remembered unhappily.

"You dare," he began, "you dare accuse me of summoning a monster—"

And then he did the last thing I expected. He jumped me.

I was so startled that he had me on my back on the bottom of the cart, his hands around my neck, before I could react. The cart tipped wildly. "I know how to fly this air cart," he grunted, digging a knee into my midsection, "and I—"

His eyes went wide and his grip slackened as the air went solid around his own neck. Gripped by a slightly tardy binding spell, he fell backwards as I pushed myself up, furious. "Suppose I turn you into a frog for the rest of the trip," I said between clenched teeth, "so you don't give me any more trouble."

But suddenly my attention was distracted. The air cart was beginning to wobble badly as it flew. I glanced downward and realized we were no longer heading back south toward Vor's valley. Instead we were heading east, much more rapidly than the cart normally flew. I gave the commands to correct the course, but the cart did not respond. Instead it picked up speed.

"This isn't the way back to the valley!" cried Vor.

"Someone else has control of the cart!" Closing my eyes against the others' alarmed faces, I slipped into the stream of magic, trying to find in the welter of influences around us the magic that made the cart ignore my commands. I found it in a few seconds, but finding it was no help. The wizards at the school had long ago worked out, by trial and error, commands the cart would obey, but someone here had specific knowledge of this kind of flying beast and had used that knowledge in the moment I had been distracted. Even a dead flying beast's skin could not resist spells shaped especially for it.

"Hold on to me, all of you!" I cried. "We've got to get out!"

Paul and Vor seized my arms at once, but Lucas clung to the cart's edge. "You mean you're going to start flying with all of us trying to hang on to you?"

That was exactly what I meant. "Yes, yes, hurry! I can't break the cart out of the attraction spell."

"And then you'll drop off those of us you don't like?"

"Come *here!*" I dragged him to me with magic and quickly started putting a lifting spell together. I had never tried to fly with three other people before.

But it was too late. As Lucas struggled in the grip of my magic, making it impossible for me to hold on to him and the other two at the same time, the cart began spiraling downward. Below us was a circular green plain rimmed with low dark hills, a dense grove of trees in the middle. We were heading for those trees.

The air cart swung low, tipping until all of us piled against one side, Lucas still struggling. With a twitch it tossed us out.

We spun out into the air, Paul and Vor nearly pulling my arms from their sockets. I applied enough lift to them to ease my arms and almost reluctantly looked for Lucas.

I caught him barely before he hit the first tree, just soon enough that he did not crash into it at full speed. But he disappeared from sight with a gratifying yell and a rapid breaking of twigs.

The air cart hesitated above us, abruptly freed from the attraction spell. I yelled commands at it in the Hidden Language and followed Lucas downward. The air cart shot off to the south, and we descended through a canopy of leaves to the thin grass below.

I came down prepared to face an unimaginable enemy but found only Lucas, green shadows, and an uneasy silence. Lucas, I was glad to see after all, seemed essentially intact. Paul and Vor collapsed without a word. The air that had been cool and brisk in Vor's valley was here sensuously warm. I closed my eyes for a second, concluding that there really must be a saint who looked after wizards.

Paul raised himself on his elbow after a moment. "What happened?"

"Someone or something wanted us down here and didn't particularly care how we got here."

"Who is it?" He scrambled to his feet.

"I don't know. I'm trying to locate him, but now that he's no longer drawing us with magic, I'm having trouble."

Paul had his sword out and looked around intently, but he had no more success with his eyes than I was having with magic. "How are we going to get back?"

"Walk to Vor's valley. I sent the air cart there as soon as it was freed from the attraction spell."

"Or we could ride," Paul suggested, which made no sense at all.

"I can't walk!" groaned Lucas. "You've broken my ankle!"

"You're lucky I saved your life instead of killing you," I said grimly. Dropping out of the sky had diverted my attention, but I had plenty of fury left. "It's entirely your fault we're here. If you hadn't attacked me, I could have kept someone else from taking control of the air cart. If it weren't for the oaths the school makes us swear to serve mankind, you'd not only be a frog but a very dead frog."

Lucas looked quickly toward Paul and Vor, but it was clear he would get no reinforcements there. "So are you just going to stand there and threaten me?" he said, attempting a sardonic smile. It was not improved by a grimace of pain.

"No. But I *am* going to demand to know why you believe that wizards are conspiring against the nobility, and why you summoned a fanged gorgos to the bishop's funeral."

He reached for his sword, but I froze it in his sheath. "I thought you'd discovered that violence against a wizard won't work, Lucas," I said fiercely, standing in front of him with my arms crossed. "And I already know most of it. It starts with *your* plan to use a gorgos to discredit both the Church and organized magic!

"You and your brother," I continued sternly, "have developed the foolish idea that the power of the aristocracy, even that of the kings of the western kingdoms, is being diminished. And you blame the priests and the wizards for this. Because you imagine that the kings could do better without their spiritual and magical advisers, you—"

"I know nothing of the gorgos," interrupted Lucas. "I'm not going to dignify such accusations with a response. But the power of kings *is* being daily diminished by wizardly scorn!" Sometime soon I really would have to find out what purported failings had led to Sengrim's final argument. Should I start suspecting Lucas of having murdered him, then deliberately replacing him with a renegade who paid no attention to the school and its oaths to help humanity?

Lucas looked as much toward Paul as me as he spoke. "Did you hear that wizard up on top of the mountain? 'Young fellows,' he called us. And it's not just scorn for our position. It's a determined effort to weaken us collectively! Even the feeblest and silliest kings are allowed to survive and flourish. Before the wizards' school, when wizards owed their allegiance to their kings rather than the school in the City, bandits and ruffians were found in great numbers, and princes could earn their spurs in combat. Then a few short wars by the strongest took care of the weak and foolish, and kings could stand proudly in their castle halls, rather than amusing themselves with illusions and fairy stories."

Paul looked toward me with a forced smile, as though trying to persuade me he had never believed such things.

"Did you consider the gorgos a fairy story?" I demanded of Lucas.

He ignored me. "Not very long ago, all my worst fears were confirmed. A nobleman from the City stopped by our castle on a journey. And this man, as it turns out, is a close friend of the Master of the wizards' school. He confirmed that the school is plotting very soon to break all purported obedience to the aristocracy!"

"The Master has no close friends among the aristocracy," I said, surprised. "Just who did this man claim to be?"

"He was a nobleman, all right," said Lucas testily. "I don't remember his name, but he had a black beard and hazel eyes—wore a big ring. And he seemed remarkably well informed on how the school operated."

"I spent all spring at the school, and I never saw anyone who—" The words died on my lips. Standing before us, where a second ago there had been no one, was a pale green woman.

She was green all over, naked skin the color of the first leaves in spring, eyes and hair a rich jade hue. She had round, uplifted breasts, a tiny waist, and almost unbelievably long and graceful legs. Clouds of dancing lights, like tiny stars, surrounded her: almost, but not quite, keeping her decent.

"Is this one of your Little People?" I asked Vor in a low voice.

"She is not little," he said with the hint of a smile. "She's a nixie."

"Of course I'm a nixie," she said in a mellifluous voice, taking a step toward us. "And I'm *delighted* that four men have chosen to visit me."

Vor turned to her, smiling fully now. "I wouldn't have said we *chose* to visit you, Lady. But you do have a charming grove."

"And even more charming treats await you, as I'm sure you realize."

"I realize that, of course, but *you* must understand that this is rather startling for all of us."

"Did you bring me here?" said Lucas, glowering balefully at her. "I am leaving *now.*"

"But you can't leave," she said with a tinkling laugh. "None of you can. Not until you've fully satisfied me. *He* knows what I mean," with a glance at Vor, "and the rest of you will find out quickly. But don't worry. You'll enjoy it fully as well!" She leaned down, breasts near Lucas's face, and kissed him on the top of the head.

Paul took an involuntary step backwards. His sword, forgotten in his hand, clanged against a root.

She said a quick word and it spun out of his grip. "No weapons here, or at least not weapons of steel!" she said coyly. "Come now, which of you would like to be the first?"

I shot Vor a despairing look. "It's late in the day, Lady," he said smoothly. "We've had an exhausting time, and, as you can see, one of us is injured. We wouldn't be able to satisfy you very well this evening. Perhaps if we could eat and sleep first?"

"Very well," said the nixie with the same coy smile. "Come with me!"

We followed her a short distance through the grove; Lucas, supported by Vor and Paul on either side, managed to hop. I came behind, trying to sort out magical influences. It was unexpectedly easy, and then I realized that this was because no magic now penetrated from outside the grove.

Under low-hanging branches were spread four beds, piled high with pillows. On tables next to each were bottles of wine and baskets of red and yellow fruit. She had clearly been expecting us.

"There!" said the nixie to Vor. "Is this what you wanted?"

"This will do most excellently, Lady."

"Then I shall leave you to your dreams." She kissed him quickly and slipped away through the trees.

Vor looked after her, rubbing his lips with his knuckles. "This will be a new experience. I've never been caught by a nixie before."

"A new experience for all of us," I said. I wondered briefly if the stories I had sometimes heard at the wizards' school, of witches and their mad lusts, were in fact garbled stories of nixies.

The others sat down on the beds. Lucas looked fairly subdued now. I was still furious with him, but it would have to wait. "I'm going to find out how thoroughly the nixie has us imprisoned," I said. "Paul, come with me. Vor, see if you can make Lucas's ankle more comfortable."

As we walked under the trees toward the edge of the grove, Paul asked with distaste, "So she expects us all to satisfy her before she'll let us go?"

"That's certainly what she says."

After a short pause, he continued, "Is flying always like that?"

"It's not usually that exciting. Generally I'm not trying to lift three other people at the same time."

Paul nodded, seeming reassured. "I'd gotten used to the air cart this week—or as used to it as one can get. It's like being in a boat; you know you're suspended far above the bottom of the lake or ocean, but you still feel as though your feet are solidly planted. But coming down . . . I was amazed you're willing to fly at all!" At least he didn't say that flying made him think of ascension.

"Maybe we can see the horses again once we get out of the trees," Paul added.

"What horses?" The prince seemed to think about horses at entirely inappropriate times.

"Didn't you see them, out on the plain? I spotted them just before the air cart tipped us out."

"I was too busy trying to save our lives to give anything else much attention," I said sharply.

"There was a whole herd of them," he continued, unabashed. "And they were running like the wind."

Before I could answer, my nose was abruptly flattened by something invisible. I stopped, rubbed my nose delicately, and reached out a hand. The air had become solid before us.

III

Paul put out his hand too and rapped on the invisible wall. "I was afraid of this," I said. "The air's been turned to glass. We can't get out of the grove, and no magic can pass in or out."

"Let's see if the barrier's impervious to steel," said Paul, drawing his sword. To my surprise, the blade went straight through up to the hilt, but his hand was stopped. "It's as though it's only a spell against humans," he suggested.

This was a new kind of spell to me, but I admired its ingenuity. By being specific to humans, the spell could allow wind and rain—and presumably birds and insects—to reach the grove, but would keep us firmly inside.

We continued our circuit of the grove. At one point Paul spotted the herd of horses in the distance, and I somewhat reluctantly agreed that they did indeed appear to be beautiful animals.

I wondered if I ought to take this opportunity of being alone with Paul to warn him against the nixie. His mother, I was sure, would want me to. Naked women making open invitations could not have been a common part of his experience. But if we made it back to Yurt alive, he would very shortly be my king to whom I owed respect. Even as a prince, he was old enough to make his own decisions.

I stopped to pick some leaves growing under one of the trees. "Herbal magic," I explained to Paul. "I've never seen this particular species before, but the old wizard of Yurt taught me enough of the magic of earth and growing things to be able to recognize a plant's properties. I hope it will help Lucas's ankle."

He helped me gather a double handful of it, and we walked back toward the center of the grove. Just before we reached the others, he turned with a smile and said, "You know, when you asked me to accompany you, I was afraid for a minute you were going to preach at me about nixies and morality. I have to apologize for even imagining you would—that's more something the chaplain would do!"

"Of course," I said, not looking at him.

Lucas was eating strawberries, his shirt off and his foot up. His undershirt had been ripped into bandages and firmly wrapped around his ankle. "I don't think he's broken it," said Vor, "but it's badly sprained."

"I think it's broken," contradicted Lucas.

"I brought some herbs that may help," I said. I soaked them in wine, because we had no water, and slipped them into the bandages as gently as I could. He grunted as I worked, as though to remind me that it was highly painful.

"If you've got such powerful magic," he said, "why don't you just heal the broken bone?"

"Magic has never been much good at altering the cycle of sickness and health," I said, sitting on the bed across from him. "You would need supernatural power to do that. Even herbal magic isn't practiced much anymore; generations ago the wizards let the doctors take over the herbs that worked reliably."

Lucas clearly considered this a feeble excuse to mask my own inadequacies. "If you're so good at transforming things into frogs, why don't you just transform me into a prince who *doesn't* have a broken ankle?"

"I could transform you into a number of different creatures," I said as patiently as I could, "some of them rather nasty, but all of them would be wounded in some way if you were." Lucas grunted without answering and lapsed into silence.

"So the nixie really is interested in *us*, as men?" Paul asked Vor. "Why would she use her magic to draw in four men she'd never seen before?"

Vor gave him a sideways look and handed him an apple. "I think this is all we're getting for supper," he said. "Where did you think baby nixies came from?"

Paul thought about this. "You mean that nixies and humans can breed? It wouldn't be like trying to breed sheep and cattle to each other?"

"Of course not. Since all of them are women, they need human men. Didn't your tutor ever teach you about nixies? I thought princes were supposed to be well educated."

Vor counted himself as a human, I thought, and yet there remained something almost magical about him, as though his people were the result of generations of breeding between humans and something out of the wild land of magic. I found myself yawning hugely. In the morning, I would have to test to see if he were stopped by the invisible wall as Paul and I had been, but not now.

"Tomorrow," I told the others, "before the nixie comes back, I'm going to try to get us out of this grove. But I can't work magic when I'm this tired." I looked rather groggily toward Lucas, but he had stretched out and was already beginning to snore. I was asleep even before my head reached the pillow.

Snuggled luxuriously amidst pillows and comforters, dreaming of Theodora, I heard a bird singing. For a few moments I was able to incorporate the sound into my dream, but at last, reluctantly, I opened my eyes. A brilliant scarlet bird hung on a branch two feet above my head, pouring out a golden song to greet the morning. It flew away as I rose on one elbow and looked around. It was already full daylight, but lumps in the other three beds showed that I was by no means the last awake.

I lay down again, hoping to recapture my dream, but the realization that Theodora was three thousand miles away, and even if she was still alive and well did not want to marry me, brought me fully awake. It had been a remarkably vivid dream, in which she had had no reservations about marrying me or about anything else. The nixie, I thought, had been influencing our sleeping minds for her own purposes.

The other three also stretched and sat up, not meeting each others' eyes. "One problem with nixies," said Vor, "is that they're not very subtle."

We had fruit and wine for breakfast; the bottles and the baskets had been replenished while we slept. "Is your ankle any better?" I asked Lucas.

"It doesn't hurt with every breath the way it did last night," he admitted, "but I certainly couldn't walk on it."

"I'm going to try to break the spell that's holding us

in the grove," I said. "Until I do, I'm afraid we're going to have to stay here—unless of course we decide to take up the nixie's offer."

"But Lucas is married," said Paul puritanically. "If she wants us all before she'll let any of us go, that means we're trapped here."

Lucas gave him a sour look, and I almost expected the older prince to say that, married or not, he could and would do anything he wanted. But instead he turned away to finish the strawberries.

"Come with me, Vor," I said. "I want your help."

"What should we do if the nixie comes back?" asked Paul in some alarm.

"Be polite," said Vor. "Call her Lady. Nixies like that. And don't even bother trying to explain that it's hard to feel in the right mood to respond to her charms when you've been imprisoned against your will. That's something nixies never have been able to understand."

The invisible wall at the edge of the grove once again met my outstretched hand. It was as impenetrable to Vor as to Paul and me. I tried several variations on dissolving spells, but none of them worked. Vor tried pushing other objects through the barrier and found they passed without difficulty. He was even able, by holding on to a leafy branch, to push most of his arm through. But as soon as he reached the rest of his body, not surrounded by leaves, the wall stopped him solidly.

"How about turning us into birds?" Vor suggested half-seriously. "We could fly through. The real birds are coming and going without any problem."

"I've thought of it," I said, entirely seriously. "The problem is, if I turned myself into anything nonhuman, I wouldn't be able to say the spell to return us all to ourselves. I'd even been thinking that I could turn the three of you into some other creatures so that you could escape, and stay here myself, but that wouldn't work either. Human magic doesn't penetrate this wall, so you would all have to remain birds."

"Could you turn us into some creature that it would be nice to be for the rest of our lives?"

I gave this suggestion more attention than it probably deserved. When I had been at the wizards' school in the City by the sea, I had often gone down to the breakwater to watch the dolphins playing in the surf. But being a dolphin would be difficult in these dry borderlands of the land of magic.

"I wish I had my books," I said. "I'm not familiar with the kind of magic that formed this barrier, and it will take me a while to work it out from first principles."

"I know what we could do," said Vor, almost playfully. I was quite sure I had never seen him being playful before. "We could all turn into nixies."

"We could *what*?"

"If we were nixies, the nixie of this grove wouldn't try to stop us from leaving, and we could pass right through this barrier. But we'd still be able to speak, so you could turn us back into ourselves once we were out in the plain."

"Transformations spells cannot be used frivolously," I said firmly, inwardly appalled. "Besides, the princes would never agree."

"I'm not sure I would agree either," Vor said lightly. "But at least it was an idea."

When we returned to the beds under the trees, Paul said, "The nixie came while you were gone. We called her Lady and managed to persuade her that we weren't in the right mood. She went away again, but now I'm wondering if she's poisoned the fruit."

"Poisoned the fruit!"

"Usually in the morning when I'm home I can't wait to get outside, to ride, to run. We slept better on these beds last night than we've slept the whole trip, so I should be brimful of energy. But now I don't feel like moving at all—and look at Lucas!"

The older prince rolled over and opened his eyes at the sound of his name. "I'm not asleep."

But Paul was right. The nixie was affecting more than our dreams. Making us feel languorous, making us playful, in a few days she would have us forgetting the world outside her grove.

"I don't think it's the fruit," I said. "I think it's in the air. I'd better work fast."

Lucas stretched and sat up. "Tell me, Wizard," he said in much better humor than I expected, "what real harm would come to us if we *did* take up the nixie's offer?"

I shot Vor a quick glance. He shook his head and said, "Complete exhaustion, but it should wear off." Paul glared at Lucas, indignant on behalf of the crown princess of Caelrhon, but the other prince ignored the look.

I took a deep breath. "The three of you can do what you like. But Paul was right that the nixie won't let us go until she's been satisfied by all of us. And as a wizard, I am bound by iron oaths." This was a prevarication, because the oaths I had taken had nothing to do with chastity. But I didn't want to explain that, in love with both Theodora and the queen, I found the nixie's advances repellent—though even that might change in a few days in this soft air.

Instead I folded my arms. "While we're all here," I said, "I want to take the opportunity to finish the discussion we were having yesterday." This at least took the rather listless half smile off Lucas's face. "I'm getting very tired of having to drag this out of you. You keep talking, Prince, about aristocrats needing to break free of their wizards. Then how do you explain waiting in the city of Caelrhon until the old bishop died, to make sure that a renegade wizard you'd hired *yourself* insulted his memory by attacking the cathedral?"

IV

Lucas gave me a vicious look; I was actually rather pleased to see that languor had not yet taken him over. But he had the sense not to try to jump me again. "I stayed in the city all summer to defend it from you!"

He seemed to mean it. "What threat could *I* possibly be?" I demanded indignantly.

"Why else," shifting his scowl from me to Paul, "would the wizard of Yurt spend so much time in Caelrhon unless planning an attack on my kingdom? Would you care to tell me, Prince, just what plot you have been concocting against me?"

Lucas feared an attack from Paul? Everything had made sense for a moment, but now suddenly all my suppositions were disintegrating.

I expected Paul to reply hotly but he only laughed, momentarily easing the tension. "Our wizard was in Caelrhon at the request of the cathedral, to defend the church against the monster some other wizard had already brought there—at Vor's suggestion."

Vor was about to reply, but I interrupted him. "Wait," I said. Try to sort it out one piece at a time. "You mean, Lucas, you weren't anticipating the gorgos at the bishop's funeral?"

"My father got a telephone call from a dark-haired girl none of us knew," Lucas growled, "saying that 'something rather striking' was about to happen in the cathedral city, and that if we considered *that* spectacular we should wait until the bishop died! I headed for the city at once, of course, but when I got there I found the gorgos had already been seen—and you had just arrived. And you wonder why I decided to wait you out?"

So the renegade wizard I couldn't find had actually sent the royal court of Caelrhon a warning two months ago, boasting obliquely of his gorgos? He must have persuaded one of the Romney girls to telephone for him; no wonder the band had left town in a hurry!

"Sengrim wanting revenge on me I could have understood," continued Lucas grimly, "for dismissing him after years as Caelrhon's Royal Wizard. But when magical dangers persisted even after he blew himself up, I realized that more of you school wizards must be involved in a conspiracy of vengeance. But the gorgos on the cathedral and *you,* Wizard, in the city made it clear that I wasn't the only target for wizardly revenge. The goal was the destruction of both the cathedral and the kingdom of Caelrhon."

"I've never plotted against anybody in my entire life," said Paul calmly. "And our wizard certainly wasn't in Caelrhon at our orders; we'd been wondering all summer when he'd come home."

One piece at a time. The wind whispered through the branches of a tree behind me. I found myself reluctantly admiring Lucas's courage. He had stayed in the city for weeks, convinced there was a wizard there seeking his own death but still determined to defend his kingdom and the church. Little wonder he had been so surly with me, both in Caelrhon and on this trip, if he thought I was that wizard! And his rapid looks around at the end of the bishop's funeral, which I had found so suspicious at the time, came from the threat of 'something spectacular'—a threat Lucas could not tell to either Paul or me since he thought we were behind it.

"You're right, Prince," I said, "that there has been a renegade wizard in Caelrhon. The only flaw in your logic has been thinking it was me." That and persuading himself that if wizards were eliminated, aristocrats could become glorious heroes out of legend, but I wasn't about to tell Lucas that. "This wizard's *real* goal is the destruction of the Church," I continued. "The gorgos's attack on the cathedral was intended as a direct insult to the memory of the old bishop." Joachim, I thought, should hear me now—or, for that matter, Zahlfast.

But I kept on coming back to the unanswered question of who this renegade might be. Any wizard could have asked Vor about a gorgos, but it would have taken enormously powerful magic to call one from this northern land to Caelrhon and then to imprison it somewhere for weeks, much less elude all my efforts to find him.

I even wondered briefly if Elerius, who had graduated far ahead of good old Book-Leech with half the effort, might have been involved. Elerius's magic would certainly be stronger than mine, and Zahlfast would respect his judgment. My old teacher's sudden and irrational conviction that priests were working to destroy wizards made much more sense if he had been told this by someone he trusted, someone who, on the contrary, was seeking to destroy priests. But a wizard with a post at one of the most powerful western kingdoms would not become involved in the affairs of Yurt or Caelrhon. And, I reminded myself, a remarkable number of young wizards had graduated ahead of me.

"There are plots within plots here," said Vor to Lucas. Unlike me, he seemed full of theories. "Someone, probably even starting while your wizard was alive, arranged an elaborate masquerade to persuade you and your father to turn against wizardry." His eyes gleamed in the forest shadows. "Who would most like to see you helpless, with no wizard to come to your defense? Isn't it most likely to be Prince Vincent, your own younger brother?"

Lucas gave a start but did not answer immediately—he *had* considered this explanation. But this was terrible! Had Vincent contracted a nefarious plot to ensure that he, and not his brother, became king of Caelrhon? And only one man stood between Vincent and the crown of Yurt, once he was married to the queen the very day after Paul's coronation: Paul himself.

"What are you implying about my brother?" roared Lucas to Vor, finding his voice at last and, I thought, roaring even louder to cover up his hesitation. He might have plenty of suspicions of his own about Vincent, but he was not going to let anyone else voice them.

I ignored him, having for the moment an even more important concern. "Paul," I said, "I want you to promise me not to ride your stallion anymore."

"Not ride Bonfire?!"

"Vincent gave him to you. He's a trap. He's planning to use that horse somehow to kill you."

Paul regarded me stiffly. "I can decide for myself what horses to ride, Wizard."

I didn't have a chance to answer. Lucas pushed himself up onto his one good foot. His hand on his sword hilt, he hopped and shouldered his way between the two of us, making for Vor.

But before he could test whether the sword was faster than the spell, Paul leaped up. "Stop it! All of you, stop accusing each other for one minute!" A stray ray of sunshine had worked its way down through the leaves and glinted on his hair. "We've all been working against each other," he announced, "and we've all got to stop! No more accusations, no more lies, no more attempts to overpower each other. We need each others' help, not just to get away from the nixie but to save your kingdom, Lucas."

I watched him admiringly. I did hope we made it home to Yurt alive, because he would be a superb king.

"So you, Wizard," Paul continued, turning on me, "have got to stop acting as though only you were wise and knowledgeable." I opened my mouth and closed it again. "Vor, you've got to think less of your revenge and more of the welfare of the city where you now live and work. And Lucas, you have to admit that you've been deceived."

It took Lucas about ten seconds to make up his mind. But then he took a deep breath and said, "All right. I agree we're going to have to work together. But first I want some reassurance, *real* reassurance, that you are not plotting to reunite Yurt and Caelrhon with yourself as king."

There was a tinkling laugh behind us. All of us froze, then turned slowly. The nixie stood surrounded by her glittering stars. She was even more alluring than I remembered.

"Come now," she said with a smile. "You had tried to tell me that you had no energy, but for the last hour you have been quarreling with each other! That seems energetic to me!"

Paul threw himself on his bed, his back toward her. Lucas let himself down more gingerly. "You're offering us something delicate and enticing, Lady," said Vor. "We may need just a little more time to let the sour taste of the outer world pass away."

"If you keep on putting me off," she said with a coy smile, "I may have to take affairs into my own hands."

I sat down, not looking at her. Trapped here in the borderlands I was powerless to find the wizard who must be behind it all: the magical attacks on Joachim's cathedral, the vague warnings I had received against priests, Vincent's abrupt wooing of the queen.

I lifted my head. Vor and the nixie were still exchanging light banter. He seemed to be enjoying their conversation hugely, but he also seemed to have put her off again. "Then I'll see you tomorrow morning!" she said and slipped away. The dancing stars lingered for a few seconds behind her.

None of us felt like talking when she was gone. After a few minutes, Lucas reached for the apples.

When the silence threatened to last all day, I said, "I guess I'd better start on my spells to get us out of here. I'll try to work fast."

I went to the edge of the grove and sat down, my back against a tree, and started probing the magical structure of the invisible barrier. Paul followed me. He pressed his face against the barrier as against a window, looking for the horses. I had closed my eyes but opened them when I heard a sharp whistle. Paul was trying to attract the horses' attention.

The herd was closer than it had been yesterday. They cocked their ears at the sound of the whistle. They were all different colors, bay, black, gray, and sorrel, none of them red roan. But they had the same light step, the same delicate noses and wide-spaced eyes as Bonfire. When Paul whistled again they turned as one and ran, manes and tails floating behind them.

V

A week passed. The second day the nixie became petulant, and I told her brusquely, "I'm sorry, Lady, but we aren't interested."

"Then you'll have to stay here the rest of your lives," she said, not smiling at all. I turned my back on her, and in a minute she went away and did not come back.

In the following days, the air seemed less sensuous, still soft and perfumed but without the overwhelming sweetness it had had when we first arrived. Languor seemed to have overtaken Lucas completely. If pressed, he would admit that his ankle was healing, but mostly he slept and ate fruit. Vor too lapsed into inactivity.

Paul and I however remained occupied. Every morning, he determinedly trotted around the grove twenty times. He also continued trying to attract the horses; by the fourth day they approached rather than ran at the sound of his whistle, but they still remained well back, snorting and flicking their tails nervously. And I wrestled with the nixie's magic.

I felt a desperate urgency to be back home, to stop the renegade wizard from doing what he was planning—or at least to be there when he did it. If he had been at all checked by my presence in the city, he certainly had nothing to fear now. His gorgos had gotten me out of the way almost as surely as if it had killed me.

If Vincent was working with him—maybe having turned against his own brother—I didn't want to imagine what he might be planning against the queen, though his plots against Paul seemed horribly clear. And I also did not want to imagine why and for what purpose he had captured Theodora, unless it was to silence the only person in the city who seemed able to detect his magic. The gorgos's attack on the cathedral at the time of the old bishop's funeral might only be a preparation for a much worse attack when the new bishop was elected. This wizard, apparently much more powerful than I could ever be, had in his control, directly or indirectly, the two women I loved, the dean, and the young man I hoped would become my king.

"Look at the stallion," said Paul, interrupting my thoughts. I looked out obediently. Only ten yards beyond the invisible barrier, the bay stallion stood watching us, pawing the ground with one foot, shaking the mane from his eyes with a proud toss of his head.

I closed my eyes again. I almost thought I understood the structure of the magic barrier now, after a week of studying it. Several times I might have had it, and several times on closer examination I had been wrong. I was having to improvise everything, and I kept having Theodora's feeling of being almost at the top and yet knowing that this time I would never make it. If I ever saw the school again I would have to relate my experiences to the technical division students as an example of improvised magic.

But this time— Quickly, delicately, I started putting a spell together, one designed specifically to overcome the spells that kept the air solid before us. I said the words of the Hidden Language and confidently reached out my hand.

It struck solidity so hard I bruised my knuckles. I probed again for the structure of the nixie's magic. The spells had all been changed.

"What's wrong?" Paul turned as I slumped down.

"She's changing the magic structure of the barrier. I'd wondered why I wasn't doing any better overcoming her magic, but now I know. As soon as I work out how to overcome one set of spells, she switches to another."

"And then can you overcome the new set?"

"Yes, in time—just a few seconds slower than it takes her to change the spells again."

There was a quick flutter of leaves, and the nixie burst into view. With a tinkling laugh, she planted kisses on Paul's lips and my own and scampered away again.

"I have an idea," said Paul with a half smile that made me hope he was not serious. "You and Lucas don't want anything to do with the nixie, and I can't say about Vor, but suppose just one of us were able to 'fully satisfy' her. Do you think she'd let us go?"

Out of several things I might have said, I chose, "When she was hoping for four men, I don't think she'd settle for one."

"Oh, I think I might be able to serve in the place of four men if I wanted to," said Paul with that same half smile.

"I have a better idea," I said. "Try to get some of your horses into the grove. They might be able to pass through the barrier the way the birds do, and maybe we could ride them out."

"Of course," said Paul in surprise. "What did you think I was doing?"

If the nixie was still nearby and listening to our conversation I had just given away what might have been our last chance. Even now she might be altering her barrier so that horses could not pass through it any more easily than could humans. Our only hope was that the nixie might never have needed spells to imprison horses.

"Quickly!" I said, low and urgently. "Try to lure the stallion in here. We have to go now! I'll get the others."

"I'm working as rapidly as I can," said Paul mildly.

But as I hurried away through the trees he started a different series of whistles, so enticing that even my feet slowed for a second.

Both Vor and Lucas were asleep. I woke them with a quick hand on their shoulders. "Come on," I said in a low voice. "We may be able to leave."

I lifted Lucas with magic before he could protest and hurried back through the trees, Vor close behind. Because Lucas was well off the ground, his head some two feet above mine, several times he got a faceful of leaves before he could duck, but I ignored his insults.

We stopped well back in the trees so as not to startle the horses. Paul was talking to them now, softly, alluringly. If the nixie was listening, I thought, she must wish Paul would talk that way to her. The stallion and a black mare were only a few feet beyond the invisible barrier.

A bird shot by suddenly, scolding, and the horses tossed their heads, wheeled, and ran. I tried to swallow bitter disappointment.

But Paul kept on whistling and calling, not at all dismayed. Most of the herd stayed a quarter mile away, but the stallion and the one mare approached again, less cautiously this time. "Come, my beauties, don't be afraid, we won't hurt you, come, my lovely ones," Paul was saying.

He held out one of the nixie's apples. The stallion snorted and stretched his neck forward, still ten yards away. He took one stiff-legged step, then another. And then he was coming through the invisible barrier.

None of us breathed. Very solemnly and deliberately, the stallion took the apple from Paul's hand and crunched it between powerful teeth. With his other hand, Paul held another apple toward the mare. For a moment she held back, then with a nicker she too stepped into the grove.

My impulse was to leap forward, to seize the horses, but even I knew that would be fatal. Paul was stroking the stallion's neck, still talking softly and constantly, his voice like a running brook where the words mattered less than the sound. And then abruptly he took a handful of mane and swung up onto the stallion's back.

The horse jumped, all four feet together, and then whirled and began to run. The prince was almost lying on the horse's back, his head down and his legs pulled up so that no part of his body touched the nixie's barrier. It parted and let them through as though it were not there.

And then the two horses were off, racing across the plain, Paul clinging like a burr to the stallion's mane. "He's not abandoning us," said Vor, but his tone made the statement almost a question.

"No, he's not," said Lucas before I could answer. "He has to accustom the horse to being ridden before anyone else can even try."

The stallion reared, trying to shake Paul off. There was nothing I could do but watch; my magic could not penetrate the nixie's barrier. The stallion came down again, Paul still firmly on his back. The whole herd swept off, galloping across the plain, and disappeared from our view.

"The nixie's not going to wait passively for two hours or two days or whatever it takes Paul to calm down that stallion," said Lucas. I thought this one of his more intelligent recent observations.

Vor seemed to think so too. "There's only one thing to do," he said with his quick, fleeting smile. "I'll try to keep her occupied."

Lucas and I both turned to stare at him. "Oh, I'll readily admit I'm not in the right mood right now," he said playfully. "But nixies, happy nixies, can put one in the mood very easily. They do say that, if you live through the experience, satisfying a nixie is something you never forget."

Lucas cleared his throat as though about to speak but changed his mind.

"The two of you are bound by oaths of marriage and of wizardry," Vor continued, "but as long as I'm back home in the borderlands, I might as well take advantage of an opportunity I'm not likely to be offered down in the cathedral city among all the priests. With a little conversation, a little wine, and a few games, I should be able to stretch it out for several hours."

Lucas and I had nothing to say. "Oh, Lady!" Vor called, moving back toward the center of the grove. "Where are you? Could you bring your delightful form closer to mine?"

He was gone. Lucas and I looked at each other. I arranged him as well as I could, his leg propped up before him, and sat down to wait.

An hour passed, and the horses reappeared in the distance. I thought I spotted a dark shape still clinging to the stallion's neck. The stallion was not running now but walking.

"It looks like he may be taming that stallion," said Lucas with reluctant admiration. "Look at how easily he's sitting now."

Paul slipped down from the horse's back, a hand still in the mane, then leapt back up again. The stallion jumped, but this time only a small jump, and Paul guided an incipient gallop back into a trot.

Then he was off the stallion's back again and moving toward the black mare. I could see him stroking her, talking to her, and then suddenly he was on her back and she was running, and the entire process started over again.

The whole herd disappeared around the far side of the grove. I thought of following them but was afraid of doing anything that might startle the horses. Paul was going to need absolute concentration to try to tame two wild beasts that galloped like something out of legend.

I wondered again where Bonfire had really come from. Having seen the bay stallion and the black mare up close, I was now certain that Paul's red roan stallion had come from these borderlands. If the renegade wizard had been up here to find a gorgos, he might have taken back a horse for Prince Vincent at the same time. I was even more convinced that that horse was a trap.

Another hour passed. I was so tense that the very tension made me yawn with exhaustion.

And then Paul was back, appearing abruptly before us, riding the stallion and leading the mare with a hand on her mane. Both kept taking nervous little steps and jerking their heads up, but they kept coming. They passed without difficulty through the nixie's barrier. Extreme fatigue and delighted pride were both on Paul's face, but all he said was, "Where's Vor?"

I let my mind slip away through the trees until I found him. Standing in the flow of magic by the edge of his mind, I called softly, "Vor. Paul's back. We're going now."

Very few people not trained in magic can hear a wizard speaking to them directly, mind to mind. But there was an abrupt stir and I returned to myself, knowing he had heard. "He's coming," I said.

"The mare's a little gentler," said Paul. "You and Lucas try mounting."

I rose up in the air, bringing Lucas with me, and set us down on the mare's back as gently as I could. Vor came out of the trees, his face ashen and running with sweat but giving us a complacent smile. Paul reached out a hand, and Vor scrambled up behind him.

"Hold on to my waist," said Paul. "All of you, keep your heads down and tuck up your feet. Let's *go!*"

Paul urged the stallion forward, and the mare followed. The stallion was out in the plain again in a second, but

Lucas's wounded leg stuck out sideways from the mare's back, and it hung up on the nixie's barrier.

Lucas grunted with pain, and I caught him just before he was dragged backwards off the horse, just before the mare bolted out from under both of us. With a firm hand on her mane and my best imitation of Paul's voice in her ears, I turned her in a tight circle and tried again.

And this time we went through, free of our leafy prison.

"Run!" cried Paul. "Here comes the nixie!"

PART SEVEN

The Bishop

I

The graceful green form stood on the edge of the grove. Waves of sensuous emotion broke around us, but we kept galloping.

When the nixie's call to us did not succeed in a few seconds, she tried to call the horses. Paul's stallion threw up its head and stopped so suddenly Vor almost slid off. The mare too skidded to a halt and looked back.

But while a dead flying beast's skin has no choice but to answer a call designed for flying beasts, a living horse can make a choice. Paul shouted to the horses and, almost reluctantly, they turned away from the grove, and abruptly the attraction spell dropped and we ran again.

Although Paul had been riding these horses hard for several hours, they showed no sign of slowing now. Half my attention had to go to the lifting spell that was all that held Lucas on the mare's back. I was not nearly the horseman Paul was, and I quickly fell behind.

But it did not matter. We were free.

After five miles, at the hills that ringed the plain, Paul pulled up the stallion. "The horses don't want to go farther," he said. "And I don't want to exhaust them." A light dampness had finally broken out on their coats.

"We'll have to walk the rest of the way. Lucas, the wizard can carry you."

None of us objected, not even Lucas, whose ankle had been healing nicely in the nixie's grove until the slam against the invisible barrier had twisted it anew. We slid to the ground and Paul embraced both horses, putting his cheek in turn against each of their necks. "Goodbye, my beauties, my lovely ones. I'll give your greetings to Bonfire."

He then turned to the rest of us. "The nixie made us fight among ourselves, but if we are going to make it home again we all have to help each other." All of us nodded soberly. Paul was clearly our leader now. I thought it a nice diplomatic touch for him to blame our disagreements on the nixie. We stumbled up into the rocky hills, Lucas hovering a short distance above the ground due to my magic, and the horses pranced away across the grass to rejoin the herd.

It took two days to get back to Vor's people's valley. Vor was able to climb up and down even the steepest inclines without difficulty, but on several occasions I had to carry both princes up a nearly vertical slope or across a crevice.

Late the second day, when cool blue shadows stretched out across the barren land, we finally reached a river, rimmed on either side with verdure, and followed it upstream until we came through a narrow divide into the valley.

Word spread quickly that we had arrived, and people came hurrying down from their homes in the cliffs to greet us. I was too tired to notice much of what was happening, except that Vor gave everyone a lively account of our exploits. Several long-fingered women brought hot stew, which certainly helped. As the stars came out, lights twinkled on all up and down the cliffs, and, as Paul had hoped, it looked like fairyland. Someone realized that, although Vor seemed prepared to talk all night, the rest of us were about to fall asleep sitting up. We were boosted up ladders and given blankets and dropped into oblivion at last.

"Vor," asked Paul, "do you want to come back to Caelrhon with us, or do you want to stay here with your people?"

The air cart, I was happy to discover, had indeed obeyed my last commands after tipping us out, and it had returned to the valley. In the morning we were preparing to fly home.

"I'll come back with you," said Vor in his normal laconic style. "The lads will want me once they start construction again."

And they might be starting again very soon, I thought. It had already been three weeks since the old bishop's death, and I did not think they would delay the election of his successor for long.

Paul echoed my thought. "I wonder if we'll be too late for the new bishop's enthronement."

"We can telephone from the mountain and find out what's been happening," I said.

And so once again, after a day of flying, we came up the icy vertical side of old Book-Leech's mountain and landed next to the little blue house. I let Paul tell most of the story.

"Well, I've heard about nixies, of course, but I've never met one," said the wizard, pouring out tea. "I'm sure you found it all a, well, *interesting* interlude." Paul blushed up to his hairline. "That was certainly clever of you, young fellow, to find a way out of her grove—guess old 'Frogs' has been teaching you his tricks, eh?"

Paul had tried to downplay his role in saving us, but Book-Leech, of course, had realized what an accomplishment it in fact was. It really had owed nothing to me, and I said so.

"I'd like to use your telephone," I said in a pause in

the conversation. "The priests of the cathedral will want to know that the gorgos has been destroyed."

I expected him to offer me the phone at once, but he hesitated before answering. "Well, you're welcome to use it, of course, but I'm not sure it's working."

"Not sure it's working?!"

"It may be because we're so far away from any other telephone," he said apologetically, "or because there's interference due to the magical influences from the north."

"But there have been wizards posted here for years—"

"Well, you see, it *used* to work. But it didn't use to have a far-seeing attachment. It was just put in this summer, and, well . . . Elerius himself installed it, so I know it must have been working at first, and now I'm afraid I've broken it somehow. I've never been any good at technical magic myself. Could you look at it? It is, after all, your invention."

I took a deep breath. I had invented the far-seeing attachment essentially by accident and still had no good idea how it worked; wizards from the technical division had had to take apart my rather haphazard spells to be able to duplicate it. "Let's look at it together."

He took it out of a drawer. "It *does* work for the school to call me. That's why I didn't realize at first there was a problem."

A quick glance at his shelves showed that he, like me, owned no books that might have helped. "If you can't telephone the City for help," I asked, "what's the point of having you posted here? I would think they would want to have this fixed immediately."

"I can usually get it to work *once*," he said, "so I could call the school if there was any sudden problem up in the land of magic. But— Well, I guess I can tell *you* this without embarrassment. I don't like to tell the school that I, a thoroughly trained wizard, can't solve a magical difficulty."

It was rather reassuring that someone who might in another year have been first in his class could also have patches of incompetence. But I myself had had so many blows to my pride over the years that I might have been willing to admit my failure in a case like this.

The two of us bent over the telephone, probing its spells, communicating mind to mind. Suddenly I thought I saw the problem. Breaking off pieces of the flow of magic with words of the Hidden Language, I adjusted the spells, reorienting the telephone within magic's four dimensions.

"There," I said aloud. "I think it should work now."

"Of course it will. That's the spell I have to use to get it to work at all. You can make one telephone call now if you like, but you won't be able to make another until tomorrow. So who do you want to call?"

I considered. I could continue to try different spells on the telephone, but they were as likely to make the instrument stop working completely as to fix it. I wanted reassurance that the queen was alive and well, but whatever Prince Vincent might be plotting he needed her so he could marry her. I needed to talk to the wizards' school, but it would have been much easier to do so without the princes standing there. One call should reassure me that no new monster had appeared in the cathedral city.

The telephone viewscreen lit up, and I saw one of the young priests of the cathedral. "Hello?" He could not see me.

"I'd like to speak to the dean. Father Joachim," I added as he seemed to hesitate. "This is Daimbert, the wizard who was staying with him." The young priest's face changed slightly. "I know he'll want to talk to me," I said urgently.

"The dean cannot speak with anyone at the present time," said the priest in icy tones.

"Then give him my message, please," I said, speaking

rapidly. "Tell him that I've destroyed the monster and will be back in the cathedral city in a week." I tried to read something in the young man's motionless face. Could Joachim have left explicit orders that he did not want to talk to me? Had the cantor Norbert decided to get revenge for his humiliation by launching a new, more deadly attack against the dean, perhaps with the active assistance of an evil wizard? "No new monsters have appeared on the cathedral tower, have they?" I asked in panic.

"No, and I trust you are not disappointed." And then he did ring off, leaving me hoping that he *would* convey my message.

"I'll send the air cart back to the City as soon as we're through with it," I said as we were leaving the mountaintop. Having not seen any other flying beasts in the borderlands, I had to give up my plan for an air cart of my own. "So the school will be able to send you more supplies whenever you need them. Swallow your pride and ask them to send out some technicians at the same time."

He nodded ruefully. But during the week it took us to fly home I gave him no more thought.

Paul and Lucas spent much of the trip working out elaborate methods to trick and overcome whatever renegade wizard was operating in Caelrhon. Vor was unable to give any more exact description of him than that he seemed fairly young and had a black beard. He commented, rather surprised himself, that he could not really recall the man's face, though he did remember his white jacket, emblazoned with yellow suns glowing by their own light, a jacket that I could certainly not remember anyone at the school wearing. The two princes speculated at some length on Vincent's role, concluding that he must have been deceived by the renegade, and drew up plans in which they were able to gallop, formidable and glorious, across all their enemies. I could have told them none of them would work.

"I'll be eighteen in two weeks," said Paul. "I hope Mother has been going ahead with the preparations without me. You were going to be at my coming of age ceremony anyway, weren't you, Lucas? I'll need you now especially, because the wizard may be planning some attack to coincide with the event."

And if the renegade wizard was planning some outrageous further assault on the cathedral, I needed to warn the Church. Once Joachim was elected bishop I hoped that I could still get in to see him in spite of the other priests' suspicions of magic-workers, suspicions doubtless increased by Norbert's experiences.

II

We reached Caelrhon at sunset and saw both the new and the old towers of the cathedral rising before us. "The Romneys are back," noted Vor.

And not just the Romneys. As well as their caravans, I saw a large number of silk tents pitched outside the city walls, far more than one usually saw for market day. I set the air cart down in front of the gates. We climbed out, leaner and much more ragged and dirty than we had been when we left, and smiled to think what we must look like to people in silk tents.

"The first thing I'm going to do," said Lucas cheerfully, "is to take a very long bath." I was giving the air cart the commands to return it to the City.

"Don't use up all the hot water," said Paul.

"I'll need to see how my lads are doing," said Vor and slipped away. The air cart soared upwards into the darkening sky.

"Save some hot water for me, too," I said to Paul. "I'm going around by the cathedral, to tell the dean not to worry about the gorgos anymore. I don't trust that young priest to have given him the message."

The construction site in front of the cathedral was

dark and still, except for the construction crew's huts on the far side. Then I heard sudden loud and cheerful voices as Vor arrived. I saw the watchman's lantern but detoured around him to reach at last the quiet cobbled street behind the church, where thin lines of yellow light came into the street from shuttered windows.

My footsteps echoed as I hurried down to the house at the end. I stepped up into the dark porch and knocked. For a long moment there was no response. Then there was a click as the door was unlocked, and a candle shone in my eyes as it opened.

I had expected to see Joachim's silent servant. Instead I saw a man I had never met in my life. "I need to see the dean at once," I said. There was probably a good reason why Joachim had someone else opening his door. "It's very urgent."

He hesitated, apparently trying to decide if I was dangerous, then nodded. "Wait here, please."

There was another long pause, and I could hear faint voices. Then the candle appeared again with someone else carrying it. He was dressed in the black vestments of a senior officer of the cathedral, but he was not Joachim.

After a panic-stricken moment in which I imagined that we had somehow come to the wrong city, I remembered seeing this man last month at dinner at this very house. He was older than Joachim, with an intelligent face if not the dean's intense expression.

"Excuse me, I expected to see Father Joachim," I managed to say.

"He is at the episcopal palace, but I am sure I could help you."

Joachim was alive, but I was too late. I tried to smile and shook my head. "Thank you, but it wasn't important. Sorry to disturb you." The priest stood in the doorway, still holding up his candle, watching me as I slowly walked back down the street.

✧ ✧ ✧

At the castle, Paul met me in great excitement. He seemed younger somehow than he had in the past weeks. "We got back just in time! They're going to elect the new bishop and have his enthronement tomorrow! Everybody's here—Mother, Prince Vincent, the old king and queen of Caelrhon. And they say that not only are all the lords of the two kingdoms here—that's why we saw so many tents—and all the bishops of the nearby dioceses, but the bishop of the great City himself! I'm afraid the castle is very cramped with the royal courts of both kingdoms, and there's hardly any hot water."

I felt swept with relief to hear that the queen was all right. Now all I had to do was find Theodora. "And have there been any more manifestations from the renegade wizard?"

"No. Lucas told me he was going to talk to his brother immediately, of course. But I've seen Bonfire, and he seems well—my knights did remember to exercise and feed him."

There was one more important point in what Paul had said. "And they haven't elected the new bishop yet?"

"Well, not really. I've just been hearing about this. They hold the official election right before the enthronement, but in fact they have to decide much earlier. It would never do to have everyone there for the ceremony and then have a split election! The priests keep the results secret, of course, but there are plenty of rumors."

"And who is rumored to have been elected?" I asked, but I already knew.

"You'll never guess. It's Father Joachim, our old chaplain! We'll find out for sure in the morning."

The morning found us all in the cathedral very early. I kept probing for another wizard in the city, but I could not find him. I also found no monsters, not even the red lizards with hands, although I had flown surreptitiously over the new tower, repeating the spell to reveal what was hidden. This absence of other wizards and of magical creatures was not the relief it should have been, because I also had not been able to detect the wizard even when Theodora had. I wondered if he planned some outrage for the middle of the ceremony or if, as at the old bishop's funeral, he would save his surprise for the end.

The church was even more crowded than it had been for the funeral, because as well as all the townspeople there were all the aristocrats of two kingdoms, with their trains. Quite a few wore their swords, a surprising sight in church. I spotted Yurt's two counts and the duchess several rows behind us. The duchess was flanked by her tall husband and their twin daughters. The girls waved at us and Paul waved back. I even saw the Romneys, in their bright red and gold best, squeezed into a back pew.

Prince Vincent sat with his own family, including his parents, his brother Lucas, the crown princess and their children, in the front pew on the far side of the church, so Paul and I had the queen to ourselves. As we waited for the service to begin, Paul continued telling his mother the story of our adventures which he had started last night. The nixie, I noticed, became changed in the telling into a rather ill-defined although still malignant magical creature.

I was almost overwhelmed to be sitting so close to the queen again, smelling her scent, seeing her smile, hearing her voice. She addressed me perfectly naturally, as she always had, and I did my best to be equally natural.

But I still glanced surreptitiously around the church, looking for Theodora. She could have been there but I would not have seen her in the throng.

Then the organ began playing, and conversation quickly died away as aristocrats and townspeople settled back as well as they could in the crowded pews. Through the great doors of the cathedral came half a dozen bishops in brilliant scarlet robes. All of them seemed quite old and highly venerable. They walked solemnly the length of the cathedral, across the mosaic Tree of Life, to stand around the altar.

When the last bishop had taken his place, the doors opened again, and all the cathedral priests came in. I looked for and did not see Joachim. But the other members of the cathedral chapter filed slowly up the aisle to stand in a group beside the bishops.

One bishop stepped forward: the bishop of the great City. I had seen him once when I was in school. The great mane of hair protruding below his mitre had been gray then and now was white, but his booming voice was unchanged.

"Dearly beloved," he began, speaking into a profound hush, "we are gathered here to observe one of the most important ceremonies of the Church, the election of a new bishop."

I rather doubted that I was his dearly beloved. Although Joachim had forestalled an incipient riot against me, after I left there would still have been strong feeling against both the magical monster who had attacked the cathedral and the wizard who "must" have had something to do with its appearance. Perhaps Norbert had tried to cover up for his humiliation by lashing out against me, even if not against Joachim, once I was gone. The City's bishop would certainly not be impressed at hearing from one wizard that another wizard was planning some sort of attack on the Church.

"In the Church, as you know," he continued, "we bishops are brothers, brother shepherds, guiding the Christian flock in the ways of God with each others' assistance and guidance. Because each bishop is elected by the priests of his own cathedral, that is the men who will serve under him, only the most holy and worthy men are sought for the position. We who are bishops know in our hearts how far we fall from the ideal, but the ideal is clear: piety, intelligence, judgment, dedication to the Lord's Word."

I became tenser and tenser, waiting for what must be coming, but a fast and irreverent magical probing still located no monsters.

The bishop opened his Bible. "The office of bishop was laid down from the beginning, and the Apostle tells us the necessary qualifications: A bishop must be blameless, vigilant, sober, of good behavior, apt to teach, not greedy of filthy lucre, but patient, not a brawler, not covetous, one that ruleth well his own house. A bishop must be a vessel unto honor, sanctified, and meet for the Master's use, prepared unto every good work."

He closed the Bible complacently, as though congratulating himself that *he* was prepared for every good work, and turned to the assembled cathedral priests. "You have heard the inspired Word regarding the sort of man whom God calls to the episcopal office, speaking through the will of the cathedral chapter. Are you ready now to elect such a man?"

"We are ready." I noticed that the priest who was apparently now dean spoke for the chapter.

"Then let your deliberations begin."

The priests filed gravely out the side door of the church. They had been gone for ten minutes, and Paul had started to swing his legs and I was wondering if there would be a recess, when they all filed back in again. This time they had Joachim with them.

I strained forward to see better. He was dressed in scarlet robes and was bareheaded. His eyes turned toward us, but he did not seem to see us.

"We have made our choice," said the new dean.

"And do you all agree in this choice?"

"We are all agreed, in the name of the Father, the Son, and the Holy Spirit." The priests spoke together, but I heard Norbert's voice loudest of all.

"Then send your candidate forward!"

The priests stepped aside, and Joachim walked slowly to the front. I would have been intimidated by those enormous black eyes in his completely sober face, but the bishop of the City met him placidly. "Joachim! You have heard the will of the cathedral chapter. Do you accede to this election?"

"If God has called me," said Joachim in a low, grave voice, "in speaking through the chapter, then I must accept, although I know in my heart I am not worthy."

I had to disagree with this. I thought he met every criteria the bishop had mentioned.

"Brother bishops!" turning to the others. "Do you accept Joachim as your brother?"

"We accept him with joy," said the bishops, all speaking together.

"And you, the People of Yurt and Caelrhon," turning to the congregation, "do you acclaim him as your spiritual father?"

There was a general affirmative murmur from the crowd.

"Then kneel down, Joachim." Joachim knelt, and the bishop took a crystal ampule of oil from the altar. He unstoppered it and poured two drops on the lowered head before him. He then took a tall gold and white hat, like his own, and fitted it on.

"Rise then, anointed of the Lord, and fellow bishop!" Joachim stood up, and the two men kissed each other on both cheeks. "Take these symbols of your office." He put a shepherd's crozier into his right hand and slipped a ring onto his left. The enormous ruby gleamed in the candlelight, the ring I had last seen on the dead bishop's finger.

"Then let us all sing Alleluia to God!"

The congregation scrambled to its feet, the organ began to play, and a great song of praise rang out. Joachim stood still, not singing. I tried to catch his eye as he was only about twenty feet away. But I doubted he saw me. His eyes were again elsewhere. He was bishop now, burdened with the souls of two kingdoms, with responsibilities that went far beyond the worries of a wizard he had known when they both were young.

When the hymn died away and the congregation sat down again, two acolytes brought forward a throne. It was heavy, and they dragged as much as carried it in front of the altar. When it was properly positioned, they stepped back and Joachim sat in it.

"My people!" he said, addressing us all. "I come to you an unworthy man, but one who will do his best to guide your souls to God, with His aid. I would now like to ask those of you who govern our people's physical bodies to come forward, to dedicate yourselves and your purpose to the same divine purpose that guides us all."

Another week and Paul could have taken part himself, but the queen was still regent. She rose, holding Yurt's silver ceremonial sword, then walked slowly forward to the altar, laid the sword on it, and knelt before the throne. She kissed the episcopal ring, and Joachim put his hand on her head and blessed her. Then he took her by the shoulders and drew her up.

"Rise, my daughter, and govern well," he said, and handed her back the sword.

She returned to her place, squeezing in between Paul and me, and then it was the turn for the king of Caelrhon. The ceremony was repeated with our duchess, then Caelrhon's dukes, then the counts of both kingdoms, followed by the castellans and the lords of manors. It occurred to me as the ceremony progressed that it would be very easy for an unscrupulous lord to use the opportunity to plunge his sword into the bishop's heart.

But everything progressed with perfect correctness. When the last lord had returned to his place, and I was starting to wonder if we might still escape without a magical attack, Joachim rose and stepped forward.

He was now only a few feet away and I was sure he saw me, though he gave no sign of recognition. Instead he raised his arms to bless the congregation.

But I did not hear his words. I stared instead at the sleeve of his robe.

It was a brand-new robe, clearly made just for him since he was taller than any of the other priests. Worked across the bottom of the scarlet sleeve were intertwined roses and crosses. They were done in a distinctive stitch, where the embroidery thread crossed three threads, skipped one, and crossed two more. That was Theodora's embroidery.

Theodora was alive and free in the city.

III

We poured out of the cathedral into the noon sunshine. "A fine ceremony, a solemn ceremony," said the young chaplain of Yurt as though he had been personally responsible. "He's a fairly young man to be elected bishop; we may not see very many more episcopal elections in this city in our lifetimes."

"Have you invited him to my coming of age ceremony?" Paul asked his mother.

"He'd accepted when he was still dean," she said, "but he may not now be able to get away from his new duties."

"Were you surprised he was chosen?"

"He was an excellent chaplain," said the queen with a smile. "You would not even have been born if he hadn't saved your father's life. I think he'll be an excellent bishop."

I hardly listened to their conversation. I scanned the skies for some new monster and the crowd for Theodora, seeing neither.

Several minutes passed, and nothing happened. Might the wizard be saving his next attack for Paul's coronation? The duchess and her tall husband, Prince Ascelin, came over to talk to us. "I haven't seen the royal family of Caelrhon in months," Ascelin said with an almost shamefaced grin and a glance in their direction. "I wonder if Prince Lucas is still not talking to me."

"But what's the problem?" asked the queen, concerned.

"We were here in Caelrhon this spring at the same time as he was. Lucas was talking about his wife—justifiably, I'm sure!—about all her beauty, skills, and accomplishments. Not to be outdone, of course, I started talking about the duchess," with an affectionate glance toward his wife. "I told him there was no one in the twin kingdoms, man or woman, who could compare to her in riding or hunting."

I paused in scanning the sky to feel briefly sorry for Lucas. When he was already feeling royal power diminished, it must have been bitter to hear himself compared unfavorably to a duchess.

"He seems to have taken it as an insult to the crown princess," Ascelin continued, a smile crinkling the tanned skin by his eyes. "He challenged me to a sword fight—a bad idea, since I would have disarmed him immediately. Fortunately his wizard stopped the fight before it even started: paralyzed him where he stood and took the sword from his hands. Lucas transferred all his fury from me to his Royal Wizard, and I was able to escape, calling apologies over my shoulder, while the prince was starting to tear into his wizard for lack of respect."

I didn't wait to hear any more. "Excuse me," I said to the queen. "I'll see you at the castle a little later." To the young chaplain I added, "I hope Joachim outlives you." And I hurried away.

Cutting around the cathedral's hill, I headed for the artisans' area to the east, the area where Theodora lived. I kept passing groups of townspeople, all in their Sunday finery, talking about the election. Normally I would have been interested in their reaction to their new bishop, but now I brushed past.

At the foot of Theodora's street I paused. I could see her door and the upstairs window. It looked dark. A black and white shape darted in front of me: Theodora's cat. I bent down, made clicking noises, and held out one hand. The cat hesitated, then recognized me and came to rub against my hand. It, at least, was happy to see me.

After a minute's petting, the cat turned and trotted purposefully up the street. At its door, it sat down and began to meow. I came up quietly behind it. The door opened. "All right, kitty, come on in."

The cat walked in, tail high. I took hold of the door to keep it from closing and found myself looking at Theodora.

Before I could think, I had clasped her in my arms and buried my face in her hair. Not until she pulled back a little, trying to wipe the tears from my cheek with one hand, did I realize I was crying.

"Daimbert?"

"Dear God, Theodora, for the last month I've thought you were dead." I seized her again as though my embrace would make her immortal.

"But I'm not dead," she managed to say, with the light, almost teasing note I knew so well. After envisioning so many horrible things, including that I had only imagined her existence, the feel of her in my arms was even better than I remembered.

"Or I thought you'd been captured by the wizard—or, or had even joined him."

"What wizard?"

We were standing just inside her half-open door. I released her enough to be able to see her face in the light from the street. "I have two very important questions for you. First, will you marry me?"

"I told you before," she said with a half smile, "a girl needs time to consider."

And a month had apparently not been long enough.

I knew the answer with the certainty of a blow to the stomach.

But I still managed to bring out my second question. "Last month there was a powerful wizard in the city, someone you could sense but I couldn't. Is he here now?"

She turned her head away, slipping for a moment into her own magic. Then her amethyst eyes met mine. "No. If he's here, he's shielding his mind as effectively from mine as he is from yours."

So perhaps I need not fear an immediate attack. Looking at Theodora it was almost impossible to imagine her working with an evil renegade. I dismissed him from my thoughts. "If you don't want to marry me, would you consider living with me, even for a little while?"

She smiled. "I suspect this conversation may take a while. If we talk here, we may be interrupted. How about if we go to the grove outside of town?"

I was naturally intrigued by this suggestion, even though I realized she had not answered my question. I rubbed my eyes with my fists, and Theodora got her key to close the door behind us. As she stepped into the street, I noticed for the first time that she wore a black and gold dress with a bright red apron and shawl.

"You were at the new bishop's enthronement," I said with sudden comprehension, "sitting with the Romneys."

She gave me a sideways smile. "I saw you with your royal court, but I was fairly sure you didn't recognize me. I was wearing a head-scarf, too. I thought the pew with the Romneys an appropriate place for a witch. Was that extremely good-looking young man your Prince Paul?"

I nodded and reminded myself not to be jealous. Whatever reason she had for not wanting to marry me had nothing to do with Paul.

She tucked her arm through mine as we walked, one more couple out for a stroll on a fine afternoon after the episcopal election. Her earrings moved in and out from behind her hair in the charming way I remembered. "Isn't the new bishop your friend the dean?"

"That's right."

"He looks very intense," she said, "as though he doesn't worry about the things that worry ordinary people, but always tries to look through to spiritual issues." I nodded again; it seemed a good assessment. "But tell me—does he ever smile?"

"He's been known to," I said, smiling myself. "But not often. He'll be an excellent bishop, but I'm afraid some of the young priests will find him hard on them."

"You've been away for weeks," she said. "Where have you been?"

It occurred to me only then that she might have been as worried about me as I was about her. "And where do *you* think I've been?" I said teasingly, using her trick of answering a question with another question.

"I knew you defeated the monster that appeared right after the old bishop's funeral," she said. "Everybody in the city was talking about it." Maybe I wasn't being blamed for as much as I'd thought. "But the rumor was that something was still wrong, or the monster wasn't fully defeated, and you had to go thousands of miles to find out where it had come from."

"Close enough," I said. "I've been up at the border of the northern land of wild magic." The borderlands seemed much less interesting at the moment than the shape of her mouth, the way she held her head, and the color of her eyes. "The fanged gorgos, the monster, came from there, and I had to take it back to destroy it."

Somehow she had me talking easily again, as I had always talked with her. While we walked through the city, out the gates, and past all the crowds and the tents and the Romney caravans toward the little grove a mile away, I gave her a quick overview of our adventures. The grass that had been long and green when we last walked here together had been browned by the summer's sun and trampled by many feet.

She was, as I had expected, fascinated by my account of the valley where everyone lived in houses built into the cliff. She was also very interested in the nixie's barrier that specifically would not let humans pass. It was good to talk about magic with someone who understood it, and who I did not feel was in competition with me.

"So what would you have done," she asked with a laugh, "if your prince hadn't been able to attract those horses? Would you have given in to the nixie's charms at last?"

I didn't reply—in part because I did not know the answer. We had reached the edge of the woods, and I prepared to fly both of us up and over the blackberry tangles.

But she forestalled me. "I've been practicing while you've been gone. Watch!"

Slowly and deliberately, her lips moving silently, she rose into the air on her own magic, went over the tops of the brambles, and disappeared from view, a delighted grin on her face. From the thump and the sudden laugh on the far side I knew she'd come down faster than she intended.

I followed her, landing more gracefully, and we walked together to the center of the grove where the spring still played and the emerald grass grew long. The air was still permeated with unfocused magic, but not nearly as strongly as I had remembered.

"Let's sit down," she said in a different voice than she normally used. "I want to tell you something." She sounded as sober as Joachim.

I had been about to take her in my arms but hesitated. We sat down next to each other, not touching. "What is it?"

"I am going to bear a child."

✧ ✧ ✧

There was a long pause. I put a hand over my eyes and called myself all the insulting names young wizards use for each other; the list was fairly long. A second-year wizardry student would have known better. But when I took my hand down I still had to ask, "And—it's mine?"

"Yes," said Theodora, less soberly, "yours— She'll be yours and mine."

"It will be a girl? You're sure?"

A small smile had again reached the edges of her lips. "Of course I'm sure. After all, I'm a witch."

This certainly ended the vague plans I realized I had been making about somehow having both her and my position in Yurt. Whatever institutionalized wizardry tolerated in its wizards, it was not being the fathers of families. "Theodora, you know I want to marry you. I'll be happy to live wherever you like."

The smile was gone again, and she took my hand. "But I never intended to marry you."

IV

Christ, this was bad. I had thought my self-esteem had suffered so many blows over the years that I was fairly immune, but I had been mistaken. I had never loved the queen as much as I loved this woman.

"Theodora, I—" I tried to find some way to phrase it delicately so it would not be an insult, and ended up not finding any and saying it baldly. "So you made me fall in love with you deliberately, not interested in me at all, only—only using me the way the nixie wanted to use us!"

"Daimbert, it wasn't like that," she said mildly.

But now that I had started I couldn't stop. "Once you had what you wanted, you didn't need me and didn't care to see me again." I had jumped up and was pacing back and forth while she sat quietly, listening. "You managed to hide from me with your damned ring of invisibility, and when I left the city you were delighted, hoping I wouldn't come back. If you hadn't opened the door for your cat without taking the precaution of peeking out first, I never would have found you."

"I'd always hoped to see you again."

But I wasn't going to be interrupted. "Of course you didn't tell me, then, that you didn't love me. You had to be sure you were pregnant first, because if you weren't you needed to lure me back for one more try."

I threw myself on the grass, my back to her. In a moment I felt a hand stroking my hair. As she'd stroke her cat, I thought bitterly.

"Daimbert, I do love you."

"Odd that you never mentioned it before," I said, but less bitterly.

There was a catch in her voice that, in a moment, made me sit up and turn around to look at her. Her cheeks streamed with tears. To my questioning look she said at last, "I feel so bad to have hurt you!"

I turned away again. This wasn't helping. The women I loved could never love me. All I could do was to make them cry when they realized how deeply I was wounded.

There was another long pause, then she began tugging at my shoulders. I allowed her to pull my head into her lap, where she continued stroking my hair, but I kept my eyes shut against her.

"Let me tell you how it appeared from my side," she said at last, her voice somewhat calmer. "I wanted to meet you from the first time I sensed your mind here in the city. And before you say anything, let me make clear that I was *not* planning from the beginning to seduce you. I just wanted to get to know a wizard."

"You were already friends with the old magician, and if you'd wanted you could have met the Royal Wizard of Caelrhon any time before his death."

"I told you, Daimbert, you aren't like other wizards. Old Sengrim would have had nothing to offer me—if he'd even cared to get to know me. I knew at once that you were the only one I'd ever come across who might be at all interested in teaching a witch his magic."

"Magic first, children second," I mumbled.

"And once I met you," she persisted, "I realized that I could gain from you far more than I'd hoped. And not what you're about to say! What I gained from you was friendship."

"Friendship," I repeated. It seemed a weak enough word.

"You're the only person I've been able to talk to about magic since my mother died. You were even interested in learning *my* magic, which I won't teach anyone again until our daughter is old enough to understand. And you're funny, and affectionate, and enthusiastic, and treated my ideas with interest and respect. Is it any wonder I fell in love with you?"

"Odd you never mentioned it before," I said for the second time.

"That's because I was hoping you weren't in love with *me*," she answered. "I knew you were Royal Wizard of Yurt, and I knew wizards don't marry. If I made it clear how strongly I felt about you, you would feel compelled to resign your position, and I also knew the conflict would destroy you emotionally."

"As opposed to feeling like this," I said with intentional sarcasm. But I did open one eye for a quick glance at her face. She wasn't crying anymore but looked down at me affectionately. I closed the eye again.

"Your stay here, I knew," she continued, "would not last long. You'd been Royal Wizard for years, but you'd only known me a short time. Before many more weeks had passed, I realized, you'd solve the cathedral's problems and go home to Yurt. I'd always hoped to have a daughter, and I knew I couldn't find anyone better to be the father."

"Then having gotten what you wanted from me, why did you hide?"

"Because you asked me to marry you."

"And you certainly didn't want to do *that!*"

"No," she said, very quietly, "because I did. If you had asked me again I probably would have agreed."

"And would you agree now?" I asked, sitting up and compelling her eyes to meet mine.

But she shook her head. "I've had a month to strengthen my resolve. Please forgive me."

I could manage no better answer than a snort.

"I'd hoped you'd forget me. Well, no, not hoped. I always wanted to see you again, and I certainly had to tell you about our daughter. But when you left the city so abruptly, I anticipated that by the time you came back and went home to Yurt you would be ready to put the whole interlude behind you. I did hope that you would at least think of me warmly sometimes."

"But I already told you I resigned as Royal Wizard!"

"And had your resignation refused. I saw you sitting with your royal court this morning."

She had me there. "Then I'll just resign again."

But she could be as stubborn as I. "No. Now listen to me. I've had plenty of time to think about this. You've been involved in wizardry your entire adult life. It's as much a part of you as your bones and skin. You're also a very good wizard, and you're respected at the school. You couldn't give up magic, and you also could not be satisfied doing odd tricks at fairs. I know you. I've heard you make disparaging remarks about magicians having to make their livings from pathetic scraps of magic, spells done for no better purpose than the entertainment of the ignorant. You'd do your best to hide it from me, because you *are* very affectionate, but there would always be a gap in your life."

It would have been easier to argue with her if she hadn't been right. "But there will always be a gap without you!"

She ignored the interruption and pushed on. "And I

thought about myself. I've lived on my own for ten years and come to value my privacy. It's been a good ten years. I have my embroidery and my magic and my climbing—though I won't be doing any of *that* for the next year or so—and soon will have our daughter."

I thought glumly that it was a sign of how much she valued her privacy that we were having this conversation here in the grove, not in her house.

"The cathedral probably won't give me any more needlework once they decide I'm a loose woman, but I'll still make a good living; I'll be able to live for months on what the priests paid me these last few weeks."

"So you don't want anyone else disturbing your life."

"That's not what I'm saying. I'm saying I wouldn't make a very satisfactory wife to a wandering magic-worker. No matter how much I loved you, I'd miss my independence, and I'm afraid I'd take it out on you. No, I think I'm the kind of person who is much better for short visits than for a permanent stay."

There didn't seem to be any way to answer this, even though I knew she was wrong. Theodora would be highly satisfactory for a permanent stay. But I considered for a moment what she'd just said. "Then you wouldn't mind if I visited you sometimes?"

"I would want you to visit as often as you could. You realize, Daimbert, there wasn't anyone before you, and there won't be anyone after you."

She smiled, for the first time in a long time. I seemed to have agreed to an arrangement that in fact I still refused to accept. But I was tired of arguing, and she had said, undeniably, that she loved me— "Is it all right if I kiss you?"

The smile widened. "I'd been hoping you'd suggest that."

The sun was low as I walked through the narrow city streets to the castle. I wondered vaguely if I was too late to get anything to eat.

Paul met me in the courtyard. "There you are. We wondered where you'd gone. You have a dinner invitation."

"A dinner invitation." This didn't make any sense.

"A priest came by from the episcopal palace an hour ago. The bishop wants you to dine with him."

"The bishop?" I repeated stupidly.

Paul laughed. "I thought you'd be flattered by the honor! There can't be many wizards asked to dine by bishops the very evening of their enthronements."

I managed to pull myself together. "Oh. Yes. The bishop. This will be a good time to warn him."

All summer I had known that if Joachim became bishop our long evening conversations would be over for good. But now he was bishop, and he still seemed willing to talk to me. I should have been delighted but felt no emotion at all. Besides, it would all be different.

"I've got something else to tell you," said Paul, somewhat sheepishly. "I know you didn't want me to ride Bonfire. But I did anyway. I can't believe Vincent meant him as a trap, and, besides, I couldn't help myself. Was there ever something you wanted to do so badly you didn't care about the consequences?"

I nodded without speaking.

"Bonfire really is as gentle as a kitten, and can he run! He's even faster than those horses in the borderlands."

"All right, then, but be careful," I said inadequately. I hurried inside to scrub my face and to brush the bits of grass out of my hair and beard.

As I walked toward the cathedral a few minutes later, I tried to recall all the concerns I had about a forthcoming attack from an evil wizard. I had feared no one in the Church would be willing to listen, but if Joachim had invited me to dinner he would certainly let me speak.

A young and rather nervous acolyte met me at the palace door, but inside I was pleased to see Joachim's silent servant, apparently forgiven for his complicity in

Norbert's plot. He nodded gravely and motioned me toward the study.

"Uh, Your Holiness—" I began awkwardly, dipping my head and wondering if Joachim expected me to kneel.

The bishop had been reading his Bible, but he immediately rose to greet me, taking both my arms in his strong grip. "I am glad you were willing to come," he said with a smile, a genuine smile such as I had not seen on his face very often. "I had been afraid you would refuse. You have been out all afternoon, I understand? You must be starving. Come into the dining room, and we can eat at once." He wore his ordinary black vestments again rather than the scarlet robes of this morning, although the ruby ring was still on his finger. He looked more comfortable and relaxed than I could remember seeing him for a long time. "And don't call me Your Holiness, Daimbert, unless you expect me to start calling you Your Wizardliness!"

The candles were lit, and the bishop's servant brought the soup. I sat down in something of a fog, but as soon as we started to eat I realized that he was right; I was starving.

"I want to thank you, and I want to apologize," said Joachim. "You removed the magical danger to the cathedral, at much greater personal risk than I had anticipated—although I should have known better. When I got your telephone message last week I drew a relaxed breath for the first time this summer."

I had to warn him that the magical danger was not all gone, but he was still talking.

"And all the time that you were marshaling your forces against the monster, I selfishly ignored you. I was so caught up in my own concerns, worrying about the bishop, worrying about whether I would be elected myself, that I paid no attention to *you.* But now the bishop is safely in Abraham's bosom, and I have been elected to succeed him, for good or ill. I think all the members of the cathedral chapter had a serious lapse of judgment, but, with the help of God I will at least not lead my flock into evil."

"As you know," I said, "I'd always thought you'd be a good bishop. And, do you remember?" with a fair approximation of a smile. "I promised you two things if you were elected. I said that I'd go to the land of wild magic, and I've done so—or at least to the borderlands, which were wild enough for me. And I promised that I'd try to work with you, to find ways that wizards and priests could stop distrusting each other."

This might be hard, I realized, since the first thing I was going to tell him was that there was an evil wizard loose in the twin kingdoms. But the servant came back before I could say anything more, to take away our soup bowls and serve the lamb and carrots.

"Put the cheese and fruit on the side table," said Joachim, "along with the rest of the wine. We can serve ourselves."

The servant closed the door behind him as he left. Joachim turned his enormous dark eyes on me. "Now I'd like you to tell me what's really bothering you."

"I'm afraid a wizard I haven't been able to find is plotting some massive attack," I said. "It was he who called the gorgos, and I can't even imagine what he's planning next."

Joachim had put down his fork and was watching my face.

"I don't know where he is now. I came back from the borderlands as fast as I could because I was terrified he might try to attack the cathedral at your election the way he did at the old bishop's funeral. Nothing happened, and I can find no sign of wild magic in the city, but that may only mean he hasn't been able to get a new monster from the north—yet. And I doubt I'll be able to get any support from the wizards' school."

The bishop nodded gravely, still watching me. "But you don't sound as though you anticipate a magical attack tonight."

"No, or at least I hope not."

"Good. Then you can tell me all about it a little later." He took a few bites, then looked at me again. "Right now you can tell me what's happened to you, you personally, these last few months. Because something has happened which has affected you even more profoundly than your fight with the monster."

I forced myself to adopt a light tone. "What makes you think something out of the ordinary has happened to me, besides of course nearly being killed by a gorgos?"

This was far too flimsy for him. "As I told you once before, I know you better than you think I do. You put me off then, but I can't bear to see you like this any longer. Something terrible has wrenched your soul, and if I'm supposed to guide the souls of this diocese I can't leave my oldest friend to suffer unaided."

I tried not to meet his eyes. "You don't need to hear all this. Half of it you wouldn't understand, and the other half you'd just say I was receiving a sinner's just reward."

"And are you?"

I looked up in spite of myself. "Joachim, I don't even know anymore."

"Then why not try to tell me?"

I took another bite of lamb—it really was very good—then pushed my plate away. "This may take a while."

"We have a while."

I took a deep breath. "It starts back when I first came to Yurt. I've tried to tell you this several times, but you never seemed to understand. Until this summer, I've always been in love with the queen."

V

I knocked on Theodora's door just before dawn. "Theodora. It's me."

She opened the door looking extremely charming in a white nightgown, her hair tousled and her cheek still bearing a crease from the pillow. "What is it?"

"I've come to invite you to Prince Paul's coming of age ceremony."

"But—" I gave her a good-morning kiss while she tried to object. "They won't want me there—they don't even know me. And Daimbert!" with an exasperated laugh. "What will the neighbors think if they see me standing here in my nightgown, kissing someone at this hour of the morning?"

"Then I'll come inside," I said cheerfully, closing the door behind me. The cat rose from the hearth, stretching itself to twice its normal length and yawning widely. "I hope you realize the neighbors will start thinking all sorts of things in a few months anyway. But don't worry about the cathedral. They won't think of you as a loose woman, but more as a woman who has been sinned against, so you'll continue to get commissions from the priests."

She rubbed her eyes and sat down, pulling a shawl across her shoulders. "What's happened to you? You look almost feverish. Did you even go to bed last night?"

"No," sitting down beside her. "I've been talking to the bishop."

"The bishop! You've been telling him about me—"

I smiled at her concern. "I certainly told the bishop the most important details, such as that you are the most wonderful woman in the world, and I love you. I didn't tell him you're a witch—the Church has long experience in dealing with sin, but even Joachim has always had trouble with magic."

"So you let the bishop condemn you as a sinner?"

"Joachim thinks of everyone as a sinner, starting with himself. He's never held it against anyone."

She started to look amused in spite of herself. I put my arm around her. "If it's any comfort," I said, "he thinks you're right, that I belong in Yurt and you here. Both of you are wrong, of course."

"Then why do you seem so happy this morning?"

"Maybe the Church has a point, that confession is good

for the soul. But I think the real reason is my relief that I'll finally be able to find the renegade wizard; Joachim has a plan to draw him out of hiding."

"What's his plan?"

Looking into her intelligent amethyst eyes, I realized that Joachim had actually been quite vague about his precise intentions. Last night, after he had listened to my long, disjointed story about the queen and Theodora, once I finally told him my suspicions of a renegade, he had said with calm assurance that locating him would not be a problem. At that point, emotionally drained, I had been glad to believe whatever he told me.

"It involves Paul's coming of age ceremony," I said, feeling light-headed. I knew I remembered the bishop saying that. Did the plan also involve Norbert? No, I was quite sure it didn't, although I had confessed my involvement in that to Joachim along with everything else. He had placidly refused to attribute any worse motives to the cathedral cantor than misplaced distrust of magic and a rather sad and petty jealousy, though he said he expected that the wizard who had sold Norbert the book, the wizard who had fostered his jealous plot, was still here in the city.

"The only problem with the bishop's plan," I extemporized when Theodora seemed to be expecting more, "is that it depends on me being as good a wizard as Joachim thinks I am, which is better than I think I am. That's why I need you to help me at Paul's coronation. I'm a member of the royal court of Yurt and can invite anyone I please."

"But I can't— How would I—"

"You're going with the episcopal party," I said. "It's all arranged. The bishop will provide a horse for you. And be sure to attend morning service at the cathedral, an hour from now. Joachim will be giving his inaugural sermon, and it's going to be highly interesting."

"If there's a dangerous renegade wizard loose," she asked, "shouldn't your school be able to help?"

"That's one of the wizard's best ploys. By having his gorgos appear on the new cathedral tower originally, he's made it appear this is something in which the school should be reluctant to be involved. By waiting until the Royal Wizard of Caelrhon had died, he hoped there would be no one here with the magic to oppose him."

I kissed Theodora and stood up to go. "The queen and prince are riding back to Yurt this afternoon. I need to go with them."

A smile she tried to suppress twitched the corners of her mouth. "It's odd that you never told me your queen was so lovely."

I sat down again. "Theodora, you have to understand that—"

She gave up trying to hide her smile. "Of *course* I knew there was a queen of Yurt, even though you never mentioned her. And I'd seen her several times over the years, and I'd certainly noticed she was very beautiful. That's why, when you very carefully never referred to her, I knew there was a reason."

"But there's never been any—" I protested.

"I knew that all along." She smiled at me, amethyst eyes dancing. "When the king of Yurt was still alive and they came here together, she and he were inseparable. Now that she's been a widow for several years she might be willing to start looking at other men, but she'd be looking for a prince or another king, not a wizard. This was all clear to me, but I could never be sure if it was clear to you."

If I had spoken to Theodora several months ago, I might have saved myself a lot of anguish. But then I hadn't known her several months ago—and might never have if it weren't for that anguish.

"It put me in a difficult position," she continued thoughtfully, "because I didn't know if you loved the queen while knowing it was hopeless, or if you'd deluded yourself that you might someday have a chance with her. I would hate to see you deluded, but on the other hand, once I found myself falling in love with you, it made it easier if I could reassure myself that your real affections were already engaged elsewhere."

There didn't seem to be any way to answer this.

"What I am truly sorry about, Daimbert," she added, "is that I never realized, not until I saw you sitting with your royal court yesterday, that you'd discovered for yourself that your love was hopeless. For a witch, it's embarrassing to have to admit I overlooked something that evident."

"You mean— It's so obvious that I had loved her but she could never love me that someone could spot it across a crowded church?"

She gave me an amused look. "Remember that witches understand all sorts of hidden feelings that ordinary mortals—and even wizards—can't know. Besides, I know you better than anyone else does."

Enough people seemed to know me better than I thought they did that soon I wouldn't be able to have any secrets at all. "But if you knew all this yesterday—you didn't say anything about the queen then!"

"Of course not. You were too upset already. But I don't know," she continued, "exactly what happened between you and your queen to make you realize your love for her was hopeless."

I looked away as I answered. "I asked her to marry me."

She made a small incoherent sound. "I'm sorry, Daimbert," she said after a moment. "No one should be refused twice in one summer."

I thought of telling her she could solve that problem for me but knew better. "And I don't love the queen. I never really loved her. I only love you."

She laughed and pushed me away. "Of course you love your queen. You have for nearly twenty years. Now hurry back to the castle and get ready for church service."

But she was wrong, I told myself. I didn't love the queen.

✧ ✧ ✧

The cathedral filled up rapidly. The visiting bishops had left with their entourages after yesterday's enthronement, but almost everyone else returned for the bishop's inaugural sermon.

After changing my clothes and drinking several cups of strong tea back at the castle, I felt almost coherent again. Among the people coming in was a woman dressed in an elegant dress of dark lilac silk. A few strands of nut-brown hair emerged from under a chaste white wimple. I slipped into the pew next to her. "You look like a castellan's lady, if not a princess," I whispered with a smile. "I scarcely recognized you as my beloved embroideress."

The dark lilac of the dress brought out the color of her eyes, even in the dimness of the cathedral's interior. "Of course," she replied. "It's not for nothing that I make my living by sewing. If I'm really going to go to your prince's coronation, I have to look suitably regal. What will happen here?"

"You'll see," I said, wondering myself. "Joachim's not just the new bishop; in some ways he's now the most powerful person in two kingdoms."

The organ's tune changed to a deep and solemn processional march, and the cathedral priests filed in, sober in black and white, led by their new dean. When they had assembled around the altar, Joachim appeared, walking by himself across the mosaic Tree of Life.

As he took his place at the lectern in front, resplendent in the scarlet robes that Theodora had embroidered for him, he appeared almost cheerful. No one who did not know him as well as I did would have noticed, for his lips did not smile, and his dark eyes were as unwavering and compelling as always. But his voice, as he read from the Bible and then proceeded to speak of the love and brotherhood that should bind mankind together under God, had none of the anguish in it I had heard so clearly at the old bishop's funeral. Rather, he spoke with both assurance and humility.

"As this is my inaugural sermon," he said, putting down his Bible, "I would like to address to you, my people, a special request." This, I thought, was where his plan began. I remembered clearly now: he had said he would lure the wizard out of hiding through an idea planted in his first sermon.

But Joachim's next words were entirely unexpected. "For too long there has been at best an uneasy truce, if not indeed outright enmity, between the Church and organized wizardry. While I am bishop of the kingdoms of Yurt and Caelrhon, I would like to see this stop."

Theodora looked at me from under raised brows, and I thought I heard an uneasy shuffling from where the cathedral priests were sitting.

"There has been talk, groundless talk, of the wizards' school seeking to infiltrate all aspects of life in the western kingdoms, of abrogating the authority of lords and even of kings." I gave the royal princes of Caelrhon a quick glance to see how they were taking it. It was their turn to shift uncomfortably in the pew.

"This talk was started by someone who is an enemy of the people of our two kingdoms! Unfortunately it has been picked up, both by some laymen who may be in the congregation today and by some officers within the Church. As of today, I want this foolishness to cease." Joachim looked at all of us with burning eyes, and his voice rose clear in the silent cathedral. "Priests and wizards need to work together, beginning at once."

This was starting to sound dangerously like heresy to me. I wondered what the bishop of the great City would say when he heard about it; relations between his cathedral and the nearby wizards' school had always been strained. I had been hoping Joachim would be bishop for forty more years; at this rate, he might not last forty more days.

"These rumors against wizards were started as a smokescreen," Joachim continued, "to try to force a wedge between institutionalized wizardry and organized religion, between the wizards and the people they serve with their magic." I did my best not to look like a wizard. "Once this wedge was in place, the enemy of all our people, inspired by the devil, was planning to attack the Church! He thought he could do so safely, because the powers of magic, that otherwise would have come forward to serve Christianity, would already have been driven away. The ultimate attack on the Church is still to come."

There was no doubt that Joachim had his audience's entire attention. "I do not know for certain when this attack will arrive but it will be soon. Therefore we must be ready, all of us, churchmen, wizards, lords, and townspeople, to oppose it together. I have already spoken to the Royal Wizard of Yurt, who has pledged his support." He caught my eye for one second. "But I also have a task for the dukes and counts and for the castellans and manorial lords who are here.

"Yesterday, on the day that I was elected, you all laid your swords on the altar in symbol of your pledged service to the Church. I ask you now to fulfill that pledge! Next week I must be away from the city for a few days, to attend the coming of age of the young king of Yurt. The royal family of Caelrhon will also be there. I now fear that someone will take advantage of our absence to stage an assault on this church. You will all remember with horror the outrageous attack at the time of the old bishop's funeral, when one brave wizard was able to save us." He did not try to catch my eye this time, which was just as well. "This time the attack may be even worse, and that wizard will be in Yurt, with me, and unable to come to the rescue.

"Therefore! I want all of you to be ready, priests with your prayers, magicians with your spells, and the lords of men with your swords. I do not know if there will be another monster as we had before, or even a flock of monsters. But with the help of God, the attack will be averted."

He stepped then from behind the lectern to bless the congregation, as calmly as though he had not just offered the olive branch of peace to institutionalized wizardry. As the congregation rose, rather shakily, for the final hymn, I thought he had managed well something I had had trouble with myself, even in talking to him: he had issued a warning against a magical attack without warning against magic.

He disappeared out the side door of the church as the organ notes died away, and the congregation, buzzing with rapid conversation, poured out the great front doors into the muddle of the construction site. Now that I had heard his plan, I did not like it at *all*. I found myself glancing up at the sky as Theodora and I passed through the doors and wondered if I would ever again be able to come out of an important service in the cathedral without looking for monsters.

"You told me the bishop's first sermon would be highly interesting," said Theodora, looking at me as though not sure whether to smile, "and you were certainly right. He spoke as though—as though he didn't care what anyone would think, either the people here or the rest of the Church."

I shook my head. "I don't think he does," I answered absently. "He answers to God and to his conscience, and it may not even occur to him that most people also answer to the opinions of others." I took a deep breath. "Come with me," I said. "I have to talk to him."

PART EIGHT

Coming of Age

I

The narrow street behind the cathedral was full of priests. They looked up in surprise as we approached, then resumed their conversations behind us. I tried to decide if they were making negative comments about Joachim, but as far as I could tell they were wondering what they could do to keep his respect.

When I knocked at the episcopal palace, the acolyte who answered first tried to make us go away, saying the bishop was busy and that we should present ourselves and whatever business we had to the priest who would be on duty at the cathedral office in midafternoon. When I showed no signs of leaving, he gestured to someone I could not see for reinforcements.

But then I heard Joachim's voice from within. "Is that the wizard? Send him in, and bring more tea."

The acolyte fell back, defeated, and Joachim's silent servant led us into the dining room. The bishop, still dressed in scarlet, sat at breakfast.

He rose and came forward to greet us. Theodora, abashed, knelt to kiss his ring. As she rose again, he took her by the shoulders and looked at her face. "Theodora," he said. "I am delighted to meet you properly at last. I've seen you often before, of course, but I never knew your name. Isn't this your embroidery on my sleeves?"

I hoped that Theodora realized that Joachim never said that he was delighted to meet someone unless he meant it. He brought up chairs for us, dismissed the servants, and poured us tea.

"Is that what you had in mind," he asked me, spreading jam on his toast, "when you said you wanted priests and wizards to stop distrusting each other?" He spoke soberly, but something about the angle of his eyebrows made me think he was enjoying himself.

"I hope you understand what you've just done," I said darkly. "Talking about how the city of Caelrhon needed to be defended didn't fool anybody. You *dared* the renegade wizard to attack you next week in Yurt, using yourself as bait to draw him out!" This was, after all, Joachim's own plan, and I knew he would sacrifice himself quite willingly if he thought it necessary. "And after putting yourself in danger like that, you then decided to preach on harmony between wizardry and the Church?"

"If there are important thoughts and attitudes that need to be changed, one should start changing them at once," he replied calmly.

"You certainly got the attention of your cathedral priests. They're standing out in the street wondering what they should now do differently—even Norbert, I'm sure. With someone else, they might have balked at the idea of becoming friends with the wizards, but they're too much in awe of you to do anything *but* agree."

"They're not in awe of me," said Joachim casually, and with what I thought was a thorough lack of insight, "just of the authority of my office." He started to refill our teacups and looked concerned that mine was still full, though Theodora had retreated from the conversation by sipping hers.

"But how about the other bishops?" I demanded. "*They* won't be in awe of your office. Aren't they going to reprimand you for heresy?" At this rate, I thought, he might not even live long enough to be reprimanded.

Joachim cocked his head at me as though wondering what I meant. "I said nothing that could possibly be considered heresy. I only preached the brotherhood of mankind and told everyone that I wanted unfounded and untrue rumors to stop." He broke into an unexpected smile. "There are advantages to being in the Church rather than connected to your wizards' school. We don't have the central organization you do; there isn't a Master like the Master of your school to whom I have to answer." There was no doubt about it, he was enjoying himself. "Bishops in council can of course discipline erring brethren, but no one could possibly call a council against me for urging priests and wizards to serve God's purpose together."

Considering how reluctant he had been to be elected bishop, I thought, he was not at all reluctant to exercise the authority of his position once he had it. "But how about you?" I persisted. "You've certainly told me enough times over the years how inferior magic is to religion."

He gave me a long look from eyes in which a glint of humor lurked. "It is, of course," he said. "But I've probably been too dismissive. After all, even wizards—strange as this concept may seem to you—are the children of God."

I shouldn't waste my time worrying about priests and bishops reacting to the new bishop of Caelrhon. Joachim as bishop might be hard for *me* to deal with. I gave up the effort and laughed. "All right, Joachim. I can tell your own personal safety is much lower on your list of concerns than it is on mine. I'll try to protect you. I have to get back to Yurt now, but I'll see you there very soon."

"And you'll be riding up with our party, I believe?" Joachim said to Theodora, who had been too overcome by the honor of drinking tea with the bishop to say anything. "Good. We shall be able to talk properly then." He rose. "I do indeed have a lot I need to do, but I have an advantage that makes many things easier for me now than when I was dean." The glint was back in his dark eyes. "I have a dean to help me!"

But before letting us out he rested a hand gravely on Theodora's head. "Bless you, my daughter," he said, "and the child that you carry."

"So you did tell him everything," said Theodora. I walked with her through the city streets to her house. It wasn't exactly an accusation, but from someone who valued her privacy as much as she did it was also not an endorsement of my night-long conversation at the bishop's palace.

"I already told you that," I said. "I had to tell him I was going to be a father because he wouldn't have let me go until he found out why I was so upset." Although I had said highly insulting things to her just the day before, I now felt I had to phrase it diplomatically. "You *did* rather manipulate me, you know. But there are all sorts of things the bishop still doesn't know about you. You can tell him yourself that you're a witch, to keep him amused during your long ride to Yurt together."

She looked at me as though wondering if I was serious. "You don't seem very respectful toward the bishop."

"Of course not. Even if we're going to start working together now, I'm afraid my habits of disrespect toward the organized Church are too deeply ingrained to change."

She started to smile in spite of herself. "I used to think it was a shame there weren't more wizards like you. Now I'm beginning to think it's just as well."

"Many wizards would agree," I replied. "But I must say I find it disturbing that you're always teasing me but treat Joachim with awe. After all, we were at Yurt together for years, and we're the same age."

She shook her head, still smiling. "You two may have once been the same age, but you've stayed the same while he's twenty years older. And he isn't royal chaplain of Yurt anymore—he's the *bishop.*"

As we walked, I kept glancing at her out of the corner of my eye, wondering if I dared ask her again to marry me. The picture of standing with her before Joachim to be married was so intensely real that I could not let myself believe it might never happen. But if I asked her too often it would become nothing but a joke between us, which she at any rate would never take seriously.

The royal party headed back through sunny valleys and hills toward the royal castle of Yurt. Paul rode his red roan stallion, but he had acceded to my concerns enough to stay within sight of the rest of us.

My eyes were starting to feel gritty from lack of sleep, and even though I knew I would be stiff at the end of the day from jouncing on an old mare, I still preferred to let her do the work of transporting me home. There was a spell I could use against fatigue, but I hesitated to use it; after its effect wore off, I always felt worse than before. I hoped Joachim would be alert enough to attend to his new duties today. But maybe people with pure minds needed less sleep.

At the moment, my thoughts kept me from dozing. I was extremely fond of the queen, I told myself, as I was of Paul, and for that matter of everyone else in the court of Yurt. The queen was just as lovely as she had always been, her nature as spirited and as affectionate. But nineteen years of daydreams about her seemed gone as though they had never existed. Even the memory of kissing her in the twilight in the fields outside the castle seemed so far away that it might have happened to different people.

Partly my daydreams had been driven out by Theodora's reality, I reasoned, and partly my unspoken imaginings had been dissipated by telling Joachim about them. But it made it much easier than I could have expected to ride next to the queen and to talk to her.

Now, if it had not been for Theodora, I told myself, I could have imagined nothing better than continuing as Royal Wizard of Yurt. I thought I would even have been able to think approvingly of the queen's marriage to Prince Vincent, if I hadn't been so sure that he was only using it as an excuse to get into Yurt and seize it for himself.

I tried to sound her out, to see if she might know something that would help me even if she did not realize she knew it. "Why did you decide to move up your wedding, my lady?" I asked casually.

She looked up sharply, the sunlight gleaming in her emerald eyes. In spite of her easy and natural manner, I thought, she *did* remember our last real conversation. But what she saw seemed to reassure her. I wasn't sure if this meant she too knew me better than I thought she did, or if it meant she didn't really understand me at all. She answered without awkwardness or embarrassment. "We just couldn't bear to wait any longer."

The sudden constriction of my chest made no sense, I chided myself, because I was now ready to hear her talk of such things without pain.

"It seems," she continued, "that all I've done recently is prepare for the two ceremonies: Paul's coming of age and my own wedding. It would have been easier, of course," she commented wryly, "if he'd been in Yurt during the last month. I let him go to the cathedral city for a few days, and next I know you've kidnapped him!"

"I apologize for taking him with me," I said, thinking that it could not indeed have been easy to make preparations for a once-in-a-lifetime ceremony when the key person in that ceremony wasn't even there. "But if it hadn't been for Paul, the rest of us might still be up in the border of the land of magic."

She looked thoughtfully toward the red stallion and

its rider, running long loops next to the road while the rest of us proceeded more sedately. "He tried to downplay it when he told me about it," she said, "but I could tell that he had been responsible for finding a way for you all to escape. Of course, I know perfectly well, Wizard," she added generously, "that you would have come up with something of your own in not much more time."

"He got to know Prince Lucas much better during the trip, too," I said, hoping to work the conversation back to Lucas's younger brother Vincent. "It's good that the two future kings of Yurt and Caelrhon should be friends."

"He tended to gloss over the dangers of the trip," said the queen with a smile, "but I could tell there were at least a few places where you might all have been killed. That's not the sort of thing a mother likes to hear about, but, now that it's all over safely, I can reassure myself that maybe he needed a little real adventure. We've always tried not to spoil him, but there's no question that he's been somewhat sheltered."

So far I was no closer to finding out anything about Vincent. I could talk indefinitely to the queen about Paul, even though he would be exasperated to know we were talking about him like this. But I still needed to know if she had observed anything about Vincent. "When I came back from the City and first met the prince, my lady," I began, "there was something about the way that the two of you treated each other which I can only characterize as *odd.*"

She gave me a surprised look, as well she might, but said nothing.

"You and he seemed happy to be together," I plunged ahead, "but I had the strangest feeling that I was watching a play, that you had rehearsed what you told me about your whirlwind courtship."

The queen blushed most becomingly and tugged at a loose stitch on one of her riding gloves. I let the silence stretch out, knowing she would have to answer eventually.

Having exhausted the possibilities of her glove, the queen glanced around to be sure no one else was within hearing distance, cleared her throat twice, and gave what I had to call a giggle. "I hadn't realized it was that obvious," she said. "Maybe we *were* acting in a play, although I hadn't thought of it that way. But it would have been rather embarrassing to admit that *I* had been courting *him*!"

"You were courting him," I repeated.

"I wouldn't tell anyone other than you," she said, which I presumed was meant as a compliment. "But this winter, when I realized that my baby boy was going to be king very soon, and it had been six years since King Haimeric had died, I decided I would remarry. I was never meant to be a nun."

I nodded but did not trust myself to speak.

"Even you going back to teach at the wizards' school," she continued without looking at me, "made me realize that the years were passing, and that if I wanted another husband I should choose him soon. Going over the possibilities, I quickly picked out Vincent. That's why I invited him to come stay in Yurt this spring."

I rode in silence without answering. It all sounded coldhearted and calculating to me, not at all like the queen.

"It sounds very coldhearted when I put it like that," she went on, as though reading my thoughts. "But I wasn't deliberately planning to marry him, because I didn't know if I would love him. Rather, I thought I would review my options, to see if I *could* come to love someone else after the king."

She gave me a quick glance, as though wondering if she should apologize again for never having considered me as a candidate. If so, she decided against it. "Vincent seemed from the beginning the most likely of the lords and princes I knew."

"So he doesn't mind that you picked him out?" I managed to ask.

"Not at all! He was highly flattered. He was just a *little* irritated with me at first for inviting him to Yurt to see if he might be the man I would want as a husband, and then being so slow to make up my mind. You see, he'd always been secretly in love with *me.*" She gave a dreamy smile that I would gladly have missed. "His only problem was his family; he said his older brother kept suggesting that this might be a chance for Yurt to take over Caelrhon. Vincent, I'm afraid, has always felt somewhat stifled living under his brother's shadow. He has no use for politics himself, of course."

This time she fell into a silence that she seemed to have no intention of breaking. I did not believe a word of it.

Or at least I did not believe what she had said about Prince Vincent, even if she thought it was true herself. Her own motivations, I thought reluctantly, might make sense. This was, after all, the same woman who had threatened her parents with becoming a nun many years ago, when they had tried to marry her to someone she did not like. If the young chaplain had started pressuring her to join the Nunnery of Yurt, her immediate reaction would have been to marry again.

And she had always loved parties and dancing. If nothing else, working her way through the eligible men in the adjacent kingdoms would have promised several seasons of festivity.

She pulled her horse over to the side of the road and called to her son. "Paul! I think you've tired your horse until mine can match him. I'll race you to the woods!"

Watching the two of them gallop ahead—the queen had always been an excellent horsewoman—I felt a profound if irrational certainty that Vincent had much more in mind than the kisses of a beautiful woman.

II

I came home to Yurt as though I had been gone for years. The trees and grass around the castle had the rich dark green of late summer. I happily reshelved the thoroughly battered books of spells that I had taken with me to the cathedral city, and from there to the borderlands, to Vor's valley, back to the cathedral city, and back home again. Now that I was apparently once more Royal Wizard, I thought I might be in control of at least parts of my life again—except for finding the renegade wizard.

Activity in the royal castle of Yurt was frantic. The staff were busy cleaning and airing all the guest rooms, as well as decorating the great hall; the knights were preparing for a tournament such as had not been held at Yurt for years; and the cook was constantly getting in and preparing the food for days of festivities. The queen's parents arrived the day after we returned, to be there for their grandson's coming of age.

Trying to stay out of everyone's way, I worked long and late on my spells, setting up magical protective barriers so that no creature could land on the walls or the tops of the towers, not even something invisible, without triggering alarms. But I wished I knew something, anything, about the wizard who had brought a gorgos to the old bishop's funeral and might be showing up in Yurt to attack the new one.

My only possible lead was the cantor Norbert, who had certainly obtained the old book of spells from a magic-worker, a fairly young, dark-bearded wizard according to his account to Joachim, a wizard wearing the same star-studded jacket Vor had described. But it had always been hard to see the scholarly old priest behind the gorgos, and he would scarcely have told the bishop all about the wizard from whom he obtained the book if he was still conspiring with him.

I took Paul quietly aside to warn him that we might see another monster at his coronation. He grinned, intrigued by the possibility. When I asked if he thought we should scale back the festivities, he only laughed. "We can't very well cancel the ceremonies unless a dragon is actually on us!"

"I don't want you out in the open when the wizard brings on his next monsters."

"But you wouldn't have me begin my rule as king cowering timidly inside," replied Paul. "Especially if it comes during the tournament we'll be ready for it, since all the knights will be in armor. Maybe this time I'll even get a chance to fight it myself, since you didn't let me last time." At least he didn't seem bothered that I had not tried to incorporate any of his and Lucas's elaborate plots into Joachim's plan to lure the renegade wizard into the open.

The rest of our guests arrived at Yurt the day before Paul's birthday: the royal family of Caelrhon, the duchess and the two counts of Yurt with all their families, and all of Yurt's manorial lords. The stables were packed, the guest rooms full and overfull; and most of the visiting knights ended up pitching tents beyond the moat.

There was a surprise when the royal family of Caelrhon rode up, for the king was not with them. The queen of Caelrhon was accompanied by her sons Lucas and Vincent, Lucas's wife and children, and a dozen knights, but not her husband.

"He's staying in the cathedral city," Vincent told my queen, holding her hands and looking at her in adoration. "Father thought he'd better be at the cathedral to defend it from attack."

If the king of Caelrhon had passed up Paul's coronation to protect the bishop's church, I thought, I hoped he would not be too disappointed when nothing happened—assuming, of course, that Joachim's plan worked.

The bishop's party arrived last of all. It was just growing

dark when we saw a small group of horses, led by a banner with a cross, emerging from the woods. Fireflies winked in the grass by the road as I went out to meet them.

The young chaplain came with me, all aflutter in brand-new vestments. I wondered how he would hold up during his first spiritual examination by the new bishop.

Joachim, Theodora, a young priest, and two knights rode up the last rise to the castle. Their horses were the only ones to arrive all day without the tinkling of harness bells. The riders listened while the chaplain rattled through his speech of welcome, full of phrases from the Bible and expressions of hope that the bishop would not find this small castle too unworthy of his attentions. But my attention was distracted. Emerging from the woods and starting up the brick road toward the castle were several caravans, lanterns swinging from them as the horses labored in the final climb.

"The Romneys," I said out loud, too startled to realize I was interrupting the chaplain until I had done so.

"That's right," said the priest who had come with the bishop, in tones of disapproval. "We passed them on the road late this afternoon. They said they wanted to be here to see the prince crowned."

This was something I had not counted on. There should be nothing wrong with the Romneys being here, and yet all my calculations were built on knowing exactly who was going to be where at all times. I shook my head at myself. I was already as tense as a bowstring, and some of the other guests were bound to do something innocent and unimportant that would throw me into a panic.

The chaplain had trouble finding the thread of his welcoming speech again. Joachim thanked him and shook his horse's reins, and his party moved across the drawbridge into the courtyard. The Romneys pulled their caravans off the road a little distance short of the tents of the visiting knights.

The queen came out to welcome the bishop, both more sincerely and more simply than the young chaplain had. Paul stood beside her, looking extremely solemn. He stepped forward as the bishop's horse was led away to the stables.

"Holy Father, I have a request to make," he said, speaking rapidly, as though afraid the bishop would walk away before he could say it. "As you know, I will be spending tonight, the night before my coronation, in prayer in the chapel. It is traditional that a priest come to counsel me at some point, and I would be honored—very highly honored—if you could do so."

The young chaplain looked surprised; I expected he had been busily preparing spiritual counsel himself for the new king.

"I would be delighted," Joachim said gravely.

A smile lit up the prince's face. "Wonderful. Come around midnight."

The queen turned to greet Theodora. The two women looked at each other for a long moment; Theodora, I expected, wanted a good look at the other woman who had refused my proposals and the queen wondered who this young woman could be although she was much too tactful to ask.

The last available room in the castle, at my request, had been reserved for Theodora. It was a small room at the top of a flight of stairs, but in the morning the windows would look into the dawn sky. With the queen's permission, I had cut some late roses from the king's garden and arranged them in vases.

"I wanted to let you know," said Theodora as I set down her bag in the room, "that the old magician is with the Romneys."

"The old magician? You mean the man who was so furious that I might be interfering with his 'making an honest living,' the one to whom you taught a little fire magic?"

"That's right. I hadn't seen him since the beginning of the summer, since even before I met you, but when we caught up to the Romneys he was riding on one of the caravans."

I nodded slowly. "I hope the worst he'll do is to make some scandalous illusions at an inappropriate time in the ceremony, but while I'm waiting for the renegade wizard this magician's magic may prove distracting."

"This is the closest I've ever seen your queen," Theodora continued. "Have you told *her* all about me as well?"

"Of course not!" I started to protest indignantly, then realized she was teasing me. "I just told her that you were an important lady from the cathedral city," I added with dignity, "who I wanted as my special guest."

"Then you'd better go out with the others," she said with a smile, "before they all start wondering just how 'special' a guest I am!"

But she kissed me before I left. As I went back down the stairs, I realized that in her own way she was as little concerned about public opinion as Joachim. She would always do exactly what she wanted, rather than what she thought others would want her to do, but as a single woman, one without any authority whatsoever, she had to avoid attracting attention to herself that might keep her from her privacy or what she had been intending.

One of the servants found me as I came back out into the courtyard. "There's a phone call for you from the City."

My heart pounded rapidly as I picked up the receiver and looked at the face of one of the young wizards of the school. "Zahlfast said that you'd asked us to call you if there was any unusual activity up in the land of magic," he said. "I wasn't sure I should call you, since nothing came of it, but then I decided I'd better."

"What is it?" I asked impatiently. The wizard who had summoned a gorgos to the cathedral city would not be casting spells from which nothing came.

"We had a call about an hour ago from the wizard who's posted up at the borderlands. He said a very small dragon had suddenly started south, but he was able to fly down and get ahead of it and put a magical barrier in front of it. When it bounced off his barrier, the dragon turned around and went straight back. I wouldn't have bothered you for such a trivial event, but Zahlfast told me you'd been very insistent."

I thought rapidly. "Do you know if the school ever got that telephone fixed?"

"The telephone? You mean the one up in the borderlands? I didn't think it was ever broken."

I took a deep and ragged breath. "Is Zahlfast there?"

"No, I think he went out to dinner. Shall I have him call you?"

I hesitated a moment, then shook my head. When I had spoken with Zahlfast the day before, he had seemed miffed that I was still worrying myself over what he considered the Church's problems. I was not going to get any help from him. "Just tell him that phone *is* broken." I rang off. I didn't need any more phone calls to tell me what would happen.

They had put Joachim in his old room off the chapel. He looked up soberly as I came in. "A monster from the land of magic is heading toward Yurt," I said without preamble.

"How close is it?" he asked quietly.

"Not close, not yet," I said, sitting down. "But if it hasn't left yet, it will be doing so shortly." I told him quickly about the strange problem with the wizard's telephone in the northern mountains, the phone which could make only one call a day.

"I should have realized then that it had been deliberately broken," I said. "And I should have insisted that it be fixed. Someone summoned a dragon earlier today, but without using a particularly powerful spell. The wizard up there turned it back, but because he then called the wizards' school to tell them about it, he won't be able to make any other calls for another twenty-four hours. In that time, anything else could—and surely will—come over the border, without his being able to give warning."

"How long will it take the monster to reach us?"

I noticed that Joachim was gripping his crucifix. "That's not going to be very useful," I said. "I know I've explained this to you before: the forces of wild magic are *not* the powers of darkness."

"And I have explained to you before," he said with a lift of one eyebrow, "that there is plenty of evil in the world that is not embodied in demons."

He was right, of course, but this seemed to me a situation where magic was going to have to be opposed by magic. "It's at least three thousand miles up to the edge of the land of magic," I said. "It took us a week in the air cart, although I'm sure a monster could fly far faster than that. I presume it will reach here sometime tomorrow."

"If it indeed is heading for Yurt," said Joachim, and I knew he was thinking of his cathedral.

"You've left your church well protected. Besides the king of Caelrhon and various knights, you've got Vor and his workmen."

"We're even better protected here," said Joachim. "You're an excellent wizard." I didn't have the heart to tell him he was wrong.

"Well," I said, "we'd been guessing something like this would happen. Maybe we should just be glad we were right. Do you think we should have them cancel Paul's coming of age ceremonies?"

Joachim shook his head. "Your renegade wizard seems to have excellent information on what's happening in Yurt and Caelrhon. If we hide, he will too. We have to get him out into the open."

I stood up. "I'm going back to my room to work on my spells. If you're working on your prayers this evening, pray for me."

III

The castle was up at dawn on a beautiful late summer day. I had only dozed fitfully after finally putting away my books. I walked out over the drawbridge for a look at the northern sky.

The grass was damp with drops of dew glinting in the rising sun. Bird songs reached me from the meadows and the woods below the hill. The knights' tents were still quiet, but I saw smoke starting to rise from the Romneys' camp. The clear sky was absolutely empty, and the fresh air seemed to promise a morning in which nothing evil could possibly happen.

When I walked back inside a few minutes later, the courtyard had already filled with lords and ladies, dressed in their best finery and talking excitedly. The frantic preparations the constable and his men had been making the last few days seemed to pay off. Soon we all found ourselves eased unobtrusively into rows according to our stations. Gwennie, the constable's daughter, grown-up and formal in blue and white starched livery, helped arrange us.

I caught Theodora's eye and smiled. Regal in lilac silk, she was attracting both curious and admiring glances.

A clear passage was left down the center of the courtyard. Talking died away as two men came out from the great hall, unrolling a long red carpet. They stretched it out through the gates and over the drawbridge, then onto the hilltop beyond. The castle's brass choir began to play, clear, bright notes, a song of triumph and joy.

And then Paul appeared. He had come down the narrow stairs from the chapel and through the great hall and now, following the red carpet, he stepped into the courtyard. He wore blue and white velvet and had a white velvet cap on his golden hair. He looked straight ahead as he walked. The brass choir continued to play, but the only other sound was the clinking of the silver spurs on his heels.

As he walked out through the gates, the rest of us moved forward to follow. A clear space had been left on the hilltop, between the drawbridge and the knights' tents. Here the constable's men had brought the throne from the great hall. Paul stood beside it, leaning on the arm, looking toward all of us and not quite seeing us.

We wizards do not have public ceremonies, coronations or enthronements, celebrations of critical turning points in one's life. When our lives changed, as mine irrevocably had, it was due to more private events.

The last notes of the processional faded away, then the members of the brass choir hurried to join the rest of us in a respectful semicircle around Paul and the queen. The greatest lords, including the royal family of Caelrhon, were at the front, with the rest of the guests and the royal staff behind them. The Romneys, I noticed, were standing in front of their caravans a little way down the hill, watching attentively.

"My people!" said the queen. Her voice and the calls of birds were the only sounds. Even the Romney children, clustered around their parents, were wide-eyed and silent. "For six years I have served as regent of Yurt. It is now time to turn that rule over to your new king. Prince Paul, my son and the son of your late King Haimeric, is eighteen today. Today he comes of age, and today he shall be king!"

Surreptitiously I again looked toward the north. If my calculations were right, we might still have a few hours of safety. Joachim stood calmly on the far side of the crowd, surrounded by the chaplains and priests whom several of our guests had brought with them.

"I swear," the queen continued, "that he is King Haimeric's son, born to be king. You all have grown to know him well, and, I hope, to love him." The queen, all in red, looked radiant. The golden circle of her crown glinted in her midnight hair. Most of the guests were looking toward Paul, but Vincent, I noticed, had his eyes fixed on her. "Do you all agree that he should be your king, to lead you in war, to lead you in peace, to lead you in wisdom and judgment?"

"We agree." "We agree." "We agree." The murmur went quickly through the crowd. Only the priests said nothing. The Church was not under the authority of kings, and therefore could not agree or disagree to their coronations. I wasn't sure of the official status of wizards here, but I certainly agreed that Paul should be king.

"Then come forward, Paul, to receive the crown of Yurt!"

He came slowly forward, pulling off his cap, and went down on one knee before his mother. The great royal crown of Yurt sat on a stand beside her. It was plain hammered gold except for the diamond set into the front.

The queen was speaking again, describing the duties of rule, but I had trouble concentrating on what she said. The disruption of the telephones, I thought, might all be a ruse, and whatever was going to attack us might not now be flying down from the north, but might instead already be here.

I knew that the gorgos who appeared at the old bishop's funeral had not just flown south that morning, for it had already been seen earlier. In the intervening time it must have been in or near Caelrhon, under a powerful binding spell, waiting to be released. What might already be here in Yurt?

I started delicately probing for magic and was so surprised I almost cried out when I found it at once. There was another magic-worker here, neither me nor Theodora. But then I realized it was only the old magician. I spotted him for the first time, standing with the Romneys, his squinting eyes almost the only part of his face visible behind his thick beard. He appeared a little less ragged than when I had seen him last; I guessed his jacket came from the Romneys. He looked in my direction as I looked in his, and, although I could not be sure at this distance, his look seemed venomous.

A spy for the renegade wizard, I thought with abrupt certainty. He had been sent here by his master to watch for the best moment to attack.

The queen had finished the formal recital of a king's responsibilities. Paul gave the formal acceptance of those responsibilities, although in so low a voice it was hard to catch the words. The queen then lifted the heavy gold crown and placed it on her son's head to the accompaniment of a flourish from the brass. "Rise then, King Paul, ruler of Yurt!"

He rose slowly, with a dignity appropriate for someone three times his age. He held both arms straight out for a moment, a silver sword in one hand and the royal sceptre in another. Then he mounted his throne and turned to look toward all of us. "With the aid of God and with your counsel," he said, in a voice clear but just a little higher than he might have wished, "I swear that I shall guard you, lead you, and rule you justly. Come forward, then, my people, to renew your allegiance to the crown of Yurt."

For the next hour, the lords and knights of Yurt came forward one by one. Each knelt before the throne and recited the fairly long oath of allegiance to their king, holding up their clasped hands to Paul. When each had finished, he put his hands around theirs, drew them up, and kissed them on both cheeks. He then presented each with a small box tied with blue ribbons. The men received silver belt buckles, and the few women, such as the duchess, who ruled in their own right received silver brooches.

The servants had melted back into the castle at the beginning of this part of the ceremony. The rest of us who did not swear formal allegiance to the king of Yurt, that is the priests, the royal family of Caelrhon, and I, stood together at one side, watching. Although as the first of the lords came forward there was absolute stillness for the oaths, as the hour went by people started talking in low voices. Delicious smells began to waft out from the castle toward us.

When the last knight had given his oath, the constable brought out a portable altar, and all talking ceased. Joachim took his place behind the altar, the constable's men passed out hymn books, and we all gave thanks to God and prayers for the health and long life of our king while the sun continued to climb in a cloudless sky—a sky still free of monsters.

At the end of the service, Paul again stepped forward. As though realizing only now that everything had gone smoothly and that he was indeed king of Yurt, he broke into his first smile of the day. "My people! I thank you again for all being here for my coming of age and coronation. I thank you for your allegiance and for your prayers. And now I would like to invite you all to the feast!"

There was applause as the guests moved toward the bridge and the castle. So far, I thought, so good. I just wondered how long our reprieve would last.

In the great hall, long trestle tables had been set up and spread with white linen cloths. I ended up at the high table, next to Paul's Aunt Maria, as I had eaten so many meals in Yurt over the years. The queen's parents faced me on the other side. Paul now sat at the head of the table, with the bishop in the seat of honor to his right, while the queen sat at the foot. The new king took off his heavy crown and set it beside his plate while the servants hurried up and down with the heaping platters. I spotted Theodora at a side table, surrounded by lords of manors and their ladies. Laughter drifted in from the courtyard, where Paul, in the spirit of hospitality, had insisted that the constable set up tables even for our unexpected guests, the Romneys.

Though there was no sign yet of trouble, I almost wished that whatever would happen would start at once, to break the tension. However, no one else appeared apprehensive. Joachim attentively followed the conversation at his end of the table, and Paul had gone from being solemn to being almost boisterous, making jokes, telling stories from his youth, and eating as if ravenous.

"It was so beautiful," said the Lady Maria at my elbow, "that I'm not ashamed to tell you the tears ran down my cheeks." I realized with a start that she had been speaking for several minutes.

The meal continued to progress in spite of my fears, with new courses, musical interludes from the brass choir, a display of tumbling by several of the Romneys, and happy conversation by everyone but me. After the trout, after the chicken, after the roast lamb, after the salads and custards and savory sausage and pies, when the servants had stopped bringing out new bottles of wine and the level of the ones on the table stopped receding about three-quarters of the way down, Paul stood up.

He waited a moment to give the conversation a chance to fade, then called for the cook to come forward. Pushed by her kitchen maids she came toward the head table, embarrassed, laughing, and highly pleased. Paul thanked her for the meal and kissed her to general applause. He then called on the constable to come receive congratulations for organizing everything so well, and issued a general thanks to all the staff.

"And now," he continued as the applause died away, "I would like to announce what you have all been anticipating: this afternoon's tournament. We will have horse races, jousting, mock battles, and trials of skill on horseback. To give you all time to prepare your horses and armor—and to digest this excellent dinner!—the tournament shall begin in three hours. Listen for the trumpet's note that will announce its beginning."

People slowly started rising from their chairs as general conversation started again. I, however, started at once for the drawbridge. If I kept my eyes on the sky, no dragon should appear without warning. I wondered if Zahlfast would come if I pleaded with him, or if it would be too late by the time he arrived. As I reached the doorway I spotted Theodora across the room, frowning in my direction, and nodded at her encouragingly.

But then I realized that all conversation throughout the great hall had abruptly ceased. All the lords and ladies stared toward me, even Paul and the queen. Their expressions were disconcerted, even worried.

They all knew, then, I thought, feeling my ears go red. No chance now to slip away unobtrusively. Somehow word had gotten around the hall that a magical attack was planned for today, and yet the Royal Wizard did not know how to deal with it. When the floor refused to swallow me I bowed stiffly to the crowd, who now seemed to be looking past my shoulder, and backed toward the door.

The duchess broke the silence. She gave a great laugh and slapped the table before her. "Well, Wizard!" she called. "You've done some wonderful illusions for us in the past, but these are the best yet!"

I felt a prickling as all the hair on the back of my neck stood on end. I whirled around and saw them, and knew what I had been expecting all day had begun at last. These were no illusions. Peering into the great hall from the courtyard were creatures like lizards, but far bigger than lizards and bright red. They crept on their bellies with the front halves of their bodies arched upwards, because instead of forefeet they had human hands.

IV

They saw me looking at them, and the one in the lead spread its red wings and began to hiss. I started desperately on a paralysis spell. It had been useless against the gorgos, but these were smaller creatures. After only two seconds, before I had the spell more than half assembled, they disappeared with a bright flash.

I darted out into the courtyard, gritting my teeth, and threw Theodora's spell to reveal the invisible into the spot where they had been creeping.

They reappeared just as abruptly as they had disappeared, closer to me than I had expected. I backed away cautiously. Their clawed hands looked powerful enough to take me apart.

I put together the final words of the Hidden Language, and the creatures all froze. I hesitated, suspecting a trick, but they were as still as stone. I probed carefully and found them trapped within my paralysis spell as though frozen in ice. Wings, scales, claws, and eyes were still and silent. Without the will or ability to move, inside my paralysis spell they could do no more than breathe.

I passed my hand over my forehead. "That was too easy," I thought. Laughter and clapping came from the great hall behind me, but I paid no attention. If a renegade wizard was planning a massive attack on Yurt, he should be able to do more than this. Might all this be an effort to lull me into a false sense of security while the real attack was prepared?

And then, abruptly, the Romney children were all around me. The oldest boy looked at me with admiration in his black eyes. "Did you make them? How do you make them move? Are they going to start moving again?" To my alarm, some of the younger children were now among the creatures, feeling their rough scales and tugging at their wings.

"I wouldn't do that," I said. "They're paralyzed now, but I can't guarantee they won't wake up. Have a look at the claws."

But my paralysis spell held. "I hadn't realized you could do real magic as well as illusions!" the boy continued.

The Romney woman with the gold teeth hurried toward us. She started shooing the children away in what

I thought justifiable concern. I reached into my pocket and found I still was carrying the gold earring I had picked up at the beginning of the summer. I held it out on my palm. "Does this belong to any of you?"

The younger Romneys, who had started moving across the drawbridge and toward the caravans, returned to cluster around me. One of the younger girls gave a squeal of delight. She flipped back black curls to show that the two earrings she was wearing were not a pair: one was a gold hoop, like the earring in my hand, but the other a simple silver stud.

I gave her back her earring to the approving shouts of the other children. Before they could all move off again, I took the older boy by the arm. "I didn't make the lizards," I told him. "I've only paralyzed them. Have you seen someone else do magic like this?" The renegade wizard, I thought, must be very close, but he was shielding his mind from me as effectively as ever.

"Of course not," the boy said in surprise. "Thanks for the demonstration!"

The other children, led by the girl with the earring, were now running back toward the caravans. "Before you go," I said to the Romney woman, "I want to tell you something."

She turned good-natured black eyes on me. "Those were the earrings she got at her naming ceremony when she was four, and she's been devastated since she lost the one."

But I was not about to be distracted by earrings. "Do you remember you told me my fortune? You told me I would meet someone beautiful and mysterious and would fall deeply in love. I wanted to tell you that you were right."

She gave a gratified smile before hurrying after the children. I turned back to the lizards.

At the moment they still seemed paralyzed, but a wizard with the powerful magic to summon them would be able to break my spell. I lifted them magically, one at a time, and carried them across the drawbridge and out onto the grass. Several lords and ladies clustered in the courtyard, watching. Opinion seemed divided on whether the lizards might be a threat or were merely part of the planned entertainment.

I had to call the school. If they could send the air cart, I might be able to ship the lizards to the City, out of the wizard's range, and where teachers with more powerful magic than mine could put long-lasting binding spells on them. I pushed through the crowd, ignoring all questions, until I found Theodora.

"Watch them," I said. "If they start to move, even the slightest twitch, call me at once. And try again to find that wizard." She looked at me with amethyst eyes wide. "Yes, they must be the same creatures you've seen when you wear your ring."

A moment later I was connected to the wizards' school. A very young wizard, no more, I guessed, than a second-year student, appeared in the glass base of the telephone. "No, Zahlfast isn't here. And the Master isn't either. In fact," in a frightened rush, "there's no one here at all. All the teachers left."

"They left?" I said incredulously.

"They left last night. I don't know where they went, but they seemed very worried. All they told us was to keep reviewing our lessons and working on our spells until they came back."

"Well, if they get back soon, have Zahlfast call me," I mumbled.

This was terrible. What could possibly have caused all the teachers to leave the school? All I could think was that the wizard had a much larger and better coordinated plan in place for today than I could possibly have imagined. I would certainly receive no help from the school, nor was I in any position to help them.

My heart pounding, I ran back outside. There was

no change yet in the lizards. Theodora gave me what was probably meant to be a smile of encouragement. My own answering smile wasn't any better.

"How did they get here?" she asked quietly.

"I wish I knew. The wizard must have brought them, but I can't find him. He may even be lurking in the castle, invisible." I slapped a fist into the other hand in frustration. "How could a renegade wizard be so good at magic? I've been trying to find him since I first heard of the problems the cathedral was having, way back in the spring, but he's been hiding from me as effectively as if he didn't even exist!"

"I'll look for him," said Theodora. "If I put on my ring of invisibility, I should be able to see what is concealed."

"And send that old magician out here too," I said. "He probably trusts you, since you taught him fire magic. Just don't mention that I'm going to take him apart if I find out he's been spying on me for the wizard."

As she hurried away, I decided that as long as I was effectively trapped here with the lizards, I ought to talk to Vincent. "Paul!" I called, seeing him standing with some of the knights, and motioned him toward me with a jerk of my head.

Then I remembered. All summer I had been trying to remind myself that he would shortly be king and that I should treat him accordingly. Now that he was king I was back to treating him like a boy.

He came over, not seeming to mind my inappropriate summons and flushed with high excitement. He still wore his blue and white velvet.

"Excuse me, sire," I said, trying to speak formally to make up for my lapse. A very quick smile crossed his face; I had never called him "sire" before. "The wizard who attacked the cathedral sent these giant lizards. I've been able to paralyze them, but I don't know how long I'll be able to maintain the spell if he tries to free them."

"We could use them as targets in the tournament," Paul suggested.

It was an appealing idea, but I didn't like the thought of the lizards coming suddenly back to life directly under a horse's hooves—maybe the hooves of the king's horse.

"I haven't had a chance to talk to Prince Vincent," I went on. "Do you know if Lucas has been able to find out anything from his brother?"

"Not that he's told me."

"Could you find Vincent and ask him to come here? If he *is* working with a renegade magic-worker, he may be planning far worse."

"Vincent himself told us that wizards have ways to make someone reveal all their secrets!" said the king with a grin. "I'll get him. And I have faith in you to stop whatever's coming."

I didn't remind him that the gorgos had very nearly killed me, and I had only been able to overcome it with a spell that was not supposed to work.

Vincent came out of the castle a few minutes later, already dressed in the padded linen shirt and trousers he would wear under his armor. Even without his finery, he walked with the grace and assurance of a prince—or, I thought, of a man who planned very soon to be king.

He poked a finger into the side of a motionless lizard. "Monsters don't stand much of a chance with you, do they, Wizard! I still remember how you knocked my sword out of my hand when I tried to tease you. I could have warned these creatures to stay away. Where did they come from, anyway?"

But I was not to be distracted. "I think you know more, Vincent," I replied sternly, "than you've cared to say about them."

He took a step backwards. "I? I know nothing about them!" He was so obviously staggered that it was hard not to believe him. However, I was successful in doing so.

"They were summoned by a wizard," I said shortly, "with whom you have been plotting to overthrow both the Church and organized wizardry and, incidentally, to seize the kingdom of Yurt for yourself."

Vincent stared at me with a complete lack of comprehension. Then he shook his head, as though not sure whether he should smile, and sat down, his arms resting on his knees and his hands hanging loose. I remained standing. It seemed I had spent much of the summer accusing people of sinister plots.

But I got a very different reaction from Vincent than I had from his brother. "Paul's been trying to tell you that you stand in the way of his real development as a king, is that it, Wizard?" he asked sympathetically. "Believe me, I never intended to turn him against you personally."

"Then what did you intend?" I demanded.

"Sit down," he said, gesturing. "We can talk more easily. Lucas came back from your trip to the land of magic all full of accusations about how I was plotting against everybody—him especially—but I hadn't expected you to believe it too."

I hesitated, then sat down beside him. The midday sun was bright on our heads and made his copper hair gleam. The lizards, frozen in positions of attack with their clawed hands upraised, stood before us.

"Sometime this winter," Vincent said, "our late wizard started playing on Lucas, telling him that there was no longer room for courage and character in the western kingdoms, because the wizards and priests between them had ended most wars and adventures. Lucas has always been worried, you see, that he was going to grow old, like Father, without ever having done anything. I myself was not so sure that the old wars were ever as glorious as they seem in the legends, but I knew better than to try to tell my brother that."

He had been staring at the lizards as he spoke, but now he turned to look at me. "One thing did seem strange, that our wizard seemed to be trying to discredit the wizards' school, pointing out such things as that there were now wizards in more and more courts, and talking about a plot to wrest control from the kings. It didn't make any sense to me for someone I knew had graduated from the school."

It didn't make any sense to me either. I remained silent and let Vincent continue.

"I guess I just never took him seriously—or I felt that if princes should distrust wizards, I would start by distrusting *him*. Then he died, of course, which made it all moot. But it certainly made a good story, and I must admit I told it to your Prince Paul."

I gave Vincent my wizardly glare, but he was looking away. As he sat here, talking in a half-amused, half-apologetic manner, I thought that, if he were not planning to marry the queen and murder Paul, I would find myself liking him quite a bit. "Paul believed you," I said.

He smiled ruefully. "That's your real problem, isn't it, Wizard." It wasn't, but I did not answer. "I'd been trying all spring to win his friendship, and it occurred to me that to give him a share in a secret, something we princes could work against together, might make him a little less distant toward me."

"You bought his friendship with the red roan stallion."

Vincent chuckled. "Come on, Wizard. You and I don't need to be rivals for Paul's affection." We had actually been rivals for the queen's affection. This conversation was getting more confused by the moment. "And I wouldn't say I 'bought' his friendship. I knew he wanted a red stallion, and when the Romneys had the horse for sale I thought I'd better buy it at once. There can't be many others like it. They knew it too—they certainly charged enough! I'd also thought, of course, that Paul was a little timid and deferential for someone who was going to be king so soon, and that if I said a few things to make him rely on himself rather than others' counsel it might help a bit. But from what Lucas told me, your trip up north did much more for him than my hints and suggestions ever could!"

Ever since Joachim first telephoned me at the wizards' school, to tell me there were twinkling lights at night on his new tower, I had been creating and disposing of a long series of theories to account for the events in Caelrhon and Yurt. Long after I knew that the original problem had been Theodora practicing climbing and fire magic at the same time, new crises and diabolical plots kept appearing. The only two points on which I was now firm was that a renegade wizard, who hated the Church, had brought a gorgos to the cathedral city, and that Vincent was trying to seize Yurt for himself.

A quick glance at the sky still revealed no dragons. "I want to ask you about that stallion," I said.

Vincent gave me a look of genuine amusement. "Lucas told me you thought the horse was a trap. It's an intriguing theory, but it's certainly not true."

"Where did the Romneys get the stallion?"

He shrugged. "You don't ask horse-traders where they get their horses. But the Romneys are right here if you want to try."

I was not yet ready to give up my suspicions of him. "If you didn't intend the horse as a trap," I asked, "how were you planning to murder Paul?"

Vincent jumped to his feet. Shock, fury, and then incredulity passed across his face in a series of waves of white and red. I saw him ready to attack me, then remember both that he was unarmed and that a sword wouldn't do much good anyway. Very slowly, he sat down again, staring at me. "Are you serious?"

It was exactly what I would have expected him to do if I was wrong. "How else did you plan to become king of Yurt?"

Both of us sat in silence for a moment, trying to sort out our thoughts. Vincent continued to stare. Below us, the constable's men were finishing preparing the lists for the tournament. A number of the knights already had their armor on and were walking back and forth between the tents, showing off for each other. The horrible certainty that I had just created a diplomatic crisis between Yurt and Caelrhon grew on me.

V

"Well," said Vincent after a minute, "maybe I had that coming, for spreading rumors about a wizardly plot against princes. But I do want to reassure you I never intended to be king of Yurt."

"Then why are you marrying my queen?" I demanded.

"Because I love her, of course," said Vincent with a smile. "I know you wizards never marry, so you probably haven't noticed, but she's the most beautiful and the most delightful and desirable woman in the western kingdoms."

The one positive thing I might be able to salvage from this conversation was the knowledge that the queen had never told Vincent about my proposal to her.

"I hope you appreciate how ironic this is," said Vincent. "My brother is terrified that when I marry your queen, Yurt may make it an excuse to take over Caelrhon. And now I find out that you have been expecting the exact opposite!"

I felt I ought to apologize but didn't know what to say.

"Look, Wizard," Vincent went on. "Let's be reasonable about this. The queen and I both want you to stay on as Royal Wizard after we're married, and I'm certain Paul really does too, even if I may have inadvertently turned him against you for the moment. When you were off at the school this spring, the queen wondered whether she might have to get a new wizard if you ended up staying there, but she also told me she hoped that you'd be back. So let's forget all this and forgive each other. All right?"

He started to rise, taking my agreement for granted, but I was not through with him yet. "A wizard brought a gorgos to the cathedral city last month, and brought these creatures here today. What do you know about him?"

He paused on one knee. "I don't know anything about this. Lucas refused to hire a new wizard after Sengrim's death, and the only other magic-worker I've spoken to since then is you." He stood up. "Now, if you'll excuse me, I really do need to get my armor on."

Without waiting for an answer, he started back toward the bridge into the castle, whistling. Just before he reached the bridge, I called him back. "Prince Vincent!"

He turned back slowly but not, I thought, particularly grudgingly. If I had been a prince instead of a wizard, I really would have wanted to be just like him. "Can it wait?"

"I have a quick favor to ask you." He came back and stood before me, hands on his hips. "Could you see if you could find the Romney from whom you bought the horse? Even though"—I just barely kept myself from phrasing it as "Even if "—"you have no plots against Paul, it's possible someone else does."

He shrugged. "All right. But I don't want to be late for the tournament!" He went off through the tents, greeting the knights and joking with them as he went. In a few moments, I saw him reemerge from beyond the tents and this time go directly into the castle. At least, I thought, I had not actually created a diplomatic rift between the twin kingdoms.

A Romney man walked slowly toward me, not uncertainly but as though he wanted me to realize that he moved at his own pace, not mine. I swallowed my impatience and waited.

He sat down next to me and adjusted his red kerchief. "A lot of the knights of Caelrhon have horses they bought from me," he said casually. "Were you thinking of buying one yourself? I'm afraid we don't have much with us right now, but I could find you a good steed by next week."

I had to admire the Romney's ability to turn any opportunity into a potential sale. "I wanted to ask you about the red roan stallion you sold Prince Vincent at the beginning of the summer," I answered. "I might want one like that—no ordinary horse for a wizard!"

He gave me a shrewd look from intensely black eyes. Neither one of us believed for a minute the talk about buying a horse. "It might be hard to find one just like that," he said. "Horses that good are scarce, as you realize. I might be able to have one in a few weeks. If you gave me a down payment now, it might make the search easier."

I abandoned the pretense of wanting a horse like Paul's. "You got that horse from a wizard, didn't you."

He looked at me in apparent disappointment, though I wasn't sure if he was disappointed at losing a sale or just at cutting our sparring short. "Well, I did," he admitted, "though I trained the horse myself. A beautiful animal it was when I got it, but wild."

"Have you seen the wizard at all recently? Might he be bringing more horses from wherever he got that one?"

He shook his head, almost imperceptibly. "I haven't seen him in months. Though of course I didn't tell him I'd buy anything he found, I think he realizes I would if they were like that stallion."

Vor, Norbert, and the Romneys had all been able to see this wizard—why couldn't I? And, I thought with a surge of jealousy, he must have an air cart of his own, to be able to transport horses from the borderlands. If I was somehow able to overcome him maybe I could have it for my own.

But this was an unprofitable line of thought. Much more

pressing was whether the horse might still be a trap, though to be triggered by the wizard himself, not by Vincent. "Thank you for the information," I said. "Do let me know if you have any horses like the red stallion again."

The Romney man returned to his caravans without pressing the issue of a down payment. At the bottom of the hill, ladies and attendants were already trying to find the best seats in the stands.

The chief outcome of my conversations was that I knew I had to find the wizard. But I seemed no closer to doing so. He must be here, but he was still thoroughly concealed. I realized uneasily that it had been some time since Theodora had gone to look for him. . . .

A trumpeter appeared in the lists below. Lifting the horn to his lips, he blew a single long blast, then began a lively tune with the rhythm of horses galloping. To general shouts, the knights around the tents mounted their horses. Paul came out of the castle, riding Bonfire. His new armor shone like silver, and he carried a plumed helmet in one crooked arm. For the tournament all weapons were to be blunted. Only the new king himself wore a real sword.

He was halfway down the hill when Vincent came out of the castle, pushing his horse to a trot. He waved as he went by. I had already seen Lucas going down, riding easily with no sign of pain from his ankle. A number of the castle staff, young Gwennie among them, hurried to join the lords and ladies in the audience.

In a few minutes the tournament was under way. The Romneys stood on the sidelines. From where I sat with the lizards, I had a clear view of the sky. I kept looking and kept seeing nothing but birds.

I heard a step beside me, jumped, and turned to see Joachim. He regarded the lizards curiously for a minute, then sat down on the grass beside me, arranging his robes around him.

For a second I considered ordering him back into the safety of the castle, bishop or no bishop, then realized he was probably deliberately making himself visible in order to bring on a wizardly attack. "These are the creatures that were moving stones around on your new tower," I told him. "They can't do any harm now, as long as they're paralyzed, but if I leave them the wizard will probably break my spell at once."

In the field below the castle's hill the first event began, a horse race. I noted that Paul had had the good taste not to participate; Bonfire could easily have outrun any horse there.

"I've just talked to Prince Vincent. I'd believed all summer that he and a renegade wizard were planning a joint attack, but I realize now that this belief wasn't the product of wizardly insights, only of jealousy. Everything I saw as signs of a despicable plot—the way he and the queen behaved toward each other, the fact that Yurt and Caelrhon were once one kingdom, even Vincent's gift of a stallion to Paul—had a simpler and more innocent explanation. All my suspicions were so incomprehensible to Vincent that he decided I must in fact fear he would turn the young king against *me.* He forgave me. But while I've been wasting my time worrying about an attack on the queen and on Paul, the wizard may be doing something horrible down in the City."

I told him about the mass exodus of the teachers from the school. Joachim nodded slowly. "But these lizards show he's not ignoring Yurt," he said. "He may be attacking on two fronts."

The wind cut silver paths through the long grass on the castle's hill and the fields below. The area of the tournament was already becoming trampled and muddy.

"But where is he?" I burst out. "Is this all? If he's here, what will he do next?"

The knights in the tournament lists were now preparing for the tests of skill; mounted men would gallop at top speed toward a ring dangling from a thread and try to thrust their lances through it.

"Theodora's looking for him," I added, then stopped, realizing that I couldn't tell him more without revealing that she was a witch.

"I was glad to have a chance to talk to her yesterday while we were riding," said Joachim. "At first she seemed shy of me, almost awestruck. I had hoped that if I became bishop I could make people realize that bishops are not like princes, men of authority and command. Rather, we are shepherds, sinners ourselves but chosen by God to help and guide other sinners. But I've been bishop for over a week, and I'm still being treated as a lord of men."

This was much too complicated to try to explain to him now. Shouts from the base of the hill showed that one of the riders was doing very well; it appeared to be Vincent.

"Theodora reminds me somewhat of you," Joachim continued, "especially you twenty years ago, when I first knew you. You both have the same sense of humor, where it's often difficult to tell if you're making a joke or not." Normally I would have been afire with curiosity to know if they had talked about me, and what they had said, but now I was too worried to care.

"What's my priest doing?" said Joachim in quite a different tone. I looked down toward some of the spectators milling around at the edge of the lists. The young priest who had come with the bishop was in the middle of a crowd of Romneys. I didn't know what it looked like to Joachim, but to me it looked like he was placing a bet.

"Maybe I should go down there for a little while anyway," said the bishop. "I cannot approve of battles, even mock battles, but I do not want to appear to be avoiding the festivities deliberately." He brushed himself off and walked quickly down the hill.

I watched him go, feeling increasingly uneasy about Theodora. But then I saw a dark lilac dress approaching rapidly from the direction of the deserted Romney caravans. At the same time a servant in Yurt's blue and white livery shot out of the castle and over the bridge. He was running and reached me before she did.

"Come right away!" he cried. "It's a telephone call from—from someone named Zahlfast! He said he must talk to you at once, about the safety of the wizards' school!"

"Theodora!" I shouted to her, jumping up. "Stay here and watch these lizards!"

"Wait! I have to tell you—"

"Tell me when I get back." I flew straight up and over the castle wall, the quicker to reach the telephone.

PART NINE

Renegade

I

Zahlfast's face looked as haggard as I had ever seen it, and he breathed hard. He stared at me blindly; he must be calling from a telephone without a far-seeing attachment.

"Thank you," he said. "I wanted to tell you we got the warning in time."

"What warning?" I appreciated the thanks but I had no idea what he was talking about.

"When I got back to the school from dinner last evening, the young wizard relayed your message that the phone in the watch-station up in the borderlands was broken. That fool hadn't told us, of course," meaning good old Book-Leech. "Instead he thought he'd try to fix it himself, though he's not competent to do so."

Zahlfast paused, then continued in something closer to his normal schoolteacher tone. "Maybe we should make a series of courses in technical magic a required part of the curriculum, rather than an elective option. Because I've never found that kind of magic congenial myself, I'm afraid I haven't pushed for it, but in modern times all young wizards really should know modern magic."

"But what's happened?" I demanded. "Where are you?"

"I'm not sure. We're in the royal castle of—" Someone behind him provided a name. "I think we're about a thousand miles north of the City."

"You and all the teachers?"

"Just three of us are here; the rest are spread out over hundreds of miles. It didn't take us long, once we'd heard that something was wrong with the phone at the watch-station, to guess that the weak attempt of a very small dragon to fly south was a feint and that something much worse would soon follow. So we tried to telephone to the watch-station at once—and got through. We could always phone *him*, which was why we hadn't realized there was a problem."

Zahlfast wiped the sweat off his brow. I almost danced with impatience. "As I'm sure you already guessed," he went on, "a whole horde of dragons had just flown up over the mountains and started south. Maybe a hundred of them."

I froze in horror. This was even worse than I expected. "Were they heading for Yurt?"

"No. They were heading for the City."

"And that's why all the teachers went."

"The dragons scattered when they met us," Zahlfast continued. "One *did* come close to Yurt—it was finally killed a quarter mile from the cathedral city of Caelrhon."

Then those waiting to protect Joachim's cathedral from danger had seen something worth waiting for. I paused. "All of you overcame them all, I assume?"

"Well, yes," said Zahlfast, with a flicker of a smile. "Otherwise, I wouldn't be talking to you. Thank you again."

"Wait, before you hang up! I have to ask you something. This spring when I left the school, you gave me a warning. You said that priests hated and feared the wizards and sought to destroy them. I know we've never gotten along well with the Church, but this was different. You were trying to keep me out of the affairs of the cathedral of Caelrhon. You have to tell me: had Sengrim, the Royal Wizard of Caelrhon, given you that warning before he died?"

"Yes, he did," said Zahlfast in surprise.

"He must have had an apprentice," I said grimly, "someone none of us even knew existed. Find him. He might be here in Yurt, or he could be anywhere. He's the one who disabled the telephone, and he's the one who summoned the dragons."

For one of the few times since I'd known him, Zahlfast looked shocked. I hung up and ran back outside. Even if the hundred dragons had not been successful in destroying Yurt or the school—or both—they had effectively kept me from having any help here from another wizard for at least another day.

Theodora waited by the motionless lizards. I had grown to despise the sight of them. "Come on," I said. "I'm going down to the tournament grounds to make an announcement. Thank God, the worst that I'd feared is not going to happen."

"Daimbert, listen to me," she said desperately.

"Tell me in a minute. The bishop and Paul and probably a lot of the others know I've been expecting an attack of dragons or worse, and I have to reassure them it won't happen."

The knights had now finished riding at the ring and had begun the jousts, the heart of the tournament. One joust had just ended; neither rider had been unhorsed, and they were waiting for the judges' decision. The queen came up to me with a rather quizzical smile as we reached the lists. "Vincent's been telling me about a very odd conversation the two of you had," she began.

But I couldn't take time to listen to her right now any more than I could listen to Theodora. "I have an announcement!" I called, then realized no one could hear me. There was a spell to amplify one's voice; it took me a moment to find and apply it. "I have an announcement!" I tried again.

This time my voice boomed out gratifyingly loudly. The queen and Theodora, who had been standing on either side of me, both took a quick step back. The riders readying themselves for the next jousts had trouble reining in their startled horses.

"I've just been talking to the wizards' school," I said to a rapt audience, "and I wanted to tell you all that an attack on Yurt has just been averted!" It was in fact an attack on the school instead, but I didn't have time to go into detail. "A hundred dragons were summoned from the land of magic by an evil wizard. But the masters of the school were able to overcome them all."

There was a rapid buzz of conversation at this unexpected announcement. The bishop looked as though he had known all along that I was an excellent wizard. The riders, including Paul on his red stallion, had their mounts under control again. The young king settled his plumed helmet over his head.

"Daimbert, you must listen!" Theodora tried again. I turned toward her. "I've found the wizard. He's right here. He's been hiding from both of us."

The pit of my stomach felt as though it had turned to ice. I grabbed her by the shoulders and turned her toward me. "Where? Where is he?"

"We should have known!" she cried in despair. "The old magician, the man we never worried about. He's the wizard in disguise!"

He had been hiding right under my nose. And I had just told him, as well as everybody else, that his most elaborate plot had failed.

"But where—" I needn't have asked. There was a crack and a flash like lightning, a burst of blue smoke, and he appeared directly before me.

The wizard's disguise of ragged robes and heavy eyebrows were gone. His white beard whipped in the wind from his spell. And I recognized him now, the renegade who had eluded me for months. It was Sengrim, the wizard everyone had thought was dead.

Theodora and the queen retreated rapidly in opposite directions. Behind the wizard I could see several horses rearing straight up at the smoke and lightning. For a second even Sengrim was unimportant. Paul's stallion had reared higher than any other horse and was going over backwards. But before I could seize him with a lifting spell, Prince Vincent had leaped forward to grab the dangling reins. With a sharp tug at the head, he steadied the stallion enough that Bonfire was able to find his balance and come back down safely. The king kicked his feet free of the stirrups and sprang off, and he and Vincent gave each other triumphant slaps on the back.

I swung my attention back to the wizard before me. "So you think you and your school are safe now, Daimbert," said Sengrim in cold fury. "But my magic is much stronger than yours!"

Behind me, I heard a strange hissing and honking sound. My head jerked around, and I saw that the red lizards, which I had been busily watching for hours, were now free of the paralysis spell and had started toward us.

Everyone in the lists seemed as paralyzed as the lizards had been a second ago, and for one horrible moment I thought the spell had been transferred to them. But they were not held prisoner by a spell, only by shock. They stared in horror from the lizards to the commanding figure before them.

And one person *was* moving, Paul. He had his sword out, the only real sword in the tournament. He very slowly advanced toward the wizard from behind.

I didn't dare motion toward him. All I could do was to give him a quick stare that I hoped was a warning—if he could even see it through his visor.

"You're so sure of yourself that you even tried to patronize me when we met in Caelrhon," the wizard said grimly.

"But I thought you were just an old magician!" I protested. If I could keep him talking for a few more minutes, I thought, desperately trying to put a spell together, I might have a chance.

"Can you cast a spell like this?" cried Sengrim. Where he had been standing there was suddenly not a wizard but a pillar of fire, twenty feet high. Enormous eyes glared down from the top, and an enormous laugh rang out from the flames. Paul had the sense to back up rapidly.

Sweet Jesus, he was good. I had never seen anything like this.

A tongue of flame licked toward the wooden stands where the spectators were sitting, and in two seconds they were ablaze. The paralysis broke as people screamed and struggled, trying to get out.

I abandoned the spell I had been working on and grabbed at what I could remember of Theodora's fire magic. The only calm person in the crowd seemed to be Gwennie, directing people down the steps away from the fire. In a moment I was able to reduce the level of the flames enough that everyone was able to get out of the stands, beating at their burning clothes.

They tried to run, but they could not run far. Sengrim had set up an invisible barrier around the lists, as strong as the nixie's, against which they shoved helplessly. The lizards were within that barrier and drawing dangerously close to the crowd. And then another tongue of flame came toward me and surrounded me. Protected from the blaze after two scorching seconds by Theodora's magic, I advanced toward the pillar of fire, one arm held out.

"Stop!" I cried out, in a voice amplified by magic. "We both learned wizardry at the school, and we're both sworn to help humanity!"

The pillar of fire seemed momentarily to contract, and I hoped for an instant that he was listening to me. But then I realized he was not reacting to what I had said. He was under attack by Theodora.

With another blinding flash of light, the pillar of fire was gone and the wizard was back. I realized that Theodora must have helped me put out the fire in the stands. In the five desperate seconds of breathing room which her magic gave me, I managed to cast a new paralysis spell toward the lizards. This time it held.

"So you think you've got a witch to help you," the wizard said with bitter scorn, not even bothering to break my new spell. He waved out the last of the flames with one hand. Clearly fire magic had possibilities I had not yet explored. "No woman can know *real* magic. Just one more sign of your true debility, Daimbert!"

"But what are you talking about?" I demanded. "What can you have against me?" Again, I had to keep him talking while I tried to put a complicated spell together. Figuring out what had happened, why he was even alive, would have to wait.

Almost everyone had pressed themselves against the invisible barrier, as far from the wizard as they could go, except for the queen and Theodora, who stayed rooted where they had been when the wizard first appeared, and Paul, who again began a stealthy approach from the rear.

"Brute force is no more useful against me than magic!" cried the wizard. "I know you're back there, knight!" He whirled and started firing knives toward Paul, real knives, no illusion, powered by magic. They clattered off his armor, sending him staggering back.

I gave up any hope of trapping Sengrim with a binding spell, or even of being able to oppose his spells individually. I briefly considered summoning him, regardless of whether summoning was the greatest wizardly sin, but then I would only have his deranged mind even closer to mine.

My only hope was to build around him a magic structure that would make it impossible for him to practice any magic within it. I had told Joachim, what seemed years ago, that I might have to put such a spell on their cathedral. At the time, I had had no idea how to do so; now, after spending the last week with my books, I might.

That is, if I even had a chance to finish assembling the spell. With Paul out of the way, the wizard turned his magic knives on me. The barrage went on for ten seconds, and I jettisoned my growing spell to repel them.

"Answer me!" I cried when the knives stopped coming. "I had nothing against you! Why are you so set against me?" I snatched up the remnants of the spell I had started building before it faded away completely.

"They always preferred you down at the school," the wizard said bitterly. This was better. I could listen to him and work on my spell at the same time. But Paul was starting again what I feared was a suicidal advance.

"They made you, *you*, wizard of Yurt nineteen years ago," he cried, "even though you'd barely been able to graduate, even though as wizard of Caelrhon I deserved to be transferred to the more senior kingdom and had already applied! And this spring they invited you, *you*, with your inferior magic, to the school to teach, something they've never offered me!"

I'd never known a wizard who lost his mind before. Normally I would have been interested in observing the symptoms.

"Even when you abandoned the principles of wizardry by making friends in the Church, the school refused to believe the worst about you!"

I almost had my spell together. If I could keep him talking just a few more seconds, if Paul would only stay back, if the spell even worked—

He didn't give me a chance to find out. "And you can't

even begin to match spells with me!" he cried. "Can you do this?"

He held both arms straight out, and lightning flashed from each hand. Thirty feet on either side of him, crevices in the earth opened up, opened directly beneath the queen and Theodora.

I had no time to think, only time to react. I couldn't possibly save them both. I grabbed the queen with magic and tossed her to safety.

As I flew toward the crack where Theodora had vanished, the pillar of fire reappeared, swirling with diabolical laughter. But as I dropped down the crevice I finished my spell and hurled it at him.

The crevice was some twenty feet deep. Theodora lay limp at the bottom. I snatched her up and flew out as the ground shifted with a roar and the crack slammed back shut.

I had him. Highly startled, the wizard stood within my trembling spell, his magic stripped from him. His barrier around the lists collapsed, and with it many of the people who had pressed against it. I dropped to the ground, Theodora in my arms. Her eyes were shut but she was still breathing.

"It won't work, Daimbert!" roared Sengrim. "I may not be able to work magic while I'm standing here, but I can walk right out of your spell!" And he proceeded to do so.

But he had not counted on Paul. The young king's long, stealthy advance had finally reached its goal. He sprang forward, naked sword in his hand, and thrust it with all his strength into the wizard's back.

Blood spurted over Paul's silver armor. He wrenched off his helmet; a stripe of red across his eyes showed where the blood had penetrated the visor. He slowly pulled his sword back out of the wizard's body and wiped his face with the other hand.

Clasping Theodora against me, I went to look. The wizard lay without moving. It all came back to me why I had taken Paul to the borderlands: I had wanted his sword arm between me and danger.

The flow of blood from the hole in the wizard's back slowed to a trickle and stopped. I turned him over with one foot. He flopped lifeless, his eyes open and empty. "Thank God," I said. "He's dead."

"My God," said Paul, his face under the blood completely white. "I've killed him."

II

The constable had, of course, arranged for a doctor to be present at the tournament. I dragged him away from attending to our guests. Due to good fortune and to Paul, none of the knights or spectators had been killed, although most had burns, bruises, or at least badly strained muscles. The worst off were two knights who had been less quick than Paul at getting off their spooked horses—one had cracked ribs and another had a crushed leg where his horse had rolled on him.

"She's going to be all right, I should think," the doctor said sourly, looking at Theodora lying stretched out on the queen's bed, absolutely still except for the faintest rise and fall of her chest. "She got a bad scare and a bad knock on her head, but her skull's not cracked, and I don't think her neck is broken. Sleep's the best thing for her. Now, if you'll excuse me—" He escaped back to the wounded knights before I could say anything else.

I had already flown madly around the castle's hill, ripping up whatever leaves and twigs seemed at all promising for herbal magic, and had made a poultice which I put on the bump on her head. The doctor had shaken his head at it but said nothing.

I took her hand. "Theodora," I said, both aloud and

directly to her mind. "It's me, Theodora." There was no response.

Joachim put his head in, as sober as I had ever seen him. "How is she?"

"The doctor claims she'll be all right. But I'm not so sure." I seized him by the arm. "Please, will you pray for her?"

He opened his mouth to say something but stopped. Instead he nodded.

"I know what you're thinking," I said desperately. "You heard Sengrim call her a witch. You think a witch is something evil, but it's not—it's only what wizards call women who know a little magic. She *does* know magic, a little magic, but she's not evil. You talked to her. You must know that. Please, Joachim."

He took a deep breath and eased his arm out of my grip. He looked at her for a moment, then turned his enormous dark eyes on me. "I realized all along that she knew magic," he said quietly. "I told you she reminded me of you. All I had been going to say was that I was already praying for her."

I sat down on the bed next to her. "Will you stay with us?" I asked timidly.

"I can't. Your royal chaplain has just told me that Paul's up in the chapel, lying sobbing on the floor in front of the altar. I've got to go talk to him." He was gone before I had a chance to answer.

The queen sat with me later that day, watching Theodora. It was still daylight, though it felt like the middle of the night. The rest of the festivities had been canceled. The castle around us seemed silent as a tomb.

"Her color looks a little better," said the queen, though I hadn't noticed any change myself.

"Suppose she never wakes up?"

"She will," said the queen positively, though she had no basis on which to be so positive. But I appreciated the gesture and tried to smile. "Thank you for saving us all again—especially me," she continued. But then she remembered that in saving her I had let Theodora tumble down the crevice. She became silent, rubbing absently at a bruised arm.

"How's Paul?" I asked after a moment, because staring at my clasped hands seemed fairly fruitless. "Have you talked to him?"

"Only very briefly. The bishop spoke with him at some length. He's never killed anyone before, of course—and as a mother I'd hoped he'd never have to. When I talked to him, he was both horrified that he'd killed the wizard and deeply distressed at the blow he thought he'd done to his honor by attacking him from the rear. He's asleep now—sleep can do a lot when someone is eighteen."

I spared Paul some sympathy. I had never had to kill anyone either, although I had come extremely close to my own death a few times. I wondered if the latter might even be preferable. Whatever Joachim had told Paul, it was unlikely to be that the sixth commandment did not apply in cases where a wizard had lost his mind.

Neither the queen nor I said anything more for a few minutes. I took one of Theodora's hands. It was warm and completely unresponsive.

"She is very dear to you," said the queen then. It was a statement, not a question, but I could hear the intense curiosity behind it.

"I met her in the cathedral city this summer," I said in answer to the question she had not asked. "It was after I'd briefly stopped off here, after teaching at the wizards' school—the visit when you told me you were marrying Prince Vincent."

She nodded, understanding what I had not explicitly said.

"Yes," I said, "she is very dear to me."

What had once been an elegant silk dress was now stained and tattered. I thought inconsequentially that if Theodora woke up she would find this highly irritating.

"I understand that your wizards' school doesn't want its graduates to marry," said the queen after a moment.

"That's right," I said. I saw the sympathy in her emerald eyes and considered sobbing with my head in her lap. "And not just the school. It's a tradition that goes back to the beginning of history. Wizards are supposed to be wedded to magic." I stroked Theodora's hand for a moment in silence. "Besides," I said at last, "she doesn't want to marry me."

The queen took my other hand in hers. She started to say something and changed her mind. But I knew what it would have been. She, like Theodora, had been going to say, with great sympathy and absolutely no offer of help out of my sorrow, that no one should have to be refused twice in one summer.

The queen was too tactful to ask more, but talking to her was better than sitting silently, watching Theodora's face for nonexistent signs of returning consciousness. "She told me she would miss her independence if she was tied to someone else, but that's not the only reason. The other reason, and I think the real reason, is that she knows that I couldn't be a professional wizard if I was married to her, and that I wouldn't be happy working illusions at fairs. She's right, but I'd be delighted to sacrifice all that to be with her. The problem is that she decided to sacrifice herself before giving me a chance to do so first."

"It sounds like she loves you," commented the queen.

I nodded. "She does, almost as much as I love her. But I know that if she recovers, she'll want to go back to the cathedral city and leave me here. I still refuse to accept this arrangement." I glanced toward the queen and wondered if what I was saying was a speech of resignation.

"She may give you no choice," said the queen, which might have been an unwillingness to accept my resignation.

She stood up suddenly to turn on the lamp. Daylight was fading at last behind the drawn curtains. The magic globe of light made what had been a dim, sad room almost bright and cozy. I could even imagine that a little pink had returned to Theodora's pallid cheeks.

"Even if she won't marry me," I said, to make sure the queen knew that I would not renew my proposals to *her*, "I will always consider myself to belong to her."

The queen looked at me, blinking in the bright lamplight. She realized there was more and waited to see if I would tell her.

I knew this was the final conversation like this I would ever have with the queen. If I was indeed going to stay on as wizard of Yurt we needed to have everything open between us, so that we could be comfortable and natural with each other and never have to discuss it again.

"There's one more thing you should know," I said at last. "She's carrying my child."

The queen went completely still, not even breathing for five seconds. Then she gave my hand a final squeeze and reached over to stroke Theodora's brow.

What had been one of the happiest and most private moments of my life, I thought, that afternoon in the grove outside the cathedral city, now threatened to become public knowledge. I reminded myself that having the queen and the bishop know about it was not the same as having it known to everyone in the twin kingdoms. I just hoped Theodora would see it that way.

This topic seemed to have run its course. "You started to ask me earlier," I said into a silence that threatened to stretch out indefinitely, "about my conversation with Prince Vincent." The queen looked up in surprise, then remembered. "I hope he told you I don't suspect him anymore."

"Yes," she answered slowly. "He did feel he'd answered all your concerns. But to suggest that he planned to murder Paul!"

I looked away. "Maybe I just have a suspicious nature. I know now I was highly mistaken. But when I learned that the wizard of Caelrhon was planning an attack here" —I felt no necessity to explain that I had not realized the elusive renegade wizard was Sengrim until he actually appeared before me— "I thought that the prince of Caelrhon might well be implicated. After all, wouldn't it make sense for someone who would otherwise never be king to want to gain a wife and a kingdom at the same time? I know now how wrong I was!" I added hastily.

"You do realize, Wizard," she said after a minute, "that I am going to marry Vincent tomorrow, and we intend to live in Yurt."

"I know," I said. "And therefore I feel I must offer you my resignation."

There, I had done it at last. This time there was no ambiguity. When Theodora learned I was no longer wizard of Yurt, she would have no choice but to marry me.

"You can't offer me your resignation," she said with the faintest trace of a smile. "I'm not regent anymore."

"Then I'll tell Paul I'm resigning."

"He would never accept your resignation. He thinks much too highly of you."

"He'll accept my resignation if I tell him I've grossly insulted his mother and her future husband."

She shook her head. The faint smile was still there. "And I'll tell him that you only imagined the insult. No, Wizard, both Vincent and I would ask you to stay on, even if Paul were not here, even if Vincent really *was* going to become king of Yurt. All I ask is that you and Vincent seek to be friends. We couldn't let the wizard get away who had saved us all from renegade magic. I can't force you to stay, of course, and *she*"—with a nod toward Theodora's still form—"may still change her mind. But please. I want you to be Royal Wizard as long as I live in Yurt."

There didn't seem to be any way to refuse this. It was at any rate unambiguous.

The queen left a little while later to go sleep in Theodora's room. I offered to move her, but the queen dismissed my suggestion. "I told you to bring her in here so you wouldn't have to carry her up those stairs. I'll be fine. And I think she'll be fine by morning." She was gone with this statement of what I considered unwarranted optimism. I stretched out next to Theodora and slept a little myself.

Toward dawn, I awoke abruptly from vague and depressing nightmares to feel a stir next to me. "Daimbert?" came a sleepy voice.

I was too overcome to answer. I put my arm tight around her and buried my face in her pillow.

When she spoke again, it was with the slightest hint of her customary teasing tone. "Are these your chambers? From what I can see, the room looks much fancier than I had imagined. Don't you think everyone will be shocked when we come out to breakfast together?"

I sat up and turned the lamp back on to look at her. "These aren't my chambers; they're the queen's. She had us bring you here. Do you remember what happened?"

Theodora closed her eyes for a moment, then opened them again. "What happened to the wizard?"

"He's dead. Paul killed him."

She lay quietly for a minute, then reached for my hand. "Please believe me, Daimbert. I taught him a little fire magic a few years ago, when I just thought he was an old spell-caster, but I never taught him *that.*"

"I know you didn't," I said. "But do you remember how you came to be knocked unconscious?"

"It's a jumble," she said after another long pause. "But—the last thing I remember is a crevice opening in the earth under my feet. And at the same time, I think—I think the same thing happened to your queen!"

She gave a jerk and tried to sit up. I pushed her gently back down. "But the queen!" she said. "If these are her chambers, what's happened to her? Did he kill her?"

"No, no," I said reassuringly. "The queen is fine. I already told you, she suggested herself that we put you here." But now I had come to the one thing I had dreaded about Theodora's waking. "I saved her. The two of you were in opposite directions from me, and I had only a fraction of a second, not time to save you both." I had my face in the pillow again. "I swear before God," I said indistinctly through the feathers, "that I love you more than I do her."

"I know, I know," she said and tentatively stroked my hair.

"But you *don't* know," I said, pushing myself up again. "I didn't even choose—there wasn't time. Afterwards, I had to ask myself why I turned to her, rather than you. And I realized" —I hoped this didn't sound like an accusation— "I realized it was because I believed you could fly."

Theodora thought about this for a moment. "I don't think I'm as good a pupil as I should be. I would have needed a few seconds to put the spell together. I can't remember even trying."

She reached a hand slowly up to the bump on her head. "Did I hit a stone? I can almost remember falling. One thing climbing teaches you is how to fall. I must not have gotten my arms over my head in time." She was irritated with herself at this lapse. "I seem to have completely ruined my dress, too," she said ruefully. "Could you help me up so I can change?"

I held her down with a hand on each shoulder. "You can't change here, unless you were planning to put on something of the queen's. And I don't want you to move at all until I have the doctor back in to look at you again. Even if your head is all right, I want to be sure about your back and your neck. And," after a pause, "our daughter."

She smiled somewhat sleepily. "She's fine. Babies are fairly well protected the first few months. And you *know* I'm a witch, Daimbert," to my worried expression. "This is something I can be certain about." She yawned. "It isn't really morning yet. If you won't let me up, I'm going back to sleep." She smiled, closed her eyes, and proceeded to do so. I turned off the lamp and sat next to her while outside it gradually grew light.

III

The queen and Vincent were married by the bishop in a quiet ceremony the following morning, and our guests began to leave in the afternoon. No one really had the heart to continue the festivities. The cook said darkly that she hoped that those of us who stayed had good appetites, or a lot of good food was going to go to waste.

Paul stood at the gates, thanking each person individually for coming and apologizing for their burns and bruises. Lucas slapped him on the shoulder in good fellowship. "Now watch yourself, young king," he said with just the faintest hint of jealousy. "You have to realize it can't all be like this. You're not going to turn eighteen, be crowned king, and have a chance to save your kingdom from peril all on the same day again!"

I thought Paul recognized the irony of having the departing guests treat as a glorious deed out of legend something that he himself considered the worst experience of his life. But he said nothing about this. Some people, however, may have wondered why he did not seem to smile.

The Romneys were already gone. They had guessed all along, I thought, that Sengrim and the ragged old magician were the same person, and they didn't care to answer questions on this topic. They also did not want to discuss the telephone call one of the Romney girls had placed to the royal court of Caelrhon of behalf of the "magician," and they did not want any further discussion on the topic of the red roan stallion. Sengrim had given it to the Romneys as a bribe or a reward for their silence, I realized, knowing that they would love the opportunity to tame such a superb horse and that they would be able to get a substantial sum from the right buyer. Vincent, I thought, must have paid them a good half of the spending money his father allowed him in a year.

We buried Sengrim in the castle cemetery, where kings of Yurt and servants of Yurt had been buried for generations. The young royal chaplain read the service with what I thought was exaggerated seriousness. Paul listened while staring expressionless into the distance, then tossed the first shovelful of dirt onto the coffin and went back to the castle without waiting for the rest of us.

By the end of the afternoon, the bishop's party were the only guests left. I went up to the chaplain's old room to talk to Joachim.

"Do you think Paul will be all right?" I asked. "I hope you haven't told him that he's irretrievably damned for eternity for killing the wizard." When Joachim didn't answer, I continued, "Come on, I know that in the past you've felt the bishop wouldn't approve if you revealed the secrets of the confessional, but *you* are bishop now."

He took a deep breath, and his mouth moved slightly in what might have been a smile. Joachim had always taken the oddest things for jokes. "I still wouldn't reveal the 'secrets of the confessional,' as you put it," he answered, "but I can tell you that I most certainly did not tell your king that he was damned for eternity. To kill is always a sin, but this world has been imperfect since the Fall, and one cannot always make a choice between good and evil. Sometimes the only choice is between one sin and a worse one. The worst possible sin for a king, sworn to defend his people, is to let them be killed. He has a stain on his soul, but he should be able to recover from it."

"I hope you explained all that to Paul."

He lifted an eyebrow. "Of course I did. Don't you have any confidence in me as a priest?" I couldn't tell if he was serious or if this was one of *his* jokes.

We sat in silence for a moment. "How long can you stay?" I asked then.

"I'll wait until Theodora feels well enough to travel; that will give my new dean a chance to get some experience on his own. I am very happy to see her recovering so well."

"As am I, thanks to your prayers."

"And to your herbal magic," he replied, "and her own youth and health, and maybe even the doctor's draughts."

I hadn't asked Theodora again to marry me, feeling that it would be unfair to press her in her weakened state, but I feared I already knew what she would say. Even without my assent, we seemed inexorably to be moving toward an arrangement where she and our daughter would live in the cathedral city while I stayed in Yurt. "But I want to ask you something, Joachim. You seem remarkably unconcerned for a bishop about an expectant mother refusing to marry."

"I thought you knew that marriage was a sacrament, created by God. The essence of a valid marriage is free consent. It would be a great sin to force someone to marry against her will. I cannot approve, of course, of unmarried women having children, but it would be even worse to force such women into marriage."

Clearly I wasn't going to get any help from *him*.

"Your child was conceived in sin, but then so were we all, ever since the children of Adam. You do realize, Daimbert, that Theodora's unwillingness to marry you gives you no license. You have repented sorely of what you have done, but it would not be true penitence if you intended to do it again. I spoke with her while we were riding here, and she agrees. Your relations from now on must be of the purest."

This was worse and worse. "But I love her!"

"In this fallen world," Joachim continued, holding me with his eyes, "love is often an opportunity for sin, but remember that love remains one of the first gifts of God to His creation."

"How would you know?" I asked bitterly. "You've never tried love yourself."

"Of course not," he said in surprise. "I'm a priest."

Considering how much trouble we had understanding each other, it was a wonder that Joachim and I were friends at all. "Now that you're bishop," I said, "you're responsible for the whole of the twin kingdoms. You can't be responsible for my soul anymore."

"Of course," he said, immediately and contritely. "Forgive me. I was speaking as though I were still your chaplain."

This didn't help. I certainly wasn't going to discuss Theodora with Yurt's new chaplain. "Don't you think you could look into getting us a different one?"

He looked amused but shook his head. "I've talked to your chaplain, and there's really nothing wrong with him, Daimbert. He doesn't have an impure mind, or whatever you once tried to tell me. He might never make a great theologian, but he's a perfectly competent priest."

I bit my lip. "I was afraid you'd say that." By talking about the young chaplain, he had made it almost too late for me to say that I had no intention of keeping my relations with Theodora of the purest. If she agreed with him, I would at any rate have no choice. Besides, I didn't want to argue with Joachim. "I hope you don't think that *I* have sunk irretrievably into sin."

He looked at me a long moment without answering. "No," he said at last. "Not irretrievably. Not that I know about. Not yet."

✧ ✧ ✧

Theodora and I walked slowly around the castle's hill in the early morning two days later. She and the bishop's party would shortly be leaving to ride back to the cathedral city.

"Before you ask me," she said, "let me tell you the answers. Yes, I love you very much and will never love anyone else. No, I can't marry you. No, I can't come live with you here, getting in your way as Royal Wizard, defying the bishop, and probably getting you into serious trouble with your school. And no, I don't want to wander around from fair to fair doing magic tricks."

This did indeed seem to answer all possible questions in advance. I put my arms around her and gently kissed the purple bruise on her forehead. "You realize," I said, "that I am going to come visit you very often."

"Of course. I thought we already agreed on that." We continued walking for a few minutes, then she said, "I do feel embarrassed as a witch that I never realized the Royal Wizard of Caelrhon was the same person as the old magician I'd known for years. What is your school going to do?"

"I haven't had a chance to tell the school much more than that he's dead. All the teachers have been up north, and I just spoke very briefly to Zahlfast last night when he returned. I need to call them again. But I've been trying to work some of it out myself. An enormous amount of Sengrim's madness was directed personally toward me."

She nodded without speaking.

"Sengrim had hated me for years. He was a good wizard, really good, or he would never have been able to master a gorgos. And he knew it, and it ate into him that no one else knew it. I've always just considered it a sign that even intelligent wizards can have errors in judgment that they asked me to teach at the school, but for him it must have been the final blow to his self-esteem."

"It can only be a small proportion of the graduates who are ever invited back to teach, even just a short series of lectures."

"That's just it. But Sengrim didn't realize how inadequate I felt. All he knew is that I've had my name in every copy of *Ancient and Modern Necromancy* for years, because of accidentally inventing a telephone attachment, and that I'd been invited back to the City and he hadn't. To plot against me without suspicion, he decided to fake his own death.

"It started with me, but it didn't end with me," I continued. "At this point I'm guessing, but I think he turned his jealousy of me into hatred for all the wizards at the school. And the Church was a tempting target, since no wizard, other than me, would be very concerned about strange apparitions on the cathedral."

"What it comes down to, then," said Theodora, "is that you and Paul have not only saved the people here but the church and your school."

"Not at all," I said in surprise. "Well, maybe Paul has. But I can't take any credit. All I did all summer, while Joachim thought I was trying to find a way to protect the cathedral from peril, was to fall in love with you."

She made a noise that was almost a snort.

"All right," I conceded, "I did get the gorgos back up north. And I found out that Lucas had gotten himself into a state where he wanted to discard both priests and wizards, and I talked him out of it. But I'm going to have to phrase it all rather delicately when I explain it to the Master of the school."

We kept on walking. "The bishop likes you," I said after a minute.

"I still find him a little intimidating," she said, "but at the same time, strangely, I find him a good person to talk to. Though one thing is odd, Daimbert. Because I'd known he was your friend I'd expected him to be a lot like you, but he isn't at all."

"The priesthood doesn't allow people like me."

She smiled and squeezed my arm. "Probably just as well. But I wanted to ask you," more seriously now, "how many people in Yurt know about our daughter. First you told the bishop, and now you told the queen! How about the teachers at the school?"

"So far," I said, smiling down at her, "we're up to two people."

"And the school?"

"I have no intention of telling them. They don't want married wizards, but if you won't marry me then the rest is none of their business. Even if I am at some level answerable to organized wizardry, I still, as a theoretically competent wizard, have to be able to make my own decisions. I'm not even going to tell them that I taught—or tried to teach—a witch to fly!"

IV

After watching the bishop's party ride away, I did not go back inside the castle. Instead I went into the old king's rose garden and sat on a bench for a while, then wandered up and down the rows of rosebushes, trying to distract myself by remembering what he had long ago told me about where he had obtained or how he had bred each one. The blue rose that he had brought back from the East was blooming: an enormous, brilliant sapphire flower. I could never forget how he obtained that one.

After an hour I came out again and looked out across the fields of home. Whatever else had come out of this summer, I seemed cured of being homesick for the Yurt of years ago. If everything had stayed exactly the same, Paul would not now be my king, and I would never have met Theodora.

Years of warding off thunderstorms during harvest time had made me aware of what crops looked like when they were ready to be gathered in. I smiled and estimated that the barley would be ripe in about a week. It was time to review my weather spells.

Off in the western sky I saw a speck approaching. My heart gave a hard thump, but that was out of habit. I knew what was coming. Zahlfast had said he would send the air cart for the red lizards. I walked around the hill to where they still stood. I was actually rather pleased with my paralysis spell, which I had not expected to last this long. But it might be hard to fit them all into the cart.

I looked again toward the speck, which was close enough now that I could tell it was purple. But something was odd about it. I rubbed my eyes and looked again, and this time there was no doubt. It was not one air cart coming but two. So much, I thought, for getting my own air cart. Sengrim must have had one which, it now appeared, the Master had appropriated for the school's use.

The two carts dipped, banked, and landed beside me. I loaded the lizards carefully, packing the heads, wings, and legs in as well as I could. There was just enough room left in the second cart for a man.

I ducked back across the drawbridge and found Gwennie. "I was looking for the constable," I told her, "but you'll do fine. I have to go down to the City but I'll be back tonight or tomorrow." I did not trust Sengrim's lizards not to come back to life if left to themselves. I had, perhaps unjustifiably, come out of this business quite credibly, and I didn't want to ruin it now.

Gwennie waved as the lizards and I took off. It took until early afternoon to reach the white spires of the City and the school perched on the highest central point. The lizards remained paralyzed the whole way. As the carts landed in the school courtyard, I thought that these creatures might prove useful after all for the students to practice their "antimonster" spells.

As I unloaded the stiff bodies, with the help of a teaching assistant and several students, the cheerful conversation and questions around me suddenly stopped and I looked up to see two senior wizards: Zahlfast and the white-bearded Master of the school.

Zahlfast walked around the lizards slowly. "Nice paralysis spell, Daimbert," he said in his schoolteacher voice.

"I know you gave Zahlfast a quick overview on the telephone of what happened," said the Master, "but I'd like to hear more. How about if you come to my study?"

Leaving the assistants to finish dealing with the lizards, I followed the Master with a cold feeling in my chest. It seemed ominously significant that the two wizards had appeared together. Although there had never been any formal announcement, it had become clear over the last few years that Zahlfast had gone from being the head of the transformations faculty to being the de facto second in authority at the school.

Inwardly I was in turmoil. While my own role in killing Sengrim, I was now ashamed to admit, had not bothered me in the slightest, it suddenly seemed highly likely to be a heavy black mark against me in the eyes of the school. No one expected wizards to get along well with each other, but killing each other was something else.

In the Master's study, I told them everything that had happened as honestly as I could, neither trying to justify or to boast, starting with the lizards on the new cathedral tower, and including the gorgos, the strangely out-of-order telephone at the watch-station, and my final spell against Sengrim. All I left out was Theodora. I ended with my guesses why he had been so jealous of me. "One thing you can tell me," I concluded. "Was he just very good at magic, or was he working with a demon?"

Zahlfast and the Master looked at each other. "There is nothing that makes us think," said Zahlfast, "that he'd taken the step into black magic."

"Good," I said. "We gave him a Christian burial."

"You may be correct," said the Master, ignoring this comment, "that he was eaten up with jealousy. I must say I'd never known a student of mine to summon a hundred dragons to attack the school. If your king hadn't killed him, I wonder what his next effort might have been—but thanks to you, we will never have to know!"

Zahlfast said thoughtfully, "I wonder if we ought to keep somewhat closer track of the wizards after they leave the school, to make sure something like this doesn't happen again. We'd seen him this spring, only a short time before he faked his death, but we believed him when he said everything in Caelrhon was fine."

"Was that his air cart?" I asked abruptly.

"Why, yes. He told us that he'd been able to obtain a purple flying beast up in the land of wild magic. I presume he got it at the same time as he was capturing the gorgos and disabling the telephone system. The cart will be very useful at the school now that he won't be needing it." Just as I had thought.

The Master leaned toward me, his hands on his knees. "So. What it all comes down to, young wizard, is that you defended your kingdom successfully from someone who knew a lot more magic than you do."

"And in the process," added Zahlfast, "you and your local bishop worked out an agreement that priests and wizards ought to stop working against each other."

I looked at him sharply. I hadn't said anything about this, as not being directly relevant.

"Yes, we've heard about it," said Zahlfast with a smile. "You weren't the only wizard in Caelrhon, you know."

"Since Sengrim was so good at magic," I asked, changing the subject because I didn't want to have to justify my friendship with Joachim, "why was he still wizard of Caelrhon? If Yurt's the smallest of the western kingdoms, Caelrhon has to be the second smallest."

Zahlfast looked as though he was going to say something

about how the school did not discuss one wizard's career with another, but the Master answered me without hesitation.

"There's a lot more to being a good wizard than being good at spells. Some wizards stay at their first posts for their entire lives, some move to richer courts in just a few years, some stay at the school as assistants, some come back to work at the school after years away. It all depends on a number of factors, including the wishes of the wizard himself, how well he's doing where he is, and what other opportunities may be available. In his case, he'd applied for other positions over the years, but none of them were quite right for him."

"Including Yurt," I said. "I still don't understand why you made sure that I became wizard here."

"We told you that years ago," said Zahlfast. "You were the best qualified person for the position."

"Caelrhon will need a new Royal Wizard now, of course," said the Master. "The king telephoned the school after the royal family realized that Sengrim really wasn't a good representative of a school-trained wizard. There is someone we had in mind for the position, and we would like your opinion. His name is Evrard, and I believe he was briefly ducal wizard of Yurt fifteen or twenty years ago."

I was surprised but pleased. "That's a fine idea. He'll be a good Royal Wizard of Caelrhon."

"And that brings us," said the Master, "to the real issue."

This was it, I thought, the reprimand for which I had been waiting the last hour. My only hope was that even if they wanted to install someone else as wizard of Yurt, they couldn't do so over the objections of Paul and the queen.

"We want you to stay here and teach at the school."

This was both unexpected and anticlimactic. "But I was just here this spring," I said. "I would have thought I did a poor enough job inspiring your technical division students that you wouldn't want me to try again already."

"It seemed like a good idea at the time," said Zahlfast, "and in fact I think those students will get more long-term advantage out of your lectures than you realize. But you may well be right that the technical division isn't the best place for you. You could teach in one of the other faculties this fall."

I shook my head. "I appreciate the offer, but I really can't. I've been away from Yurt much too much this year anyway. Paul's just become king, and he needs his Royal Wizard with him as he adjusts to his new responsibilities."

"Maybe you don't understand what we're saying," said Zahlfast. "We're not asking you to stay at the school for a series of lectures. We're asking you to join the permanent faculty."

This was certainly not what I expected. I looked from one to the other, my mouth doubtless gaping. "But—" Out of several things I might have said I chose, "But I thought the two of you were going to punish me for being implicated in the death of another wizard."

Zahlfast started to chuckle. "So you told us the whole story, expecting at any moment that we would accuse you of being a traitor to organized wizardry?"

"And you're not going to?" I said cautiously.

"Haven't you been listening?" asked the Master, the twinkle in his frost-blue eyes pronounced. "The school certainly doesn't want its graduates killing each other, but the first oath you all take is to serve humanity. Very few wizards are ever asked to join the permanent faculty. We very much want you."

I had again the feeling that I had irretrievably lost my way, but now it was worse. Not only had I become lost wandering in a wood, but the forest floor itself had been whipped out from under me. "But I have just been talking to the queen about my position," I said. This point at least was firm. "She and King Paul very much want me to continue as Royal Wizard of Yurt."

Zahlfast waved away this objection with a hand.

"I have to warn you," I went on, "I'm as interested in establishing cordial relations with the bishop of the twin kingdoms of Yurt and Caelrhon as he is with wizardry."

"That is in fact part of it," said Zahlfast. "Maybe we've been too dismissive in the past. Even though religion is inferior to magic, priests are still part of the humanity we serve. I can't abide the bishop of the City myself, but he won't be bishop there indefinitely. We'll be in the City far longer than he is, and when his successor takes over it might be a good time to start establishing better relations. You'd be the perfect person to do it."

"So, what do you say, Daimbert?" said the Master cheerfully. "We want you to join us permanently at the school, not because you're good at certain spells, but because you're a good wizard. You're not like most wizards, but more and more we've come to realize that that can be an advantage. We'll even let you have a hand in choosing an appropriate young wizard to succeed you in Yurt. Will you do it?"

"No."

Not an explanation, not an excuse, just a straight negative. The monosyllable hung in the air, out before I even had a chance to consider. But I had no intention of calling it back.

Zahlfast looked both startled and disturbed. "Maybe we haven't explained it clearly enough."

"You've made yourself very clear," I said. "But I wouldn't be a good teacher." This wasn't the only reason, but it would do for a start. "If I were going to train young wizards, I'd have to know five times the magic I do. The only way I got through the lectures this spring was by emphasizing ways of thinking rather than content. Even after close to twenty years past my own graduation, there are probably major areas where the average new graduate knows more than I do—and I don't just mean in the technical division."

Zahlfast looked at me thoughtfully. "Encyclopedic knowledge of spells isn't what makes someone a good teacher of magic. If that was all that was required, we wouldn't even bother teaching—we'd just make the students memorize *Thaumaturgy A to Z*. It's only the bad teachers who think they know everything. Every good teacher has stood in front of a class one time or another and felt like a fraud trying to explain something."

This did not at all accord with my memories of the enormously knowledgeable teachers at the school. It slowly sank in that I really was being asked, and by people who recognized a major proportion of my shortcomings, to come back and be their colleague.

"We can start you off easily," said the Master, "just give you classes where you feel comfortable already. You will, after all, be the most junior wizard on the faculty by a considerable margin, and we don't want to overburden you. What do you say?"

"It's still no."

I wondered if I had looked as distressed to Theodora when she kept refusing my proposals as the two older wizards now did. "I recognize the honor," I said. "In fact, I'm almost overwhelmed by the honor. And I recognize that every wizard has a duty to institutionalized wizardry to serve it as best he can. But I can't leave Yurt."

"Why not?"

"I love the people there."

They looked at each other as though hoping the other would understand. "Maybe there's something you haven't thought about," said Zahlfast slowly. "Wizards live far longer than ordinary humans. If you become too close to the people there, you'll just be hurt when you have to leave them behind."

"Fine," I said. "Invite me to the school in fifty years."

In fifty years, Joachim and the queen would be dead, and Theodora and Paul, assuming they were still alive, would be happily watching their grandchildren grow up and would no longer need me. In Theodora's case, I reminded myself, they would also be *my* grandchildren. I had a sudden doubt whether fifty years would be long enough.

Zahlfast thought the same thing. "If you decide to stay in Yurt because of the people, Daimbert, you do have to realize that new people are going to appear, and they may engage your affections as well. Now you say you want to stay in part because of your king—King Paul, isn't that right?—and yet I don't think he was even born when you first went to Yurt."

"We're asking you," said the Master slowly, "because we think you have unique abilities that ought to be put to the use of wider wizardry."

I shook my head. "It wouldn't work. You're hoping that I'd be able to open communications with the bishop of the City. But I have no inherent ability to make priests give up their suspicions of wizards. All I have is my friendship with Joachim, the new bishop of Caelrhon. If the church and wizardry are going to start working together, you'll have to start with him and me, not with the bishop of the City and a representative of the school."

I could have added that the reason I had, even if highly reluctantly, let Theodora refuse to marry me was because she thought I would be more happy and comfortable as Royal Wizard of Yurt. I had not given up life with her and our daughter to go live in the City.

"You sound quite definite," said the Master.

"I am quite definite. You seem to think I'd be good for the school because I'm different from most wizards. Maybe I'm also different in that I don't consider a post here the most desirable thing in the world."

"I'm afraid this isn't what we expected," said the Master.

"That's all right," I said, forcing a smile. "It wasn't what I expected either."

"You seem fairly firm about this," said Zahlfast, "but give it some thought. It will be fine if you want to change your mind."

"I will indeed give it some thought," I answered. This was an understatement. "Don't forget to ask me again in fifty years."

"Then let me ask you something else in the meantime," said the Master. "Is there something we could do for you or give you? You may not appreciate this properly, but you did save the school from tremendous peril by your warning."

I thought for a moment. Everything I had hoped for this summer had reached a dead end. Even though Joachim and I might still be friends now that he was bishop, I would see him even less than I had before. The queen was lost to me forever, and Theodora did not want to marry me. There was just one thing left I had wanted.

"Yes," I said slowly and smiled. "You can give me one of the air carts."

EPILOGUE

I took off in my air cart in late afternoon, but instead of heading toward Yurt I flew southeast from the City. With Sengrim's death, everything seemed wrapped up to everyone else's satisfaction, but not to mine. After half an hour I saw a castle's towers rising before me in the darkening air. More than twice the size of the royal castle of Yurt, it perched on a high pinnacle above a fertile river valley. As I approached magic lamps winked on in all the windows.

The air cart stopped abruptly, jerking me forward. The wings continued to flap, but we made no progress. I probed for spells and discovered that the air had been made solid: impermeable, as far as I could tell, to any sort of magical flying creature, but not, I discovered as I thrust an experimental hand through, to me. It looked as if someone had been taking lessons from the nixie.

I set the air cart down at the base of the rocky pinnacle and ascended the steps, my heart beating fast. Guards with halberds barred my way at the top. "I would like to speak to Elerius, your Royal Wizard," I said, but already I could see a black-bearded figure coming up behind them. He must have been warned by the triggering of the protective spells he had set up to guard his castle from creatures from the land of wild magic.

"How delightful to see you, Daimbert," he said, as hearty and welcoming as good old Book-Leech on the mountaintop in the borderlands. I just wished I could believe him equally sincere. "Come to my study. And I understand that congratulations are in order!"

Then I had reached him before the news that I had refused the position at the school. "I turned the Master down," I said casually. "How much of a role did you play in setting up the offer?"

This startled him. He stopped dead in the middle of asking a deferentially hovering servant to bring us tea, then whisked me up the stairs into his study and slammed the door. I had never seen so many books in one place in my life. In a moment Elerius had regained his cheerful composure, but I could tell it was not the same.

"Zahlfast and the Master must have been quite surprised!" he said, smiling while his hazel eyes looked me over intently. "How could you refuse an offer to join the permanent faculty—something they have offered no one in thirty years? Is Yurt so charming, or do you have your eye on a bigger kingdom somewhere else? Or," and he paused for a few seconds, "is that witch in Caelrhon more appealing than the City?"

That was the final evidence I needed. That he would threaten—even obliquely threaten—to blackmail me meant I must have information about him that he wanted kept secret.

"Don't smirk, Elerius," I said quietly. "You can guess and insinuate all you like. But if you push me too far I'll just tell the Master I'm leaving organized wizardry to spend the rest of my life doing illusions at fairs—after I tell him that you were behind Sengrim every step of the way."

We were interrupted before he could answer by the entry of servants with tea. It was quite a production: four servants in livery, one to open the door, one to carry the teapot, one to carry the tray with cups and spoons, and one to carry a plate of gingerbread puffs baked in brightly colored foils. I bit into one when it became clear that the servants would not go until everything had been found satisfactory. Not bad, although Yurt's cook's were better.

Elerius had had time to prepare his response by the time the servants finally left. "I *did* befriend Sengrim a few years ago," he said good-naturedly, pouring tea, "back when he was trying to persuade the school that we needed to do more with fire magic and no one else would listen to him. Everyone at the school knows about that. But that hardly means I was 'behind him every step of the way'!"

"It means you brought a fanged gorgos to Caelrhon which nearly killed me," I said, looking at him levelly over my teacup. "Sengrim would never have managed that on his own. He had to be working with a demon—and Zahlfast said he wasn't—or else an extremely good wizard. Theodora—the witch you seem to know about—touched a wizard's mind in the cathedral city, but this wizard was not anyone she recognized. And that means it wasn't Sengrim, not even in his disguise as the old magician. Both the cathedral cantor and the construction foreman mentioned dealing with a wizard, but somebody *young*, not old like Sengrim."

Elerius's teacup gave a sudden rattle in its saucer. I looked at him sharply but he only smiled, waiting for me to continue.

"And then Zahlfast and the Master seemed well informed about the bishop's inaugural sermon, saying there was another wizard there. They didn't say who, but it must have been someone they trusted. You knew all along I was in Caelrhon, because you sent me a letter urging me to leave, realizing full well it would have exactly the opposite effect; I should have been suspicious at the time that you even knew I was there. The Master forgave me for being indirectly responsible for Sengrim's death. Did you think he would forgive you for being directly responsible for mine?"

"You were never in serious danger, Daimbert," said

Elerius, passing the gingerbread puffs. This wasn't how I remembered it. "I was of course interested to see how you would do against a gorgos with your particular style of magic, but I was there, disguised, among the townspeople." The image of a face I had seen in the crowd, past Lucas's shoulder, as I lay on the paving in front of the cathedral suddenly clicked into place. "Another minute in your fight with the gorgos, or another move by Caelrhon's crown prince, and I would have had to intervene." I didn't like his timing; there hadn't been any minutes or moves to spare. "And you would never have been in any danger at all if you hadn't been so precipitate. Sengrim was intending to defeat the gorgos himself—with my help, of course."

"You say Sengrim intended to overcome a gorgos he had himself brought from the land of wild magic," I said slowly, peeling foil with fingers that I kept from trembling by sheer will. "You realize, Elerius, that this makes no sense whatsoever. So far you've helped a renegade wizard turn on his own employer, attack a cathedral, summon a hundred dragons from the land of magic, and nearly kill scores of people at the coronation of the king of Yurt. This is scarcely suitable in the school's best graduate! I came to talk to you before telling the Master any of this, but if you don't have an adequate explanation I'm heading straight back to the City tonight."

Unless you imprison me, I thought, keeping my thoughts well shielded, or unless you instructed the servants to poison the gingerbread puffs.

"A good idea, talking to me first," said Elerius with a remarkably genuine smile. "I know there have been a few occasions in the past, Daimbert, where you ended up looking like a fool. It's this habit of acting on instinct, you know. It may serve you well in your personal sort of improvisational magic, but it's a poor guide in ordinary affairs. No sense letting the school think they had a narrow escape when you turned down their position!"

I waited silently, knowing he would have to say more. Outside it was fully dark, and the magic lights were reflected in the windows. On the wall hung Elerius's diploma from the school, nearly six feet long, with his name written in letters of fire at the top and the lower half dense with mentions of honors, distinctions, and areas of special merit. Stars twinkled all around the edges. Mine in my chambers in Yurt had my name and the twinkling stars and nothing else.

"Sengrim, as I mentioned," Elerius said at last, "first came to my attention several years ago when he was trying to persuade the school that they ought to offer at least a series of lectures on fire magic—with him teaching it, of course. The Master wasn't interested; there's that one course I occasionally teach myself on the old magic, and he seemed to feel that was enough. Besides, I believe he wasn't sure Sengrim would be an appropriate mentor for the young wizards—he was acting rather strangely even then. He wouldn't even say how he'd learned fire magic. . . ."

"I know how he did," I said shortly. "Go on."

Elerius lifted sharply peaked eyebrows at me but continued. "I was interested myself, however, both for my own course and because I believe wizards shouldn't reject anything that might prove useful. And that's why Sengrim came to consider me his friend, and why he turned to me this spring when he quarreled with his prince, pretended in a fit of pique to blow himself up, and then decided rather belatedly to try to reestablish himself at Caelrhon. I agreed, somewhat reluctantly I must say, to Sengrim's plan to prove to his king and prince what a good wizard he really was. I have to admit I originally thought his plan as nonsensical as you do: first to bring a monster from the land of magic and then to overcome it in a very public setting to show his competence, amazing everyone by his extremely timely return from the dead. But when it became clear that he would do it with or without me, I decided it would be better to help."

"So you decided after talking to the construction foreman," I said slowly, "that a gorgos would serve his purposes nicely, and you helped him go up to the borderlands and capture one—as well as a horse for the Romneys, who he was afraid might reveal that the ragged old magician in the area was in fact the supposedly deceased Royal Wizard in disguise. You helped with that disguise too, didn't you—something thorough enough to fool even another wizard. Just out of curiosity, exactly where near Caelrhon did you manage to imprison Sengrim's gorgos?"

"There's a little grove a mile outside of town, a grove thick with unchanneled magic. It wasn't difficult to channel it, to make a chamber in the ground under the spring where the gorgos could be bound until it was wanted."

I closed my eyes for a second. I had been heedless of a number of things the day I went there with Theodora.

Elerius poured out the last of the tea. "I'm afraid, Daimbert," he continued, "that you rather spoiled Sengrim's plan for him. It was supposed to end with him triumphantly telling Prince Lucas that even the bravest and most able kings needed wizards to protect their kingdoms from wild magic, and being welcomed again into the royal court. Instead it ended with the prince threatening to kill *you*. Even though it could just as easily have been him, rather than feeling gratitude for your fast action Sengrim became extremely bitter toward you. And I understand the two of you had had some sort of earlier misunderstanding?"

I did not deign to answer.

"He was already furious with the school," Elerius continued, "which he thought had unfairly given you opportunities he deserved himself. I seemed to be the only school-trained wizard he trusted as he started imagining plots against him from the faculty and trying to create counterplots. At any rate, at this point it became obvious that he was growing seriously deranged, so I thought it best to distance myself from him. The rest, including the dragons and the unfortunate attack on your king's coming of age festivities, was entirely his own work. I was pleased to hear that you had once again triumphed."

He fell silent but looked at me as though waiting for my reaction. "So this is your entire story?" I said at last. "The story you would have told the Master if I accused you of being involved with Sengrim?"

"Of course. Truth is always wisest."

"What about the rumors of the school plotting to put wizards in every castle and manor to seize control from the aristocracy?"

Elerius shrugged. "Rumors are always flying on one topic or another."

"How do you explain leaving to his own wild devices a wizard you thought had become deranged?"

"You know I have no authority over any other wizard." Elerius shook his head regretfully. "I have sometimes tried to persuade the Master and Zahlfast that the school needs tighter discipline, but as long as they keep only a loose, almost informal organization, there is really nothing a wizard can do in a situation like this." He set down his empty cup and rose briskly to his feet. "Well, did you plan to return to that little kingdom of yours tonight, Daimbert, or would you like to stay here? I'm sure a set of chambers could be arranged."

I gave him my best wizardly glare from under my eyebrows and remained seated. I had suspected Theodora of manipulating me coldly, Lucas of bringing the gorgos to Caelrhon himself, and Vincent of plotting to murder Paul and the queen. All of them had managed to talk me out of my suspicions. But *someone*, if not the princes of Caelrhon, had been working with Sengrim. And I would not give up these suspicions so easily.

Elerius looked down at me quizzically. "I'm sorry, Daimbert. I should have realized when I saw you devouring the gingerbread that you had not had any dinner. Shall I order you a tray?"

I was not going to be talked out of valid suspicions and I was not going to be patronized. "Sit down," I said as though this were my study rather than his.

Surprisingly, he sat down at once. Emboldened by this small triumph, I leaned forward, still glaring. "Let me point out a few things that your explanation doesn't cover. You were not just trying to assist Sengrim in a plan to recover his position. You were using him for your own purposes."

"And what might these purposes have been?" Elerius asked as though I had suggested something rather amusing.

"You want to establish a firmer organization at the school. Zahlfast told me that at the beginning of the summer, and you just said the same thing yourself. The best way you knew to make the school draw tighter together was to make it feel threatened: threatened by an embittered wizard turned renegade, by a church that hated wizardry, by aristocrats threatening to dismiss all their wizards, and by dragons coming over the border. This all started without any help from you, when Prince Lucas quarreled with his Royal Wizard because Sengrim stopped him from a fight in which he would have been bested at once. But you took advantage of the situation because it fit in well with your own long-term plans. Did you think I would not find out that you yourself had installed the far-seeing telephone on the mountain at the borderlands—the phone that wouldn't work?"

"I heard about that," said Elerius easily. "But the spells for the far-seeing attachment have always been a little haphazard. Didn't you invent it yourself, Daimbert?"

I ignored this latest jab. Yurt's own telephones had worked perfectly for years.

"And what better way," I continued, "to make the school feel itself beleaguered by the church and the aristocracy than actually to make certain that it was? You showed up at Caelrhon's royal court in disguise, telling the king you were a City nobleman who had learned of the school's 'plots' against aristocrats, plots you invented in the hope—nearly realized—that threatened royal courts would turn against the school. I had been wondering for some time who this purported aristocratic friend of the Master's might have been, and I only realized now, when you mentioned being in the cathedral city, that Lucas's description matched you. I gather you play the nobleman well, Elerius. Haven't I heard some strange rumors about your parentage? Perhaps a birth on the wrong side of the blanket in some royal castle . . ."

But he did not take the bait, only following me intently, his eyebrows slightly raised, almost as though—pleased?

I pushed on. "By having me, a wizard, in the city of Caelrhon all summer even if no other wizard was in evidence, and by having the gorgos appear at the old bishop's funeral, you were certain the priests would blame the monster on institutionalized magic. Your only miscalculation was not taking Joachim into account—the dean of the cathedral, now bishop. He's the most powerful churchman in two kingdoms, but he's also my friend."

"That is something about you I have found intriguing, Daimbert," Elerius said as though in calculation.

"And which you mentioned to Zahlfast when urging him to hire me permanently at the school. This is the one aspect I haven't worked out yet: why you want me on the faculty, when your ultimate purpose is to reorganize the wizards' school—with yourself in charge!"

Elerius leaned back in his chair and laughed. "This is even better than I imagined, Daimbert! I enjoy watching your mind work. So now you suspect me of going renegade and hatching a plot to overthrow the school?

You really should have your friend the bishop say a suitable prayer of gratitude that you didn't take this story to the Master!"

"It's more subtle than that," I said, watching him without smiling. "You aren't like Sengrim; you haven't lost control of your mind and your magic. You haven't even forgotten your oaths to help humanity. If you had, by now I'd probably either be dead or a frog—or both.

"This was all carefully planned," I continued. "You meant no harm to anyone, or at least that's what you tell yourself. But you have a vision of a drastically reorganized wizards' school, one in which the students follow a highly structured, highly rigorous program—a program from which I would never have graduated—and where the school continues to maintain careful control even after the young wizards have taken up their posts. Through no coincidence, *you* would be at the head of this school."

I paused to let him say something, but he only continued to listen, intent tawny eyes holding mine and an indulgent smile on his lips.

"Hints of danger from priests and aristocrats, you realized, would not be enough to give you the chance to remake the school in your own image. But again Sengrim gave you an opportunity. You knew I would work out eventually that he brought the gorgos to Caelrhon—and that even if he had overcome his bitterness toward me enough for rational conversation, he would have been too proud to mention your role in helping him. So you decided—and quite rightly—that if dragons attacked the school Sengrim would be blamed for that too."

"Then *I* am supposed to be responsible for those dragons?" He was still giving his indulgent smile.

"Sengrim could never have called that many by himself. He was in Yurt, with the lizards he had learned to master several years ago, when someone else brought dragons over the border. You didn't go to help the masters fight them even though your kingdom is so close to the City. You have spells of your own around this castle that would have warded off dragons. I'm sure you were able to persuade yourself that none of the faculty would actually be killed, that fighting dragons in the City streets would be messy but not actually fatal if everyone kept their heads and worked together. But a battered school with a badly wounded faculty would need someone to step in and take charge, someone who would quickly assure that wizards, rather than being just one of the 'three who rule the world,' would be the only rulers."

The late summer evening was growing cool in this tower high above the plain. Elerius snapped his fingers, said two words, and lit the kindling in the fireplace. The flames quickly caught the dry wood. When he looked toward me expectantly, I said a few words of my own in the Hidden Language to light a tiny cascade of flames in the air before us.

"Not bad, Daimbert," he said appreciatively as they flickered back out of existence. "Did you come here then to match spells with me?"

I shook my head hard. "Your spells are better than mine. I've always known that. That's why I want to know why you seem to want *me*, whose only strength is in improvisation, in a school that you plan to remodel as rigorous, standardized, and monolithic."

"Don't assume your imaginings about my 'plans' are real, Daimbert," he said slowly, looking into the fire and not smiling any longer. "You have speculation but not a shred of evidence. If you tried to take any of this to the Master, you realize, I would only deny it all, and you would come out looking an even bigger fool than you did all those years ago at Zahlfast's transformations practical."

He spoke so soberly that for a moment I began to doubt my own reason, and I wished wildly for Theodora's ring of invisibility so I could escape before I embarrassed myself any further.

"But," and he turned his eyes sharply toward me, "let's assume for a moment that you're right."

I took a deep breath and let it out again.

"Don't you think the idea deserves better than your dismissal? For generations before the Black Wars, the aristocrats controlled the western kingdoms and used their strength and even their wizards against other kings and lords. The result was the bloody wars that so sickened the old wizards that they, contentious and individualistic as they were, finally banded together to stop the fighting. So we know that aristocrats can't be allowed to make the great decisions. And the priests with their prating about sin and morality would not be any better. So who does that leave but the wizards?"

"Why does *anyone* have to rule the world?" I demanded. "Why can't the townsmen rule their towns, the kings their individual kingdoms, and the priests their churches?"

"Since in fact we *already* are the ultimate rulers," Elerius went on without answering my question, "then it would be best to plan ahead, rather than simply reacting to events. The Master did an excellent job in setting up the school in the first place, coordinating the teaching of wizardry, making sure young wizards learned magic's responsibilities as well as its spells. But the time has come to think of the next necessary steps. Those of us of the next generation, trained in the school and its methods but with visions of our own, are ready to go beyond the victories already won." He paused and smiled. "You realize, of course, I am speaking hypothetically."

"And what would I, hypothetically, have to do with all this?"

"You and I have crossed paths before, Daimbert," said Elerius thoughtfully, stroking his beard. "You have an uncanny knack of disrupting my plans. If I actually had intended to use dragons to attack the school, then I might be quite angry with you for warning Zahlfast in time. *Some* wizards in such a situation, I might imagine, would realize that you had most likely not told anyone in the City that you were coming here, and that with the king of Yurt thinking you were still at the school, the school thinking you were back in Yurt, and the witch in Caelrhon thinking you had loved her and left her, it might be a *very* long time before anyone came to my kingdom to ask awkward questions. . . ."

"So far," I said evenly, clenching my fists until the nails bit into my palms, "you have tried denial, blackmail, and threats. All this has done is make me more certain than ever that I'm right."

"And you're holding out for bribery?" Elerius asked, showing his teeth in a smile. "Since this is all hypothetical and indeed quite imaginary, I can say honestly that you are providing me one of the most entertaining evenings, Daimbert, I have had in a long time. But I was about to add that I am not one of the wizards who reacts simply by eliminating all potential opposition. I already told you that I believe one should not reject anything that could prove useful. Anyone who has the ability to thwart me—even if not always intentionally—has strengths it might be best to have on my side."

"This is the bribe, then?" I asked, fists still clenched along my sides. "I get hired onto the permanent faculty of the school now, in part so you can keep a closer eye on me, and then you promise that when you take over I can stay?"

"Wouldn't you find this a tempting bribe, Daimbert—if I were making one?"

"No. I am Royal Wizard of Yurt. And I do not want to be part of any attempt to control the rest of the world. I know you are a better wizard than I could be in a thousand years, but even you can't control it. If I have thwarted you, it's not because I have outmaneuvered you. It's because the world, and that includes me, is much too messy and unpredictable, impossible for even the best wizardly planning to guide successfully." I rose abruptly to my feet. Get out while I was still alive. "Thank you so much for tea, but I should get home to Yurt tonight."

Elerius rose too and went to the door, the gracious host, to see me out. I followed him, feeling sweat trickling down my neck. Almost. I was almost out of here to safety. But he paused with his hand on the latch.

"Don't take accusations to the school, Daimbert, when you have no proof," he said quietly. "You can take pride in having kept organized wizardry unchanged if that was your goal. But I would still like to be your friend. Think over these ideas how the school might be improved. Anyone who can overcome a fanged gorgos with spells that shouldn't work, become friends with a bishop, and make such imaginative and highly romantic guesses about what I might have been planning, deserves closer study!" He opened the door. "Have a pleasant trip home—but keep in touch."